ALSO BY SCOTT WESTERFELD

SWARM

SCOTT WESTERFELD

MARGO LANAGAN · DEBORAH BIANCOTTI

SIMON&SCHUSTER

First published in Great Britain in 2016 by Simon and Schuster UK Ltd
A CBS COMPANY

First published in the USA by Simon Pulse, an imprint of
Simon and Schuster Children's Division, New York.

1 3 5 7 9 10 8 6 4 2

Simon & Schuster UK Ltd
1st Floor, 222 Gray's Inn Road
London WC1X 8HB

www.simonandschuster.co.uk
www.simonandschuster.com.au
www.simonandschuster.co.in

Simon & Schuster Australia, Sydney
Simon & Schuster India, New Delhi

A CIP catalogue record for this book
is available from the British Library.

PB ISBN: 978-1-4711-2491-4
EBOOK ISBN: 978-1-4711-2492-1

Printed and bound by CPI Group (UK) Ltd, Croydon, CR0 4YY

MIX
Paper from
responsible sources
FSC® C020471

Simon & Schuster UK Ltd are committed to sourcing paper
that is made from wood grown in sustainable forests and support the Forest
Stewardship Council, the leading international forest certification organisation.
Our books displaying the FSC logo are printed on FSC certified paper.

For everyone whose power
is being tested

So much power.
So few limits.

SWARM

CHAPTER 1
SCAM

"YOU LOOK *GREAT* IN THOSE JEANS!" ETHAN SAID.

He handed the guy a flyer.

The guy did *not* look great in those jeans. It was abundantly clear he'd gone commando just to fit into them. His legs would probably never bend again.

But Ethan didn't care. He was in a good mood, and the whole world was going to benefit. He moved on, scanning the crowd.

It was the last Saturday night before Christmas, and Ivy Street was buzzing. The clubs were about to open and everyone was ready to dance.

"Hey," Ethan said to a young woman in a purple feather boa. "Don't feel bad. Your boss is a total idiot."

She took the flyer. "How'd you . . ."

Ethan shrugged. *How* indeed.

"And, girl, purple is your color!" he enthused.

She beamed at him.

He was practically *singing* tonight.

Of course, it wasn't Ethan talking. It was his other voice. The one that always knew how to get Ethan what he wanted. And tonight all he wanted was for everyone to feel as happy as he did. So the voice was telling them whatever they needed to hear.

He moved on, feeling the happy. Letting the happy light him up from inside.

It was almost *weird* feeling this good, but for once his life was turning around. With the Summer of Suck in his rearview mirror, Ethan was free and clear. No more worrying about bank robbers and drug-dealing mobsters. No more being grounded by his mom. Even the other Zeroes were laying off their usual Scam bashing, treating him like part of the team.

And then there was Kelsie. After the kidnapping and the near-death experience inside the exploding building, she'd been pretty PTSD. Add in the despair of losing her dad and, well, it had been bad times.

But now she was on the up and up. Sometimes even happy. And if she was happy, then Ethan was too. *Seriously* happy.

"Your mom got you a Raystar 47 for Christmas!" Ethan heard himself say. He had no idea what that meant, but in front of him some guy's eyes lit up like a pair of horny fireflies. He must've *really* wanted that Raystar.

"Hey, how'd you even—" the guy began.

Ethan gave him a flyer and kept moving through the crowd.

Kelsie had settled easily into the Zeroes. *You're my family now,* she'd told Ethan shyly, and he'd practically gone super-nova with pride. Kelsie liked being with other people who had powers. She liked DJing at the Dish, exploring what she could do with a dance crowd. She didn't even mind Glorious Leader's endless "training."

One time Kelsie had said she was only in Cambria until she had enough cash to go find her mom in New Orleans. But she was still here, so maybe Kelsie had *another* reason to stay in Cambria. Someone she didn't want to leave behind.

Ethan hoped so, anyhow.

"Hey, you!" the voice cried as Ethan handed some short-ass kid a flyer. "You should totally tell her how you feel! Love is in the *air*, dude!"

Ethan blinked, playing back the words in his head. Was that a sign? That was a stretch—the voice *never* talked to Ethan directly. But this was one of those nights when anything seemed possible.

Okay. He'd talk to Kelsie tonight, right after the Dish closed.

"Whoa." The kid was wearing that familiar, startled expression everyone did when the voice plumbed their secrets. "You know about my stepmom?"

"I . . . wait. Your *stepmom*?" Ethan switched to his own

voice. "Forget I said anything, kid. Seriously, abort. Abort!"

He snatched back the flyer. Kid was too young for the Dish anyway.

Glorious Leader—*Nate*—had sent him over to Ivy Street, telling him to rope in people who were young and ready to dance. But if some fourteen-year-old kid turned up at the Dish, they'd all blame Ethan.

It was a reminder to focus, to not get swept up in the happy. Especially later with Kelsie. If he used his Zero voice to confess his feelings, Kelsie would know. So he had to use his own clumsy, fallible Ethan Cooper voice.

This flyer thing was the perfect warm-up. Hitting all these people with good news made him feel expansive and confident. On top of the world.

In fact, he was doing such a good job that he was almost out of flyers. But it wasn't quitting time yet.

If he was going to talk to Kelsie tonight—which he definitely *was*, no chickening out—he needed a huge, happy, agreeable mob in the Dish. Because then Kelsie would be so hooked into the passion and thrill of the crowd that she'd see the truth. *Yes, Ethan, I'm totally in love with you, too. I always have been. Since the moment you showed me I wasn't the only one in the world with a power!*

Which sounded unlikely, now that Ethan played the words in his head. But if she didn't say exactly that, at least she probably wouldn't say anything too soul-crushing.

Kelsie would never make him feel bad.

More flyers, then, to amp up the Dish tonight. *So many flyers.*

Ethan headed for the Office-O on the next block.

The place was practically empty.

He passed an old dude dozing behind the counter and headed to the back, where the copiers were lined up under the fluorescent lights like small armored vehicles. There was a young couple, Ethan's age, dressed for a night out in Ivy Street's club scene. The guy had a funky half-shaved haircut, and the girl wore a black frilled skirt.

Not Ethan's bag, but definitely the kind of people that Nate wanted at the Dish. Once he had more flyers, the voice would make their day telling them how awesome they looked.

He paused at the first copier, but it was flashing PAPER TRAY EMPTY. He tried the next copier. Same. Ditto the third. He scanned the row of copiers. All the red lights were flashing.

Okay, that was irritating. He looked around for someone in a blue Office-O shirt to help him.

Then he heard the *ka-chunk* of a paper drawer being slid out, and he turned to the young couple. The guy emptied the copier tray and took the paper to a paper cutter at the end of the row. The girl lined up the pile and began slicing.

What the hell?

Ethan stepped forward and cleared his throat. "Um, guys?

They sell paper here, you know. You don't have to take it from the copiers."

"Don't have any money," the girl said.

Ethan frowned. Like they could walk out of here with a thousand sheets of Office-O paper under their arms for free?

But if Ethan started arguing, he'd disturb the happy that filled him. So he smiled and let himself have a moment of wanting paper. Wanting the guy to *give him* some paper, and be glad about it.

The voice took over. "Dude, I need to make some copies. And you'll be interested in why."

The guy pulled the paper drawer from the last machine, ignoring Ethan. He was skinny, but tall, and carried himself like he wasn't afraid of anyone.

"There's this club that's special, if you know what I mean."

That got the guy's attention. Ethan held up his one remaining flyer.

"Coolest underground place in Cambria," the voice confirmed. "With the hottest DJ and the sweetest crowd. Just help me out with some paper so I can make sure there's a *super*-big party there tonight."

The guy smiled, like Ethan was suddenly an old pal. "That sounds great, buddy. Knock yourself out."

He slid the full tray back into the last machine and stepped back with a bow.

"Hey, thanks," Ethan said in his own voice.

That was the thing to remember about the voice. It didn't have to be a brutal weapon to do its thing. It didn't have to cut people down. As long as Ethan maintained a high level of affection for all humankind, the voice was happy being a sweetheart.

Maybe that was the key to superpowers. Not taking them too seriously. Not taking *yourself* too seriously.

Like, using your power for good or something.

He laid down his last flyer, swiped Nate's credit card along the card reader, and let the machine do its thing. While it rattled off a few hundred copies, Ethan slipped a lozenge from his pocket and stuck it in his mouth. A voice-induced burn was building in his throat.

But getting a good crowd for Kelsie was worth it.

Six months was a record for him. His previous longest crush—Mari Prendergast, freshman year—had lasted about a week and a half. So this wait made him even more certain that Kelsie was the real deal.

He'd almost blurted out his feelings a dozen times in the days and nights after her dad died. But grief had given her a kind of thousand-yard stare, like she was lost inside her own skull. Trying to talk romance at a time like that would've been cruel and unusual.

So he'd waited until things had calmed down for everyone.

The copier clattered to a halt. Ethan gathered his flyers and handed one to the couple at the paper cutter. He unleashed the voice to give them a last dose of happy.

"You'll love it, guys. And best of all, they'll never see you coming!"

Okay, that was pretty out there. But no weirder than the voice's stepmom advice earlier.

The couple looked surprised too, but Ethan just nodded and smiled like everything was normal. He headed for the door.

CHAPTER 2
SCAM

IT WAS EVEN BUSIER BACK ON THE STREET. THE stores were open late tonight and people were frantic with last-minute Christmas shopping.

Next to the Office-O, Ethan spotted a girl peering at a retail-window display of robot Santas. She had white-bleached hair with a strip of magenta over one ear. Perfect.

"Party at the Dish tonight." He held out a flyer with a smile. "Great for your next post!"

Ethan squirmed as the words came out. Nate didn't want anyone putting stuff about the Dish online.

The girl turned toward him, befuddlement fading into a look of recognition. "Hey, it's *you*."

Ethan swallowed the voice down. "Um, sorry, who . . ."

But he knew who she was.

She grinned. "Been to any good bank robberies lately?"

Sonia Sonic. The girl he'd met on the cold marble floor of Cambria Central Bank last summer. The girl who'd videoed his Zero voice in action and posted it for the entire world to see.

That girl. And the stupid voice had just gone and promised her more material!

He tried to hide the flyer, but Sonia yanked it away from him. Lightning fast, she snapped a picture of it with her phone.

Ethan was seriously screwed.

Nate had warned all the Zeroes to keep a low profile, and specifically to avoid Sonia Sonic on pain of death. Those were Nate's exact words: *pain of death*, which sounded like some pretty serious pain.

"I knew it!" Sonia said. "You're up to something, right? You and your freaky friends?"

Ethan tried to look like he didn't know what she was talking about. But all the Zeroes read Sonia's feed regularly.

She was practically a career weird-hunter now. She'd been posting about inexplicable crowd events ever since the bank thing. She might not have been present for the police station meltdown last summer, or the riot on Ivy Street the next night, but she'd interviewed a lot of people who had been.

And, like most of Cambria, she'd witnessed firsthand the mysterious glitch at the Fourth of July fireworks show a week later. After that she'd started tracking outbreaks of crowd madness from Seattle to Miami to Santa Rosa. Her theory was that all these events were related, and that Ethan and his friends were part of some strange conspiracy.

She was mostly wrong, of course. For a start, most of the Zeroes had never even been out of Cambria. There was no conspiracy, even if it was pretty clear that there *had to be* other Zeroes out there causing trouble.

But six superpowered teens experimenting on people in an illegal nightclub? Now *that* story would blow all of last summer's crazy out of the water.

Sonia leaned forward conspiratorially. "You know, that bank video was the biggest thing to happen to me ever. People all over the country read my posts. I've had calls from journalists, even a senator from Washington State. I'm, like, a celebrity now!"

"Glad my humiliation was useful to you," Ethan said.

For weeks after she'd posted that video, Ethan hadn't been able to go anywhere in Cambria without being recognized. Which was the opposite of useful with a power like Ethan's. When your superpower was lying, it didn't pay to be famous.

In fact, none of the Zeroes needed Sonia's attention. It'd be a lot harder to influence people if they knew that crowd magic was nudging them along.

Sonia scanned the flyer. "What kind of club name is the Petri Dish, anyway?"

"It means you're not welcome there," he said.

"Why not, exactly?"

Because the Dish was the Zeroes' hideaway, a place where they could experiment with their powers. (Hence the stupid name.) They kept it underground for exactly three reasons—no media attention, no cops, and no Sonia frickin' Sonic.

Of course, Ethan didn't say any of that. He could only unleash the beast. He hated to, because the voice had been in such a happy place today. But the safety of the team was more important than his own good mood.

"Because you really *don't* want to be seen in public with that hair," he heard himself say.

Sonia opened her mouth, but nothing came out. The voice was an expert at getting that reaction.

"Sure, I can see you were going for magenta with that stripe. But right now it looks more like a shade of Life Saver. Flamingo Musk, maybe? Or Cat Vomit Rosé?"

"Stop even talking!" Sonia cried. "This is GothLyfe Full Metal Magenta! You can't *get* more magenta than this."

But the voice was cruising now. It burned with a fierceness he hadn't felt in days. As if all the happiness it had flung out into the world had been a warm-up for the real deal.

"Maybe it was this morning, sweetie. But unless you want to be known as Sonia Salmon Head—"

"Why are you doing this?" She glared at him, eyes glistening.

Ethan could feel the voice rising up, ready to go again. But with a searing effort, he managed to choke down the next insult.

This wasn't what his power was all about. It wasn't who he *was*. Not anymore.

"Sorry," he croaked.

As he warred to keep the voice silent, Sonia's expression shifted.

"Wait a second. This is exactly what you did in the bank. You made that robber go crazy, just by talking to him."

"I . . . um," Ethan managed, still struggling. "Pink hair . . . bad."

"I am totally coming to your club," she said grimly. "There's nothing you can say to stop me."

And with that, the voice died a silent death in Ethan's throat.

That was the thing about his power—it knew when to quit. If there was nothing to say that would get Ethan what he wanted, the voice went to sleep.

Looked like Sonia was coming to the Dish.

He swallowed, wondering how to explain it when he got back.

Hey, Nate, remember the one person you told me on pain of death not to invite? Yeah, well, check out her new hairstyle!

"Okay. But let me take you." Maybe he could get ahead of this. "My girlfriend's the DJ. Kind of."

"Kind of your girlfriend, or kind of the DJ?"

"Definitely the DJ," he muttered.

"Okay." Sonia flipped her striped hair over an ear. "I'll make sure to check out your girlfriend's mad skills."

She made *skills* sound like it had *Z*s on the end.

Maybe Kelsie could charm Sonia out of posting about the club. She could work anyone who was willing to be part of a crowd.

"I think your hair's pretty cool, actually," he admitted.

"You are a *freak*!" Sonia grinned and linked her arm through his. "But you're not so bad, when you're not going psycho. And hey, we're practically Cambria royalty, right?"

A familiar voice called from behind Ethan. "Hey, everyone! Free shipping for your Christmas packages!"

Ethan turned. It was the guy who'd been stealing paper in the Office-O. He was in the doorway, shouting at the people on the street. His girlfriend stood beside him, warming her hands in the folds of her frilled skirt.

"Seriously!" she added. "Mail your Christmas presents here and now. We've got packing supplies! Wrapping paper! FedEx forms! We'll spring for it all!"

A crowd began to gather, their arms full of shopping bags. They all looked tired and hopeful enough to believe in a Christmas miracle.

The guy lifted his arms above his head. He had a thick wad of cash in each hand.

"Huh," Ethan said. So much for them having no money.

"Quit stalling and let's go," Sonia said, dragging at his elbow.

"Does that seem weird to you?" Ethan asked, pointing at the couple.

"Ethan, I know weird, and that's nothing like it. Free stuff always pulls a crowd." She stared at her phone. "But this *is* weird. Whose phone is this?"

"Isn't it your—" Ethan began, but a convulsion struck his throat, like his Adam's apple was expanding. "I should forget she'll never I'm not good enough how could I—"

Ethan stopped talking. His throat felt like someone else's, and his voice sounded like someone else's too. But worst of all were the words he was saying. They weren't *his* anymore, after all that time he'd spent learning to speak, even though the voice could do it better. Suddenly his words felt like someone else's, and he couldn't get them out right.

He tried again, "I just want what I can't but it's something I never—"

This wasn't the voice going haywire. No. It was his own voice—his Ethan Cooper voice, the one he'd spent his whole life trying to claim—somehow turned alien inside his own mouth.

Panic roiled his gut.

"I tried but it's never wanted to know everything—" This was *not* him talking! Even his lips and tongue felt wrong, like a dentist had shot him full of novocaine.

"Brain fart again?" Sonia asked, dragging him away from the Office-O crowd. "Come on. Because I'm still going to your nightclub, even I have to take you to the psycho ward first."

Ethan turned to her, his mouth working to explain but no sound coming out.

Finally he managed to shout, "Mesopotamia!"

It was his code word, something he'd chosen when he was a kid—a fail-safe, in case he ever had to make sure it was him talking and not his other voice. He hadn't needed that word since he was ten.

"You are *so* random," Sonia said calmly.

"Hello? Hello!" Yes, the pall was lifting. The words came out almost normally, and his throat felt like his own again. "Sorry, I didn't recognize myself for a minute there."

Sonia was frowning at her phone again. "Yeah, I know what you mean. Come on, this Dish club of yours isn't going to investigate itself."

Ethan let Sonia propel him away from Ivy Street and toward the Heights. He handed out a few more flyers as they walked, but he couldn't use the voice with Sonia watching. After what had happened, he wasn't sure if he wanted to speak at all.

Right now all he wanted was for Nate to not be on the door when he rolled up with Sonia Sonic in tow.

CHAPTER 3
BELLWETHER

THERE WERE TWENTY-SEVEN PEOPLE IN LINE. NOT enough to open the doors.

Nate hated clubs that let customers in too soon, forcing them to jangle around in too much space, forming half crowds and feeble connections.

Not while he was working the door.

Besides, keeping the crowd waiting gave him time to take notes on who was showing up tonight. Hipsters with chunky glasses—local residents, probably. A group of women in designer jeans, alight with the wary bubbliness of slumming it in the Heights. The usual underage contingent who knew that the Dish never turned anyone away. Well, except people visibly messed up enough to alter Kelsie's vibe.

The Petri Dish was a controlled experiment. Every variable mattered.

For example, the male-to-female ratio of the line was getting a little high. Nate texted Ethan: *No more groups of guys.*

For most of the summer and fall, Nate had spent his weekends with Kelsie on Ivy Street—taking notes, asking questions. Determining the best night of the week to open, the right mix of young and old, the minimum number of people required for serious dancing to break out.

Thirty-one in line now. Still not enough.

The Curve started at around six people, but everything the Zeroes had accomplished this summer showed that bigger crowds were better. More meaningful. More *powerful.* So every night he waited for at least forty people before opening the doors.

Nate had never particularly liked nightclubs. But now that he had his own, he realized that most of their problems were easily corrected.

Being in charge always made the difference.

"Hey, dude," a girl shouted from halfway down the line. She was wearing a purple feather boa. "Don't tell me it's *full* in there already. Let us in!"

The energy of the crowd centered on her, then shifted back to Nate. He gave them a smile, focusing all those restless shimmers of attention.

"Five minutes," he called out. It settled them a little, but it also sharpened their anticipation. People finger-combed their hair, reapplied lipstick. At the front a guy reached over to straighten his boyfriend's tie.

Two couples, white teenagers trying to look chill about being on the bad side of town, joined the end of the line. Thirty-five now. Very close. Nate pulled a little tighter on the web of attention from the crowd, drawing it to himself.

These were his favorite moments, keeping the crowd on edge like this.

But then his focus frayed a little—a police car was cruising past, the officers inside it taking a long, hard look.

The Petri Dish was in no way legal. Chizara had brought the electrical system up to code, and the owners of the once-derelict theater were happy to take a cut of profits. But there was no liquor license, no *anything* license, and no contracts. Just a web of informal arrangements.

On paper the Dish was a private party, a gathering of friends in a rented space. Presumably Ethan's voice and Nate's charm could sell that story, keeping Nate's police record spotless. But the theory hadn't been tested yet.

The police car kept moving, but Nate wondered if he should open the club now. Having a crowd hanging around outside was a little too conspicuous. Especially since the Cambria PD was officially focusing on crowd control, thanks to the strange events of last summer.

Of course, crowd-madness stories were popping up everywhere. Flash mobs, rampant teenagers, and unexplained riots were all the rage lately. It was pretty clear that there were other people with superpowers out there.

Which irked Nate just a little, the idea that he and the others weren't the only Zeroes in the world. But at least his crew was learning to use their powers in a systematic way.

Maybe those other groups didn't have Bellwethers to guide them. Maybe he was meant for bigger things.

Another couple had just joined the end of the line. Thirty-seven now.

But what was Ethan doing back so soon? The crowd wasn't big enough to open, and Nate needed another twenty by the end of the hour, to keep the build consistent with last month's.

Mierda. It figured Ethan would never understand the *controlled* part of a controlled experiment. His dereliction of duty probably had to do with the girl beside him. She had silver hair with a magenta streak and was waving her sparkly phone around, snapping pictures. Exactly the sort of trendy cutie that Ethan always widened his eyes for, when he wasn't busy pining for Kelsie.

Though this girl looked oddly familiar . . .

Nate went to the end of the line, ignoring the glimmers of confusion from the crowd. *Where's the door guy going? Isn't it five minutes yet?*

"Uh, hey," Ethan mumbled as Nate approached. "This is Sonia."

"Nice to meet you. Ethan, is there any reason you're not . . ."

Nate's words faded—Sonia . . . *Sonic*? The one person in all of Cambria who was committed to exposing the Zeroes. And here she was, taking a picture of Nate.

"Can I ask you some questions about your nightclub?" Sonia asked, keeping the phone steady as she talked. Not photos—*video*.

"It isn't my . . . ," he began, but it was too late. Sputtering denials and raising his hand to cover the lens would only make him look guilty. He had to get her inside the Faraday cage of the Dish before the video was backed up to the cloud.

Which meant she had to keep shooting.

"It isn't so much a club as a party." He smiled for the camera, then turned and beckoned her to follow. "Would you like a tour?"

Sonia nodded happily. Ethan opened his mouth, but nothing came out. Good. Nate didn't need the voice butting in.

"This is only our third event," he said. "We always open the third Saturday of the month."

That would have to change now, of course. But they could always scare up a new crowd. And switching the schedule around would make it harder for the police to crack down on them.

"I've heard it's the best party in town," Sonia said. "Can I ask what makes it . . . special?"

Nate almost lost his smile at that last word. Sonia Sonic knew a little too much about the *specialness* of the Zeroes.

Way too many people read her posts since last summer, and she was getting D-list Cambria famous. Nate even heard people murmuring her name as he walked her back to the front of the line. She was a problem, and would continue to be a problem.

But first things first—Nate had to deal with her phone. Sonia didn't like posting without pictures.

"We're just about to open," he said as they reached the doors. "But maybe get a shot of the line first. Big crowds are good PR."

"Right. Of course." She turned back and lifted her phone high. Everyone was stirring to life, attention and anticipation crackling off them like sparks from a hot wire. A couple of people waved for the camera.

While she was busy shooting, Nate opened the door and signaled for the bouncer waiting just inside. The guy was a mass of muscle, too intimidating to keep in plain sight this early in the evening.

"Take a message to Chizara," Nate said softly.

"Of course, Mr. Saldana," answered the Craig, his eyes brightening. The Craig had a thing for Chizara—or for *Crash*, to be accurate. A thing that was not unlike worship.

"This girl can't leave with her data intact." Nate nodded at Sonia. "Phone equals brick."

The Craig frowned, but by now he was used to the Zeroes saying strange things. "Got it, boss. That girl—brick her phone."

Nate gave him the full wattage of his approval. Incorruptible and unimaginative, the Craig was the perfect employee for an illegal nightclub. He would never betray Crash, not since he'd seen her destroy the Parker-Hamilton Hotel with a wave of her hand.

Craig was already halfway to the lighting booth, eager to deliver the message.

Nate checked the door line again. Another three had joined the end.

Forty on the nose. Perfect.

"Shall we?" he said to Sonia, then gave Ethan one last baleful look and opened the doors of the Dish.

CHAPTER 4
CRASH

THE CROWD SPILLED ACROSS THE DANCE FLOOR, already bopping to Kelsie's background trance music.

Chizara set two of the rainbow lights spinning, on slow—it was best to start off basic, then build through the evening. In the DJ booth beside her, Kelsie fiddled with the turntables, flipped though stacks of vinyl. Chizara leaned back, waiting for her to make the next move.

In the crowd a few people stared at their phones, shook them, then shrugged and shoved them into their pockets. Chizara grinned. Was the Faraday cage the best invention ever or what?

She looked up reverently. Against the stucco ceiling of the old theater, a fine metal mesh sparkled in the rainbow lights. It was amazing how something so full of holes could keep out the awful roar of signals, the painful chatter of repeater towers and wifi spilling from surrounding buildings. Here in the Dish, all of it was silenced.

Chizara shivered—how easy it would've been to gloss over Bob's words that time at work, instead of asking idly, *Faraday cages? What the hell are those?*

Why hadn't she researched signal blocking before and found out that a metal mesh was the answer to all her problems? She could have built her own personal cube of silence any time.

Of course, like her mom always said: *A man with a good roof never gets used to the rain.* If Chizara had grown up with a Faraday cage wrapped around her room, she'd never have built up her resistance. These days she was pretty much fine with phones—the average crowd wasn't the prickle bush it had been even a few months ago. But the silence inside the Dish felt truly luxurious.

She stretched her arms in the cramped lighting booth. Being pain-free was a fantastic feeling, and the fact that she'd built this sanctuary herself only made it sweeter.

The Petri Dish was Chizara's design. She'd figured out how to build the cage, how to wire the place with analog sound and lighting, avoiding the buzz of networks.

Sure, the Craig and his musclemen had done the heavy lifting, setting up light towers and trusses, hanging that old mirror ball and the spotlights and strobes that made it magic. Bob, her old boss at the shop around the corner, had given her lots of tips, and Bob's friend Justin, a disco king back in the eighties, had sold Nate most of the equipment and found them other good cheap retro stuff.

But the final word on everything had been Chizara's.

At the moment the mirror ball and the UV strobe were the high points of the light show. But she wanted to install one of those wild tumbling UFO lights one day—maybe two, at either end of the dance floor.

The thought made her thirsty for more dazzle. She switched on a couple of white spotlights and set their narrow beams swinging randomly around the space.

One spot flashed past the Craig. He was shouldering through the thin crowd toward her. With intent, not just for a chat. He liked to talk tech with Chizara—well, he'd talk anything with her, but the tech was his usual excuse to start a conversation. He was always bringing up lighting ideas he'd seen at the clubs on Ivy Street.

Most of his suggestions called for digital controls, though. She wasn't going to taint her refuge with that networked dreck. She had to keep telling him: *The Dish is pure analog, Craig, remember?* His hold on her superpower was shaky. Sometimes he almost believed in it, but mostly he just seemed to think she had a terrific sense of timing around demolition sites.

"Zup, Craig?" she called out over the music.

"Message from Mr. Saldana."

"Uh-huh?" Chizara suppressed a grin at the massive guy's respect for Glorious Leader.

The Craig jerked his head toward the dance floor. "Girl out there, he wants you to make sure to brick her phone before she leaves."

Chizara's eyebrows went up. "Which girl?"

"See over there, standing next to Ethan? The one shooting video."

Chizara reached her mind into the clunky workings of a swinging spotlight, nudged its electricals so that the gears turned the way she wanted for a moment. She squashed down a little spurt of pride. All her practice meant she could go low-tech now, pushing around fat, sizzling electromagnets as easy as microchips.

She held the white beam steady on the girl for a couple of seconds, isolating her from the rolling-box colors. "Cool hair. Makes her easy to—wait, that's Sonia Sonic!"

She felt a stab of sick nerves. Cambria's self-appointed weird-hunter had been sniffing around since Scam had super-powered his way out of the police station last summer. Sonia was always ready to post about unexplained crowd behavior and system failures. She was onto them.

So who the hell had gone and told her about the Dish? Who'd *brought* her here, for goodness' sakes? What kind of dumb-ass . . .

Ethan noticed the lingering spotlight and shot a guilty look toward Chizara. Of course.

"Sonia who?" the Craig asked. He never went online unless he was running short of supplements.

"An old friend." Chizara moved the spotlight away before it got obvious. "Tell Mr. Saldana I'll take care of it."

"Need the Craig to bring her closer for you?"

"Nope. I got it." She winked at him, deadpan.

"You got some kind of phone zapper?" He tore his gaze from her and checked around the booth, eyed the cupboardlike switching box with its fat ribbon cable going to the light board.

"Nope." She pointed to her temple. "It's all in my head."

Craig gave her his *Are you really magic?* look—half fear, half awe. "Uh, if you say so. I better get back on the door."

As he walked away, Kelsie shouted from the DJ booth next door. "You ready to tear this up, Crash?"

Chizara gave her the thumbs-up, then blanched the crowd with a couple of flashes from the wide white floodlights. Arms went up all over the dance floor, and Kelsie kicked in with her first track, the driving beat taking and shaking them like streamers on a cheerleader's pom-poms.

Chizara spun the other rolling boxes into action and added some flashing spots, lancing mauve-white light among the dancers. That would keep them busy for three minutes. Kelsie's shakedown track was never a long one.

She squinted across the bouncing crowd. There was no

need to hurry with the phone-fritzing—Sonia looked like she was settling in. She stowed her phone in a tiny sequined bag on her hip and stepped out onto the dance floor.

Chizara tracked her vivid hair through the crowd, nudging a spotlight here and there to keep Sonia in sight. All the dancers' phones, hunting for signal, jumped and shimmied in pockets and purses. It was like looking over a night-lit city with a constant rippling earthquake going on.

It would be quite a challenge, homing in on the floating speck of that one phone.

But that was the point of the Petri Dish, wasn't it? To be a safe place for the Zeroes to challenge themselves and their powers.

Chizara kept a firm eye on the silver-and-magenta hair and felt for the dim dot of the phone that matched the girl's movement.

Next door, Kelsie cued up another track. One beat faded into another, and Chizara sent a new mix of lights sweeping across the dancers. She and Kelsie had rehearsed their transitions for days before the first Dish party two months ago—now Chizara hardly had to think about them. She could concentrate on Sonia.

Who was right up close, bouncing in front of Kelsie. Getting out her phone again, taking photos. She held it up and started a panorama of Kelsie on the decks, Chizara in the lighting box, documenting all the Dish's operations.

Chizara sent her Crash brain into the phone. The minuscule maze of electronics lit up, so pretty and fine compared to the brute gears and tungsten flares of spotlights. Where was the action happening? Where were the sounds and images flowing into the memory?

Ah, there. Like babies in a nursery, all in a row. Waiting to upload to the cloud as soon as the phone escaped the confines of the Faraday cage.

Crash applied the burning needle tip of her power, turning the phone into a sparkly brick.

But as her mind slipped back into the good-times vibe Kelsie was sending out, Chizara felt a little jolt, a hiccup . . . something she didn't like.

She looked down at her hands. They hovered over a board full of switches and sliders. The labels—*RB1, VNSP SET*— suddenly made no sense whatever, even if they were in her own neat handwriting.

She was supposed to be in control of all this. But—

She sent her mind through the circuitry, but it was like a map of an alien city, meaningless, lit with random pulses. She should know her way around this stuff. Hadn't she *built* it? But now it meant nothing. She knew nothing.

She froze in panic. The alien city stretched out in front of her, surging, quaking. Nothing connected. What was it all for? What was *she* for? Her heart raced faster than the music's pounding. Lights zigzagged in automatic patterns, gleaming on the mesh and the scarred-plaster walls of the Dish. She was supposed to rule those lights, not let them wander—she was supposed to take hold and move them.

But she didn't—

But they weren't—

Then the familiar logic of the systems drifted back into place, and they were suddenly what they should be, what they'd always been—the cables streaming power, the thousands of feet of wire fanning in and out of the two glowing hubs of music and light that she and Kelsie commanded. Whatever glitch of her brain had taken them away from her had gently handed them back.

Sweat broke out cold all over her, and a breath shuddered into her throat.

What the *hell* had just happened?

CHAPTER 5
ANONYMOUS

THE SPOTLIGHTS STILLED A MOMENT, AND THIBAULT looked up.

Chizara stood stiffly, her hands like snatched-back claws, as if she'd just gotten a shock from the lighting board. Her attention was snapped ropes of light, flailing around her head.

Thibault dropped from his bar stool, ready to run and help her.

But then she lowered her hands to the sliders again. Her attention reattached to Kelsie, to the crowd, to her job. The spots restarted their jagged dance across raised arms and faces.

Thibault sat back, still watching her.

As Kelsie smashed through to a new track, Chizara followed flawlessly, her lights a roving counterpoint to the beat. Everything back in its place.

It was a pleasure to watch those two rocking the crowd, to see the connections divide endlessly across the dance floor, a stable cloud of diffuse light over everyone, no single strands lasering between individuals. They were one big multibodied animal, one mind, one heart, everyone lost in the music and the movement, no one resisting, or making a move on anyone, or breaking out and making trouble.

At times like this, Thibault's power almost felt like a gift. Maybe he could never join that web of connections, but he could *see* them like nobody else in the world—except Nate, of course.

And being on the sidelines wasn't all bad. Crowds were like clouds of smoke—it was easier to understand their shape from the outside. He could see things as they truly were here, not be swept up in Kelsie's dance euphoria.

Someone had to stay free of her grip, to intervene if needed. Thibault was the club's secret bouncer. If Craig was the battleship, he was the stealth fighter.

Flicker was behind the bar, moving confidently in the familiar space. Tonight she wore a zebra-striped dress, easy to spot through anyone's eyes she happened to borrow.

She was busy stacking cans under the counter. The Dish had only one ancient refrigerator, and by design the cold beer always ran out early. As Nate said, a sober crowd was better for practicing their powers on.

This crowd was younger than usual, everyone out of school

on the last Saturday before Christmas. Thibault recognized a lot of faces, though. He'd made an effort to memorize the regulars. He wanted to know this place as well as he'd known his last home, the Hotel Magnifique.

A girl caught his eye, swaying through the crowd, her hair dramatic white and magenta. Seriously? Sonia Sonic? Why had Nate let her in, when she was practically stalking the Zeroes?

Ethan was trailing after her. Okay, Nate must have told him to keep an eye on her.

"You thirsty?"

Flicker handed a bottle of water across the bar, fully aware of him even with all these people around. Amazing.

It was icy in his hand. The last cold one, no doubt.

"Thanks."

She dipped her head at him. "Let's see if I can hold on to you when people start lining up."

"No big deal if you can't."

"Oh, but I will." She ran a finger down the inside of her left arm. Earlier, upstairs in his room, he'd moved his lips slowly along that same line, making her shiver. Breathing her in. And she hadn't forgotten it.

Damn it, why did the Dish have to be open tonight?

Even after half a year, it astounded Thibault that he had a girlfriend, someone who remembered his name and what kind of coffee he drank. Someone he'd happily wear this ridiculous red leather jacket for, just so she could spot him more easily in a crowd. She even quoted Zen koans at him sometimes.

Like whispering, *Attachment leads to suffering,* with her lips next to his ear, her hands on his skin. Right now Thibault was fine with being attached, to this girl and this place and these people. He had a home, upstairs in the old theater office. No more ripping off hotels. He even had a roommate, Kelsie, who wasn't completely surprised when she ran into him making breakfast in the mornings.

For the first time, he was part of something—this group experiment where the Zeroes could hone their skills without breaking police stations and hurting people.

"This is a pretty tight set," Flicker said.

Thibault nodded. "Mob gets better every time."

Beyond the haze of crowd connections, Kelsie was a tiny figure with giant headphones clamped around her blond curls. She danced in her skintight silver dress, lining up the next track. She'd wound up the crowd pretty high—shiny faces and open mouths. Maybe she should ease up some?

Right on cue she switched to a gentler track. Thibault grinned. The first time the Dish had opened, she'd exhausted everyone in the first hour. But she was learning.

Released from her thrall, the crowd's awareness flickered about like bugs' antennae, brightening as people greeted friends or eyed alluring strangers. Some drifted toward the bar, eager for the cold beer while it lasted.

Flicker's awareness of him faded, but it would come back.

Thibault slid off the bar stool, watching the dance floor empty. Sonia Sonic was standing in the center, looking around at the unused stage of the old theater, the box seats full of Chizara's lights, the rickety stairway. Checking *everything* out.

Was Nate really okay with this?

Sonia took out her phone, held it up, then frowned.

A flickering beam of attention arced toward her. Chizara, half smiling in the lighting box. No, not Chizara—Crash.

Thibault joined in the smile.

"What do you mean, only beer?" someone bellowed nearby. "My girl wants champagne!"

Thibault turned. A tall, skinny guy leaned at Flicker across the bar. The nearer half of his head was shaved, and the girl beside him was all makeup, boots, and frilly skirt, her hands on her hips. Their attention was like two shining pickaxes sunk into Flicker's face.

How had Thibault not noticed these two before? They had trouble written all over them.

"Sorry," Flicker said cheerfully, sight lines multiplying as the guy's voice drew everyone's attention. "It's five-dollar beer or a buck for water. And we're not even legal for beer, really."

The girl looked super bored. The guy shrugged and reached into his jacket and pulled out cash—a *wad* of it, like something out of a comic book. Thibault hadn't seen that many bills since the summer, when Scam had stumbled into Nate's place with Craig's duffel bag of drug takings.

The guy dumped the cash on the bar and strolled the length of it, drawing the bills out in a line like a card dealer spreading a deck. Then he grabbed his girlfriend's hand and pulled her back through the crowd. "Come drink your five-dollar beer, bitches!" he called out. "We're gonna dance!"

The bar crowd changed in a microsecond. Attention flashed thick on the bills; hands grabbed and people surged forward. Flicker stepped back, looking dazed.

The crowd had been one big magical beast on the dance floor, built with all Mob's care and skill. Now it fragmented into a hot mess of individuals, needy and clamoring. A koan tolled in Thibault's head: *Even a shower of money is no satisfaction.*

See? The money was already gone. People started calling for beers and water and snacks, the bright lines of their attention stabbing at Flicker. A guy pushed past Thibault, straightening a little stack of bills and aiming for the door.

"Okay, that is not cool," Thibault said, going after him. The cashed-up guy might have been an asshole, but this was an out-and-out thief.

He reached the guy just as he was shoving the cash into his jacket pocket. Chizara was playing the UV light across the room, and the security strips flashed at Thibault like the bills were signaling for rescue.

37

He rescued them, right out of the guy's hand.

The thief swung around. Thibault chopped away his attention before it had time to land on him. The guy's outraged look turned to bewilderment.

"Who the—?" He checked his empty pocket, scanned the crowd.

Stashing the money in his own pocket, Thibault cut away through the dancers to find a jostle-free place to stand against the wall.

The rich guy and his girlfriend were in the middle of the dance floor. They stood face-to-face, holding hands, gazing into each other's eyes.

Thibault's breath caught—the bright bar of attention in the air between them was so raw and intense. They were the center of each other's universe. But it wasn't what he had with Flicker—this was something stronger, darker. He felt a quiver of fear.

Kelsie cross-faded into a new, stronger beat, like she was responding to the sudden passion on the dance floor. People cheered, and connections started to melt together as they fell in with the rhythm, the crowd beast reforming.

Good. Maybe these two could repair the damage they'd done by throwing their money around. People were already spilling back onto the floor, whirling to the irresistible music. Thibault found himself bobbing his head in time.

Chizara took the lights down, following Kelsie's lead. Now

it was almost black inside the Dish, except for teeth and white T-shirts throwing back the UV light, and a few spotlights slithering over the crowd—

Then one more shaft of light as the couple began to slowly spin, and their ultrabright connection scythed out, slicing through the room, a fiery blade.

This wasn't just love.

These two were Zeroes.

The beam of their connection struck Thibault, and he stumbled, all meaning draining from the world.

CHAPTER 6
MOB

THIS WAS THE PART KELSIE LIKED THE BEST—WHEN the crowd *really* started dancing.

They were right on the edge of out of control. Familiar faces from her Ivy Street clubbing days and a bunch of new people too. She was ready for them. Tonight she'd blend her music and her power to create the most awesome dance party Cambria had ever seen.

The boom frames on the big speakers beside her rattled, sending the bass like a heartbeat through the floor of her DJ platform. She let the energy fill up the room like a flood, carrying her away.

She amped the bass, then flipped her bulky headphones off one ear to hear the whooping and hollering.

She leaned against the wave of eagerness from the crowd.

She needed this. It was only here, in the DJ booth, that she could forget about the stupid mess of her life. The flashbacks to last summer stopped when the vinyl was spinning.

She bent over her turntables, matching the next track's tempo to the remixed pop song already playing. Then she reached out into the crowd and cross-faded between decks. . . .

In one voice, the crowd roared.

The savage delight of their reaction was that of an animal let off the leash. The wilder they got, the wilder Kelsie felt. The farther she went out on a limb, the more they wanted to follow. Her spine was a hot white spotlight shining right out through the top of her skull.

Dad would've been so proud. He'd barely recognize her, up here in the DJ booth five feet above the dance floor. Close enough to be part of the crowd, but separate, too. Working the room with her music and magic.

A thought stabbed through her—if only she'd gotten him help years ago.

The energy in the room darkened, Kelsie's loss spilling across them. She eased back, counting out a long breath. The panic attacks had begun the night Dad died. She was getting better, though, with the Zeroes' help. Her roomie—Thibault, that was his name—was teaching her the Middle Way.

When she'd started DJing two months back, the crowd kept carrying her off, and she'd forget that she was supposed to control the music. Songs had stuttered or faded out into embarrassing pauses.

Tonight she wouldn't miss a beat. She'd make the Zeroes proud, and pay them back for taking her in. She was one of them, even if she hadn't been practicing her power as long.

Chizara's lights swung toward the middle of the dance floor and landed on a couple. A girl and guy eye-banging each other as they danced, oblivious to everyone else. Kelsie felt a pang of envy. They were lost in their own world. She wondered if she would ever be part of something so private and intense.

But it was weird. Around the couple the crowd was growing restless and shaky. Like they sensed something they couldn't be part of. The intensity in the room became rough and unpredictable, and someone stumbled across the dance floor. Suddenly nobody seemed to know what to do with their bodies.

Kelsie gasped, feeling the crowd's shakiness reach out for her.

She could fix this. Something light and simple would drag them back from the edge, the kind of thing that got played during time-outs at a basketball game.

Kelsie reached for the crate of vinyl, but something weird happened—she couldn't recognize the first album she pulled out. The artist and track names were in some kind of alien scrawl. The pictures turned to slush, spreading across the crate and infecting every cover until they were all unreadable.

Beside her the decks seemed to turn into mouths with sharp pointed teeth. She leaped back before they could snap off her hands.

"Oh my God!"

Her confusion crashed against the weird tides of energy on the dance floor, forming a feedback loop of pure panic. The music from the speakers jolted—two mismatched beats colliding, like a dogfight breaking out.

Out on the dance floor the crowd became an angry sea, and the music turned to screams. The Dish filled with a monstrous shape where the dance floor had been.

Kelsie was alone up here, and all the darkness in the world was spread out below.

She couldn't recognize anything—or anyone.

CHAPTER 7
FLICKER

THE MUSIC SKIDDED, TWO SONGS TANGLING, Kelsie making a rare mistake.

Flicker was on her knees, feeling among the cans in the refrigerator, fingers searching for cold aluminum. None of the beers felt like they'd been inside for more than a minute or two. Best to close the door and let the fridge do its thing.

"It's warm, sorry," she said, standing up and handing the guy a can. She slid her vision into his eyes, saw that he was handing her a ten, and gave him a five from the cash drawer stuffed full of money from that rich guy a minute ago.

What an asshole. Compensating much?

She bounced her vision around the bar—nobody was staring at her, waiting for a drink. But the eyeballs out on the dance floor were twitching, everyone a little unsteady on their feet. Pre-Christmas jitters, maybe?

She searched for Anon's red leather jacket, something familiar to hold on to.

Wait—Anon wasn't his real name.

Weird. She'd lost it somehow. By reflex her fingers went to the bracelet around her right wrist. Braille letters were punched into the band of leather. They settled slowly into meaning.

T-H-I-B-A-U-L-T.

Flicker played the sound of it in her mind, liltingly French.

When she'd picked braille back up a month ago, it had slid back into her fingers, feeling easy and right. It was a handy way to leave notes for herself, since her boyfriend's involuntary superpower happened to be erasing memories.

The air shook again, interrupting Flicker's thoughts. More mismatched tempos blared from the speakers, like a collision of two marching bands in a parade.

Shit. It wasn't like Kelsie to keep blowing transitions like this. And the two beats were *still* flailing against each other.

Flicker cast her vision out into the crowd, trying to catch a glimpse of the DJ platform.

But everything looked *wrong*. . . .

Dancers usually stared down at their feet, or up at the light show, or at attractive strangers. But the eyes out there were darting around in a panic, like someone trying to find a snake in their bedroom.

Over the juddering music, Flicker heard anxious cries of confusion building. She could almost *smell* the fear of the crowd.

And the dancing had turned to flailing . . . like something out of a demented puppet show. Limbs and torsos jerking around, pulled by invisible lines of force. Like everyone's brains had been glitched somehow and they'd forgotten how to use their own bodies.

She caught a glimpse of Kelsie on the DJ platform, huddled in a corner by her records, arms wrapped around her knees. Chizara stared at her light-booth controls, confused and terrified. The lights were swinging through the same patterns again and again, stuck in a loop as random as the music.

Whatever this was, it had hit everybody, which meant it must also be affecting . . .

Flicker cast her vision around, looking for him. He was wearing something special tonight. Right—a red leather jacket.

She found it a moment later, on the dance floor with all those hideously jerking bodies. His movements looked just as wrong, glitchy and uncoordinated.

But the worst thing was his face. He was a fake.

What was he *supposed* to look like? Flicker ransacked her

memory. His eyes, his chin, his smile? All those carefully memorized features looked wrong to her too. They matched this impostor out on the dance floor, but not her own inner sense of *rightness*.

And she'd forgotten his name. Not just the tricky real one—his code name too.

Flicker's fingers went to her wrist, searching the band of leather. But again her mind failed her, the dots refusing to resolve into letters.

Braille was gone too.

Something in this club was messing with her brain—with *everyone's* brain.

She had to get out.

Flicker switched off her vision, turned from the seething dance floor, and ran the length of the bar. She jumped the boxes she'd stacked there this afternoon. Which meant her memory wasn't broken, just her ability to *recognize*.

She rolled under the flip-down door of the bar, shouldered the push bar of the emergency exit, and tumbled through, into the back alley full of garbage bags and broken glass. The smell of piss and old cigarettes hit her like a fist, but something clicked back into place inside her brain.

"Anon," she said with relief. "Thibault."

Even better, she saw his face. The pale half-moon of his ear peeking out from beneath dark hair, the line of his jaw when he smiled.

Here outside the Dish, she was herself again.

Nate was out in front working the door, maybe beyond the reach of whatever was happening inside. And clear of Crash's Faraday cage.

Flicker pulled out her phone, held down the home button for voice control.

"Call Glorious Leader."

CHAPTER 8
BELLWETHER

"SOMETHING'S HAPPENING." FLICKER'S VOICE WAS tight, panicked. "It's bad."

Nate frowned, still scanning the line of waiting people. Another twenty exactly. He'd been about to let them in and bump the crowd.

"What do you mean?"

"Everyone's moving wrong. And I can't think straight."

"Wait. What?"

"Crash and Mob are freaking out," Flicker went on breathlessly. "It was hitting me too. I couldn't even remember Anon!"

"Isn't that—"

"No, not just the usual. I couldn't *recognize* him."

Nate turned and faced the door to the club. It sounded like Flicker had overdosed on too many dancing eyeballs. A smaller version of this had happened the first night of the Dish.

"Stay behind the bar," he said. "I'm coming in."

"Don't! I'm out back—had to leave." He heard Flicker's breathing slow as she got under control again. "Seriously, Nate, it's not just me. Something's going wrong in there. Like, our powers got tangled up or something. Or Mob's got everyone in some kind of weird-ass feedback loop."

Nate shook his head, refusing to believe. Nothing had changed from last month or the month before. This was a *controlled* experiment.

"Someone's going to get killed!" Flicker cried.

"Okay. Just stay where you are."

"Be careful."

"I will." Nate slipped his phone back into his pocket, wondering what had gone wrong. The other times Flicker had overdosed herself with a crowd's vision, she might've been dizzy, but she'd known what was happening.

He turned. "Craig? Don't let anyone in till I tell you."

"You got it, Mr. Saldana" came the firm reply. For a moment Nate considered bringing the Craig along for protection. But if someone's power was really going haywire in there, he didn't want those massive limbs flailing around.

Nate opened the door.

Inside the Dish, the crowd had been shattered into a thousand pieces. There was no unity, no form, no connection. Even the weblike structure of a leaderless rabble was missing.

The music was a train wreck, two songs playing at once, and the dancing had descended into a horror of twitching limbs. Mob was huddled on her platform, terrified.

Fear was the only force that bound the room together. Nate could feel it in his bones, panic and confusion, along with something deeper and more cutting—loss of self, of meaning.

The source of the nightmare was easy to spot. In the center of the dance floor a couple whirled around each other. A guy with a half-shaved head and a girl in a frilly skirt, a white-hot beam of attention streaming between their eyes.

Nate had never seen a bond so intense, so brilliant. It scythed out into the crowd as the couple spun, keeping everyone else severed and detached. As if the pair had sucked up every glimmer of connection in the room and focused it between themselves.

They had powers.

As the beam of their connection cut across him, Nate felt it a hundred times worse, like a blow. The certainty of where he stood—here in the Dish, among his friends—began to falter. Everything seemed unreal, as if the nightclub, the crowd, even his own body had been replaced by counterfeits. Everything he knew was ashes.

He raised his hands to take control—but his confidence crumbled inside him. The dazzling line of attention between the couple was too bright, too strong for him to seize the crowd away.

For that matter, did he possess any power *at all*?

Suddenly the notion seemed absurd, that he could bend people toward himself, take a crowd's attention and focus it on any goal. In the presence of this radiant pair, it seemed impossible.

He was a nobody. And this place he and his friends had made had turned into a hell of jerking, terrified bodies.

"No," Nate said. This place was his. He knew every inch of it.

There was a fuse box across the dance floor, behind Chizara's lighting booth. From there he could shut off the lights, the sound, everything, and bring this nightmare to a halt.

This was *his* crowd, *his* club, *his* experiment. And if he couldn't keep control of it, then he would send it crashing into darkness.

That certainty propelled him across the dance floor. The crowd was blown apart, disconnected and detached, like the losing side in a bar brawl. For the first time in his life, Nate found himself bumped and shoved, threatened by flailing limbs and frenzied bodies.

As he reached the fuse box and swung it open, the last few embers of his confidence sputtered. He felt like a little kid in front of a fire alarm, with no right to pull this handle.

His focus was flowing out of him, his ego sucked away into the gyre of the couple whirling in the middle of the dance floor. This was their room, their crowd, *their* music making the air shudder around him.

He was worthless, a fraud.

They had taken everything from him.

With his last shred of certainty he reached for the big red lever and pulled, plunging the Dish into darkness.

CHAPTER 9
CRASH

EVERYTHING WENT DARK, NOT JUST IN THE DISH but in Chizara's mind. All those glowing lines of current she'd built winked out. All those pulses of energy stilled. Only faint traceries of empty veins were left, vague maps she was no longer responsible for.

She was Crash, but she hadn't crashed this. Someone had cut the power to the whole building.

And cut the power to the mob, too. That awful ravening roar had given way to shouts of fear in the sudden darkness. Chizara nearly cried out herself, with relief. She had her mind back, her confusion having switched off with the lights.

She ran her fingers over the control board. She recognized every switch and slider by feel. Order was restored.

But not out on the pitch-black dance floor. The crowd was

in motion, pressing against the base of the lighting booth, setting it shaking beneath her feet. Then the rush went the other way, and there were noises of glass smashing, screams, and names called out in the dark.

What had happened to the Dish, her refuge? This was supposed to be a safe place, where the Zeroes could do no harm.

Chizara remembered the tremors she'd felt after crashing Sonia's phone. Then this earthquake, a thousand times stronger. Had Kelsie fed some kind of panic loop into the crowd?

Chizara fumbled for the light-box door, wrenched the catch open, and felt her way carefully down the stairs.

Phone lights were flicking on, showing a fallen lighting truss, overturned stools and tables. Tears of shock and terror, even blood—a big cut down that guy's arm, a girl pinned under the truss, screaming as people climbed over it.

"Go around!" she shouted, pointing past the truss toward the main entrance. A few of them obeyed, and started to guide the others, and Chizara edged toward the DJ platform.

She climbed up, pulled out her phone for light, and found Kelsie huddled, wide-eyed, against the crates of vinyl records.

"Are you okay?"

"I'm not sure." Kelsie stared out into the distressed dancers.

"What happened?" Chizara bent and took hold of Kelsie's shoulder. "Did you have some kind of seizure or something?"

Kelsie stared at her. "You think *I* did this?"

"The music went wrong first, then—"

"It didn't start with the music. We had them going great, but then . . ." Kelsie stared at her hands. "I couldn't recognize anything. Not my decks, not the records, nothing!"

"It wasn't you," came a voice from the darkness.

Chizara swung the light. "Nate!"

"There were two of them." He swept the beam from his own phone over the crowd. "Dancing in the middle of the floor."

"Wait," Kelsie said. "I felt them. The ones who were totally into each other?"

"And using powers. Something that cut through everyone's connections. I could *see* it."

"What?" Chizara said. "You mean Zeroes did this—on *purpose*?"

"Won't know until we find them. If I turn the fuse box back on, can you get the work lights up?" Nate asked. "No music, no spinning spots. Just stop this panic!"

Chizara nodded. "Work lights only."

Nate headed off into the darkness, and Chizara took Kelsie's hand. "So, other Zeroes have finally come to town. Sorry I blamed you."

"No, I totally lost control."

"Me too. Whatever they are, they're powerful."

"They broke the crowd into little pieces."

"It's okay. We'll fix it." Chizara felt along the dead pathways around the room, getting ready for the electricity to flow again, but also trying to spot the two new Zeroes.

Now that the terror was over, she was pissed. How dare they come in here and—

A *chunk* sounded in Chizara's mind as the room tried to reignite around her. She held the power back from the DJ system, from all the fancy lighting tech, and let it through to the room lights.

For a moment everyone's faces were naked in fear and confusion, mouths agape in the stark, ordinary light. But then they saw where they were, the shape of the room, where the exit was. Some recognized friends, and everyone started pulling themselves together.

Nate jumped onto the old theater's stage and stood, arms wide, calming the crowd. "Sorry, everyone. We've obviously had a technical malfunction."

The hubbub quieted. Gratefully, Chizara submitted to his Glorious Leader charm, and she felt Kelsie's hand relax in hers.

"But it's all under control now," Nate went on. "Just make your way toward the exits, please—take it slow, so no one gets hurt."

Then he signaled across the room to Chizara and Kelsie, and pointed.

"Yep, that's them," Kelsie said.

A tall white guy with a half-shaved head was shoving people out of his way. His girlfriend was tiny, but just as pushy.

"They look pissed about getting shut down," Kelsie said.

"Not as pissed as I am. All that energy we had going with

the crowd, they stole it. Sucked it away like, I don't know, dance-mob vampires."

Nate was still onstage, keeping everyone calm. But he was watching the pair with fascination. He probably wanted to quiz them on how their power worked and ask them to join up.

Chizara just wanted to kick their asses.

"I'm going after them." She pulled away.

"You sure?" Kelsie called out, but Chizara had already plunged into the crowd, slipping through the still-addled mob.

The crush grew heavy around the entrance, and the two were way ahead of her.

"Hey," Chizara shouted. "Stop those two! They did this!"

Terrified faces turned to gawk at her.

The girl turned too, tugged on the guy's hand.

"We know what you did!" Chizara cried.

The guy didn't look guilty at all, or even nervous, like he'd just been busted for using a superpower. He only rolled his eyes, picked up his girlfriend, and pushed harder for the door. She flopped over his shoulder as if unconscious.

"Please," he cried out. "My girlfriend's hurt—let us through!"

Calmed and made orderly by Nate, the crowd opened up before them.

"Oh, come on," Chizara cried. "Really?"

The girl, her open eyes two slits, blew a kiss back to Chizara.

"Craig! Stop those—"

The kiss hit, and the walls towered and tipped sideways. Since when were all these people a different species from her? And why was the sky covered with that sparkling metal mesh?

Chizara almost puked at the awful strangeness of it.

It took a shaky, dreadful moment for the weirdness to pass. No one around her looked confused. The girl had blown her reality-twisting kiss pinpoint-straight at Chizara.

And the couple were almost out the door, the crowd closing behind them.

Chizara set her jaw and kept shoving forward.

Long seconds later, she reached fresh air. It screamed with signals, everyone's phones springing awake, a cloud of angry wasps storming her.

Through the pain, a familiar mass of muscle loomed. "Craig! Lift me up!"

"Yes, ma'am." The Craig's meaty hands clamped her hips and lifted. From two feet above everyone else, she scanned the crowd. Nothing.

Then some white guy grabbed her arm. "That way, Crash!"

She stared down at him.

Right. Flicker's boyfriend—forgettable guy.

He pointed across the road. The tall guy and his girlfriend were darting into an alley between the used-car lot and an abandoned tire warehouse.

"Okay, Craig, I got 'em!"

Chizara's feet hit the ground. Flicker's boyfriend was already ahead of her. She overtook him at the corner, and she would overtake those other two as well.

The crowd and their painful phones fell behind as she ran full tilt, anger powering her on.

CHAPTER 10
SCAM

SOMEWHERE IN ALL THE CHAOS, ETHAN HAD BEEN shoved into a wall.

Which was good, because it was the only thing that kept him standing. He leaned there, gasping, trying to remember how to breathe. Wishing his eyeballs would stop rolling around in his skull. He had a nauseous, dizzy sense that his limbs had been rearranged.

"My freaking *hand*!" someone screamed beside him.

The Dish had been transformed. No music, only shouts and sobs. And instead of Chizara's light show, the place was lit with the stark white bulbs they used for cleaning up.

There was a stranger beside him. No, it was Sonia, a magenta streak falling across the center of her face. She was holding her right wrist, and she was trembling.

Shock. That was what it was. That was why Sonia was shaking. Why he couldn't focus his eyes.

Nate was on the stage, telling everyone to calm down, but it was only halfway working. People staggered across the dance floor like they couldn't understand their own bodies. Elbows and knees everywhere. One guy was crawling, like he didn't trust himself to walk. His nose was bleeding onto the floor.

"You okay?" he managed, but he wasn't sure Sonia could understand him. His voice felt weird and jerky, like he was saying someone else's words. Like that moment outside the Office-O.

"I think I sprained my wrist." Sonia's face was pale. "What the hell just happened?"

"I have no idea!" He looked at the DJ booth. Kelsie was up there, huddled in a corner.

She needed help, but he had to ditch Sonia first. He let the voice fly, wishing Sonia would leave him alone.

"You should get to a hospital."

"Hospital? For a sprain?"

"If it swells up, you could get permanent nerve damage."

"Seriously?" She stared at her hand, probing it gingerly.

The voice got all concerned. "It could ruin your typing forever."

"This sucks. First my phone breaks, and now this. I should sue you guys!"

Ethan swallowed. Maybe the whole permanent-nerve-damage line was overkill. It'd be bad enough if Sonia posted about a crowd freak-out at the Dish. But if she took them all to *court* . . .

The voice picked up his uncertainty and went dumb. But Nate's spiel was working, and people were moving toward the door in an orderly way. Sonia drifted along with them, glaring at her hand.

Ethan ducked into the crowd and headed for the light booth. He had to make sure Kelsie was okay.

The weirdness hadn't completely gone. Every step Ethan took felt like it was in the wrong direction. As if someone had imposed a completely different floor plan on the building.

Black spots filled his eyes, swimming in formation every time he moved his head. But he could see Kelsie on the floor of the DJ booth, her arms wrapped around her knees.

Had she caused this whole crowd disaster with some kind of feedback loop?

He climbed up to the booth. "You okay, Kels?"

"Ethan," she said slowly, like recognizing him took effort. "Did you see them?"

"See who?"

"There were people in here, with powers. They took our crowd away, sucked it dry."

Just the words made Ethan feel like he was going to puke again—new powers with evil intent. But at least it hadn't been Kelsie.

"Nate saw them feeding off the crowd," she said. "It felt like we were being cut to pieces. Crash went after them."

For a sudden, awful moment, Ethan felt alone. All the other Zeroes had crowd powers—so they'd seen what had happened, had felt it. But all he'd gotten was motion-sick.

"Is that Sonia Sonic?" Kelsie groaned. "Perfect. We're screwed."

He turned and found Sonia waiting below the DJ booth.

"The exit's too crowded," she called up. "Hey, were you just trying to get rid of me?"

Ethan turned back to Kelsie. "Gotta deal with this. Glad you're okay. Hey, later we should . . ."

He bit down on his words. This mess had clearly wiped their talk off the agenda—the serious talk about major feelings.

Crap. He was *never* going to tell her.

He jumped down from the booth.

"Is she okay?" Sonia asked.

Ethan nodded. "Come on, let's get you a cab."

"She's cute," Sonia said.

A siren sounded outside, and Ethan groaned. Whether it was cops or an ambulance, the voice was probably needed now. Nate had put him in charge of keeping the authorities off their backs.

Of course, Nate had probably never imagined a meltdown quite the size of this.

"Crap! Sonia, we have to get out there."

"Wounded coming through!" Sonia called through gritted teeth, holding up her wrist.

People parted, and soon they were outside. Ethan sucked in brisk December air, and his head finally cleared. Plenty of the crowd had spilled out already, and there was a police car rolling up.

"Crap," Ethan said. Everything was toast.

A wall with ears stepped in front of him.

"What the hell happened in there?" the Craig asked. "First everyone goes nuts, then Chizara comes pounding out, chasing down some kids!"

Ethan had never seen Craig's face this pale before. He put a calming hand on the guy's massive shoulder.

"Don't know, Craig. We'll figure it out. You seen any cabs?"

"I can call one. But first," Craig said, jerking a thumb over his shoulder, "local constabulary."

"Don't sweat it. I got this." Ethan inclined his head toward Sonia. "Get her in a cab and pay. Okay?"

"Leave it with the Craig."

As he went toward the police car, Sonia tried to follow, but the Craig stood in her way. Ethan didn't bother looking to see who won that contest.

Two officers were getting out of the police car, adjusting their duty belts and looking over the crowd.

Come on, voice. Whatever it takes to get rid of these guys!

One of the officers swept his flashlight across the departing Dish patrons, who looked dazed and terrified, like their whole world had come undone. Exactly the kind of expression cops loved to take an interest in.

Ethan moved in, thinking about how much he wanted them to go away.

"Officers." The voice sounded so casual, like all three of them were drinking buddies.

The first cop looked Ethan up and down. He was tall, with forearms like hams. "You know anything about this club, kid?"

"Club? It's more like a private party." Ethan recognized Nate's line from before. Nice of the voice to keep it consistent.

The other cop sidled up to join his partner. He looked mean and tired. "Either way, seems kind of like a disturbance of the peace. Underage drinking, from the looks of it. And some bad trips?"

To Ethan's surprise, the voice took a simple route. "Officers, what's it gonna take to make this go away?"

"Getting straight to business, huh?" the short one said.

Ethan shrugged. The voice always knew what it was doing.

"How about one gee for the inconvenience?" it said.

Shit, that was a lot of cash. Also, Nate was going to be pissed about bribery. And if Ethan's *mom* ever found out . . .

The tall cop turned to his partner. "He serious?"

"How about two grand right now?" the other one said.

"Cheaper than taking the rap for causing grievous bodily harm, say."

The voice didn't even try to haggle. Which meant there was no point. "Two grand it is. You stay right here, officers. I'll be back."

Ethan gave them a conspiratorial wink and spun on his heel.

He felt sick. A thousand dollars had seemed impossible, and now it was *two*? There was no way the Dish had that kind of money lying around, not this early in the evening. Nate could get it, but not out of his pocket.

But the smaller cop was right—it was cheaper than lawyers and bail. And there was no telling what these guys were capable of if they didn't get their money. Ethan had to get rid of them before they changed their minds.

Inside, the crowd had thinned out. Ethan elbowed through the stragglers toward Flicker at the bar.

"Ethan. Have you seen . . ." Her voice trailed off.

It took him a second. "Teebo? Nope. But, long story, I need money to bribe some cops. Like, two gees?"

Flicker straightened slowly. "Um, did you talk to Nate about *bribing cops*?"

"Nope. But it's kind of too late for Glorious Leader to weigh in. They're already waiting."

"Shit." Flicker sighed. "Normally, you'd be screwed. But some guy bought for the whole bar."

"Sweet," Ethan breathed. At last something was going well tonight.

"More like weird. Felt like he did it to be mean." Flicker shook her head. "It didn't make sense."

Ethan didn't want to know. "So give us two gees of it?"

He lent her his eyes, dutifully watching as she scraped the cash drawer into a paper sack.

"No idea how much is in there," she said. "Think it's enough?"

He let the voice answer, pleading with it for the simple truth. "It'll make them go away."

Hmm, that wasn't completely reassuring. But at least it meant the cops would be okay with the money for now.

"The guy didn't even look that rich," Flicker said thoughtfully. "More like he just wanted to throw away money."

"To throw away money," Ethan repeated, remembering the couple paying for strangers' shipping at the Office-O. "Did he have a shaved head and a girlfriend in a black frilled skirt?"

"Half-shaved." Flicker nodded. "Somebody you invited?"

"I guess. Anyway, I gotta go deal with this." He hoisted the bag and went back outside.

The cops were at their car. The tall officer took the bag without looking at Ethan and shoved it under his seat, like bribery was a fast-food order he was picking up.

"Nice doing business with you, kid." He swept a gaze over the Dish crowd. "But keep these tweakers off the street."

Ethan kept his mouth firmly clamped shut. Let the guy think what he wanted. So long as he left them alone.

As the cops drove away, Ethan breathed a sigh of relief. He glanced around to see if anyone was watching.

Sonia was gone, and Craig gave him a thumbs-up. Yeah, great. They'd hear from her soon enough, either in a post about crowd madness in an illegal nightclub, or in a court of law. But it wouldn't take Sonia to make this disaster famous. People were taking pictures, calling friends.

Nobody was going to forget the night the Dish turned into a zombie free-for-all.

CHAPTER 11
ANONYMOUS

THIBAULT RAN HARD AFTER CHIZARA. HE HAD longer legs, but he could barely keep up.

Beyond her, passing streetlights lit up the tiny girl and the tall guy as they fled between the warehouses. This was the only road that cut across the rail line up to Hill Street—it was like they'd planned an escape route.

Were they local? No, Thibault would have spotted them before. They weren't exactly wallflowers.

Powers, he reminded himself. They had *powers*.

But what the hell kind of powers *were* they? It had been scary enough losing control of his own body. But worse was how his mind had slipped. For a moment he'd stared straight at Flicker and forgotten who she was.

What kind of power made the *rest* of the world forgettable?

Thibault leaped over a yawning pothole. He wished Chizara hadn't scared them off. He could've followed them, found out where they lived.

Instead they were having to run them down. And a black girl chasing two dressed-up white kids? Through the Heights, at night? Any cop cruising by would escalate the situation faster than Thibault could intervene.

Now they were running down Morton Road, broken streetlights and gang tags flowing past on the dim walls. After four months living at the Dish, Anon knew the neighborhood. Syringes glinted and cigarette butts speckled the puddled ground. Pairs of sneakers hung by their laces from wires overhead.

The warehouses were giving way to smaller blocks of cheap apartments. Guys were clumped on corners and stoops, and from the balconies grandmas and worn-out grandpas in fleece jackets watched Chizara pound by. The smell of sewers vied with cigarettes.

The street forked at the burned-out corner store, and their quarry took the longer way. Thibault cut right onto the shorter, ran two blocks, and skidded out in front of them.

He threw up his arms and braced for the collision that would bring them down.

But the guy spotted him right away, leaned in, and shouldered him aside. Thibault went stumbling back, his breath knocked out. He flailed for the passing girl, but her ringed fingers knocked his hand away.

Weird. They'd seen him so fast, even in the darkness.

Also, ouch. Those rings were spiky.

Chizara ran past as he flexed his hand. She threw him a fraying look over her shoulder.

"Nice try! Come on, there they go!"

Running on, Thibault glimpsed the gleam of a boot buckle as the tall guy dodged down an alley. Ha—that alley went nowhere.

By the time Chizara and Thibault reached the corner, an engine was roaring and clamoring between the narrow walls. Thibault slowed, but Chizara overshot, caught in sudden headlights.

Her feet pedaled and she nearly fell, but she recovered, flinging her arms out wide.

A shiny black Ford convertible lurched out of the alleyway, headed straight at her.

But Crash raised a hand, and the gnashing of locked-up brakes joined the screech of tires. The engine choked and died as the car's chrome grille stopped just short of Chizara's knees. A cloud of exhaust drifted across her, and Thibault smelled the stink of rubber.

Nope. These two weren't locals—this car did *not* belong in the Heights. It was hugely long, like 1960s long. Its silver trim gleamed against the black, and its interior was all bloodred leather, impeccably restored.

The guy swore, turning the keys uselessly.

His girlfriend just looked irritated.

"Quit it, would you?" she said to Chizara. "Don't you know that's bad for the engine?"

Chizara didn't answer. She looked as stunned as Thibault felt.

These two weren't surprised by her power. Not at all.

The guy spoke up. "Look, give us our car back, okay? Or my girl messes up your head."

So *she* was the one with the power. Was the guy just some rich boyfriend?

Chizara recovered her cool, laid a hand on the steaming hood.

"Messing with me won't fix your car. It stays a doorstop until you tell me something. Where do you guys get off, playing with powers in *our* club?"

The girl twinkled her fingers at Chizara, her silver rings gleaming. "Oh, you had plans for those dolls?"

"Seriously? *Dolls?* You could have killed someone!"

"Don't be so dramatic." She gave Chizara a makeup-laden eye roll. "What were you planning to do, just let them dance all night?"

"Yes!" Chizara cried.

As they spoke, Thibault made his way around to the passenger side.

The guy looked bored. "Let's call it even. We messed with you, you messed with us. I mean, what do you think it feels like, getting shut down right in the middle?"

"Yeah, you couldn't have waited another minute?" the girl said. "We'd have given your dolls back."

Chizara glared at them. "What were you even *doing*?"

"What do you *think*?" the girl said. "Do people not know about the birds and the bees in this shitty town?"

Chizara stared at them. "That was sex?"

"That was foreplay," the guy said. "Wait till you see the news tomorrow night."

"Yeah, lotta dolls going to be crying. Sniff." The girl dabbed at her eye with the back of her wrist. "Now, are you going to start this engine, or do I have to knock your universe silly?"

Chizara stood tall. "You don't have a crowd to work with."

The girl smiled, tapped her head. "I keep that juice stored up, right here. Just like you do. And if you force me to prove it, I'll make your crazy permanent."

That didn't sound good, and Chizara looked like she wasn't going to move.

Thibault crept closer, ready to grab the girl from behind if she tried anything.

The guy turned around and looked straight at him. "And that goes for you, too."

Thibault froze.

Chizara stood aside, waved her hand. Something clicked under the hood and then the engine shrieked to life.

"Thanks for playing!" the girl shouted.

The guy spun the wheel expertly, pulling the Ford out of

the alley. With a rattling engine fart it shot off toward Hill Street. It bucked like a nervous show pony at the corner and swerved out into the traffic.

"Oregon plates," Thibault said.

Chizara grabbed his arm and pulled him along the street.

"We should follow them. You got any money for a cab?" She skidded to a halt. "Oh, right. You never need cash. And my bag's back at the Dish. Damn it."

"Wait. I do have some." Thibault pulled the bills from his pocket and gestured after the car. "The money that guy threw on the bar."

Chizara stared down at it, then met his gaze. "Um, okay. But that's not money."

He looked down. He was holding out a fan of white rectangles. The paper was the right size and shape for bills, but it was blank.

He flipped them over and back—they stayed blank. "They were twenties, I swear. That guy slapped them down on the bar in a big wad. He was spending like it was . . . play money."

Chizara just stared at him.

"You had the UV lights going. I *saw* the security stripes!"

She nodded. "So it's not just her."

"They've both got powers," Thibault said.

CHAPTER 12
MOB

KELSIE PACKED AWAY HER VINYL WITH UNSTEADY hands.

Nate had bought it all for her, laying down a cool two grand in a record store in San Francisco, like money was nothing. That Justin guy had sourced the turntables from a retro website. They were secondhand, finicky and temperamental, the most beautiful and demanding things Kelsie had ever owned. Before tonight they had looked exactly like hope, like an end to everything unloved and lopsided in her past.

But now the Dish was a wreck. Strings of lights that had spanned the walls lay in glittering pieces on the floor. The few chairs in the club had been smashed, including an old couch of Dad's. Crushed beer cans and broken plastic cups were everywhere. Ethan was dutifully collecting them in a garbage bag.

Everywhere was evidence that people had fled, leaving behind coats, sweaters, phones—thrown off or forgotten in the terror. Even with only four Zeroes in the Dish, Kelsie could feel the feedback loop of shock. The invasion of new powers had shaken everything they'd built—the safe haven where they could hone their skills, the trust of their crowd.

"Let's go over this from the beginning," Nate called to everyone from one of the last unbroken bar stools. "From when they showed up here—"

"They were at the Office-O first," Ethan said, pausing with a crushed beer can in his hand.

Nate turned to him. "When?"

"Just before I came back. I had to print more flyers, and those two were there. I gave them one."

"So inviting Sonia Sonic wasn't enough," Flicker said. She was pacing in front of the bar, her worry a cold shiver on the group's spine.

"I didn't know they had powers!" Ethan cried, and then his voice dropped. "But they were acting kinda weird."

"Weird how?" Nate asked.

"They said they didn't have money, but then they paid for everyone's shipping. Like, they yelled to people on the street, telling them to come in and get free stuff!"

Flicker broke in. "And the guy bought beer for the whole bar."

"So why throw money around?" Nate asked. "To get the crowd churned up?"

Even with only four of them there, Kelsie felt his methodical focus in the energy of the room. She grabbed hold of it gratefully, pushed it through to the others. Nate really could be glorious—smart and attentive to everything you told him, like you mattered more than anyone else in the world. *What kind of speakers do you need? How sprung should the dance floor be?*

Of course, other times he was more like the ruler of some tiny country, making speeches and building statues of himself.

The door of the Dish burst open.

It was Chizara, bright-eyed and panting, like she'd run a mile. The Zeroes' feedback loop blossomed with her bright, loose energy, and Flicker ran to wrap her arms around—

Thibault, Kelsie reminded herself. She'd been doing so well remembering him, but now everything in her mind slipped and spun, not connecting right.

"Did you catch them?" Nate asked.

"I stopped their car," Chizara panted. "But that girl threatened me with a lobotomy if I didn't let them go."

"We were going to follow them in a cab," Thibault said, pulling free of Flicker's embrace. "But all we had was this."

He pulled a sheaf of blank paper from his pocket.

Everyone stared at him, uncomprehending.

Kelsie eased back their group focus, letting Thibault's energy in. When she'd first joined the Zeroes, she'd thought he was a cold spot in the room. But he had a mellow, solid presence, once she'd learned to feel for it.

"This is from the money he threw down on the bar," he said. "Away from *him*, it was just blank paper."

"Whoa," Flicker said. "It looked real. And I saw it through *everybody's* eyes."

Nate stood. "Money. The ultimate shared hallucination."

Somehow Nate always managed to sound like he was hosting a nature documentary.

"Say what now?" Ethan asked.

"Money is a social construct," Nate said. "It needs a crowd's agreement to make it work, to turn paper into something valuable. Haven't you ever found it weird that pieces of paper are valuable, just because of the numbers printed on them?"

"Um, no," Ethan said.

But Kelsie was nodding.

Money had always seemed like a game to her and her father, except when they were out of it. Even then, Dad had usually found a way to get more—at any moment, he had a bunch of cons going. Their friend Fig had said that Jerry Laszlo worked harder at conning people than if he'd had a regular job.

"Oh, wait," Ethan said, looking pale. "This is not good."

"It's *fascinating*," Nate said. "And that's why he offered to pay for everyone's shipping, and drinks! If his power's like ours, he's only rich when there's a crowd around him!"

"Crowd funding," Thibault said drily. "We should call him Kickstarter."

"Or Coin," Nate said.

"They're just *jerks*." Chizara rolled her eyes. "And you want to give them superhero names?"

"Uh, I think we've got a bigger problem than his name," Ethan said. The energy in the room spasmed, focusing on him. He looked like he'd been busted cheating on an exam. "Because I totally bribed some cops with a bag full of that money."

Nate stared. "You . . . what?"

"Did you just say you *bribed cops?*" Chizara cried.

"Technically, it was the voice that bribed them," Ethan said. "And *technically* I didn't bribe them at all. I just handed them a bag of blank paper in exchange for going away."

"Oops," Flicker said.

"The cops were all smooth about it. They didn't even look in the bag!" Ethan's fear was pulsing through the group, setting off an alarm in Kelsie's head. "But the moment they try to buy doughnuts, they're going to be *pissed*!"

Nate held up a hand, and everyone went quiet.

"What are they going to do, report us?" he said. "They took a *bribe*. We can pay them real money later."

"Easy for you to say!" Ethan cried. "You've never had cops on your tail!"

"Except for the time your mother brought two detectives to my home, after you called me from a police station asking for *help*." Nate turned away, and Kelsie felt him shutting out Ethan's ragged, anxious energy. "What's more important is that we just discovered two more powers in the world, and we let them get away!"

"Not for long," Thibault said. "They're planning something tomorrow. Something worse than this."

The feeling of being invaded flowed through Kelsie again. She wanted to lash out, punch someone, protect her territory.

"Don't they care about keeping their powers secret?" she asked.

"I'm not sure they care about anything," Chizara said. "Except each other, and that eye-banging thing they do."

"When they got started on the dance floor, everything looked wrong," Kelsie said. "My records, my turntables. I couldn't even recognize our crowd."

"I couldn't understand my lighting system." Chizara shook her head slowly. "Everything I built was like someone else had put it together and I didn't know how it worked."

"I couldn't recognize Flicker." Thibault reached out to curl his fingers through hers.

"Ditto," Flicker said. "And I couldn't read braille anymore. Or remember your name."

"I think her power was leaking a little at the Office-O," Ethan said. "Sonia was staring at her phone funny, and I couldn't recognize my own voice. Like, my *real* one."

"Wait," Chizara said. "They used a power on you, and you led them *here*?"

Chizara's anger spiked through the Zeroes. Kelsie tried to steady them, but her own anger spilled into the loop.

Nate stood up and cleared his throat, and that steadied everything. "So her power is like Thibault's. He disappears by disrupting attention, cutting himself free of the social web. Maybe she cuts those connections for a whole crowd instead of just herself."

"But she doesn't cut them," Thibault said. "She *steals* them. It's like she sucks away all the attention in the room, focuses it between her and him."

Kelsie said, "It's not attention she steals. It's more personal."

"Right," Nate said, picking up the thread. "Your turntables. Chizara's lights. Ethan's voice. For Anon and Flicker, each other. She takes your understanding of what's important to you—maybe even your *love* of it—and makes it hers."

"Which is why people go crazy," Flicker said. "She glitches your connection to the thing you love."

"Good name," Ethan muttered. "She's a total Glitch."

"Yeah, perfect," Chizara said. "Now that she has a code name, problem solved!"

Nate paced slowly. "Opposites attract. Coin takes something worthless and makes it valuable. And Glitch takes whatever's most valuable to you and makes it meaningless. But what do they get out of it?"

"The birds and the bees," Chizara said. "Her words, not mine."

Nate stared. "You mean it's just sex? Like, for *fun*?"

Kelsie felt her anger at Glitch and Coin turn, kicking out jaggedly into the group. "*Fun* is why most people come to nightclubs, Nate. Experimenting on people is not a normal thing!"

She felt bad as soon as she said it. Nate was all about control. So for him, experimenting with their superpowers probably seemed like the responsible thing to do.

She relaxed, easing back into the spiral of frustration in the room.

"Maybe they do this because they're in love," she added softly.

Chizara shook her head. "Not love—*foreplay* is what the guy said. For the big event they're planning tomorrow. We have to stop them."

"We have to *explain* things to them," Nate said.

Chizara laughed once in disbelief.

Kelsie shared a look with her. That was Glorious Leader for you—always saying *we* when he meant *I*.

"Do you remember *us* six months ago?" Nate reasoned. "We did worse than kill the buzz at a nightclub. We stole money from drug dealers. We broke a whole police station, and—"

"And someone wound up in a coma," Chizara agreed. "But we didn't do it on *purpose*. Does this look accidental?"

She waved a hand, and the lights ignited to show him the battered and smashed club. The wreckage of the only home Kelsie had anymore.

The others were quiet. The brighter lights showed the bloodstains on the floor.

Nate spread his hands, trying to pull their gazes back to him. "Our Zeroes powers are hard to understand. Maybe they're just confused. Or scared."

Kelsie felt everyone focus on him. His curiosity overwhelmed her anger in the feedback loop, until she felt herself agreeing too. Her power suddenly felt small in the face of Nate's will.

"We can help them," Nate continued. "We helped you, Kelsie, right?"

He gave her one of those direct Nataniel Saldana gazes, the kind that made her feel like no one else in the room mattered. Kelsie dropped her gaze.

"We just have to let them know they're not alone," Nate said softly.

"They know all about powers, Nate," Chizara replied. "They even knew what I was doing to their car. And they called normal people *dolls*. Like they're nothing but toys."

"Whoa," Flicker said softly. "That's cold."

"That's not the same as being evil," Thibault said, always ready to find a middle way. "Maybe they're experimenting too. But their powers make a bigger mess."

Kelsie felt the Zeroes fracture as people took sides. Doubting themselves and each other. Doubting if what they were doing here at the Dish was so different.

"Uh, guys?" Flicker said. "I've got two sets of eyeballs approaching the door. And I think they're cops."

Fear shot through the room.

"Anon! Lock it!" Nate hissed. "Everyone, stay quiet. It's not like they'll get a search warrant to collect a bribe. I'll deal with them later."

Thibault stepped back from the door just as a rapping sound filled the Dish. Knuckles first, then a billy club hard and sharp against the door.

After everything tonight, it was all Kelsie could do to keep herself from curling into a ball again. The rapping kept coming, and it was like someone had sawed the endings off her nerves— the Dish felt invaded all over again.

But Nate was right. After a few long minutes, the cops gave the door one last frustrated blow.

"We'll be back!" one of them called, and then came the sound of them driving away.

Kelsie wondered how she would sleep here tonight.

CHAPTER 13
FLICKER

"MORE CHURROS?"

"No, gracias." Flicker put a hand on her belly, signaling the surrender of her appetite to Mrs. Saldana's Sunday breakfast.

"Are you sure?" Gabby asked.

Flicker was *mostly* sure. In Gabby's rapt vision, the churros glistened with fried-on sugar . . . but Flicker managed to shake her head.

"Nate and I can clean up. You guys are going to be late for church."

"Milagrita," Mrs. Saldana said, always a little amazed that Flicker wasn't completely helpless. Annoying from anyone else, but not from Nate's mom, who actually believed in miracles.

She cleared the girls out of the kitchen—no more churros if the guest wasn't hungry—and set them to getting ready for church. As Gabby flounced down the hall, Flicker jumped into Nate's eyes.

He was staring at his tablet, results for a search on *crowd psychosis*.

"Enjoying Glitch and Coin's previous work?" she asked.

"Yeah, we need to know what makes them tick." He scrolled through more results. "How good a look did you get at them?"

She shrugged. "Lots of eyes, all jittery."

"Were they our age?"

Flicker considered this. All the Zeroes in Cambria had been born in the year 2000, which was a pretty odd explanation for superpowers, but it was all they had.

"Maybe," she said. "But they're more jaded. Harder than us, like they've seen a lot of bad stuff."

"*We've* seen bad stuff," Nate said. "Kidnappers! Bank robberies!"

"It's not a competition," she said sweetly.

Nate lifted his gaze to her face, and Flicker was surprised to see how fresh she looked. Last night had tripped her out, like it had everyone else, but this morning the excitement of finding new powers in the world was in her veins.

Or maybe that was just Mr. Saldana's sweet, strong coffee.

"Whenever they were born," she said, "I wouldn't call them mature."

Nate expelled a sigh. "They didn't care who got hurt, did they?"

"Or who saw them do their recognition-stealing thing," Flicker said. "If they keep pulling that shit, people are going to know there are superpowers out in the world!"

"It's not just them." His eyes dropped back to the screen. "There's this study going around—it says crowd madness is way up in the last couple of years. There's already some senator calling for a task force. He wants to link it to terrorism, of course."

"Oh, great." Flicker felt the caffeine rushing in her bloodstream. "So we can expect a visit from Homeland Security."

"Maybe not today. But it looks like there's a *lot* of other Zeroes out there, and some of them aren't as disciplined as we are."

Flicker laughed. "*Disciplined?* Like when Chizara crashed half of downtown? The only reason everyone in Cambria hasn't figured us out is nobody believes in superpowers."

"Sonia Sonic does," Nate said. "We should be seeing her post about the Dish anytime now."

"Have you checked yet?"

"Every five minutes."

Flicker sighed. Chizara might have bricked Sonia's phone, but there would be plenty of other pictures from last night's disaster. Nobody evacuated a nightclub without taking a few selfies along the way.

It sucked. The Dish felt like home now, and Glitch and Coin had turned it inside out. Almost as if exposing the Zeroes had been the point of last night's attack.

She stood up and began to stack the breakfast dishes by feel.

Flicker had eaten almost as many meals at the Saldanas' as she had at home, and she knew her way around the kitchen. Which was just as well, with Glorious Leader glued to his screen.

"I wonder why those two warned Chizara that they're making more trouble today," he said. "Are they going to hit more clubs tonight, or did they show up just to piss on *our* territory?"

"Maybe they're addicted to that eye-banging thing," Flicker said, and felt an odd twinge of jealousy go through her. Glitch had sucked up all the recognition in the room, everyone's understanding of their world, of *themselves*, and had channeled it all into a bond between herself and Coin.

Which was a shitty and selfish thing to do, of course. But to have *that* as your superpower—seeing your boyfriend with a crowd-crippling intensity—sounded better than stealing other people's eyes just to catch a glimpse of him. . . .

Most days Flicker had to work just to remember Thibault's real name. It didn't seem quite fair.

But she couldn't say all this out loud, especially to Nate.

"Maybe they won't wait for tonight," she said, lifting the stack of dishes.

"What do you mean?"

"It's Sunday, only three days till Christmas—the clubs will be empty. Check if there's anything happening during the day."

"Huh." Nate began to type at his tablet.

Flicker navigated to the kitchen sink by the feel of sunlight streaming through the window behind it. The dishes settled heavily on metal, and she found the sponge where Mrs. Saldana always left it.

"Maybe we've gotten too wrapped up with the Dish," she said. "A nightclub isn't the only kind of crowd, right?"

Gabby padded past the door in stockinged feet, the hem of her Sunday dress swishing.

"Like, there's church," Flicker said.

"Mass would be a weird place to get your rocks off."

"Okay. But there's also farmers' markets, movies, football games, pizza-eating contests . . ." Flicker dried her hands. "There must be *something* going on in this town."

When Nate didn't answer, Flicker jumped into his eyes. He was searching *Cambria events today*.

"Okay," he said a moment later. "How about the annual police-versus-firefighters hockey game?"

"So much weirder than church," Flicker said with a laugh.

"But the rivalry between first responders is *primal*," Nate said. "And those guys Scam bribed last night will probably be there. We have to deal with that, too."

"But it doesn't seem like Glitch and Coin's scene." She sat down, reaching for the coffeepot in the middle of the table. "What else?"

Nate poked at his screen some more, and Flicker left his eyes for the stillness of her own brain.

"Hey, Nate," she said a moment later. "You know who keeps track of what's going on in Cambria? Sonia Sonic."

Nate snorted. "So we should ask *her* for advice?"

"Why not? She's going to post about the Dish no matter what. Might as well take this chance to charm her." Nate started to interrupt, but Flicker didn't let him. "Like you said, people are going to figure out superpowers sooner or later. We might as well have someone telling our side of the story."

"Sure, but Sonia Sonic? Cambria's third most popular social-media maven? Why not the *New York Times*?"

"Because they won't listen. And Sonia already *gets* it." Flicker shrugged. "Plus, she'll know what's going on today off the top of her head. We don't have time to fart around."

When Nate didn't answer, Flicker pulled out her phone. "Go to her site. There's a number for anonymous tips."

"But—"

"Look at it."

"Flick . . . ," he began, but then sighed and obeyed.

A moment later Sonia answered, "Yeah?"

"This is Flicker. Nate Saldana's friend."

"Um, Flicker . . ."

"The blind one. Is your wrist okay?"

"I guess." The surprise in Sonia's voice settled a little. "Are you calling to tell me what the hell that was last night? Or to warn me to keep quiet? Because I won't! My wrist is so bad, I can't even lift this coffee!"

"Sorry about that," Flicker said. "But we don't quite know

what happened, exactly. We're investigating, and I think you can help us."

"How?"

"We need to know something—what's the biggest event in Cambria today? Like, what's drawing the largest crowd?"

"I *knew* it," Sonia said. "It's always in a crowd with you guys, which means it's related to everything else that's been happening!"

"Maybe . . . I mean, yeah, probably." Flicker tried not to imagine the disapproving look Nate was giving her. But hell, if a US senator could figure it out, Sonia could too. "And the same thing that happened last night might happen again today. So tell me about everything big going on in Cambria."

"What do I get out of this?" Sonia asked. "Like, will you finally explain what you are?"

"Um, I have to consult with Nate on that. For the moment, this is about keeping more people from getting hurt."

There was a pause. "Well, if you're going to play that card, I guess I don't really have a choice. There's an indie horror movie premiere, and some stupid hockey game. But I'm headed to the only event that matters—the big wedding at Hart's Castle."

Flicker smiled. *Now* they were getting somewhere.

"Give me details," she said.

CHAPTER 14
ANONYMOUS

HART'S CASTLE WAS DECORATED FOR THE WED-ding, but it was still a castle, a *fortress*, brought stone by stone from Europe by some rich guy a hundred years ago. Pennants flew from battlements in the ocean breeze. Flowers and banners were draped over the arched gateway where metal teeth hung, waiting to clang down on intruders.

Coming up the red carpet with Flicker, Thibault tried to breathe through his nervousness. He'd lifted an invitation from two wedding guests at the back of the line, but what if the couple were famous enough that he and Flicker couldn't pass for them?

There were *real* celebrities on this carpet. The watching crowd's attention swept this way and that, like long grass in a helicopter's downdraft.

Flicker laughed. "Man, people just glue their eyes to these B-listers!"

"And take pictures," Thibault said uneasily. "Nate's going to go ballistic when he sees we walked down the red carpet."

"Easiest way in." Flicker took a spin, whirling the hem of her long red dress. "And haven't you always wanted to?"

Thibault was about to say *never*, but Flicker took his hand and said, "Sonia Sonic. One o'clock."

Yep, there was Cambria's social-media queen, right by the gate, her silver-and-magenta hair gleaming.

Thibault frowned. "I feel like we should hide."

"Relax," Flicker said. "Sonia told us about this wedding."

"I know. But Nate's new strategy of working with her seems like a *really* bad idea to me."

"It was my idea, actually."

"That doesn't make it any better."

The crowd's attention had been clumped thickly on the woman in front of them, so tall and beautiful that she *had* to be a model. It let go reluctantly as she went through the gate, and searched the line for a new target. Thibault snipped it from himself, but it lingered on Flicker a moment.

"Who even is that?" asked a woman behind the rope.

"No one," said her friend.

The words sent a jolt of anger through Thibault. He was used to being ignored, but since when did not being famous mean you weren't real?

But Flicker squeezed his hand and smiled beatifically back at them all.

Also near the gate was a guy holding up a big heart-shaped sign: I'M STILL HERE FOR YOU, K-MO! Other people waved white roses and little white flags with the couple's names.

But not everyone was here to celebrate. Farther back, a small pack had been corralled together by security. Their biggest banner said NICE DAY FOR A RED WEDDING. No tall guy with a half-shaved head, though.

"Observation," Thibault said. "Crowds not always awesome."

Flicker shrugged. "Don't read the comments."

A sudden gasp filled the air, and the glittering attention snapped away down the hill to where the limos pulled up at the start of the red carpet. In the vacuum left behind, Thibault and Flicker walked unnoticed between the heavy wooden doors.

The forecourt of the castle was even busier. Guests filed through, bodyguards and assistants peeled off to the staff area, wedding staff fussed and consulted, and security looked menacing in suits and headsets. A pile of white gift bags leaned unsteadily. The air was thick with darting arrows of attention—curious, nervous, dutiful, watchful, bored, all kinds.

At the head of the guest line, the greeter held up a hand to stop them, then put his finger to his wired-up ear to listen.

"If this doesn't work," Thibault murmured, "stick close to me."

Flicker's grip tightened in his.

The greeter finally beckoned them forward, and Thibault handed the invitation over.

"The Gormans!" His gaze skated straight off Thibault and onto smiling Flicker. "Welcome!"

Okay, the Gormans were fellow nobodies, then. The guy laid the invitation on the neat stack beside him, and his assistant tapped the screen of her tablet and nodded.

"Please follow the Rose Path to the chapel," said the greeter with a suave sweep of his arm, already looking at the guests beyond them.

"Oh, I had a question," Flicker said, and their attention swung back to her. "Does *everyone* get a gift bag?"

As the greeter answered, Thibault sliced away every glimmer of the staff's attention, stepped closer to the assistant, and tapped the grayed-out GORMAN X 2 on her tablet so that it brightened again.

Then he reached for the discarded invitation on the stack.

A few minutes later Thibault was back at Flicker's side on the Rose Path. When he took her hand, she smiled at him without a moment's surprise.

"Look," she said. "They dug up the whole lawn to plant roses! Did you get the invite back to its owners?"

"Yep. Used one of Kelsie's distraction moves. It's handy when your housemate's a pickpocket."

She laughed. "Like you need it. Come on, I found a place for us to sit."

She drew him into the side porch of the chapel. Hungry gazes crisscrossed the air inside.

"Whoa," Thibault said. "Too much fame."

"I know. It's like *Entertainment Weekly* threw up in there."

A beautifully groomed couple was just entering the chapel. The space around the guy practically fizzed, and the quick hiss of whispers faded into awestruck silence as everyone's gaze latched onto him. Man, how would it feel, being *bombarded* like that?

The guy ignored everyone, fixing his own attention on the ushers. The woman, clearly more comfortable with fame, smiled and waved to a friend, diamonds sparkling on her hand.

Thibault shook off his own awe, not at these celebrities—he didn't watch a lot of TV, especially not reality shows like K-Mo's—but at celebrity itself, its hypnotic effect on a crowd.

Man, Glitch would just *love* to suck the starstruck adulation out of this gathering.

"See them anywhere?" he asked.

Flicker paused, sifting through the web of gazes shimmering around the chapel.

"Not yet," she said. "There's space upstairs. Think that's far enough away to not get Glitched?"

Thibault looked up over the sizzling attention arcs. In the

choir loft, the organist was playing background music, and the choir sat waiting in white angel gowns.

"Perfect," he said. "Quick, before someone throws us out for not having Daytime Emmys."

"It's cute that you know what Emmys are," she said, leading him to the staircase at the back. With everyone feasting their eyes on more glamorous guests, Flicker was practically as invisible as Thibault.

She walked a little tentatively, still scanning the chapel for Glitch and Coin. But Thibault knew how to guide her.

"Spiral staircase ahead. But I'll catch you if you fall."

"Ooh, romantic." She hiked the front of her dress up and started to climb.

Upstairs, the choir sat in steeply raked seats, their attention cascading over into the main chapel, star-spotting like everyone else. They barely noticed a couple of wedding guests creeping up to join them. Thibault followed Flicker up to the highest seat in the house.

It was like sitting on a cliff top. Down below, dappled by all the stained glass brought over from Europe, sat rows of astonishing hats, sharp haircuts, and fabulous hairdos. Among them everyone's stares formed a fine living net, bright against the shadows. Some people tried to play it cool, only sneaking glances. The truly famous didn't care who else was here. They sat in big asterisks of arcing attention, all flowing in, none out.

"Smell those flowers!" Flicker whispered in his ear.

"Kind of hard to breathe, huh? Everything's so over the top."

She elbowed him. "Seriously? You don't think it's sweet?"

He shrugged. "I can show someone I love them without cutting down a field of flowers. But I might be tempted to hire a choir. For a *very* special person."

She leaned closer, coiling her senses around him. "Oh really?"

"Yes, but someone too mature for schoolgirl fantasies about red carpets and celebrity weddings."

"God, you really suck at weddings," Flicker groaned. "We might as well have gone to the hockey game."

Thibault tried not to laugh too loud. "I wish Nate had sent us to the horror film. No jacket required."

"Hey, I *like* you in this jacket." Flicker adjusted his collar.

"I'm returning it tomorrow. I can't steal anything that cost five hundred bucks." He surveyed the shifting net of attention over the congregation. "Anyone down there with a shaved head?"

"Not yet. Kind of dizzying, all those eyes *swooping* to the door when anyone walks in."

"Creepy, huh?" Thibault watched as the sheaves of sight lines bent to some new spectacle below.

"But wouldn't it be kind of fun, getting all that attention? I mean, if your superpower *wasn't* disappearing."

"Right. Because I'd totally love paparazzi stalking me." He

shuddered. "This whole wedding has convinced me that forget-
tability is my natural element."

"Well, *I'm* not gonna forget you." Flicker smiled and
bumped him with her shoulder.

"Don't even joke about it."

"Oh—" Her eyebrows went up again. "Here comes the
groom!"

Some hoots and a little applause echoed up from below.
The choir rose from their seats with a swish of robes and a rustle
of hymnbook pages.

"Oh my God, and the bride!" she said in a whisper-squeak.
"I hate her show, but she looks *amazing*!"

Flicker's attention was fraying fast, joining everyone else's
focus on the front door down below, and Thibault felt a little
stab at his heart as she pulled away.

"Not as amazing as you," he said, and kissed her, just to
keep her with him a little longer.

The organist struck a triumphal opening chord. The choir,
ignoring the two teenagers lip-locked in the back pew, took a
breath as one and burst into song.

CHAPTER 15
BELLWETHER

"GEE, NATE. GREAT IDEA." ETHAN SLUMPED BACK IN his plastic seat, hunching his shoulders. "Bring me to a stadium full of police. No way *that* could go wrong."

Nate shrugged. "I told you to wear a hoodie."

"So those cops can just shoot me and say I looked threatening?" Ethan pulled his cap down harder. It only made his ears more conspicuous. "No way."

"Just keep your eyes open," Nate said. "You need to see those cops before they see you."

The horn sounded, echoing through the stadium, and the players skated out onto the ice to raucous applause. The lines of attention in the giant space converged into a spiky mass as all eyes turned toward the rink.

The stadium hosting Cambria's annual police-versus-firefighters hockey game was almost full. Every off-duty police officer in town was guaranteed to be here. Including, hopefully, the two that Ethan had bribed with fake money last night.

Nate wanted to find out who they were, to offer apologies and make restitution *before* they showed up at the Dish again.

While Ethan looked for the cops, Nate scanned the stadium for Glitch and Coin. First responders didn't seem like the right crowd for their recognition-vampire act, but who knew? Maybe the fact that half these guys were carrying guns would be an even bigger turn-on.

Nate wasn't sure what he could do if Glitch skated onto the ice to wield her power on the crowd. Was he strong enough to pull the focus off her? Last night he'd barely kept his own ego together.

"I don't even *like* hockey," Ethan whined. "You should have sent me to the horror movie with Kelsie."

Nate didn't bother answering. Ethan's crush was old news, even if he was too chickenshit to tell Kelsie about it.

With another blast of the horn, the puck dropped, and the geometries of the game exploded before Nate.

Sports on TV always bored him. But live was way more interesting, watching the players' attention slice great sizzling arcs across the ice. Nate knew nothing about hockey, but the plays unfolded with a logic that was written in the air.

Maybe he should give being a coach a try someday. It was

big money, and sports always looked good on college applications. They were even a path into politics.

The problem was, you had to actually *play* the stupid game first. And taking orders from some other coach was not Nate's thing.

"You boys enjoying yourselves?" came a voice from behind them.

Nate turned, and found four older men in police blue behind them.

"Yes, sir," he said.

"Who you rooting for?" the man continued.

Nate realized he was dressed in a black jacket, and Ethan in a dingy khaki coat. Everyone else in the stadium was wearing either cop blue or fire red. Nate had sensed the tribal conflict from five blocks away, and the stands had self-organized into colored clumps as they filled.

If Glitch used her power in a situation like this, what would happen? Would an actual cop-versus-firefighter war break out? Or would everyone be unable to recognize their own tribe?

"Just watching the game," he said mildly.

"No opinion at all?" the man goaded.

Ethan turned around. "Well, frankly, you guys are toast. The firefighters' wings, Rodney and Overland, have the best wrist shots in Cambria. They can dig pucks out in battles on the boards, and have enough speed to make your defense back off. Your guys are reacting rather than playing aggressive, which is why, five minutes in, you've only had possession for a minute twenty-three and it's two shot attempts to zero."

The four cops didn't say a word, and Ethan turned back to face the game with a bored sigh.

"Like I said, toast," the voice finished.

As the silence behind them stretched out, Nate fought back a grin. Maybe it was Ethan who should go into coaching. Seemed like about 78 percent of sports was talking a good game of bullshit.

But when Nate's attention returned to the game, he found that the voice was right. The firefighters really were keeping the police on their heels.

"They're not in this section," Ethan said.

"Maybe we should move." Nate pointed at the big clump of blue off to their left.

Ethan sighed, but stood up and sidled toward the aisle.

Nate chose seats at the front of the swath of blue, so they could see the faces of the fans behind them.

"Perfect," Ethan said, craning his neck around. "Nothing conspicuous about *this*."

Nate didn't answer. It was tough for him here too. All that attention flashing overhead, just begging to be grabbed and twisted and *used*. But Nate had to watch it bounce around pointlessly on the ice.

What a waste, all that focus wrapped around a piece of rubber.

"Well, well, well" came a familiar voice from Nate's right. "I *thought* that was you guys."

Nate looked up and found Detectives Fuentes and King making themselves at home in the seats beside Scam. The same cops who'd interviewed Scam after the bank robbery, and who'd followed up with Nate after the police station disaster.

"You two never struck me as hockey fans," King said.

Before Ethan could launch into another discussion of the cops' wings, Nate said, "We support Cambria's first responders in all their civic endeavors."

"Uh-huh," Fuentes said, then leaned back to talk to the men in the row behind. "These two really been watching the game? Or do they look like they're up to something?"

The cops behind them shrugged, and one said, "Didn't really notice."

"Didn't notice?" Fuentes pointed at Ethan. "But this guy here, this guy is *famous*. He's the kid in the bank video! You know, the one who talked smack to Jerry Laszlo's crew so bad that they all started shooting. And *this* guy," he pointed to Nate, "was the guy he called afterward. Like he was his lawyer or something. I never even asked—*are* you a lawyer, kid?"

Nate nudged Ethan. "Get rid of them."

"I don't know, detectives," Ethan said, his voice slipping into a smooth, superior drawl. "If I had Internal Affairs all over my precinct house, I wouldn't be worried so much about who's got a law degree."

"Wait," Nate said. "What?"

Ethan smiled, the voice still rolling. "Just last week Detective King here had to testify in front of a grand jury. Not about herself, of course. She's *squeaky*. But that doesn't mean the rest of the force is clean."

The horn sounded as the first period ended, and the crowd gave a ragged cheer. But the little zone around Ethan stayed dead silent. The cops behind them all stood up together and shuffled away, muttering about beer.

Fuentes himself was stunned into silence, but Detective King was drilling white-hot attention into Ethan.

"And did you hear this from your mother the DDA? Because grand jury proceedings are supposed to be *secret*."

"Um, no," Ethan croaked in his own voice, then went smooth again. "It was from a reporter at the *Herald*. Janice something. She's going to run with the story in a couple of days."

The two detectives stared at Ethan, unblinking but uncertain.

"And now I think we need some hot dogs," Nate said, dragging Ethan to his feet and down the row of empty seats. "Enjoy the game, detectives."

Fuentes and King watched them go.

Ethan glared at Nate as they walked. "Nice job getting my mom in trouble. Why did I even listen to you?"

"You're right. We should have just walked away."

Ethan swore. "You think they bought that stuff about the reporter?"

"It must be convincing, or the voice wouldn't have used it."
Nate's eyes swept the stadium. Now they *really* needed to find
the two cops Ethan had bribed.

"I hate that Fuentes guy," Ethan said. "At least I put a fire-
cracker up his ass."

"Yeah, great," Nate said. "But if the Cambria cops are being
investigated for corruption, this just got a lot worse. Or are you
okay with your mom watching a surveillance tape of you committing bribery?"

Ethan froze. "Oh, crap. But it's not bribery if you just hand
over blank paper, right?"

Nate shrugged. "Questions like that are generally left to a
judge and jury."

Ethan gawked at him.

"Just keep your eyes open, Ethan. I'll look for Glitch and
Coin, and you look for those two cops. We need to find out if
you're already screwed."

CHAPTER 16
MOB

KELSIE USUALLY LIKED HORROR MOVIES.

She liked the roller coaster of emotions. The queasy antici-pation during the credits, the thrill of those first fake scares. Then the building dread as things got serious. Connecting with a good, focused crowd of movie fans was like living inside a story.

Which was great, depending on the story.

"It's not a slasher film, is it?" she asked Chizara. "I hate those."

She didn't need any more challenges to her central nervous system. She was twitchy enough as it was.

"You're scared of blood?" Chizara looked over her shoulder at the audience. "Then why are we in the front row?"

"Because this is where real movie fans sit! People in the

back always have other stuff on their mind, like making out and snarking." Kelsie gave a shudder. "But slasher fans . . . not my favorite crowd."

Chizara looked at her with something like pity. Kelsie didn't like pity. It made her feel small. She'd fought against everyone's pity when Dad died. Losing him was bad enough.

"I think it's more like a thriller," Chizara said. "And given that it was shot in Cambria, and about half this audience were extras in the movie, we'll probably all be laughing most of the time."

"I'm okay with that."

Kelsie could feel a thrum of expectation in the theater. No red carpet outside, only a couple of local reporters, and this "premiere" was in the afternoon, with regular movies showing tonight. It was a very low-budget film, as if any other kind of film would ever be shot in Cambria.

Still, it was sold out. She'd had to call on her friend Mikey to score the tickets.

"You think Glitch and her boy toy will really be here?" Chizara asked, twisting in her seat to survey the crowd behind them.

"Hopefully they're sleeping off last night's carnage." Kelsie wasn't in the mood for a superpowered throwdown today.

Alone in her room at the Dish last night, she'd kept reminding herself that there was someone else in the building, even if she couldn't always remember his name. Plus, a bunch of friends were just a phone call away. She wasn't on her own, not really.

Still, she hadn't slept much.

The lights dimmed, and Kelsie let herself be buoyed up by the rising anticipation.

This was the first time she'd been alone with Chizara. Of the other Zeroes, Chizara always seemed to be the most withdrawn, even a little wary of the rest of them. Like she wasn't sure superpowers were such a good idea.

Which was the opposite of what Kelsie had thought. Until last night.

The thing was, she trusted Chizara the most of all of them. Maybe it was because she was so careful with her power. At every step of creating the Dish, she'd worried about safety, and about whether Nate's "experiments" were going to hurt anyone.

There was also the connection Kelsie felt when she and Chizara ran the Dish's music and lights together. The rush of guiding the crowd through its ups and downs, of riding that beast, was shared between them, wordless and intense.

Kelsie never related to people very well one-on-one. But with Chizara it all happened through the crowd itself.

It was almost like three kids daring each other into bigger and braver dares—two of the kids were Kelsie and Chizara, and the other was something huge, the sum of all the people on the dance floor. Between them they could turn a room into an oasis of pure dancing bliss.

"Emergency exit's right over there," Chizara said, pointing. "You know, in case Glitch does show, and I have to shut down the lights."

"I'll make sure to stay close to you," Kelsie said. "But I hope they've got better things to do today."

Chizara turned around again, searching the faces of the crowd. "I don't know. Last night looked pretty much like they thought messing with *dolls* was the best thing ever."

Kelsie thought back to the summer, to clambering with Ethan through that building full of drug-fueled highs and lows, her dad wretched in the middle of it. "It's like addiction. It eats away at people until all the good stuff is gone."

Dad had always worried that Kelsie would fall into drugs, but he shouldn't have. She'd felt how lonely and isolating a life like that could be.

Besides, if she was feeling low or scared, she only had to find a happy crowd to take her away. That's why she loved dancing, malls on holidays, school bus trips, and baseball games.

"Maybe." Chizara sounded uncertain. "When I crash things with my power . . . sometimes I don't want to come back from that."

"Me too. With dancing."

Chizara hesitated. "So, you know how Nate says we should text everyone if we see Glitch and Coin?"

"Yeah?"

"We do that," Chizara said. "Right after we beat them to death."

Kelsie almost laughed.

"Kidding." Chizara shrugged. "Sort of."

"So you don't think Glitch and Coin are good people who just haven't seen the light?" Kelsie said, mockingly.

"Nate's light? Doubt it." Chizara grinned. "I think they're jerks who don't give a damn about anyone, dolls or otherwise."

Kelsie nodded. None of the others had felt how good the crowd had been last night, how ready to pop. But then those two had turned it all into a nightmare.

For a moment Kelsie let their anger spread out into the expectant crowd. And somewhere a few rows back, someone called out, "Hey, jerk! That's my seat!"

Kelsie dragged her rage back in, quashing it as the opening credits started to roll. She took deep breaths until she was back in control.

Chizara looked at her.

"Just letting off steam," Kelsie said.

"That must be nice," Chizara said. "When you're angry, you can make the world angry."

"I don't always let out what I feel." Not since her dad had died. "I have to be careful."

"As long as you don't let Nate push you around." Chizara's voice sank to a whisper as the film began.

"But pushing people around is *his* superpower." Kelsie stifled her laugh.

Nate could be intimidating. It was good to have Chizara in the group. Someone strong enough to stand up to him.

Of course, Chizara's power had forced her to be strong. While they were building the Dish's Faraday cage, she'd talked about how technology was pins and needles to her. Like having a thousand itches and she couldn't scratch any of them.

The movie was a little slow to begin, following some girl on what looked like a normal day—walking her dog, getting money out, shopping. The only scary part was that the camera was stalking the girl, watching from behind bushes, or pulling back out of sight when she turned around.

"Great. Shaky cam," Kelsie whispered.

Chizara's grin shone in the light from the screen. "Thought you said the front row was awesome!"

Kelsie didn't answer. She didn't mind shaky cam herself, but there were always people in a crowd who got nauseated. Plus, it was jarring seeing the familiar streets of Cambria through the stalker-cam lens.

"Distract me?" she pleaded in a whisper.

Chizara leaned closer, her words a breath against Kelsie's ear. "Okay. What's up between you and Scam?"

Kelsie shrugged. "He's a good guy."

"Yeah, sure. If you like pathological liars."

Kelsie sighed. She knew most of the Zeroes disliked Ethan. Watching his voice work could be downright unnerving. But she could tell it and the real Ethan apart. They all could. So why freak out about it?

"I wouldn't have met any of you guys if it wasn't for Ethan."

"I guess we owe him for that, at least," Chizara said begrudgingly.

"He's not my type, if that's what you're asking," Kelsie said.

Chizara looked kind of relieved, even as she said, "It's okay if he is. I mean, I'm not judging. Seriously."

Kelsie was about to insist that he *wasn't*, but a surge came from the crowd as the movie shifted gear. The stalking camera had gotten closer, moving up behind the girl.

She felt the crowd's excitement roll over her. In turn she opened up the feedback loop and gave back some of her own desire to be distracted and entertained. Maybe she and Chizara were supposed to be keeping watch for Glitch and Coin, but Kelsie couldn't help joining in with the audience. Becoming part of the excitement.

Then a jolt went through her—it hadn't come from the crowd, but from deep inside her.

"Hey," Chizara said, "isn't that the Parker-Hamilton in the background?"

Kelsie stayed silent, hoping it wasn't.

"I guess they shot this last summer, before it was demolished."

Kelsie couldn't answer. She remembered her dad tied up,

the countdown to the hotel's demolition ringing in their ears. She'd thought she was going to die there too.

Chizara was looking at her. "Kelsie?"

Kelsie gripped the armrests. She felt sick.

She shut her eyes against the sight of the doomed hotel. But it was too late. The flashbacks had started. Tied up in a car trunk, a bag over her head. Then strapped to a concrete pole on an abandoned floor of the hotel. Her dad nearby, beaten nearly to death. Too far away for her to reach out to him.

Her dad in the hospital. Her dad dying. Dead. Gone.

She started to sweat. This sequence played out in her dreams sometimes, but never when she was awake.

The world began to spin around her. And with it, the theater crowd spun too. Her fear flooded out into the room. The movie soundtrack grew ominous, dragging them all along with it.

Kelsie opened her eyes, taking deep breaths. Trying to put herself back in the story. The fictional story. The one on the screen, not the one playing over and over in her head.

This movie was about someone else. A nameless girl on-screen. It wasn't about Kelsie.

But then the stalking camera made its move, closing swiftly in a parking lot. A bright, shiny needle went into the girl's neck. She swooned, and was shoved into the waiting trunk of a car. . . .

"Oh my God."

Panic flooded Kelsie. Her hand shot out and gripped Chizara's arm.

She tried to stand, but the shaky darkness of the trunk had swallowed her will. By now the whole crowd was swept up with Kelsie, her fear roaring and rebounding off the movie theater's walls.

The nightmares she'd been swallowing for six months came tumbling out.

CHAPTER 17
CRASH

CHIZARA FOUGHT FOR CONTROL.

Kelsie's fear spilled over from the next seat, ricocheting around the theater. It was much stronger than the images on the screen—tightening ropes, the villain's cold-lit face—and the stings of foreboding music.

The fear made it harder to bear the hundreds of needling phones in the audience behind her, and the knot of itchy pain in the back of her head from the multichannel speaker system. With Mob's power drenching her, Chizara had to consciously fend off every spike of tech.

She held Kelsie's hand tight. On-screen the trunk lid slammed shut, and Chizara felt the thump of Kelsie's fear in her gut.

"It's all right," she muttered.

"No." Kelsie shook her head. "It's not."

In brief scraps of screen light Chizara made out Kelsie's staring eyes. With each jangle and scrape of the soundtrack more fear was welling out of her.

But it's her *fear, not mine,* Chizara thought, ferociously trying to keep the two separate. *Kelsie's fear of . . .*

Of course. Last summer. Sack over the head, trunk, tied wrists—this was the worst day of Kelsie's life all over again. This crappy movie had let those bad memories loose. Chizara felt them reaching deep inside her, blotting out her rational mind.

With a massive effort she twisted from the screen to the audience. People clutched each other, blank-faced and cowering in their seats. A few called out curses, prayers, each other's names, from mouths square with terror. And the fear kept ratcheting up.

"You've got to control this, Kelsie!" Chizara called out over the noise.

"How?" Kelsie gasped.

At least she wasn't screaming, *I can't!* Nate's training had brought her that far.

"Look at me, Kelsie!"

But Kelsie's eyes were locked in horrible communion with the screen. Above them people were howling now, scrambling along the seat rows. Chizara wanted to howl and scramble too. But if she lost control, she'd crash everything, plunge the theater into absolute blackness, brick every phone, panic everyone so much worse.

"You're *okay*." She forced the words through gritted teeth, made her terrified self listen. "You can deal with this."

Someone tumbled between her and Kelsie, making straight for the exit. Other people followed, jumping the rows, their phones zapping Chizara in the head as they passed.

Okay, time to deal with this herself.

She looked up at the beam of light flashing the terror-soaked images on the screen. Her mind followed it back into the projection booth. A tiny bright complex of electronics unspooled those jittery images, syncing them to a dozen rumbling speakers. . . .

It would be so easy to blot out the whole system in a single swipe.

Stay calm. Only what's necessary.

She didn't even crash the projector, just doused the bulb. She didn't blow the whole audio setup, just knocked the optical track sensors offline. Done.

But it made the theater darker, and the crowd still roared and fought to get away. Chizara found the circuit for the house lighting and sent a surge at it. The lights flickered on for a moment, then popped all at once. Wisps of smoke and tiny showers of glass shards disappeared into darkness.

Damn. Not enough control. The only light came from the exit signs and people's phone screens.

Kelsie's hand had gone limp. Closed eyes. No expression. Her fear had hunched her down so hard that she'd slid half off her seat, maybe passed out. But the feedback loop was still coursing through her and the crowd.

She must be caught in a nightmare. Chizara had to get her out of here.

She slid her arms under Kelsie's shoulders and knees. The girl was slim, like she burned up everything she ate with dancing.

Chizara had to force herself toward the front emergency exit. She still saw shadows of images on the screen, a primal aversion lingering behind her eyelids.

At the exit door she turned and pushed backward against the bar. The heavy door swung out.

Into daylight.

A grubby-looking alleyway—but anything was better than the boomeranging fear in the movie theater. Chizara carried Kelsie away, the panic fading into the soft burn of wireless transmissions, normal for downtown Cambria on a Sunday afternoon.

She looked for a place to put Kelsie down before her knees gave out. As well as wobbling with fear, they ached from the optical and power cables funneling stuff back and forth under the asphalt.

At the alley's end was a sidewalk lunch place, closed for the weekend—although an LED sign by its door spelled out

O-P-E-N, letter by letter, over and over, with an irritating tickle in Chizara's brain. Outside the café stood curly iron seats and tables chained to the ground.

As Chizara carried her in among the chairs, Kelsie began to stir. "What the . . ."

"Shh, everything's okay."

The seat farthest from the tickling sign could hold two people. Chizara sank onto it and settled Kelsie beside her.

Kelsie swayed, blinking at the curly chairs like she'd landed in a parallel universe.

"Where are we?"

"Outside the movie, remember? You passed out."

As if to remind her, the distant emergency exit swung open and a few girls sprayed out, mascara streaked down their faces.

Kelsie watched them intently. "Oh, yeah. The car trunk."

Through the whine of receding phones Chizara felt a scatter of fear-drops hit her psyche. Kelsie was shedding panic like a dog shaking off water.

Chizara put an arm around her. They were both trembling with relief and leftover fear.

"I never realized," Chizara finally said, "what you and Scam went through back in July, the Bagrovs kidnapping you. Trying to *murder* you. I guess I was too busy reveling in my big crash . . ."

She looked away, feeling again that epic moment when she'd brought the Parker-Hamilton down. It *had* been pretty

121

amazing. But Kelsie hadn't even seen it. She'd been in the ambulance, taking her dying dad to the hospital.

Kelsie fixed her with her big green eyes and sealed Chizara's hand between both of hers. "You saved me."

Chizara smiled. "I don't think you were in serious danger. You weren't in the crush."

"No," Kelsie said, her breath going ragged. "Last summer, I mean. In that hotel. You saved all of us, me and Ethan and Nate and—even my *dad*, for a little while . . ."

Tears sprang to her eyes and her pale face crumpled. Two tears fell hot onto Chizara's wrist.

Kelsie covered her face. Words and tears wormed out between her fingers: "And I never even said thank you!" She was crying too hard to go on.

Chizara put her arms around Kelsie and pulled her in, resting her chin on Kelsie's blond curls as the girl sobbed and shook. Sounded like these tears had been a long time coming.

Chizara held on tight, rocking her. She hadn't embraced a friend like this since grade school. And it had been a year or so since Ikem had gone from accepting her hugs to acting like they gave him an electric shock. But she was doing the right thing now, holding this girl, she knew it. She'd wait out these tears, her head getting jabbed from that damn sign and her butt aching with the city's workings.

Let Kelsie cry just as long as she needed.

CHAPTER 18
FLICKER

THE CHOIR SANG BACKUP WHILE THEY KISSED.

It was always new, feeling her lips against Thibault's. Some part of her brain always forgot how good it was, though her body remembered. But Flicker was fairly certain that this whole choir-singing-while-kissing thing had never happened before.

Harmonies filled the air, their reverberations and echoes mapping the vast open space around them. The choir pushed out all other sound except for Thibault's breathing, which grew quick and shuddery as she ran her fingers up inside his shirt.

She allowed herself a little peek at the couple standing at the altar. All eyes were on them, and they really were beautiful. They looked way too happy for this marriage to be the loveless attention grab that the tabloids claimed it was.

Their lips parted, and Thibault murmured, "See anything?"

"What makes you think I'm even watching?" Flicker asked, guiltily shutting off her power. God, K-Mo's dress was amazing, though.

"Because that's why we're here," he said. "To keep an eye on things."

"Come for the stakeout, stay for the make-out."

Flicker could feel the cringe travel all the way through Thibault's body. Yeah, that was one she should have run past the stupid-meter *before* saying it out loud.

"You're such a poet," he said with a laugh.

"Sorry. Mood killer!"

He didn't argue, settling back against the pew.

The choir came to the end of its opening song. An expectant hush settled over the chapel, full of coughs and shuffles and the wingbeats of a hundred fluttering cameras.

"We are gathered in this place to celebrate true love," began the officiant. He wasn't a real preacher, Flicker had read somewhere, but just some actor friend with an online certificate. She vaguely recognized his voice from a beer commercial.

The sermon was full of platitudes, and the congregation's eyes drifted from the happy couple to check out hats and outfits. Flicker caught a few faces that seemed familiar, but only with the tugging familiarity of minor celebrities.

Anon's hand was in hers. It *was* a little tricky, keeping hold of him with so many people around.

She leaned closer. "Looks like the eye-bang twins aren't showing up."

"Have you checked outside? Maybe they couldn't get in."

"Yeah, maybe." If anything, the crowd outside was the bigger target.

Flicker flung her vision farther, into the jumbled viewpoints surrounding the chapel grounds. Most people were staring at the loudspeakers hidden among piles of flowers, no doubt listening to the officiant's words.

Then Flicker caught a glimpse of something odd.

The security guard at one of the side entrances was slinking away from his post, looking back over his shoulder. She jumped into his head—his eyes were darting back and forth as he moved away from the crowd.

"Okay. This is interesting."

Thibault held her hand tighter.

The security guard was pulling something out of his jacket. An envelope, stuffed full.

He opened it up . . . and stared.

His fingers rifled through it, growing more and more agitated. Blank paper was evidently not what the guy had expected to find.

"Shit," Flicker whispered. "Coin bribed a guard."

"So they must be—"

"Hush. Listen . . ."

Down in the congregation, something was changing. The

tenor of the crowd, the totality of all those coughs and shuffles and whispers, was shifting into something nervous. Flicker could almost smell the twitchiness coming over them, like a herd of animals sensing a predator nearby.

The fake preacher was building to the climax of his mini sermon, unaware.

But then he said, "Jacob, do you take Kirsten to be your lawful wedded wife?"

The familiar words drew the crowd's eyes to the altar.

There was a long pause before the answer came. Way too long, and the hush began to fray with worried whispers.

Then finally the groom's voice rang out—

"Who the hell *are* you?"

A gasp went through the chapel, and Flicker flung her vision back into the crowd. They were all staring up at the not-so-happy couple.

"Who are *you*?" K-Mo shrieked. "Who are all these *people*?"

The words set off another astonished gasp, this one mixed with cries of fear. From the viewpoint of the crowd, Flicker could only see the backs of the guests' heads.

She sent herself into the officiant's vision.

He was staring out past Kirsten and Jacob, his gaze drawn to a couple striding up the aisle. Coin wore a beautiful gray suit in a vintage cut, and Glitch a crimson dress and tiny hat nodding with feathers. They climbed the stairs to the altar, then pushed aside the bride and groom.

They locked eyes, and Flicker found herself drawn into Glitch's vision.

It was like nothing Flicker had ever experienced, staring at someone with such surrender. Without any glance away, without even blinking.

She felt her own will being pulled into the vortex below. The attention, the recognition, the desperate *need to be seen* of all those fame-obsessed people gathered in the chapel, all of it was swept up into the glorious stare shared between Glitch and Coin.

"Get down there and stop them!" Flicker murmured to Thibault, but he was already gone.

CHAPTER 19
ANONYMOUS

BY THE TIME THIBAULT GOT DOWNSTAIRS, THE crowd had exploded.

Fancy hats were knocked askew, perfect hairstyles mussed and snagged, designer outfits twisted and rucked on the struggling, fleeing bodies.

The neat sheaves of wedding fascination had blown apart into hundreds of strands. Faces jigged about, pale with fright and confusion, everyone suddenly alone in an unrecognizable universe.

Thibault dodged and weaved closer to the altar, where Glitch and Coin stood eye-locked to each other, sucking up all the recognition in the room, all the meaning and familiarity. And as he drew near, Glitch's power began to tweak at the edges of his mind.

What was he doing here again?

He clenched his teeth, trying to stay on course. He was a Zero, here to protect people. And those two up front were Zeroes too. This was only a superpower at work, not some existential crisis surging up from his—

Oof. A random fist caught Thibault right in the guts. He doubled over and sagged against a pew.

This was even worse than the panic in the Dish. Why was it so *violent*?

Thibault stared up at the lashing snakes of people's attention. A moment before, those hungry gazes had been magnetized, great bundles of them, onto famous faces.

Of course. The pecking order was gone. All fame, status, and celebrity had been erased, and that loss had sent everyone reeling into mayhem.

Thibault could barely make out the two figures at the altar, one tall and one tiny, both hands joined. Their connection fizzed bright between their eyes, their world-shattering love for each other.

He could feel Glitch's power working on his mind, trying to suck out the sense to fuel her loop with Coin. *Who am I?* one part of him was whining. *Am I anything at all?*

Whatever. *Zen for Beginners* had been asking him that for years.

"Wisdom tells me I am nothing," he muttered, stepping up onto the seat.

He leaped from pew to pew, past abandoned hats and handbags and scatters of flower petals. Four bridesmaids stood frozen, wide-eyed, at the front of the chapel, arcs of attention waving from their heads like bright inchworms seeking another foothold.

"I am nothing," Thibault managed, jumping from the front pew.

He slipped as he landed on the floor, one hand brushing cold marble before he righted himself.

"I am Anonymous." The word was meaningless in his mouth.

The connection between the two at the altar sizzled and spat. It was trying to drink his mind, his very self.

Just. Keep. Going.

But then the girl's firm, fervent voice struck a steady note against the cries and struggles of the terrorized crowd:

"I, Ren, take you, Davey, to be my unlawful wedded husband."

Thibault stopped dead. The somber words lifted the hairs on the back of his neck. She'd stopped playing dolls with the congregation and turned utterly serious.

"To have and to hold," she went on. "No matter what crazy shit happens. Rich or poor, healthy or sick as dogs, or cut to pieces by the swarm. To stay by each other's side *till death us do fucking part*! Whether that's tonight, or tomorrow, or next week."

Davey stood straighter with every word. He beamed his attention back at her so fiercely it crackled.

Thibault felt his will spiraling away from him into the strand of pure recognition, of deep, bitter loyalty between the two. Why was he here again? Was it just to witness this?

"What you said," Davey murmured. "All of it."

He slipped an enormous glittering ring onto the girl's hand.

"*Grab them, Anon!*" a high voice shouted.

Thibault looked over his shoulder. Up in the choir loft a girl in sunglasses and a red dress was waving at him. Behind her the choir stared down, bewildered.

The girl's attention was complex, multiple, angling at Thibault through the choir's eyes and those of a few people standing dazed among the pews. He'd seen that done before. Who—

"Anon! Knock them over! Shake them apart!" she yelled.

Anon? Yes, he knew that name, he was sure—

"Remember who you are!" the girl cried. "*Your parents left you at the hospital!*"

A shock went through him—of fear, of thirst, of aloneness, of knowing he'd been forgotten. He grabbed at the scrap of memory.

"I am nothing." He climbed the altar stairs. Coin and Glitch—*Davey and Ren*—were still locked on each other's eyes.

Davey was saying, "For richer and poorer, but we'll be *plenty* rich—"

Thibault thrust his hand out, severing the bright bar of attention between them, erasing them from each other's consciousness.

They stumbled apart, stunned and speechless.

All at once the rioting crowd froze, staring at each other in astonishment. Then, in the silence, paired shrieks of pain echoed through the chapel. The couple had both fallen to their knees.

Thibault caught Davey by the shoulder before he tumbled over.

"Sucks, doesn't it, having your brain messed with?"

The guy stared blankly up.

"We need to talk," Thibault said. "You two and me and some friends of—"

The blow came from behind, a *thwack* against the base of Thibault's skull. He stumbled down the carpeted steps and fell to the cold marble floor, clutching at consciousness, hands in the air to ward off any further blows.

It was Ren. She dropped the Bible back onto the lectern.

"Come on, Davey. Let's *go*!"

As Thibault rose shakily to his feet, the two ran toward the door.

CHAPTER 20
ANONYMOUS

THIBAULT JUMPED DOWN THE CHAPEL STEPS AND dodged through the confusion.

"A bomb go off in there?" a security guard cried, backing off, arms wide as if to catch all the milling guests. Sirens started up in the distance as Thibault darted under the guy's arm.

Davey and Ren were already halfway down the lawn, running hand in hand among astonished caterers and event staff.

As Thibault pursued them down the slope, the babble and wail of wedding guests grew behind him. Excited reporters rushed at them, and a few strands of attention even lighted on Thibault. He sliced them away.

Photographers were all over the place, manically gathering footage. One lifted his camera at Ren and Davey, but Ren waved a hand at him. The camera dropped from his grip and thumped into his chest. He staggered back, gaping in confusion.

Ren laughed as they ran, bonded to Davey with a bright shaft of affection. They dashed through a gate in the castle wall and on toward their black-and-red convertible parked outside. Davey skidded to a stop at the car, opened the passenger door, and put out a courtly hand for Ren. She low-fived it as she dropped in.

Davey closed her door, then ran around and jumped into the driver's seat.

They paused to exchange a long, hungry kiss, pulsing with the light of their bond. That left Thibault time to launch himself over the trunk and land in the backseat. He chopped away the startled attention from the two, then lay down along the seat.

A moment later the Ford's engine caught and roared.

"Later, suckers!" Ren cried as the car screeched away from the curb. Her hat fluttered in the wind and then flew back and landed on Thibault.

He stayed down until they were around the corner of the castle, out of sight of any photographers. Then he sat up, snipped away a scrap of awareness from Ren, and slid across to where the rearview mirror wouldn't catch him.

Media trucks and catering vans sat parked along the high gray crenellated wall, all the pomp and expense of the ruined wedding on display.

"How sad were all those poor K-Mo fans?" said Ren, shaking out her hair.

"We should crash a wedding every Sunday." Davey slung his arm along the back of the seat, and Ren tipped her head back on it.

"Nah, just B-listers'," she said. "I love the way they feed off each other's faces."

"I know, right? I could feel that wannabe vibe even before you hit me with it."

"And today has *nothing* on the honeymoon." Ren leaned over and kissed Davey's cheek, lighting a little spark between them. "Love in the desert on Christmas Eve!"

The car sped up as they took the access road onto the freeway. The air filled with shuffling strands of other drivers' attention, watching traffic and counting down exit signs.

A few police cars shot past on their way to the castle, setting the two laughing again.

"Late again, losers!" Ren cried.

Thibault scooted to the middle of the backseat and stuck his head up between the two.

"You guys seem pretty pleased with yourselves," he said.

Davey flinched, his hands tightening on the wheel. But Ren just looked at Thibault levelly.

"Great. Another stalker. Or are you the same one from last night?"

Thibault didn't know what to say to that, which made her sneer.

"What? Did you think you were the only one in the world?"

"Stalker." He shook his head.

"Do you prefer 'Forgettable'?" Davey adjusted the rearview mirror. "Or maybe you think you're some kind of homegrown ninja?"

Ren snorted. She and Davey both kept their eyes trained on him—Davey in the mirror, Ren with an unabashed stare. They knew how to stay focused on him.

Because they'd seen an Anonymous before.

There were more of him in the world.

He shook the dizzying thought away and kept his voice firm. "What the hell were you doing back there?"

Ren hooked her elbow over the seat back and grinned. "Getting married. What did it *look* like?"

"It looked like you trying to get someone killed."

She snorted. "We were doing those reality-celeb morons a favor. The whole world'll be talking about this!"

"Yeah, but you trashed someone's *wedding*," Thibault said. "I heard your vows. They *meant* something to you."

"Our vows are none of your business," Davey growled, and shook his head. "Stalkers. Always snooping."

"And always so judgy." Ren turned away, now watching Thibault in the rearview mirror. "You followed us last night, too, didn't you? You were there when that black chick bricked our car. You must be one of those losers who runs the Petty Dish, huh?"

"Petri Dish," Thibault said.

"That's right. Still can't believe you only sold beer." Ren's eyes were coldly amused. "I mean, you guys blew up a *police station*. We figured you at least knew how to party."

"You knew about us?" Thibault barely got the words out. It was too much at once.

"You weren't exactly in stealth mode," she said with a laugh. "You've got your own pet weird-hunter and everything. So we decided to pay you a visit."

"What, just to mess with us? To bring down our club?"

"Look, we didn't know you *ran* the place. Our kind aren't usually old enough to own a nightclub. Or stupid enough."

"*I* knew, from the music vibe," Davey grumbled. "I told you that DJ was bad news."

"*Our kind.*" Thibault swallowed. "How many of us *are* there?"

She shrugged. "Who knows? Had four of us in Portland. Including a guy just like you, a Stalker. Maybe more than one."

"Yeah." Davey laughed. "It's not like you can line Stalkers up and count them."

Thibault eased himself back against the seat, his mind blown by the guy's matter-of-fact tone. There really were more people like him. People who shared the constant fight to be seen, to be remembered.

He wasn't alone.

Glitch was watching him carefully, almost pityingly. "You don't know much, do you?"

Thibault shook his head.

"Well, don't worry about us. We're not sticking around to piss in your cornflakes. We've got a honeymoon party to get to." She put her hand on Davey's shoulder. Her wedding ring was a heavy blend of jewels and silver leaves. Bought with fake money, of course. "Don't we, Husband?"

Silently Davey laid his hand on hers, his eyes still on the road.

"That Stalker guy you knew," Thibault said. "Is there any way to find him? If I went up to Portland, say. What's his name?"

"Like we'd remember a Stalker's name!" Davey narrowed his eyes at Thibault in the mirror. "Also, he got killed."

Thibault stared back. "You guys are just dicking with me."

"Poor baby." Glitch reached back and patted Thibault's knee. Then she fixed him with her eyes, her black hair thrashing around her face in the wind. "I've got some advice for you. It might save your life, so listen: That stuff we pulled at your club? All the other big stuff you've done? It attracts attention. The wrong kind."

"You mean, like, the government?" Thibault said.

She laughed. "The least of your worries. Here's what you and your friends gotta do—spread out wide and keep moving. Don't hang around together. Leave town."

"Leave *town*?" He glanced around. They were practically out the other side of Cambria already, headed east.

"Don't stop anywhere for long. Be a moving target."

Davey's reflection refused to meet his eye. Ren's gaze had him pinned back against the seat. Their connections made a perfect triangle, all three sides equally bright and firm.

"A target for *what*?" Thibault asked.

Ren got a faraway look in her eyes. Her plum-painted lips closed tight, like she was afraid of what might come out. Then she spoke. "For the guy who killed our Stalker friend. He's after us, and we just waved a big red flag telling him where we are—where *you* are. He's not picky. He'll chew up anyone who's got a power." And her eyes pinned him again.

"And you waved that flag here? *Why?*"

"It was kind of your wedding present to us," she said. "You guys are a diversion so we can relax on our honeymoon. Thanks for that!"

Thibault stared back at her. "If we're a diversion, why would you warn us?"

Davey gave a braying laugh. "The longer it takes him to hunt you guys down, the farther we can run. So *try* not to die too fast. How many are you?" He lifted his chin to peer at Thibault in the mirror.

"Six."

"Beautiful." Davey hit the brakes, pulling onto the shoulder. The wheels sent up a cloud of dust around them. "Six of you should distract him for a good long while. Go tell your pals to spread out."

"What? You're just dumping me here?"

"We didn't *ask* you to come along," Ren said.

Thibault looked around—this was miles out of town. And Flicker was still in the middle of that disaster. He had to get back to her somehow, especially if there was some kind of Zeroes killer around.

But he also had to know. "What does he look like?"

"He looks like a thousand zombies." Ren kept her expression absolutely bland. "Every one of them hungry to rip you to pieces."

Thibault matched her expression. "Really."

"Yeah, really."

Davey thumped the steering wheel. "Got a long drive ahead of us, dude. And it's already a long walk back. You Stalkers kind of suck at hitchhiking."

Thibault sat up on the back of the seat and swung his legs over the side. "Thanks for the, uh, advice."

He stepped off onto the empty road.

Davey looked straight ahead, his attention a clear beam at Ren. Her eyes were boring into Thibault like lasers.

"No problem," she said in a flat voice. "Take care, dude. And keep your eye on that DJ."

She rapped Davey on the shoulder and he threw the Ford into gear. They took off with a squeal of tires, kicking up a cloud of dust, like they didn't trust Thibault to disappear all by himself.

CHAPTER 21
BELLWETHER

"THEY MUST HAVE KNOWN ABOUT US SINCE LAST summer," Thibault said. "When we blew up the police station. They saw Sonia's posts and came looking for us."

Nate watched the others' attention sharpen. It was tricky for Thibault, taking the floor like this. Usually at meetings with all six of them, he only interjected from the corner. But there he was, up on the riser in the front of the home theater, trying to hold their attention.

The fact that Nate's little sisters had decorated the theater for the annual family viewing of *Frosty the Snowman* probably wasn't helping. But for the moment Thibault had the Zeroes riveted.

"They've known lots of people with powers," he said. "Some in their hometown, and probably others along the way. Even someone like me."

"Whoa," Ethan said. "Another Anonymous?"

"Yes. But Ren called him a Stalker."

"You gotta admit that's a cooler name," Ethan said.

Flicker stared at him. "Thibault's not a stalker!"

"I didn't mean as in 'crazy ex-boyfriend.'" Ethan sank into his chair. "More like Death-Stalker, the supervillain."

"Go on," Nate said, drawing the room back together. Ethan was trying to be part of the team, but his talent for scattering the group's energy was undiminished.

Thibault's voice went soft. "Ren said he's dead now. Someone killed him."

There was a moment of stunned silence, the lines of attention that held them all together sharpening in the air.

"Maybe they did it themselves," Chizara said. "They have that whole Bonnie and Clyde thing."

"It wasn't them," Thibault said firmly. "The killer is after them too. That's why they left town. They keep moving all the time—they're on the run."

Chizara leaned forward, her attention steady on Thibault. "So they pissed somebody off *besides* us? Big surprise. They're assholes."

Thibault shook his head. "They didn't blow up the Dish just to be annoying. They planned every bit of it, so that this killer knows about us, too. We're a diversion."

"Holy crap," Ethan said. "You mean there's, like, a Zeroes killer out there? And we're decoys?"

Fear surged through in the room. Nate felt it echo from Kelsie into a feedback loop. But Chizara was already on it, reaching out to take Kelsie's wrist.

The fear dropped back a little.

"Is this guy like us?" Nate asked. "Does he have a power?"

Thibault shook his head. "Not sure. But Ren said to stay away from each other, that we'd be easier to find in a group. So maybe this guy can sense people with powers. I guess that's a power in itself."

Nervous attention arced through the room again, but Nate kept his voice firm. "We need to know more about him. We have to find Glitch and Coin."

"They were headed east," Thibault said. "They're planning something special for their honeymoon."

"Honeymoon?" Flicker snorted. "You know, I don't think a marriage is official when you hijack someone else's wedding."

A flutter of laughter went through the room, and Nate scribbled her a quick note: *Good move. Keep them laughing.*

Thibault wasn't smiling. "You saw them up there, Flick. They were taking it pretty seriously."

"Why get married if a killer's chasing you across the country?" Ethan asked.

"Because they're lying about the whole thing," Chizara said. "They're just trolling us."

"Or because they don't expect to make it," Thibault said.

143

"Maybe you were right about them being Bonnie and Clyde."

Nate spoke up before that thought took hold. "If they took the wedding seriously, then they'll take the honeymoon seriously too. Something with a big crowd."

Thibault nodded. "Ren said it would be in the desert, Christmas Eve."

Nate stood up. "The day after tomorrow. Not long to figure this out. But maybe we can get Sonia to help us."

That got another laugh, and for a moment the room seemed steady. Until Ethan opened his mouth.

"Great. A Zeroes killer. *Just* what I wanted for Christmas."

"It'll be okay," Nate said, stepping onto the riser. "We'll track those two down, find out more, and deal with this. Thank you for that, Anonymous."

A moment later Nate was alone on the stage, with Thibault a wavering presence in the back row of the theater. As he slipped from their minds, the fear caused by his bad news subsided a little.

"In the meantime, we have another problem." Nate steadied himself as the center of their attention. "At the hockey game, Ethan was using his voice to ditch some cops, and it mentioned an investigation. Internal Affairs. In other words, the police department is looking at itself."

"The voice could've been lying," Chizara said.

"I wasn't trying to scam them," Ethan said. "I was trying to piss them off. And you could tell from their faces it was true."

"So they're investigating dirty cops?" Flicker asked. "Like, cops who take bribes?"

"Yep," said Nate. "And it's a secret investigation, like with wiretaps and maybe *bugged cop cars*."

"Oh," Kelsie said, and everyone looked at Ethan.

"Yeah," he said.

Chizara let out a strained laugh. "Just so you know, my police station–destroying days are over, Ethan."

"Gee," he said. "Thanks for the confidence builder, Crash."

"We're not going to let it get that far," Nate said firmly. "On the way out of the game, Ethan finally spotted our two corrupt cops. When we made contact, they were pretty pissed, but it's not like they could do anything in front of hundreds of other policemen. I've set up a meeting for tonight."

"To give them real cash?" Kelsie asked. "What if they're under surveillance?"

"Let me guess," Chizara said. "That's my job."

"Exactly," Nate said. "You'll check for hidden cameras in their car. If you find anything, maybe it's not too late to erase the footage from two nights ago."

"Maybe," Chizara said. "But maybe Ethan's mom is already watching video of him handing over that bag of money."

"*Fake* money!" Ethan corrected.

"Or maybe those cops got turned," Kelsie said quietly. "And tonight's just a setup to arrest us all."

"Anybody else remember what happened last time we

tried to pay somebody off?" Flicker said. "Two of us got kidnapped."

Everyone looked at Ethan again, and Nate could feel their fear curdle into anger. They blamed Ethan for his voice, for the way it dragged them all in whenever he went down. They always would.

"Best. Christmas. Ever," Ethan said.

CHAPTER 22
SCAM

HAVING JESS HOME WAS GOOD, IN MORE WAYS than one.

Mom was relaxed with Jess around. Like she could finally take her eyes off Ethan, now that his big sister was here. As an added bonus, Jess was a girl, and she dated girls. Which made her a walking encyclopedia of girlness.

And what Ethan really needed right now was some advice on girls. Because he needed to talk to Kelsie *before* he was arrested for police bribery.

"Say you thought you were about to die," Ethan began.

"Mom's not going to kill you."

"Kill me for what?"

Jess shrugged. "Whatever it is you did this time."

They were outside under the mountain oak tree in back of

the house. When they were kids, Dad had tied a swing to one of its branches. They'd stay outside until dark, until Mom was so tired of yelling for them to come in for dinner that she'd have to drag them into the house.

The swing was long gone. Ethan leaned back against the trunk, staring at the branch where it used to hang, wishing his life was still as simple as it used to be, back then. He sat with his back to the trunk. Jess lay on the ground looking up at the sky, rubbing an apple on the hem of her shirt. Even on leave, she was wearing faded army khakis and a T-shirt with FORT JACKSON emblazoned across a very angry cartoon dog.

This conversation wasn't going to be easy. He had to use his own words, because Jess had been calling bullshit on the voice for as long as he could remember.

"Aren't you cold?" Ethan asked. "My butt is frozen."

"I like the cold." Jess bit into her apple. "It burns calories. Like a mini workout."

"Say you thought you were going to go to jail—"

"What did you *do*, Ethan?"

Ethan swallowed. It wasn't like he could tell her about the crooked cops, or the cash drop in front of the Dish tonight, or any of the rest of the mess he was in.

So he said, "It's a hypothetical, okay? You're going to jail, or dying, or whatever. But first you want to tell someone how you feel about them. You know, romantically."

Jess's face crinkled into a grin. "I see where this is going.

You finally found a girl to tame the wild Ethan Cooper lust?"

"You know, it kind of cheapens it if you put it like that."

"Wow. You're serious."

Ethan was. Tonight he had two tasks. Pay off Murillo and Ang, the cops he'd bribed with Coin's fake money. And tell Kelsie Laszlo he was in love with her, no matter what. He'd promised himself the same thing last night, of course, before two superpowered dickheads had butted in.

But this time Ethan was for real. It was happening tonight.

Unless the crooked cops shot him. Or took him to prison. Or the Zero killer who was out there somewhere showed up.

"Forget it," he said, standing up. "Let's go in. It's way too cold."

"Mom told me to keep you out here," Jess said. "Two detectives are here, talking to her."

"Crap! Are you serious?" Ethan peered through the living room window, and saw the familiar round outline of Detective Fuentes. No doubt his partner, Detective King, was with him. Were they here to arrest him for bribery already? Why *else* would they visit Mom at home? "Why isn't she talking to them during office hours?"

Jess shrugged. "Must be secret DDA stuff. What're you doing?"

Ethan had drawn his hoodie down over his eyes, and was standing on tiptoes.

"Watching. I know those guys."

Jess took another bite of apple and talked around it. "*They* gonna kill you?"

"No. They're the detectives who were hassling me last summer."

"When you went AWOL?" Jess groaned. "Do you *know* how much stress Mom heaped on me that week? You're lucky she can't afford military school."

"Don't even joke about that!"

Dad used to always threaten Ethan with military school. Like they could train the voice out of him. But the voice would have *loved* a place like that. It thrived in situations where men shouted meaningless macho crap at each other. Ethan's brief high school football career had proved that. He couldn't run, catch, or throw, but he could talk booyah like nobody's business.

He might come back from military school an empty shell, but he'd probably have a ton of medals.

Jess was smiling. "Maybe I should go in there and invite those detectives to Christmas dinner."

Ethan ducked back down beside Jess, nearly dislodging the half-eaten apple from her hand. "Are you crazy? They hate my guts."

"Okay, okay." She was laughing now. She sat up and moved so she was shoulder to shoulder with Ethan. "Forget them. Tell me about this girl. What's she like?"

Ethan sighed, wishing he could just forget Fuentes and

King. He hoped they didn't mention the hockey game to Mom. She'd never believe he'd gone to a sporting event for the fun of it.

"Her name's Kelsie," he said. "And she's really cool."

"So, not like you."

Ethan ignored that. "I've known her for six months, which is way too long for some stupid crush. So it's real, right?" He didn't wait for an answer. "And also about time I tell her how great I think she is. But I think maybe she's too good for me."

Jess stopped chewing on her apple. "Ethan, you have the worst self-esteem of anyone I know. If you ever joined the army, they'd use you for target practice."

"Is that supposed to help with the self-esteem thing?"

Jess chuckled and ruffled his hair. He *hated* when she did that.

"Okay," she said. "So you want to tell this girl how you feel, but you're worried that she thinks you're the lamest person she knows."

"I guess, yeah."

"First things first," Jess continued. "Why are you into *this* girl in particular? That's usually a good place to start."

"She's totally pretty."

"I hope there's more to it than that."

"She's smart and has great taste in music."

Jess looked bored.

Ethan started speaking faster. "And we've been through a

lot. Like the first time we met, she saved me from this guy who was going to beat me up."

He could still see Kelsie in the doorway of Thibault's hotel suite, come to warn them about the Craig. Sparkling in a clubbing dress and matching high-tops like she'd just stepped out of a music video.

"So she's big and strong like your sis, huh?"

Ethan had to laugh. "Not exactly. She saved me with a heads-up, not a beatdown. And then I saved her from being alone. Because there's this stuff she and I share—secret stuff." He hadn't planned on doing this tonight, but why not? In a couple of hours, he could get killed or arrested. "She's kind of like me."

"Like you, how?"

"She can do weird things." When Jess raised an eyebrow, Ethan added quickly, "I don't mean in a kinky way. I mean . . . she has a superpower, like I do."

Jess tossed the apple core across the lawn. "So you're a superhero now?"

"Not a hero." That word was ridiculous, at least in relation to Ethan. "But you know how I can spew out all kinds of stuff I shouldn't know? When I talk like that, it's a superpower."

Jess didn't blink. "If that's what you want to call it."

"That's what it is," Ethan said. "I don't even know what I'm going to say when the voice talks. The words just *come* out of me."

"Listen, little bro. I've known since you were three that there's something oddball about you." Jess paused, like she was thinking her words through carefully. "Like, there was *smart* you and there was *good* you. But smart you is a faker. That's why smart you was always getting into trouble—"

"Smart me still gets into trouble," Ethan muttered.

"But the bigger problem is that *good* you, the guy that doesn't try to be smart—the guy that's kind of sweet and actually cares about people—*that* guy keeps being stomped on by smart you."

Ethan blinked. Whenever he used the voice around Jess, she looked at him like it was a moral failing or something. It was nice that she realized he was a victim too.

"So what do I do about it?"

"You fight back. Stand up to it. To beat this smart-mouth guy living inside you, you got to stop being so smart all the time and just be . . . you."

"You want me to be stupid? That is the suckiest advice I've ever heard."

"Yeah, well." Jess shrugged. "I don't get asked for a lot of romantic advice. All I'm trying to say is that it's time for you to grow up, Ethan Thomas Cooper. Be a man, or whatever."

"Now I *know* you're being sarcastic," Ethan said. "Can you check if those detectives have left?"

Jess sighed and stood, craning her neck to look in through the window. "Nope, still there. They probably *are* talking about you. I mean, that's your real superpower—supremely pissing off Mom."

"Just forget I said anything." Ethan stuffed his hands in his pockets. It really was freezing out here, but no way was he going inside for a dose of stink-eye from Detective Fuentes.

"Aww, look," Jess crouched and wrapped an arm around his shoulders. She pulled him in closer to her warmth. "Superpowers or not, if she's half as awesome as you say she is, this girl will be glad you said something."

Ethan smiled weakly. "Thanks, Jess."

"Just don't mention the cape in your closet."

Ethan pulled away and punched her in the arm.

Jess laughed. "Ow! Superstrength!"

Ethan punched her again, harder, and Jess howled in fake agony.

"Listen, I can prove it," he whispered. "I can say exactly the thing that'll convince you that smart me is a superpower."

Jess stopped laughing. She smiled at him the way Mom used to when he was little and said crazy stuff—indulgently.

"Okay, prove it. If you do, I will forever be the humble Robin to your Batman."

Ethan tried to stare down his big sister. But she was older than him and smarter and more badass and totally unconvinced.

He let his mind fill with the urge to tell her something that no one else knew about her. Something that she'd never told anyone, not even her closest buddies in Afghanistan when IEDs were going off around them or whatever.

Something that would blow her *mind*.

The voice obliged. It roared up into his throat so fast it nearly winded him. It filled his mouth and latched onto his jaw and grabbed hold of his tongue.

"So, Jess," it said. "You're into *guys* now?"

Jess's eyes widened. "Holy freaking shit. How did you—"

"Crap!" Ethan shouted in his real voice. "You gave me that lame advice and you don't even *date* girls anymore? Since when do you like guys?"

"Just this one guy, actually. It's complicated."

Ethan nodded. Pretty much everything was.

CHAPTER 23
CRASH

OUTSIDE THE DISH, DUSK FELL OVER THE STREET. Chizara, wearing dark clothes, waited in the shadows by the corner of the nightclub.

So many happy people lined up out here on Dish party nights, excited to submit themselves to Mob's crowd magic. But tonight it was just a cracked concrete wasteland, blown trash collecting in the corners.

The perfect place to meet a couple of corrupt cops.

Or a Zero killer.

Chizara shook that last thought out of her head. She didn't believe anything Glitch and Coin had to say. They just liked freaking people out.

Ethan kept stepping out from the club's front door, checking the street. Flicker and Nate were right there behind him, out of sight, though Chizara could feel their phones fumbling for a signal. But was that a third phone, just inside?

Right. Flicker's boyfriend . . .

Anon. *Anonymous! Hold it in your head! He's right there in front of you.*

He actually *lived* in the Dish, didn't he? Just like Kelsie.

Kelsie had stayed up in her room. Her crazy childhood had made her leery of cops, especially dirty ones. After the horror movie yesterday, they'd walked and talked half the night. Kelsie had been surprised at Chizara's guilt about Officer Bright getting beaten up last summer. How did that square with the Dish paying out bribes to cops? she'd wanted to know.

It doesn't, Chizara had replied grimly.

Kelsie had shrugged. *If you ask me, you can't trust dirty cops.*

Engine noise rumbled along the street, and Chizara shrank back into the dark. The patrol car's shadow slid along the concrete, blurry in the dusk, and a tire crushed a beer can in the gutter with a metallic crackle. She felt the car's constellation of electronics glide to a stop.

Man, cop cars were crammed with gadgets. It felt like a gleaming blanket of itchy thorns dragged across her body. She was careful to keep everything spinning, but how sweet it would be to crash the whole shebang.

Ethan came out from the Dish and walked toward the car. No sign of the voice's confidence in his gait, just his own pale-faced, weasely self. He carried the money in a brown paper bag that practically shouted, *Criminal activity!*

He was slouching more than usual. *If you imitate the crooked, you become crooked,* her mother always said.

Chizara closed her eyes. She had a job to do.

She sent her mind into the car, feeling her way along the glowing lines inside. From the outskirts of the roof lights, siren, and engine she moved in toward the central fortress around the driver. That glittering little city was the computer mounted by the seat, for looking up license numbers. That shiny thing, the way it split, must be the radio and handset.

And there was the video system, cameras facing forward to record traffic stops. It was running now, the data streaming into a chip. But dirty cops would be aware of their own dashboard cam and would keep it pointed away from anything incriminating. Not what she was looking for.

She could hear Ethan and the two cops murmuring to each other. Ethan sounded like he was *apologizing*. What a coward.

Whatever. She took a soundless step to the edge of the corner, where the signals were clearer, and sifted through the dashboard electronics, the GPS, the radar speed gun, the license-plate reader . . .

Maybe there was no hidden camera. Maybe Murillo and Ang weren't under suspicion.

Man, it was such a *tangle* in there. . . .

Then she found it. An electronic eyeball, no bigger than

a chickpea, was set in the shadow of the dashboard—a microphone, too. Pointed back at the driver, both were busy funneling signals into that tiny box behind them. And that was where the data stopped, it looked like—no pathways ghosted out into the air. The system was designed to be silent, undetectable if the car was swept for bugs.

So the incriminating images were waiting for someone to manually download the data.

Hopefully that hadn't happened in the last day.

Chizara pushed her mind closer to that little memory box, her jaw tight. If she broke the car, the cops would be stuck here, wondering what had happened.

It was like reaching into a fire to pick up a hot coal. Delicately, with exquisite care not to touch anything else, she reached for the paining ember.

She snuffed it out. But crashing it gave her no relief—so much other e-stuff pecked and chittered inside that car, inside Chizara's head.

Check your work, Bob's voice reminded her gently. She probed the empty space she'd made in the brilliant labyrinth of the car. Not a glimmer. Everything that needed to die was dead, and nothing else was broken.

When the investigators found that precision damage, they'd guess that Murillo and Ang were hiding something. That was the only reason Chizara had agreed to any of this—the missing data would throw suspicion on them.

She retreated back along the side alley, breathing slowly as she recovered from the precision work.

Scam and the cops were still talking, but Chizara wanted the car and all its fancy tech *gone*. How long did it take to hand a sack of money over?

Finally she heard the voice calling smoothly, "Thank you, officers."

The engine surged and some of the electronics brightened, shafting pain through Chizara's head. The vehicle's glittering constellation moved away.

She poked her head around the corner. Ethan was waving, like those cops were his favorite uncles or something.

A minute later all of them were outside. Even Kelsie, who must have been watching from her window upstairs.

"So, Crash, was there a recording?" Nate asked.

"There was. There isn't anymore." She shrugged. "At least not in that car. Someone could have downloaded the data already. Who knows?"

Chizara let herself enjoy the expression the words created on Ethan's face.

"It's only been twenty-four hours," Nate said. "If Internal Affairs inspected every police car in Cambria that often, the whole force would know something was up."

"Those two cops weren't worried," Flicker said. "No nervous glances over their shoulders. They don't have a clue about any investigation."

"Perfect," Nate said with a nod. "Good work, Crash and Scam."

"Thanks," Ethan said. "But now those guys want fifteen hundred every time we open."

Nate gave them all a theatrical shrug. "The Dish isn't about money."

Rich people said that a lot, Chizara had noticed. Nothing was ever about money when you had more than enough.

"They won't be satisfied," Kelsie said softly from the shadows closer to the club. She was still looking down the street after the police car, like they might turn around and come back. "Blackmailers never are."

Ethan stepped closer and put an arm around her. "It's okay, Kelsie. Whatever happens, the Zeroes can fix it. We had a plan and it worked. Right, guys?"

"Hey, we found Glitch and Coin." That was Anon, taking Flicker's hand. "And we'll find them again."

"Exactly," Ethan said, pulling Kelsie a little closer. "It's all handled."

Chizara felt a shimmer of annoyance at Ethan's glomming onto Kelsie without asking. She was about to say something to break up the self-congratulation party when a voice called out from across the street.

"Hold it right there, baby bro!"

Everyone turned.

A woman stepped out from darkness, and the streetlight lit

up her buzz cut. She looked like Ethan, but like Ethan stretched out to six feet tall, with some serious muscle pumped in.

"Oh, crap," Ethan said.

The woman strode at him across the street. And from her own experience of being an older sister, Chizara knew that this one was *mightily* pissed off.

CHAPTER 24
CRASH

"WHAT THE *HELL* DID I JUST SEE THERE?"

Without meaning to, Chizara took a step back into the shadows.

Jess towered over Ethan, big, strong, and loud.

"Nothing!" Ethan whined. "Just talking to some guys I know."

"Some guys in uniform? Just talking and then *handing something over*? What the hell was in that bag? Drugs? You got a meth lab going here or something?" She shot a look at the Dish.

Nate, Flicker, and Kelsie had retreated just like Chizara. They stood in the doorway, looking guilty, as if this bellowing artillery trooper had guessed exactly right. The Dish did look derelict enough to be a meth lab, at least from the outside.

Scam stood straighter. Jess saw the move and slapped him on the arm.

"Don't you *dare* use your smart mouth with me. No wonder you kept talking about getting killed. That's what happens when you mess with *drugs*!"

"I only gave them *money*," Ethan whispered. "And would you mind not shouting it for the whole street to hear?"

Jess took hold of Ethan's shoulders and gave him an outraged shake. "You know Mom's investigating the police, right? If there weren't so many witnesses, I would be inflicting such serious bodily injury on you, Ethan Thomas Cooper."

Chizara felt the brick wall of the Dish against her shoulder blades. She'd backed off as far as she could.

Jess was like Mom's Look personified, with an army cut and a buttload of righteous rage thrown in. The Virgin Mary would have felt guilty standing here.

And Chizara was far from blameless. She'd just used her power to erase evidence of police corruption.

What had she turned into?

It was like Jess had slapped her awake, bulldozing the whole fantasy world she'd been living in, built of wishful thinking, Zeroes loyalty, and all her shiny new toys in the Dish. Her moral Faraday cage, keeping out the stings of guilt and conscience. A way to keep doing her experiments on unsuspecting crowds.

Mom would *not* be proud.

Nate stepped forward and stuck out his hand. "You must be Jess."

Chizara felt his power mute the volume of her conscience. There were six people here—plus Anon—enough for Nate to play Glorious Leader all he wanted.

"Ethan's sister, right?" Nate pressed on.

Jess must have felt his power too. A little of the fight went out of her. But she still looked reluctant about shaking hands with him.

"Yeah," she said. "Just lucky, I guess."

"I'm Nate Saldana. This is my nightclub."

Chizara felt the little charge of awesomeness he'd injected into the word *nightclub* and fought not to feel impressed.

"Pleased to meet you," Jess said automatically, and submitted to a handshake.

Nate gave his best class-president smile. "I can't offer you any meth, alas. But let me introduce Chizara, our head technician."

Chizara found herself drawn out of the shadows, into the glowing sunshine of Nate's gaze.

She smiled and shook hands. "Nice to meet you, Jess."

"And this is Riley, in charge of inventory."

Jess took in the dark glasses and white cane, and her angry expression faltered a little more. This blind white girl with excellent posture didn't match her expectations of a meth cook somehow.

You had to admit that Nate was pretty damn *good* at this.

"And Kelsie, our DJ," Nate finished.

Kelsie's smile reverberated through the group. She'd spliced her power onto Nate's to bring everyone to a happy place.

Sometime soon Chizara had to give her some tips on resisting Glorious Leader, just so she didn't turn into his power-boosting puppet.

"Why don't you come in?" Nate said to Jess. "Ethan's been a huge help in getting this nightclub off the ground. You're going to be proud of him."

"Um, okay." Jess looked at her little brother. "Since when did you work at a nightclub?"

"I don't just work here," Ethan said in his own raggedy voice. "I'm, like, a founding member. In charge of publicity."

"You're sixteen!" Jess looked around at them all. "None of you are twenty-one. This club is totally illegal."

"Technically, it's more of a monthly private party," Nate said. "And that money was a donation to the policemen's fund."

He turned and walked into the club, pulling the group in his wake, like they all had fishing lines attached to the base of their spines. Mob and Bellwether together were hard to resist.

As she crossed the threshold, Chizara relaxed a little, the Faraday cage working its magic on the phone signals.

"Check out this dance floor." Nate strode into the middle and spun around, like he was on the mountaintop in *The Sound of Music*. "We built it especially for the club. Employed a lot of locals."

The work lights were up, revealing the Dish as a dusty, dark theater with metal-mesh walls. But with Nate radiating enthusiasm, there was a definite magic about the place.

Suddenly Chizara found herself eager to get in the light box and fling some watts around the room. How had she ever doubted that this space, this *home*, was worth protecting?

"You should come next month and see it in action," Nate said.

Chizara had to keep herself from nodding in agreement.

"I'll be shipping out." Jess was obviously trying to stay pissed at her brother. "And I know what a club going off looks like."

She turned slowly, stopping when she saw the bar.

"You sell alcohol? Well, I can see why you were worried about dying." Jess turned to Ethan. "Because Mom *will* kill you if she finds out about this."

"You're not going to tell her, are you?" Ethan squeaked.

Jess's face was like a cartoon of the conflict in the room—the righteous big sister with the supreme self-confidence of a soldier, fighting the tide of Mob's and Bellwether's combined powers.

"I *should* tell her about all this, especially since you're paying off cops." Jess slumped a little. Fighting the whole room's enthusiasm had to be exhausting. "Still, this is the most ambitious thing I've ever seen you do."

That was probably true, though Chizara figured it was a low

bar. What else ambitious had he done? Maybe stealing thirty thousand dollars last summer, but that had been an accident.

Ethan was beaming from the praise, though. A smile slowly replaced the panicked expression he'd worn since his sister's appearance, and his hand reached out and took Kelsie's.

A bunch of stuff happened then:

Jess saw the handhold, and amusement crossed her face.

Ethan smiled back at her and leaned pointedly into Kelsie's shoulder.

Kelsie looked from brother to sister and then back to brother—he was giving her a dopey grin now. She stepped away from him, putting herself shoulder to shoulder with Chizara.

Everyone saw it. And because they were all connected, everyone felt it too: the stomach twist of Mob's puzzlement. Even the politician's smile on Glorious Leader's face froze.

Jess's smile evaporated too, replaced by the wariness of a combat veteran sniffing out an ambush.

"Wait a second," she said. "What the hell is going on here?"

"Um" was all Nate could manage at first; then he rallied. "What do you mean?"

"This club. Since I walked in here, my head's been jerked around. It's like some kind of psy-ops shit is going down!"

Chizara didn't know what *psy-ops* meant, but she had an idea.

Then Glorious Leader did exactly the wrong thing. He spread his hands magnificently and doubled down. Chizara felt the force of his will flooding the room.

"Our humble party space isn't really equipped for psychological warfare," he said. "More for dancing."

But his laugh sounded hollow in the empty club.

Mob wasn't with him anymore. She was looking at Ethan, her power sputtering with uncertainty.

"Shit. *You're* doing this," Jess said, staring straight at Nate. Then her eyes went to her brother. "You were telling the truth about powers, weren't you? Which means that you . . ."

She looked at Kelsie, then took a few quick steps backward— and bumped straight into Anonymous.

Jess spun around. "Holy crap. Another one?"

Anon looked stunned for a moment, then made a chopping gesture, stepping deeper into the corner. Chizara's awareness of him fizzled.

Jess turned back to the group.

"Do *all* you little fuckers have superpowers?"

No one answered. Ethan must have told her about the voice. And about Mob, too, it seemed.

Again Chizara saw the Zeroes from the outside, from beyond the loyalties and friendships. They manipulated people. They experimented with crowds. They broke things.

They were pretty evil, really.

All Nate's charm had gone from the room.

"Come on, little brother." Jess stepped warily back into the group and took his arm. "We're getting out of here. These people have been messing with your *mind*."

"No they haven't—" But he was being dragged across the dance floor, and against her strength he didn't have a chance. Out they went, the door slamming behind them.

Chizara stared at the others. Kelsie sent her a confused look, but no one else would meet anyone's eye.

The silence was broken by the scrape of a bar stool. The pop of a beer can.

"Why do you guys keep telling your families about your powers?" said a voice. Anon, by the bar.

"Because it helps," Flicker said gently, taking the can from his hand. "In the long run."

Slowly the rest of them drifted to the bar and settled on stools. For a while no voices distracted Chizara from the phones in their pockets gently searching for a network that the Faraday cage wouldn't let them find.

"Ethan and his sister will figure things out," Nate finally said. "Or she'll ship back to Afghanistan and have more important things to worry about."

"You think she'll tell their mom?" Kelsie asked. She looked nervously at the door of the club. "She's a prosecutor, right?"

Chizara put a hand on her shoulder. "It's okay, Kels. Cops aren't going to start streaming in."

Nate nodded. "Jess was right when she said that the Dish

is the biggest thing Ethan's ever done. She's not going to take it away from him."

Chizara felt his confidence leaking back into the room, but she wasn't certain. There was no telling what Jess would do next.

And even if she didn't spill Ethan's secrets, they still had to worry about Internal Affairs, a crazed killer on their trail, and a whole new bunch of Zeroes bubbling up across the world.

CHAPTER 25
BELLWETHER

"IS THAT HOMEWORK?"

"Yeah, always." Nate turned from his laptop screen to face the door of his room. Gabby stood there, wearing a pink tutu and a look of genuine outrage.

"But it's Christmas break!" she cried. "High school is messed up."

He smiled at her. "Sucks to be old."

Gabby waited there, not daring to come in without an invitation. She looked bored and restless, and Nate had hardly seen her since Glitch and Coin had arrived in town, so he said, "Come in."

He shut his laptop on an image of a riot in Seattle.

"Feeling better?" Gabby asked.

"A little," Nate said. All day he'd pretended to be sick, dodging the family's holiday preparations to search for upcoming events. Christmas Eve was tomorrow. He didn't have much time to figure out where Glitch and Coin's "honeymoon" would be.

The easy part was finding the trail of mass hysteria they'd left from Portland to Cambria. They'd hijacked concerts, movies, even a high school play. And they'd never hidden themselves. It was more like they were *trying* to be found, which made Nate wonder if a killer was chasing them at all.

Though maybe Chizara was right, and they were in love with their own love story. Like Bonnie and Clyde, wanting to leave a mark before they were extinguished.

The problem was, nothing suggested where they'd be headed next. Would their honeymoon involve a college football game? A midnight mass?

But Glitch had mentioned the desert. Crowds gathered in the desert for what? Balloon races? Burning Man?

"I got you the best present ever," Gabby said. "So you *have* to get better."

"I'd never be sick for Christmas, silly," Nate said with a smile. His sisters always competed over who could get the biggest reaction from him on Christmas. So far, no one had beaten Gabby's silver business-card case of two years ago.

"I think you'll like my present too," he said. He'd gotten all the girls *lucha libre* costumes, handmade in Mexico.

"Mamá wouldn't take us anywhere decent to shop," Gabby went on. "She says malls are too loco this year."

Damn. If their mother had started to notice that crowd behavior was changing, no wonder the US government was getting involved.

"She's right," he said. "Christmas crowds are big, and you are small."

"Pfft." Gabby made a muscle pose. "I'm big! My friend Engrácia got to go all the way to the Desert Springs Mall to shop. It has three hundred stores!"

"Whoa. You could get me a present at each one."

"You wish. Engrácia had to line up all night to get in at five a.m., but she said it was worth it! It just opened last month."

Nate leaned back, staring at his sister. "Sounds really . . . crowded."

"Yeah. They have early-bird sales every day. But it's all the way in Arizona."

"Like, the desert?"

Gabby nodded, and Nate turned to his computer. *"Mierda."*

"How come you forget English when you swear?" Gabby asked.

"It's a bad habit I got from Flicker." He lifted the screen again and opened up a new window. "Did you say Desert Springs Mall?"

"Uh-huh. Are you going to get me a present there?"

"Maybe." Images spilled across Nate's screen—a shiny new mall out in the desert, a giant three-story fountain in the middle, fireworks every morning at opening time. And lots of exhausted-looking customers lined up outside, with sleeping bags and camp stoves.

A Christmas Eve riot waiting to happen. Almost a straight shot east of Cambria, about eight hours' drive at legal speeds.

Nate looked at the clock—almost ten p.m.

Which meant the Desert Springs Mall was opening in six hours.

"Thanks, Gabby," he said, reaching for his phone. "But I gotta go. You just reminded me: I need to do some shopping with my friends."

CHAPTER 26
BELLWETHER

"WHO'S SNORING?" NATE DEMANDED, HIS HANDS tight on the wheel.

He was pushing the Mercedes at ninety miles an hour, his eyes locked on the moonlit road ahead. He'd been driving all night, and the snoring sound was making his eyes heavy.

"It's Thibault," Flicker's tired voice came from the backseat. "For the third time."

"Huh." Did Anon's power work while he was asleep? Or was Nate's brain just too exhausted to remember anything?

"Wish *I* was snoring," Ethan said from next to Flicker.

Nate dared a glance at the GPS—twenty minutes away. It was four forty-five a.m., and the mall opened at five. Even Nate's tired brain could do that math.

"We're not going to make it," he said, nudging the car a little faster.

"We'd be on time if you hadn't forgotten Anon," Flicker muttered.

Nate frowned at her in the rearview. "You should've noticed he wasn't in the car earlier!"

"I'm not my invisible boyfriend's keeper."

"If we're going to be late anyway, maybe you could slow down?" Chizara was squashed into the front passenger seat with Kelsie, clutching her arm nervously. Kelsie looked like she loved cruising at a hundred miles an hour.

"Every second counts," Nate said.

"You're going to get us killed," Chizara said. "And we don't even know if this is the right place!"

"*I* do." Nate pushed the speedometer needle a little higher.

"Jess is going to kill me anyway when she realizes I snuck out," Ethan said. "Or worse, tell my mom! If you dragged me all this way for nothing, I'm going to . . . sleep all the way home. But *angrily*."

"Listen," Nate said. "We know they were headed east, and this place has the biggest crowds within a day's drive of Cambria. Thousands of people, twenty times the size of K-Mo's wedding!"

"Big sale crowds are pretty horrible," Kelsie said. "I steer clear of malls between Thanksgiving and New Year's."

"At least all our practice missions are actually going to pay off," Flicker said tiredly.

"What if *all* mall tramplings are caused by Zeroes?" Kelsie said.

Nate didn't answer that. The thought of a horde of Glitches and Coins out there—walking disaster zones—was too much to handle on no sleep.

Flicker stepped in. "I'm pretty sure people getting trampled was a thing before any Zeroes were born."

"Right," Nate said. "We're here to *save* people, not trample them. *Who the hell is snoring?*"

Flicker groaned. "It's Anon! Should I just remind you after every snore?"

"Wake him up already! This mission starts in . . ." He checked the GPS again. The increase in speed had shaved some time off. "Eleven minutes."

"Unless you roll the car," Chizara said.

"There's no traffic," Nate said, but he eased off on the speed a little. She was right—they were going to be late anyway. He hoped Glitch and Coin weren't planning to attack while everyone was cramming into the mall's entrances. They were assholes, but hopefully they weren't *trying* to create a bloodbath.

"Where am I?" came a tired voice from the backseat.

"Big Christmas sale," Flicker told Anon. "Glitch and Coin evil. Us saving people."

"Oh, right."

Nate smiled. He wished he had his folder of notes.

December 24—Addled by sleep, Anonymous briefly forgot a thing that everyone else remembered.

The road was climbing ahead, a soft swell in the desert. Three minutes to five a.m. and they were six minutes away. The dark sky ahead showed hints of red, but it couldn't be the dawn yet.

"Um, guys?" Kelsie suddenly said. "There's a serious crowd up there."

Nate slowed the Mercedes as they crested the hill. The road ahead was crammed with taillights. The traffic jam led straight to the giant glowing ramparts of the brand-new mall, its floodlit parking lot solid with vehicles, its entrances choked with thousands of shoppers. Their combined focus shone like a flaming battering ram.

"They're so hungry," Kelsie murmured softly.

The nearest taillights were drawing close. Nate put the Mercedes into four-wheel drive and steered it off the asphalt onto the rough surface of the desert. Scrubby plants started to thwack the front bumper, and Chizara's hand smothered a cry of alarm.

A firework streaked high into the air above the mall, then flowered out red, white, and blue. Even from here, with pebbles pinging off the bottom of the car, Nate could hear the crackle of it, and crowd's cheering. It was five a.m. exactly, and the Desert Springs Mall was open for business.

CHAPTER 27
FLICKER

"YOU SEE THEM ANYWHERE, FLICK?" NATE SAID.

Holding tight to Thibault's arm, Flicker cast her vision to the front of the throng.

Way ahead, sprinting for bargains, were the people who'd slept all night at the entrance. They carried sleeping bags and pillows, and one girl clutched a ragged teddy bear under one arm. Their wide-eyed gazes darted among the giant banners hanging from every storefront.

XMAS EVE SALE

80% OFF EVERYTHING

GOING OUT OF BUSINESS!

That last one seemed a little far-fetched, given that the Desert Springs Mall had been open for all of a month. But this crowd seemed ready to believe anything, to *do* anything, to give themselves a shot at a bargain. Nate's Mercedes was one of a dozen cars parked illegally by the doors.

So far it all looked normal enough, if a crazed Christmas Eve sale could ever be normal. No sign of Glitch and Coin.

"Nothing yet," Flicker said.

"I've found the central junction box." Crash's voice came from ahead of the rest of them. She sounded less nervous here than she had in the car. "What do you need, Nate?"

"Close the roller doors. Keep anyone else from getting in."

It took a moment for Crash to answer, and Flicker's ears filled with the squeak of a thousand sneakers on freshly waxed tile, the bouncy Christmas music piping through the store, the aahs of appreciation as the mall's atrium skylights came into view.

"Can't do it," Crash said. "The roller doors have some kind of safety mechanism—you need a physical key. What about turning off the escalators?"

"No! We *want* people upstairs, as spread out as possible." More sneaker squeaks, more Muzak. When Nate spoke again, he was facing a different way. "How do they feel?"

"Excited, exhausted," Mob answered. "But the main thing is . . . *greedy*. I'm trying to calm them down, but the music's too damn peppy."

Flicker agreed with that. Christmas disco was bouncing off the walls like sound waves of made of tinsel and glitter.

"Where's the music controlled from?" Scam asked.

"Second floor, at the rear," said Crash. "I could crash the sound system."

"Don't. I'll talk them into changing the tunes." Scam's voice faded as he peeled off.

"Try for classical," Mob called after him. "Something soothing!"

"You got it!" he called back.

As Anon guided Flicker around a group of chattering kids, she realized that the six of them were working together as a team.

She brought her vision back to the group. Mob's face was alight with the crowd's shopping madness—frazzled, tense, spoiling for a fight at a bargain rack. Crash and Bellwether wore determined expressions, on the same side at last. As a passerby's vision slid past Anon leading her, Flicker smiled.

"Spotted the targets yet?" Nate asked her.

"Yeah, really," Anon said beside her. "Because if they aren't here, I'd rather be anywhere else."

"Hang on." Flicker cast her vision out again, letting the questing viewpoints of the surging crowd spill into her head.

She saw hands rifling clothes racks, fingers tying sneaker laces, smoothies spinning in blenders, credit cards sliding through readers, a thousand price tags being checked. Darting from eye to eye, she began to understand the vast but simple layout of the mall—an entrance at each compass point, four wide passages surging with the crowd, all leading to the center, where a shining glass-and-metal fountain soared above a broad square plaza.

The huge structure drew every eye, filling Flicker's vision. It looked like a gigantic metal octopus with too many tentacles, each studded with shards of mirror and flashing colored lights. A hundred spouts sprayed and misted and tumbled water down into elaborate tiers of receptacles. Yet you could walk under the whole contraption without getting wet.

The fountain was possibly the tackiest thing Flicker had ever seen, but viewed from a thousand different vantage points, she had to admit it was impressive.

And there at its center, underneath its spreading arms, two familiar faces smiled at the oncoming crowds.

"I see them! Right in the middle, under the fountain!"

"Let's move it," Nate said, and Anon pulled Flicker along faster.

She kept her vision on Glitch and Coin. "He's got a backpack. Stuffed full of paper, I bet."

"A rain of cash will turn this crowd bad," Mob said. "They all feel so *entitled*. They waited all night, or got up crazy early. They want their bargains—they want free stuff!"

"How many people close to Coin?" Nate panted. "Enough for his power to work?"

Flicker sent her vision skittering around the fountain, taking in every angle.

"Not yet, but they're headed in from all directions. All he has to do is yell *Free money!* and he'll be good."

"Sorry, Flick," Nate said. "But we have to run!"

"Fine with me!"

She tightened her grip on Anon's elbow and slipped into Crash's eyes. Chizara was scanning the ground ahead of their feet, in seeing-eye-human mode, just like during their old training missions.

After seven hours in the car, it was good to run, darting around benches and mall directories and pop-up stores selling sunglasses and cheap watches.

A few breathless minutes later, the others slowed.

Crash gasped as she looked up from the tiled floor to gaze at the fountain. "I could crash the *heck* out of that."

"Not yet," Nate said. "And whatever you do, keep the lights on in here!"

"Duh."

The couple beneath the fountain were dressed up as usual, but today's finery was brighter. Glitch wore a purple satin dress, and Coin's suit was shiny black. Perfect outfits for attracting attention in the middle of the flashing, bubbling fountain.

A crowd was gathered now, and Coin swung his backpack off his shoulder and pulled out a wad of paper.

Flicker jumped into his eyes. In his hands the rectangles of white crawled with fine lines of dull green ink. The familiar shapes of presidents and seals began to appear.

"He's about to do it," she said.

"At least let me kill the fountain lights," Crash begged. "They're gnawing my skin off."

"Sure," Nate said. "But we need a way to push people back. Anything that keeps the Curve from kicking in."

"I'll try," Crash said.

"Anon, get in there and separate those two." Nate's voice was full of Glorious Leader confidence. "If we can stop them from locking eyes, maybe Glitch won't do her thing."

"You got it." Thibault squeezed Flicker's hand, then slipped away. She felt his absence with a momentary pang, then shook off the feeling and threw herself into Coin's eyes.

He was climbing now, hoisting himself up onto the lowest arm of the fountain. The money in his free hand was fully formed. No presidents after all, just a solid stack of Benjamin Franklins staring up at Flicker.

"He's going with hundreds." As Flicker spoke, Coin flung a plume of money high into the air.

She pulled back, putting her vision into the galaxy of eyes already watching—and moving in.

"Oh, shit."

"Relax," Crash said from beside her. "I got this."

CHAPTER 28
CRASH

FOR CHIZARA, A SHOPPING MALL DECKED OUT IN full Christmas bling was torture.

It was like carrying a vast, intricate, burning-hot jungle gym on her shoulders, with added angry-bee clouds of Christmas lights. It was hard to think straight, to home in and find the right pain among millions.

The excruciating beauty of the central junction box was a big distraction. Phone stings scraped across her as frazzled shoppers scrambled for the money fluttering down around the fountain.

Beside her Mob whimpered, vocalizing the crowd's exhaustion and greed.

"Just another ten seconds." Chizara dragged her mind off the junction box and back to the fountain's workings.

Incredibly, the thing was only half active, most of its ghostly pathways dark and barely visible through the flashing, hurting bars of signal. How spectacular, how painful, would it be in full flow?

That sparkling cluster in the fountain's center governed the lights' color and intensity. Chizara sifted through the hard drives, the synchronization system, the galaxy of fluttering LEDs . . . so much stuff, so much *pain*—

She crashed it all, just to clear her head.

With the lights' buzzing silenced, she could see the water system, the pumps and valves and gauges, big and crude after the lacy electronics. She put a mental finger on every piece of piping, every relevant connection.

Coin was perched in the curving steel. Glitch stood below, dancing in the rain of cash. If her brain-glitching power kicked in, they would all be helpless.

It was time to throw the switch.

With a grunt of effort, Crash shut off every valve inside the fountain, at the same time pushing the impeller pumps up to maximum. To do that without crashing the rest of the mall took all her focus, like playing Twister while flipping pancakes. Sweat sprang out cool on her face.

Inside the fountain, gauges wailed at every juncture—pressure was building, going critical. But in the rain of free money, no one even noticed that the fountain had gone dark and still.

Then a hissing came from somewhere at the top—the

built-up pressure had popped a valve open by sheer force, sending a sparkling mist into the air.

"Get ready," Chizara said to Mob, and let every valve go.

Cold water exploded from dozens of spouts, spewing in all directions under pressure. People shrieked and ducked away on all sides. The fake cash lay plastered sodden to the floor, suddenly a lot less tempting.

Even at this distance, Chizara felt a spatter of drops hitting her face. A diabolical Crash laugh burst out of her chest.

The peppy Christmas shopping tunes chose that moment to switch to a somber drone of cellos and brass.

"Go, Scam!" said Mob, and pointed. "And check out poor Coin!"

Crash laughed again. Coin was curled at the top of the fountain like a wet cat up a tree, his arms wrapped protectively around the backpack. Clumps of bills dropped from the soggy mass of green paper in his hands.

But the eruption of spray lasted only a few seconds. Crash kept the impeller wheels spinning, but this thing was designed to be a fountain, not a water cannon. She shut the valves and wiped her face.

"I'll build it up and hit them again in a minute."

The crowd looked confused by the bait and switch of free money and cold water. People stomped about, complaining, squeezing out skirts and pant legs, but they still wanted that wet cash on the floor.

But Crash had one more trick to play.

She reached up into the air-conditioning, dragging the thermostat way down and setting the fans to full blast. Icy air gusted into the fountain plaza.

People backed away from the fountain and the puddles around it, grimacing at the sudden cold. And, as the crowd fell below some crucial density, Coin's money turned back into worthless white rectangles of sodden paper.

"You!" Glitch was pointing straight at Crash from beneath the fountain. "You're that chick from the nightclub!"

Crash, her legs trembling under the weight of the mall's electronics, still had the strength to blow a kiss at Glitch and raise the middle finger of her other hand.

CHAPTER 29
ANONYMOUS

THIBAULT WATCHED AS THE FAKE MONEY FADED.

The crowd fell back. Their strands of frustrated attention stuck to the bills, stretching and shimmering . . .

Until, *snap!* Their collective focus disintegrated, flitting about in bewilderment. And all that cash was now sodden, sloppily scissored rectangles of plain white.

The crowd stared at each other and at the blank bills. Had it all been some kind of optical illusion? A trick?

Time to move in. If the crowd was thin enough for the money to fade, Ren wouldn't have much power either. Thibault had to get her someplace private before Davey jumped down to help.

He pushed forward past a soggy couple, their eyes tethered tight and bright to the wet paper in their hands.

"Some kinda magic trick," the guy said. "What a rip."

Two mall security guards were waving the crowd back from the fountain. Perfect.

Thibault snuck up behind the skinnier guard and gently unlooped the handcuffs from his belt. Then he ran a big, fast semicircle within the cover of the crowd, past their cranky faces, their angry fists.

Davey was on the lowest arm of the dripping fountain sculpture, watching Ren's advance on Crash. Thibault darted across the wet tiles, vaulted onto the long steel arm.

Davey turned to look—too late. Thibault had clapped a handcuff on his wrist and locked him onto a steel branch.

"What?" Eyes wide, Davey pulled on the cuff. "Are you out of your *mind*?"

Thibault jumped down before the guy could think to throw a punch.

"Ren, help!" Davey cried. "Stalker dude! Six o'clock!"

Ren spun around, her focus locking on Thibault.

"I see him," she said.

He tried to chop her attention away, but it snapped right back onto him.

The steel rang under the rattling handcuff. "Get the key off him, quick!"

Ren stepped swiftly backward into the crowd's edge, then flung out a hand at Thibault—

And the world stopped making sense. It became random

patches of color, twists of texture and tone. Thibault closed his eyes, but eyelids didn't make sense either, and the sounds around him turned foreign and frightening.

His mind fled in all directions. Insanity was only seconds away.

Cold water hit Thibault right in the face. His eyes flew open and he recognized the fountain, all its spouts erupting. And over there was the girl who'd glitched him. Her black hair doused flat as a winter witch's, Ren held her ground, alone, enraged, as the rest of the crowd fell back.

Nice timing, Crash.

Before Ren could recover, Thibault slid-splashed across the floor and grabbed her arm, twisted it behind her back. He pinned her other arm and dragged her away from the remains of the crowd.

"Put me down, you piece of—" Her boots thudded into his shins, sending flashes of red pain across his vision.

Streamers of curiosity and concern from the crowd latched onto Ren as he carried her away. With no chopping hands free, he tried to *will* them away, but the two security guards had spotted the howling girl and were coming after him.

"Ladies and gentlemen!" a sudden voice boomed across the mall. "I hope you've all enjoyed our little show!"

It was Nate, halfway up the escalator, hands in the air, his Glorious Leader aura shining. The attention of the crowd, of the security guards, even of dripping, angry Ren, switched to him in an instant, ready to listen, ready to trust.

He spoke to their uplifted faces, selling them the crazy idea that this was some great entertainment, and not the Zeroes' usual superpowered train wreck. There was even a smattering of applause—people *wanted* to be rescued from the crazy. They wanted things to make sense.

Thibault wrenched his mind free from Bellwether's thrall and dragged Ren off down an empty hallway. At first she kept struggling, but then she hung still, every muscle in her drenched body wire-taut. He felt the faintest wavering at the edges of his perception.

"Sorry," he said. "No crowd, no glitch."

"Give me the key to those handcuffs! I'm serious!" Her boot whumped into his shin again.

"Ow! Quit kicking! I haven't *got* it."

"You can't leave him *trapped* there. I'm begging you!" She strained to looked toward the fountain.

"Relax. With Glorious Leader talking, security won't even notice him."

"Security?" She convulsed—was she laughing or crying? "Do we *look* like we give a shit about *mall cops*?"

"We just want to talk to you two. Without a crowd around."

"You okay, Anon?" came Flicker's voice. She and Mob were following them down the hallway.

"Not too close," Thibault called. "Her power could kick in."

"Oh my God, you've got your whole *crew* here? Are you crazy?" Ren exploded again, kicking and struggling. "Didn't I say, specifically? He can *smell* us in a group!"

"Who can?" Thibault suppressed a shiver—the mall was suddenly cold, and he was wet through. "You mean your killer?"

Ren let out a wail. "If you morons figured out where we'd be, Swarm will too! Find some bolt cutters, a saw! We've got to get Davey off that thing!"

"Um, she's just bullshitting, right?" Flicker said. "To make you let go?"

"I don't think so." Mob's face was pale and stiff. "Something's coming. Something really, really bad."

CHAPTER 30
MOB

KELSIE FELT IT ROAR THROUGH HER BODY.
Something had hooked into the greed and confusion of the
crowd, dragging them into a deep, hungry rage.

It was a knife in her brain, pulsing with every heartbeat.

She stared past the fountain. The people clustered around
Nate on the escalator had begun to fall away, like a tide dragged
out before a tsunami. The wave itself was building farther back,
more and more people massing together.

Flicker's voice was faint. "You're not doing this, are you?"

"No," Kelsie said.

"And it doesn't feel like Glitch," Flicker said.

"It's Swarm!" Glitch cried from where Thibault held her,
halfway down the exit hall. "What are you waiting for? Get
Davey and let's get *out* of here. You have no *idea* what's coming."

Kelsie had more than an idea—she could feel it. She was *becoming* it, swept into the blazing anger of the crowd. They began to jitter under Swarm's control, jerking and shaking like sand on a drum. Their teeth rattled and their breath came in furious, shuddering sips of air.

Crowds had always felt like a big, dumb animal to Kelsie. But this one was more like a hive of bees—shivering and buzzing, many-bodied, single-minded.

Glitch broke free of Thibault's grasp and came hurtling down the hallway, knocking Flicker sideways. Kelsie spun and seized her, the swarm roiling in her gut. She wanted to shake the life out of Glitch. She wanted to shove her so hard into a wall that her skull would crack—

She stopped herself just in time, extinguishing the fury that burned in her muscles.

"She's right," Kelsie whispered. "We should run. Right now."

Glitch jerked out of her grasp. "The hell we will! Not without Davey!"

"I'll get him." Thibault shot past and Glitch followed, both of them headed for the edge of the trembling crowd.

It was moving as one . . . *swarming* toward the fountain. The central mass was dense and packed, but the periphery seethed with activity—people sparking out from the core and back in, almost a blur.

Under the fountain, Davey writhed against his handcuff, like he was trying to pull off his own hand.

His terror made Kelsie's mouth water. The greed of the mall crowd had shifted into another kind of hunger.

There was Nate, coming down the escalator with a mad confidence, his hands raised in the air as if he could stop the swarm. He bellowed out something that Kelsie couldn't even hear through the roar in her head.

She grabbed Flicker's hand, trying to speak—

He can't win. They'll kill him.

But the fury had taken her again—her jaw was locked tight. She tried to tear herself out of the feedback loop, but anger and thirst and even bone-rattling lust pulled her back in. She wanted to be part of this murderous crowd. Nothing else mattered.

As the buzzing edge of the swarm reached Coin, the fountain erupted, water spraying in all directions. Chizara was nearby, a hundred spinning lights pulsing to life around her raised arms. Kelsie expected an answering spike in the swarm's energy—confusion, hesitation—but there was only that deep, wrathful desire roaring through her body.

"Move it, Stalker!" Coin shouted, his voice shrill as the core of the shivering crowd drew closer. "Get me out of here!"

"Hang on!" came Thibault's voice. As he breached the seething outer edge of the swarm, Kelsie lost sight of him, her awareness faltering.

"It's not working," she managed to say through clenched teeth.

"I can't see shit," Flicker muttered. "Their eyes are twitching all over the place."

Kelsie glimpsed Glitch staggering as a passing man slammed her with his forearm, saw her go off balance as someone else shouldered her. Dozens of people were splashing through the fountain. Glitch was falling—

No, some guy had caught her and was holding her up. Anon, coming back into focus as he dragged her from the swarm. Chizara was beside them.

"Don't save *me*," Glitch yelled. "Get *Davey*!"

"I can't get through!" Thibault shouted.

Flicker's voice carried above the din. "Nate, bail out!"

The main body of the swarm had reached the escalator. Nate had abandoned his Glorious Leader pose and was running upward and away. But the first grasping hands of the mass were just behind him. Ethan stood frozen at the top of the steps until Nate jerked him into a run.

Flicker called again, calm steel in her voice. "Crash! Escalator!"

Chizara turned and raised an arm, letting out a sharp, barked laugh just as Nate reached the upper floor. The tendril of the swarm that pursued him began to slip and tumble, falling back as the stairs reversed.

Flicker sank her fingernails into Kelsie's arm. "Mob! Come back to me. Can you control them? Can you do *anything*?"

Kelsie tried to find some other emotion to send into the

crowd, but she had nothing but hunger. She moved to get a better view of Coin, because she didn't want to miss a moment of his terror. She wasn't Kelsie anymore. She wasn't even the Mob she knew.

"No," she said, half to Flicker, half to herself.

"Please!" came a long wail from Glitch. Anon had dragged her back to the hallway entrance. Chizara was right behind them—

But so was the livid border of the swarm. A woman took a passing swipe at Chizara—she ducked and kicked out, sending her attacker sprawling.

Thibault pointed down the hallway. "You guys run for that exit. I'll go back for Davey."

"You won't make it," Flicker said.

"In a crowd that big I'm—"

"Dead!" Flicker yelled, grabbing at his jacket. "Swarm *killed* the other Anonymous, remember?"

Thibault looked back at Davey. "But we can't just—"

"Too late," Mob said, horrified and exultant.

The swarm had reached the fountain.

"Screw this," she heard Crash say, and the mall plunged into darkness. The crowd was unswayed. In the eerie green light of the exit signs, they continued to shake in silent convulsions, their jittering eyes shining, the water glittering as it splashed up around them.

A pulse of energy went through the swarm, sweeping

Mob up into their vast greed. The pack seethed forward, setting upon Coin, feeding on his fear. They wanted to destroy him.

Someone pulled her, staggering, down the hallway, even as she felt every moment of the murder behind her—the clothes tearing from his body, then clumps of his hair, his skin. She felt sick and elated as bones bent and snapped. Dimly, she heard him screaming, and even that felt good. The swarm's energy slipped from gluttony to a gulping satisfaction. . . .

Then the screaming stopped, and Kelsie felt a moment of perfect, satiated bliss before she realized what the silence meant.

Coin was dead. Davey was dead.

There was a flutter of confusion from the mob. In his moment of ecstasy Swarm had lost control, long enough for the crowd to drift apart into individuals, to register what had happened. . . .

Kelsie felt their hunger turn to horror. The spike of revulsion hit her like a blow. Closer in, the Zeroes were a mess of shock and panic.

"Oh God," Flicker groaned. Of course, she'd had a close-up view.

Kelsie tried to reach out and refocus the energy of the crowd, but whoever was at its center grabbed hold again. He swallowed their terror and spat it back out, turning it into a fierce new appetite.

He wanted Kelsie next. She could feel it.

But not to kill her. Something worse.

"Run," she croaked.

They crashed through the exit doors, into a diffuse pre-dawn darkness. The air outside was cold and fresh, but sour bile rose in Kelsie's throat. She tumbled forward, dry-retching as she ran.

The swarm was right behind them, funneling into that narrow hallway. They were still furious.

Every mouthwatering ache of hunger, every shameless craving for the hunt—she felt it. She wanted to take refuge in the build and swirl of the swarm's feedback loop.

"This way," Flicker said, her voice hoarse and shaky. They ran along a short access road, back toward the mall's main entrance. "Crash, can you start Nate's car?"

"Easy." Chizara's voice was flat, grim, and absolutely under control.

Glitch was still sobbing. But she shoved Thibault away and ran on her own.

"Nate and Scam are at the south exit." Flicker's phone was at her ear. "We can pick them up. Is that crowd still after us?"

Kelsie hesitated. The farther they got from the mall, the

more she could breathe. Slowly she felt herself detach from the bitter beauty of Swarm's domination.

Bloodlust still sang in her veins, but it wasn't the swarm. It was something inside her. It had always been inside her, and now it was awake.

"He's falling behind," she panted. Maybe the blackout had thrown him off. Maybe he wasn't that fast. Maybe he was full. "But keep running."

She didn't have to tell them twice.

CHAPTER 31
ANONYMOUS

"STOP THE CAR!" FLICKER ELBOWED THIBAULT, hard. "Gonna throw up!"

Nate pulled over. Thibault flung open the door, and Flicker jumped out, stumbled away, and fell to her knees among the rocks and scrubby desert plants, heaving.

Thibault followed, kneeling beside her, holding back her hair. She heaved again onto the stone-strewn sand.

"It's okay." His own voice was shaky. "Get it all out."

He'd felt sick just glimpsing the attack on Davey, but Flicker had seen everything in close-up, through a hundred different eyes. The thought made Thibault want to puke himself.

Flicker looked up at him, breathing hard. The connection between them hung bright and steady on the night air.

"You okay?" he asked.

"No," she said hoarsely, wiping her mouth with the back of her hand. "I wish I could puke out my memories."

"I know." Thibault dropped his head, trying not to think of Davey's face, his blank panic as he rattled the handcuffs.

"How far are we from the mall?" Flicker said, leaning back on a rock.

"At least five miles. Too far for that crowd to follow on foot."

Thibault hadn't known. How *could* he have known he was helping kill a Zero? His shins burned where Ren had kicked them.

She was in the backseat of the Mercedes, still sobbing and swearing. The others stood around the car, not a single strand of attention glowing among them. They had all disappeared inside their own heads.

Thibault swung his gaze up at the vast desert sky. The randomness, the separateness of the dimming stars, their complete lack of emotion, was a relief. No one could gather them up and turn them into a deadly swarm.

Flashing lights pulled Thibault's gaze down to the valley. The mall was lit up like a stage show. An ambulance wailed along the exit road, and all sorts of emergency vehicles clustered around the main doors, their lights pulsing nausea into Thibault's stomach.

There was no getting around it. He'd left a Zero out to die.

Flicker shifted on her rock, spat into the sand.

"I'll get you some water," Thibault said. Glorious Leader

always brought bottles on training missions. Suddenly that seemed incredibly thoughtful—and also incredibly naïve.

"Thanks," Flicker said.

Back at the car, Nate's face looked like an old man's. Ren's sobs were easing to gasps. Kelsie sat shivering on the ground, her head in her hands. She would have *felt* the crowd's murderous rage, not just seen it.

Beside her crouched Ethan, looking confused. He'd only glimpsed it from the top of the escalator. Lucky bastard.

Would the killer have gone on picking them off if they hadn't run? Or did one Zero last a long time, like a mouse in a snake's gullet?

Thibault brought Flicker the water. She rinsed and spat and rinsed again, while he kicked dirt and gravel on top of the vomit.

"I knew crowds could be scary," she said. "But I never thought I'd see someone get *killed* by . . . oh, shit. Anon, incoming!"

Fists hit Thibault before he had time to turn around, nearly knocking him into the dirt-covered vomit. He ducked and caught sight of Ren's metal rings making arcs of starlight at him. He tried to slice away her awareness, but her hatred blazed too sharp and hot.

"*You* did this!" Her voice broke with tears as she thumped his chest. "You killed Davey!"

Chizara was suddenly there, grabbing Ren by the shoulders. But the girl spun around, flailing at Chizara's face. Flicker jumped up and joined the struggle, and scuffed-up dust swirled in the predawn light.

"He couldn't even run!" Ren shouted raggedly. "We could've gotten away—"

"Enough!"

They all fell back from each other, because it was Nate speaking.

"Could have gotten away from *what*?" he said.

Ren laughed bitterly. "What? You didn't see him?"

"I saw the crowd change," Nate said. "But who was doing it? There was no center, no focus."

"That's how the guy works. He's in their *heads*." She glared at Thibault, eyes brimming with starry tears. "We told *this* idiot everything you needed to know!"

Everyone's attention latched onto him, and Thibault took a step back.

"You dropped a bunch of hints! Then you threw me out of your car!"

"We told you to run, didn't we? We told you to stay away from other people with powers! And you *followed* us? And dragged along all your special friends, with their half-assed *talents*?" Ren spat the last word, but the fight had gone out of her. She shook off Chizara and Flicker and stumbled away among the rocks, taking everyone's attention with her.

She stopped at the sight of the glittering mall and reached out to it. "We were meant to die together, Davey!"

Kelsie let out a moan, and Thibault felt the group's pain sweep into his body. He barely stayed standing.

"Scam?" Nate said softly. "See if you can get her talking."

Ethan looked up. He was still next to Kelsie by the car.

"Seriously, *now*?"

"We need to know what kind of threat we're facing."

Ethan sighed, but he slowly crossed to Ren. He stood hunched and uncomfortable beside her as she wept.

A moment later he relaxed, the voice's confidence seeping into his frame. Thibault could hardly hear its murmur.

"I know how you feel."

"*Bullshit* you do!" Ren pushed Ethan hard in the chest.

He staggered back but recovered, and the voice continued calmly, "My dad left us when I was seven. It sucked."

Ethan looked up at the Zeroes, like he hadn't expected anything like that, anything so true, to come out of his mouth.

"You guys had a bond," the voice went on, coaxing a faint thread of connection out of Ren. "Anyone could see that."

Ren wept harder. Ethan was his awkward self for a few moments, squirming and throwing nervous attention threads back at Nate.

But then Ren wiped her eyes.

"My whole life . . . ," she began brokenly. "My power was just a game, a trick I played on people, screwing with their heads. I used it to get out of trouble. Or to get other people *into* trouble."

"I hear you. That's my power in a nutshell." *That* was weird, hearing the voice talk about itself. "But with Davey it finally made sense, right?"

Ren wiped her cheeks with her fingers. "Yeah, I leveled up when I met him."

"Leveled up." Ethan nodded. "Like your power turning inside out."

"He helped me figure it out." Ren hugged herself, gazing up at the stars. "How to put the stuff I stole from everyone else—all the shimmers between them and the world around them, everything they know and love and understand—into *our* connection, Davey's and mine."

"That must feel awesome," the voice said.

"You have no idea," Ren said softly, totally wrapped up in herself, no attention fraying off her anywhere. "*No one* gets to feel as close as we did. Not in all of human history."

"Like one person in two bodies."

"Best sex ever." Her voice broke again.

"Amazing," said the voice, with very un-Ethan-like wonder.

Thibault turned away. This was *not* cool, the voice playing the shrink, drawing Ren out in front of half a dozen strangers. But he was still listening.

Nate was motionless, his attention fixed on the two silhouetted against the paling sky.

"What I do, it only messes people up *while* I'm doing it," Ren was saying. "Plus maybe an hour or so. But for Davey and me, it *sticks*, you know? Doesn't fade like his money. But it's not like we could do it in secret." Her voice cracked, and she buried her face in her hands again.

"It left a trail for that . . . predator," Ethan said, and the word sent a chill through Thibault.

"We tried to keep safe," Ren sobbed. "We should've stayed away from people—in a place like *this*!" She spread her hands around at the desert hills and pleaded, "But we *need* crowds, to be who we are!"

"Just like Quinton Wallace needs them to kill," Ethan said.

"*Just* like that—Wait, how did you know his name?"

"We know a lot of things." The voice was at its smooth best now, almost hypnotic. "We can protect you. You'll be safe with us."

"Are you kidding?" Ren turned and sent a spike of hatred at Thibault. "One of you left Davey chained up like a sacrifice! And you've got a baby Swarm waiting to happen."

"Kelsie isn't like that. She's only—" The voice's soothing murmur sputtered out, and Ethan yelped, "Wait. What?"

Ren stared over her shoulder at Kelsie, and the Zeroes' attention followed, glowing wires across the lightening air.

"Mob is a . . . a Swarm?" Ethan's real voice broke on the last word.

"She will be," Ren said. "I felt her working the crowd in your stupid nightclub. Quinton used to pretend he was like that, the life of the party. The guy who loved parades. But he was just waiting for a mean and hungry crowd to come along. . . ."

A sparkling line of attention came from over by the car. Kelsie was listening now.

"You won't have long now," Ren whispered. "She's seen how fun it is to kill people with a crowd— especially people like us. Quinton says *we taste the best*."

Kelsie looked so small there, her arms wrapped around her legs, her face streaked with tears. Thibault couldn't imagine her ever harming anyone.

"Kelsie's not dangerous," Ethan said in his real voice. "That's . . . nuts."

"When your power flips inside out, it happens all at once," Ren said coldly. "You won't recognize her."

"You don't know her!" Ethan cried, his face turning red and angry. "You don't know anything. She would *never* . . ."

He sputtered to a halt, but his anger stayed, and Thibault saw him make the decision to use the voice. It broke past Ethan's squeaky outrage in merciless attack mode.

"You *should've* died with Davey. That's what you promised him, that you'd be there together at the end. But no, he died all alone, while you waltzed away! Cry all you like, but it doesn't change the fact that you left your man—your *husband*—to—oomph!"

Nate had punched Ethan in the stomach. The bright bar that had joined him to Ren blew to powder, and he crumpled to the ground.

"*You* morons made me break my promise!" Ren spat down at him. "If you'd stayed away, we could've kept running! But no, you had to *find out* shit, didn't you?" She was yelling at Nate now. "You had to follow us and *save* your poor little dolls from our evil plans!"

The world began to swim around Thibault. The stars above looked wrong—what was the point of them, how did they *fit*, what sense did their patterns make?

Damn it. There were seven of them gathered out here, enough to make a crowd.

Thibault scrabbled after the fraying meaning in Ren's rant.

"You had to come rolling out here in a big ball of Swarm bait! Nice work, superheroes! It's great that you guys are such a *team*, you know? I hope you stick together like freakin' glue until he tracks you down and tears you *all* apart, just like he did my *Davey*!"

And with that name, all the stars went out, all the world went out, and Thibault didn't know who, what, or where he was for a long, dark time.

CHAPTER 32
SCAM

ETHAN'S THROAT WAS FULL OF SAND.

His mouth was full of sand too, and so was his nose. He coughed, snorted more sand, then coughed again. He was lying facedown in the desert scrub.

He rolled over, and the inside of his eyelids turned bright red. Full daylight, and it'd been just before dawn when he'd hit the ground.

Shoot, how long had he been lying there?

Glitch had really done a number on him. It was like his whole body had forgotten how to stand up.

If Swarm attacked them now—

Crap, *Swarm*! Ethan jerked upright, heart pounding.

"Kelsie?" he slurred.

The Zeroes lay in all directions, spread out as flat as pancakes on the red dirt. But there was no sign of Swarm. Not yet, anyhow. Apart from the whistle of wind, the place was eerily quiet.

Ethan half crawled, half dragged himself over to where Kelsie lay beside Chizara, her head on the other girl's knee. Kelsie's face was starting to turn rosy in the sun.

When Ethan checked her pulse, she murmured sleepily.

"Phew." Ethan looked around.

Chizara was breathing evenly, like she was asleep. Flicker lay beside a large rock, her long hair and skirt fanned out around her. Nate had crumpled into a very un-Nate-like pose, one leg caught under him and one kicked out in front. Teebo lay alone, facing the sky with one arm across his chest.

"Anybody dead?" Ethan rasped. Then he spat sand at the ground beside him.

Damn. This was the third time this week he'd been glitched, but at least his voice was working. His real voice, the one he'd lost that first time outside the Office-O.

Speaking of Glitch, where *was* she?

And where was the Mercedes?

"Yo! Zeroes!"

Flicker stirred first, gathering herself together to sit up. "Scam, show me everyone."

Ethan obligingly swept his gaze across the Zeroes, giving Flicker a panoramic view of their collapse.

"Shit," Flicker said.

"You're welcome," Ethan replied. His stomach still hurt from where Nate had punched him.

Why had Nate punched him again?

Oh, right. He'd let the voice go to town when Glitch had called Kelsie a baby Swarm. Which was total crap, because Kelsie would never let a crowd turn a guy into mincemeat.

Ethan shuddered. He'd only caught a glimpse of the fountain before Nate had pulled him into retreat. There was nothing recognizably Davey left. Just bone and blood and mess. Lots of mess. And a lot of people covered with it.

"Give me a look at the mall," Flicker said.

Ethan obediently turned until he could see the Desert Springs Mall in the distance. The parking lots were practically empty. Only a few abandoned cars, a half dozen fire engines with their lights flashing, and government-issue black SUVs, all the same. An ambulance was pulling away slowly, and a dozen news trucks with telescoping antennae stood corralled a mile away.

There was no swarm headed this way.

"Okay," Flicker breathed.

Ethan pulled at his shirt, trying to release some of the sand from his collar.

The others were beginning to move. Slowly, like vampires at sunset.

"Where's Nate's car?" Flicker asked.

"Pretty sure Glitch took off with it."

Ethan had almost gotten through to Glitch—or the voice had. There'd been a total connection over the whole love thing. But then she had started in on Kelsie and he'd let loose. Bad move, now that he thought about it, but no reason to punch a guy.

Flicker was next to Thibault, tracing a hand down his arm until he stirred. Kelsie and Chizara were awake now too, blearily leaning against each other. Which just left one more Zero.

Ethan crossed to where Nate lay. He wanted to kick the guy. He was supposed to lead them all into glory, not leave them knocked unconscious in some desert. He grabbed Nate's shoulder and started rocking him, watching his chin roll left and right.

Nate reached out to push Ethan aside.

"Scam?" he croaked.

"I think we're past code names," Ethan said tiredly. "The mission is over. We lost."

That got him. Nate sat up and looked around. "Is everyone okay?"

"Nobody dead," Ethan replied, though when he got home, Jess was probably going to fix that oversight.

"Mierda." Nate clenched his jaw. "She left us here. Where Swarm could have taken us while we were unconscious."

"Um, maybe." Ethan cast a quick, fearful glance toward the mall.

"He wouldn't," Kelsie said, her voice cold. Her eyes were

fixed on the mall. "There's no fun in eating unconscious people. There's no fear to feed on."

The rest of the Zeroes went silent.

Ethan shivered. He totally could've done without knowing that. And he could've done without knowing that *Kelsie* knew. Like she'd been in Swarm's head somehow.

"Maybe we got far enough away," Nate said, like he hadn't heard Kelsie. "Hard to lead an angry mob for miles across desert. Is anyone still glitched?"

"I'm fine," Flicker said. "Not sure about Thibault, though."

"The sky's still wrong," Tee said, sounding like he had a hangover.

"Crash?" Nate called. Then he hesitated. "Mob?"

Kelsie was silent. She just kept staring down at the mall.

"We're fine," Chizara said, for both of them. She reached out to brush Kelsie's hair from her face.

"We are *not* fine," Ethan said. "We're in the direct path of a psycho. With no ride home!"

"Ethan, just shut up, okay?" Flicker sighed.

"Well, it's not like we can hitch a ride back to Cambria!" Ethan felt himself getting hysterical. "And my sister said she'd kill me if I did anything out of line, which I think applies to driving all night to attend a mob killing!"

"Stop it!" Nate cried, his expression pleading.

Ethan stared. He'd never seen anything like that expression on Nate. The guy almost looked afraid.

The others were eyeing Kelsie, who was still frozen to the spot.

Ethan waited for the moment when Nate—the reigning charisma champion—would grab hold of the Zeroes and focus them all on a new plan, dragging them away from thoughts of death and defeat. But Nate was quiet. The one time they could've really done with a leader, and he had nothing to say.

Ethan reached in to the voice for something to shake Nate out of his funk. If he could just get Glorious Leader back on track, the others would fall into line.

He opened his mouth, but nothing came out.

For one blind moment he was scared his power had been glitched for good. But he could feel the voice sneaking away down his windpipe. Apparently it had decided Nate's funk was immune to mere words.

Or maybe Kelsie's sadness was too strong, and would keep them captive forever in a superpowered feedback loop of despair.

Both those options sounded pretty terrible.

It was Flicker who broke the spell. She got to her feet and said wearily, "Let's go home."

"Good call, Flick," Ethan said. "One question: How?"

She turned to him, looking more pissed than anything else. Her voice came out dangerously gentle. "I don't know, Scam. Got any ideas?"

In that moment Ethan really wanted Flicker to not hate

him. He wanted her to lead the Zeroes to safety. He wanted to go home. He wanted all that more than he'd ever wanted anything.

And with that fervent desire, the voice leaped right back up into Ethan's mouth like it had never left.

"We head back to the mall!" it said. "Whose turn is it to steal a car?"

CHAPTER 33
BELLWETHER

THE CAR CRASH HAD STOLEN WAS FAST, BUT IT wasn't a Mercedes.

Nate hadn't called the police yet, or Papi. The Mercedes had a serious theft prevention system. It could be shut down remotely, or tracked, and he couldn't risk Glitch winding up in prison.

Not after what she'd just lived through.

What they'd all lived through.

Everyone was quiet in the back, tired and stunned, consumed by what they'd seen. Kelsie's mood sat over them, thick as smoke from an oncoming wildfire.

Nate wished someone would talk. He didn't want to think, to process what had happened.

What he'd *let* happen. What he'd been unable to stop.

A Zero had been torn apart, right in front of his eyes.

Swarm was stronger than anything Nate had ever seen before. His hold on that crowd had been steely, brilliant. What kind of purpose drove that awesome hunger? Beside it Nate's ambitions looked paltry, his power a plaything.

Dolls, he thought, revulsion deep in his belly. Revulsion and *fear*—he was truly afraid, and he didn't like it.

But his power had been useless. When Swarm had taken over the crowd, Nate had tried to claw every strand of their attention toward himself. *Stop. Listen to me. Heed.* But no one in the lethal mob had even spared him a glance.

Maybe if he'd been down in the melee instead of up on the escalator, he could have matched Swarm's willpower with his own.

Of course, they might've torn him to pieces instead of Davey.

As it was, all the Zeroes' powers combined hadn't been able to save the poor guy.

Losing Papi's Mercedes was nothing compared to the hole that Swarm had punched in Nate's world.

When rain began to mist the windshield, Flicker finally broke the silence.

"The sad thing is, we finally got it right. All your training worked perfectly, Nate. We saved that crowd from Glitch and Coin."

"But not the other way around," Nate pointed out.

"And what if he comes for us next?" Ethan said. "We don't even know what he looks like!"

"Did you see him, Flick?" someone asked—Thibault, of course.

As she considered the question, Nate felt the energy in the car grow tense. Mob was echoing their fear, their horror. She'd been in the crowd's mind for the long, awful minutes of the murder—and on top of that, Ren had called her a baby Swarm. Could Nate summon the energy to even *start* bringing her back from that?

And what if Ren was right? He couldn't get his mind around what that might mean.

"There were hundreds in that crowd." Flicker's words came slowly. "But yeah, I think I spotted him."

She hesitated, and Nate concentrated on steering. Suddenly everything felt dangerous—his fatigue, the rain-slicked road, even Flicker's voice. Was that Mob's emotion, or his own?

"There was a guy near the back," Flicker said. "About our age."

"Born in 2000?" Nate hadn't asked Ren her and Davey's birthdates. An opportunity to learn, missed. Everything he could have found out about Coin's power, gone for good.

"Yeah, probably. And about my height," Flicker said. "Kind of preppy. He had a little suitcase, one of those rolling ones. He was super neat, in this blazer and long pants. White socks. Terrible haircut. And he was skinny, like not-eating skinny."

"Why do you think he was in charge?" Anon asked.

"He was the only one not . . . not *buzzing*, is all I can call it. And he had this smug little soft smile on his face, like he was keeping a secret." Flicker paused. "He was enjoying it, like Glitch said."

"Don't call her that," Anon said. "Her name's Ren. His was Davey."

Silence fell again at those names, and Nate felt his will petering out. What did it matter who'd done it, beside the appalling fact that it was done? The pictures flashed across his eyes again, the blood leaping, the *force* it took to break a person—

He clung to the wheel. *Just watch the road. Just do your job. Just get these people home alive.*

CHAPTER 34
BELLWETHER

"WE LOST A ZERO," NATE BEGAN. "THAT CAN NEVER happen again."

He stood in front of them on the dance floor of the Dish, his hands out, trying to draw in their attention. But the pose had nothing behind it. He was spent, waiting for someone to laugh at him.

"We didn't *lose* Davey," Anon said. "We *killed* him. *I* killed him. The handcuffs were my idea."

Ethan groaned. "Who *cares* who screwed up worse? That guy's coming for the rest of us. We have to get ready!"

"Ready? But we don't know anything about his power," Chizara said. "I mean, besides the obvious—he makes crowds kill, and Bellwether can't stop him."

All their bright, needy focus turned toward Nate, and he had to fight not to look away.

Six against one, and they'd lost. What kind of leader let *that* happen?

"We should just skip town!" Ethan threw a shimmering glance at Kelsie. "Split into pairs, maybe. Hide out in the wilderness. That guy's helpless without a crowd to do his dirty work."

"So are we," Nate said, trying to sound calm as he fought off panic. "Alone, we're nothing."

"Yeah, but I'd rather be nothing and *alive!*" Ethan argued. "Beats dead superhero any day!"

Chizara sat forward, throwing out a whip of attention. "*Your* power would work fine in some hick town, Ethan. Not so much the rest of us. And you expect us to just ditch our families? And everything we've put into the Dish?"

Nate looked at her, trying to feel pride in how the night-club had bound her to the group. But all his strategies seemed inconsequential now.

Flicker's voice broke in: "We need a better plan than running away."

Everyone's attention brightened on her, hopeful.

"We could throw Swarm off our scent," she said. "Create some sort of crowd disturbance a few hundred miles away."

"Wasn't that Ren and Davey's genius plan?" Ethan asked. "It didn't work!"

"Because Swarm can sense us," Anon said. "Especially in a group. We shouldn't do *anything* together."

Before the group's feeble strands of hope could fall to the floor and die, Nate spoke up. "Ren and Davey could have been wrong about that. We found them without any special powers, and they found us. Swarm knows how to search the internet, just like we do."

"Then we're dead, thanks to Sonia Sonic!" Ethan said.

Nate didn't answer, didn't give Ethan so much as a glance. He had to take control and give them some solid hope.

"Swarm's been following Ren and Davey this whole time. He's obsessed with them. Even when they came to Cambria and painted a target on our backs, he didn't take the bait."

"Which was *us*," Ethan mumbled.

Nate ignored him again. "He may see that job as only half done, and keep looking for her."

It sounded so cold-blooded, and so flimsy—nobody's attention was tightening in his grasp, not even Flicker's.

"And even if he's bored of chasing her," he forged on, "he's just as likely to be distracted by some other bunch of people with powers. Zeroes are popping up everywhere."

Too many words. He was practically babbling.

But they were still listening, at least. They must all desperately want to believe.

Then Kelsie said, "He won't go anywhere else. All he wants is me."

It was like ice water drenching the room. Those were the first words she'd spoken since they'd stolen the car.

"What do you mean?" Chizara asked.

"He wanted me, after he killed Davey. Not to kill me, though. He wants me to join him."

Her cold dread echoed through them, and Nate felt the spine-creep of Kelsie's feeling singled out, like a wolf was staring at her through the trees. He tried to speak, but the feedback loop was too strong.

"Because I'm like him," she added softly.

"Is that what you really think?" Chizara said, and Nate was amazed she could fight Mob's fear. "Or are you just scared it's true?"

"Oh, it's true," Kelsie said, but as she stared back at Chizara, her voice rose a little. The question in it made a space where Nate could jump in.

"You can't be sure of that," he said. "And Swarm doesn't know where you live, Kelsie. That mall is hundreds of miles from here."

It had taken all his effort, but here they were, in his hands again.

"All he knows is that you're part of a big group of people with powers. Which means we should split up." He saw Thibault glance at Flicker. "Or at least stick to small groups. No more than two Zeroes together, maybe."

Damn. Babbling again.

"What about when Ren and Davey were here?" Chizara said. "If anyone puts up pictures of that night, he could recognize us."

Anon spoke up. "Last I checked, Sonia was still posting about the wedding. Much bigger news than a nightclub riot. We got lucky there."

Even from Anonymous, the words resonated in the group. They all wanted to believe they'd been lucky. That they might keeping being lucky.

But Nate's own heart was aching at the thought of splitting up the group he'd worked so hard to bring together. He needed to keep them here just a little bit longer.

"We should do something about that stolen car. Wipe it down for fingerprints, for a start."

"Buckets are in the storage closet," Flicker said. "We need detergent, too."

The connections broke apart, full of bright relief at doing something practical.

But again Kelsie let loose a cold rain.

"I hope Swarm does come here to Cambria."

"Are you nuts?" Ethan sputtered.

She looked older, grimmer. "I hate what he did to that crowd. He took all those connections, those human bonds, and made them *evil*. I hate that he gets to walk away from killing one of us. We should deal with him ourselves."

Nate knew that he should speak now, say something to defuse the others' alarm. But he didn't have it in him.

"Well, I'm totally okay with someone *else* handling that," Ethan said. "I've got a big sister to pacify and Christmas presents to wrap."

A relieved sparkle of laughter went through the room. Ethan's good-natured cowardice had broken Kelsie's spell.

But his outburst also reminded Nate of the sobering fact that it was Christmas Eve. How the hell would everyone get through Christmas after what they'd seen today?

CHAPTER 35
ANONYMOUS

THIBAULT THREW HIMSELF INTO THE BUS SEAT
next to Flicker and stared past her out the window. The winter sun still lay behind dark storm clouds, and the world was
a featureless gray.

Flicker leaned against him, her sight lines winking out as
she turned her vision off. Her other senses clouded around
Thibault, registering his shape, the textures of his clothes and
skin, the rise and fall of his breathing. Was she taking comfort
from what she found? For him their clasped hands were the
best and sanest thing in the world right now.

The bus ground on toward Flicker's house. He was going
to stay the night there, but then . . . he didn't know what. He
couldn't live at Flicker's forever, however much he wanted to
protect her. And if Swarm was out there hunting for groups of

Zeroes, the safest thing was to keep everyone separate.

"I keep worrying about fingerprints," she murmured.

"Tell me about it." The six of them had spent an hour wiping down the interior of the stolen car. Then Thibault had taken and dumped it a mile away from the Dish and walked back. The cops might not know what to make of a murderous mall riot, but they'd sure be interested in a car hot-wired in the parking lot a few hours later.

"Anything to preserve Nate's spotless police record," Flicker said.

"I'm more worried about his confidence. I've never seen Nate run out of steam like that."

"We're all a little freaked out."

"Freaked out?" A short, harsh laugh escaped him. More like traumatized. Heads full of a horror movie they couldn't unwatch. "When Kelsie was talking about Swarm wanting her to join him, I was waiting for Nate to step in and take it down a notch. And he just stared at her, like . . . game over. Glorious Leader, totally choking."

Flicker pressed her lips together, and the warm cloud of her senses withdrew from him. Maybe he'd said too much.

She and Nate had a connection that went back before the Zeroes, to when they were little kids. And they'd had that near romance bubbling beneath the surface until Ethan's voice had snuffed it out two summers ago. It was the only thing Flicker didn't like to discuss with Thibault.

"And when she was talking about dealing with him ourselves," he said softly, "it almost sounded like she meant killing him."

"I was wondering about that," Flicker said. "But then I thought, *Come on, not Kelsie*."

"Yeah, sure. But remember, she grew up around criminals."

"I guess." She put her head on his shoulder, her senses reaching for him again. "Let's hope we never find out what she meant."

He nodded wearily. Bad enough to watch Swarm commit his bloody murder. But to see a *friend* do the same . . .

"I've been thinking about something," he said. "Ren and Davey remembered their friend, the Stalker guy. So if anything happened to me, the chances of you remembering me are pretty good."

She gripped his hand painfully tight. "Don't, Thibault. Just—"

"I mean, they couldn't remember his name. And they laughed at me when I asked about it."

"We're good, okay?" Flicker took his other hand and made him touch his name in braille on her bracelet. "I've always got this."

He heard Ren's voice echoing in the chapel: *Till death do us fucking part!* She'd meant those words. Anyone who knew about Swarm would have to take death seriously.

He pushed the thought out of his mind, lifting his gaze to

the passing suburban houses outside, their mowed lawns, their brick porches, the Christmas lights decking their gutters. In a weird way, being mindful of the present was a lot easier when you didn't know what horrors tomorrow could bring.

Thibault's phone beeped.

"Ten bucks that's Glorious Leader," Flicker said. "Full of great ideas, twenty minutes too late."

The message read: *Is this you?*

"Whoa," said Thibault. "That's my mother's number."

"Holy crap. She's never called you before, has she?"

"Never!" Thibault's chest went tight around his heart. "I put my number in her phone, last time I was there, like you said I should. But I never thought she'd—"

The phone beeped again.

I was wondering if you were coming tonight. Saw ur present for me.

The words connected then, and pleasure washed over Thibault.

"It's Emile. My little brother!"

"Whoa." Flicker's listening tendrils brightened. "How did he remember you?"

"I snuck in and left a present under the tree for him." It actually hurt Thibault's face to smile, he hadn't smiled in so long. "Something for his rock collection, just like on his birthdays."

"He remembers!" Flicker said. "That's amazing."

"We've always had a good connection. Sometimes on his birthday he even—"

The phone beeped again.

Um, RU real?

Thibault stared at the message. Another appeared.

Mom saw the present too. She keeps asking me.

"Something wrong?" Flicker asked.

"Not sure," Thibault said, then texted: *Asking about ME?*

Ellipses pulsed for a long moment before the answer appeared. *She keeps looking @ old photos and talking about you. And crying. Dad doesn't know what to do.*

He read out the text, and they both sat silent for a moment.

"You should answer," Flicker finally said.

"How? Should I explain that Mom's not crazy? It's just my superpower?"

"Tell him you'll be there tonight," said Flicker. "He needs you. *They* need you."

Thibault shook his head. "It's Christmas Eve. It'll suck. They always have people over, and they can barely see me in the crowd. They'll just forget tomorrow anyway."

"But they must remember *something*. This proves it!"

"Emile remembers the presents I leave," he said. "The rest of them remember the pictures on the wall. But not *me*. Just a bunch of confusing clues."

"You should try," she said. "Would you rather be sitting alone in my attic all night? I have *my* parents' party, remember?"

"Oh, yeah. I was planning on lurking in the corner."

"Lurking is right," Flicker sighed. "It'll be too crowded to meet my parents again. But they'll be asking about you, as usual. My dad has this joke that you must not be real. Hearing that one's going to *suck* tonight."

"Damn. Sorry."

"It's not your fault." She took his hand again. "It's just that Mom and Dad *really* want to meet you. They don't know they already have. I feel like I have to throw them a bone somehow."

She turned to face to the window, but her senses stayed in a cloud around him. In a way this slim cut of hope was thanks to her. He never would have thought to put his number in his mother's phone if Flicker hadn't shown him it was possible. Possible that he would be seen one day—*recognized*—by the people he loved.

By the family that had lost him.

Zen Buddhism said that attachments were the source of trouble, of pain. And for most of Thibault's life that had proven heartbreakingly true. But look at this bond with Flicker—and now with Emile. Being unattached was for chumps.

He turned back to his phone.

See you tonight, kid.

CHAPTER 36
SCAM

ETHAN HAD NEVER BEEN SO GLAD TO BE HOME.

He was sunburned, he was tired, and there was sand *everywhere*. He felt like he'd been flattened by a cement truck. Repeatedly.

Just inside the front door he listened carefully for Mom and Jess.

No sound.

Good. Nobody home. There was just the *slightest* chance Jess hadn't checked his room this morning. Maybe she thought he was sulking in there, playing video games. That was his usual response to fights with her, after all.

He started upstairs toward his room, leaning heavily on the bannister. His hopes rose a little with each step.

If Jess had any clue he'd snuck out for this many hours,

she'd be on him like stink on a skunk already, right?

Which he did *not* need. He was so exhausted he felt like he might throw up. He just needed sleep.

He reached his door and opened it just enough to slip through. Then he closed the door silently and rested his head against it. He'd made it. Thank crap. He was safe. He was ninja stealthy. He was—

"Where the hell have you been, Ethan?"

—busted.

He spun around. There was Jess, glaring at him from the end of his bed.

"Aw, crap." Ethan slumped. "Listen, I'm beat—"

"Not my problem," Jess replied. "We have to talk."

Ethan almost laughed. "Seriously? You've been avoiding me for nearly two days and *now* you want to talk?"

"I've finally figured out what I need to say," she said. "So yeah, this conversation happens now."

The adrenaline of watching Davey get killed had worn off, and Ethan felt like his entire body was in meltdown. He was pretty sure he'd lost an entire layer of skin to the sand in his clothes. There was no way in hell he could talk to Jess now.

Come on, voice. Get Jess off my back so I can get some shut-eye.

Ethan opened his mouth, but the voice said nothing.

Defeated, he sat on his bed, as far from Jess as he could get. Since the night she'd followed him to the Dish, he'd been walking on eggshells, hoping she wouldn't tell Mom about the crooked cops and the payoff and the illegal nightclub and, hell, maybe even his superpowered friends.

And now, on the very day when he just wanted to crawl into a hole and hibernate for the rest of winter, *now* she needed to talk?

"You snuck out," Jess began. "Middle of the damn night, the day before *Christmas Eve.* Was it to meet your superfriends?"

"We're not that super. We got our asses kicked." He sighed. "We all should have stayed in bed."

"You should have stayed *home*," Jess said, sounding hurt. "I only get a few weeks with you guys."

"You weren't even talking to me!"

"And *then* you come back, looking hungover and covered in . . ." She ruffled his hair. "Sand? Did you go to the beach?"

"The desert." Ethan smoothed down his hair and scratched at the sunburn on his neck. "Thought you'd be an expert in desert by now."

"What the hell? How far did you go?"

Ethan leaned against the wall. He was dizzy from dehydration, and his whole body was still trembling from the after-effects of panic. At any moment the exhaustion could make him tip sideways and somersault out his bedroom window. But even that probably wouldn't get Jess off his back.

"You wouldn't understand," he said.

"Don't pull that teenage crap with me."

"Sure, Jess. As soon as you drop the grown-up act," Ethan snapped back. "*You* were a teenager two years ago."

She leaned into his face, like he always hated. "Spill it, kiddo."

"I had to meet my friends, all right? Sometimes there's important stuff we have to do. As a team. We look out for each other and have each other's backs. You know, like in your unit."

Jess snorted. "We drop ordnance on bad guys. What were you doing? Bribing cops?"

"The bribing is not a regular thing."

Except the voice had promised Ang and Murillo fifteen hundred a month. But with Swarm out there killing Zeroes, there was a pretty good chance the Dish was dead anyhow.

"Oh, really," Jess said. "And yet Mom said you knew about some secret Internal Affairs investigation. You mentioned it to those detectives at a hockey game. Since when do you like hockey?"

Ethan tried to come up with something truthful to say. Some way to explain that Internal Affairs was the least of his problems. That crowds of creepy mind-controlled human slave-bots were ripping people to pieces in fountains.

Then it came to him, almost like the voice had said it.

"This is way bigger than that nightclub," he began. "Sort of like when you get back to Afghanistan, and you have to make hard decisions. Like, someone's driving straight at you, and maybe it's a car bomb or maybe it's an innocent family."

She nodded, still suspicious. Probably because he was quoting one of her stories exactly, which was the kind of thing his Zero voice would do. Except that he wasn't using the voice. He was going it alone on this.

"Well, today we had to make exactly that kind of decision. We had to drop everything and drive all night to stop people getting hurt, and we probably saved a bunch of lives. People will go home to their families today because *we* were there."

Jess narrowed her eyes, but Ethan was on a roll.

"And maybe when those people get home, they'll have to ride out all the bullshit judgments their families are waiting to heap on their heads too. But whatever. Me and my team finally did something good!"

"I thought you said you got your asses kicked."

Ethan's rant gave out on him.

"Uh, that too," he admitted. "One guy died."

Jess stared at him. "Crap, Ethan! One of your friends *died*?"

"Not quite." The exhaustion and fear hammered on Ethan, twice as heavy as before. "I mean, he was kind of evil. But he was a guy like us, with powers. He was torn apart by this way more evil guy. It's complicated."

Hell, he hadn't even met Coin—*Davey,* he reminded himself—and Ethan had been up in the control room when Swarm had done most of his work. But he'd glimpsed that fountain afterward. And he'd seen the damage it'd done to the others—Kelsie especially. Like she hadn't been through enough.

Jess said, "And this doesn't have anything to do with those cops?"

Ethan almost laughed. "Totally different ball game."

"Jesus, little bro, what've you gotten yourself into?" Her voice was gentle.

Ethan shook his head. Even if he could explain it, Jess would never understand. A superpowered guy who killed other superpeople was probably one too many supers for her.

The Zeroes themselves had no idea what to do next, not even Nate. They didn't know whether to run and hide, or *create diversions*, whatever that meant. Or stay put, keep separate, and hope Swarm went in another direction. After Ren, hopefully.

He didn't want to talk about it. He didn't even want to *think* about it.

"With power comes responsibility, or something," he mumbled. "Anyhow, go ahead, tell Mom everything. I don't care anymore. So long as I get some pillow time."

He tried to lean back on his bed, but Jess lunged forward and hugged the breath out of him. "Ethan, if you get into any more trouble, I'll kill you."

"Get off me!" he gasped.

"Unless Mom beats me to it." She reached up and ruffled his hair, keeping him trapped in her arms. "And if she calls me one more time about *anything* you're doing wrong, I'll tell her everything. The cops, the payoff, the nightclub, the superposse.

I'll make sure she puts you in solitary confinement for the rest of your life."

"Got it." The words came out as a strained whisper.

"And if you ever need anything, I don't care what, you come to *me*! Not your crazy-ass friends."

"You bet. Now please. Let me breathe."

Jess eased up, but only slightly. "I love you. Idiot."

"Your love is painful," he gasped.

Jess kissed him quickly on the cheek. "I got one more thing I have to say to you, and I don't want you to freak out."

"Perfect intro, Jess."

"That girl you're into? Kelsie, right? You should know something." Jess leaned forward. "She's totally into that Chizara chick."

"Wait. What?"

Jess gave him a final squeeze. "Old-school gaydar like mine doesn't lie, kid bro. Those girls are into each other. Be cool with it."

Ethan felt a stab of pain right through his sternum. "She's into girls?"

Jess gave him a lopsided shrug. "One girl, anyway. Sorry to break it to you."

"It's cool, I'm just . . ." For a moment he wasn't sure *what* he was.

Dead in the water before he even began.

He'd never felt so stupid and so freaking bereft.

"Romance sucks," he said.

"Be bigger than that, little brother," Jess said softly.

"Sure." Ethan nodded, trying to reassure Jess as much as himself. "No, of course. I mean, I guess I'm just . . ."

"Surprised? Disappointed? Heartbroken?" Jess supplied, ever helpful.

"Tired," Ethan said. "Seriously tired."

But when he was less exhausted and less traumatized by the mallpocalypse, he was going to be really upset over Kelsie.

Until then, he didn't want to be awake anymore. He grabbed a pillow and pushed it between his shoulder and the wall, leaning into it.

"Just when I thought my life couldn't get any worse."

"Ethan, are you going to be okay?"

"I'll be great," he said, with more conviction than he felt. "There's always room in my life for extra suckiness."

Jess put an arm around him. "Life is complicated."

"Check," Ethan muttered. "I got *complications* coming out the wazoo."

Jess still looked worried, so he tried to grin like it was all a big joke, but he wasn't feeling it. The grin died on his face.

Kelsie was not into him. Kelsie would never be into him.

"But hey, don't worry about me." He leaned back on his mattress at last, pulling the pillow over his face. "I'll be fine."

"Roger that," Jess replied. She grabbed his ankles and dragged his feet up onto the bed. Then she left quietly.

Ethan rolled until he was facedown with his eyes clamped shut.

Kelsie and Chizara. Chizara and Kelsie.

Sure, Crash was hot, he had to give her that. But she was also a Goody Two-shoes, the most straitlaced person Ethan knew.

Kelsie might be sweet and caring, and she always wanted everything to turn out okay. But she was also an awesome pickpocket, card shark, and car thief. How were the two of them ever going to fit together?

Not my business, he reminded himself.

He was not going to dwell on his misfortune. He was going to be happy for Kelsie, because love was pure and selfless. Love was being happy when someone you loved was happy, and— *aw, hell.*

"Could be worse," he muttered into his mattress.

He racked his brain for a way it could possibly be any worse. Then he rolled to his back and stared at the first stars peeping in through his open curtains.

"At least she's not into Nate," he told himself.

His phone chirped—a text. He groaned and reached out to grab it. Probably more bad news.

The message was from Flicker.

Will you be my boyfriend tonight?

Ethan slowly sat upright. "What the actual fuck?"

CHAPTER 37
FLICKER

"IS HE HERE YET?"

"No, Mom," Flicker said. "But for the tenth time, I'll tell you when he is."

She lifted the tray of cheese from the kitchen table. The smell of gouda and a sharp cheddar rose up, and the little rye biscuits that Lily liked.

"Riley, let me get that."

"Gotten!" Flicker hoisted the platter onto her shoulder. "I've done this before. Like, at many previous parties."

Her mother sighed. "Sorry. It made me nervous then, too. Go forth and be empowered!"

Flicker smiled at the timeworn joke and felt a sudden rush of affection for her mother. Just knowing a Zero killer was out there had turned her family's annoying habits precious.

But as she reached the kitchen door, her mother added, "He's not one of those boyfriends who's always late, is he?"

"Never. Except when he gets arrested."

There was no one else in the kitchen to see her mother's expression, so when no laugh came, Flicker assumed the worst.

"*Kidding*, Mom! He'll be here any minute."

Another sigh. "Well, good. It's just that you and Lily have been talking about him for ages. Your father and I should have met him before now."

Four times, Mom. Four times.

A thought came crashing in—if Swarm came to Cambria, they might never get to know him at all. If Flicker had learned anything from watching someone die, it was that death didn't leave room to fix things in the future.

"Are you okay?" her mother asked.

"Yeah." Flicker's voice came out broken. She turned so Mom couldn't see her face, and pushed out through the swinging kitchen doors, back into the hubbub of the party.

She kept her vision off, steering herself through the chatter by sound. Like every Christmas Eve, there were about thirty people here—mostly relatives, comfortingly familiar. Aunt Melissa was telling her safari stories again, and the usual arguments about politics were keeping her uncles busy.

This was exactly what Flicker needed after the chaos of the last few days. As a bonus, the gathering sounded much too happy to turn into a Zero-eating swarm.

She was about halfway across the living room when one of the cousins popped up beside her.

"Oh, let me get that, Riley!" The tray was lifted from her shoulder.

A flash of anger went through Flicker—God, she was fragile tonight. But she managed not to lash out at Samantha, who never remembered to use *Flicker* instead of *Riley*.

Flicker only smiled sweetly and drifted away. Where *was* he? What if he'd gotten lost on the way?

Now *that* would be typical.

Lily's high heels came clicking over. "What did Mom want?"

"To bug me. Because the boyfriend isn't here yet."

"Ha. If she only knew."

"Hush." Flicker gave her sister a punch. "You *know* this is a last resort, Lily. They keep asking!"

"Yeah, well, if you had a *normal* boyfriend, we wouldn't have to lie to them all the time."

Flicker sighed. It wasn't like she was lying to hide anything horrible. It was just that Mom and Dad only remembered their conversations *about* Thibault, not the boy himself.

It all felt suddenly so trivial, when there was a Zero killer to worry about.

"I don't want a normal boyfriend," she said simply. "I want Thibault."

The name came easily. The thought of losing him had kept him stuck fast in her mind all day.

"Hey, lighten up," Lily said.

Flicker managed a weak smile. She hadn't told Lily anything. It was like, if no one else knew, maybe Swarm didn't exist, maybe Davey's death hadn't happened.

Like this was a perfectly normal Christmas.

The doorbell rang, and Flicker jumped into the eyes just outside on the porch.

Yep. The point of view was at the right height, and the hands pulling back from the doorbell button had those familiar bitten fingernails.

"It's him," she said, already in motion toward the door.

"I hope this works." Lily was close behind.

"Me too," Flicker said softly.

Then, if the worst happened, at least her parents might remember her having been normal for this one night.

CHAPTER 38
SCAM

ETHAN WALKED THROUGH FLICKER'S FRONT DOOR, aware of every gaze on him.

He hoped he looked like a regular guy about to spend Christmas Eve with his girlfriend. He felt like roadkill.

"Thanks for doing this, Ethan," Flicker said quietly.

"Don't mention it."

Being at Flicker's was better than being alone at home. When he'd woken up after a few hours' sleep, he'd found a note saying Jess was out on a last-minute food run, and Mom was probably at work. The house felt empty and creepy. He kept imagining a thousand zombies crashing through the door.

"Hey, *Scam*," Lily said quietly.

He gave her a conspiratorial smile. Flicker didn't hide anything from her twin sister, not even her friends' superpowers.

So Lily had to know that Ethan was perfectly equipped to be a fake boyfriend.

"You remember Ethan, don't you?" Flicker asked, loud enough for other people to hear.

"Oh, yeah. I remember your *boyfriend*," Lily replied. The sarcasm hadn't left her voice.

Flicker blanched at her sister's tone. The voice had to fix this fast.

Get her off my back. But be nice, so she likes me.

"Lily," the voice said gently, "you know I could never get between you and your sister. I'm not smart enough, or funny enough, or sweet enough. I'm just here to help Flicker out. Okay?"

Lily softened a little. "Whatever, Ethan. Just don't do anything rude. Our mom *wants* to like you."

"Moms always like me," the voice said sweetly.

You had to hand it to the voice. It had some stone-cold cojones.

"Okay. Let's put that to the test." Lily turned away, walking toward a group of adults at the far end of the room.

Ethan hated tests.

"Lily's not a big fan of powers," Flicker said.

"These days, I feel where she's coming from."

A woman in waiter's black-and-white carried a tray of mini franks on toothpicks past, and Ethan grabbed a couple. Suddenly he wanted to eat like there was no tomorrow.

Which there might not be. Depending on what Swarm did next.

He looked around the room. Flicker's family sure had a lot of friends. There were at least two dozen people here. Including some very cute girls who were smiling at him.

Ethan smiled back. Smiling felt good.

"Um, those are my cousins," Flicker muttered. "And you're supposed to be my boyfriend."

He blinked a few times. He hated when Flicker got in his eyeballs like that. "I was looking at the decorations!"

He swept a determined gaze along the tinseled walls to prove it. The halls were seriously decked in this place. It was like Martha Stewart had exploded here.

Flicker snorted. "Tell it to my mom. Incoming."

Lily was on her way back, and in her wake was a Hallmark mother, complete with frosted hair and a sweater covered in reindeer and snowflakes. She pushed ahead of her daughter, adroitly stepped around a life-sized Santa, and swooped on Ethan.

"You must be the young man we've been hearing so little about!" The joke sounded like it had been saved up for a while, but her smile seemed genuine. "How do you pronounce your name again? Tee . . ."

Her voice faded into puzzlement.

"Ethan," Flicker said. "And you've already met him. He came to a barbecue two summers ago."

"Of course!" She looked like she didn't remember him at

all. But that was probably because Nate had been at that same barbecue. With Nate around, everybody else was backdrop, even if they didn't have Anonymous powers.

"I was the quiet one," Ethan's voice explained. "You know what it's like, having a crush on the cutest girl at the party."

Ethan felt himself blush. He sounded like a total dork.

The voice was saying, "You have a lovely home, Mrs. Phillips."

After the heartfelt talk with Jess, it was a relief to be back in passenger mode. He let the voice compliment Mrs. Phillips on everything from the decorations to her taste in Wedgwood, whatever that was.

"Well, aren't you polite?" Mrs. Phillips gave Ethan's shoulders a squeeze. "We're sorry your family couldn't come."

"Uh, thanks."

Ethan had never forwarded the invitation. The whole act would've been way too complicated, and he didn't want to use his power in front of Jess.

"My mom had an urgent case to work tonight," the voice said. "You know, trying to get an innocent man out of prison for Christmas Day."

Mrs. Phillips looked impressed.

Ethan was impressed too. That last part might have been kinda dramatic, but at least the voice was sticking close to the truth. His mom working Christmas Eve was about the only tradition his family had.

Of course, she was really working on the Internal Affairs investigation, just in case Ethan needed another thing to go horribly wrong in his life.

"Let me get you a cup of eggnog, young man," Mrs. Phillips said. "And I'll wrap up some cake later to take home to your family."

She disappeared into the crowd.

Ethan was totally going to eat every piece of cake she gave him. Probably before he got home.

"I suppose rum in that eggnog would be too much to ask for," he muttered to Flicker.

"No way. You need to stay sharp," she said. "My family's circling like sharks tonight."

"Seriously? You think *this* is tough?" he asked. "We need to swap families for a week."

Offers of drinks and cake and mini franks on toothpicks were not a thing in Ethan's house, not even at Christmas. The holidays had been pretty nonfestive ever since Dad left. Jess always bought Ethan a shirt from the same store and Mom gave him a hundred bucks for new games. Dad sent a card with a twenty in it most years, but not every year. Not this year.

Ethan was struck with an insane urge to call his father, maybe give him a last chance to act paternal.

Flicker touched his shoulder. "How are things with Jess?"

"We talked. She's not going to tell Mom and she didn't kick my ass."

Ethan was counting that as a win-win, in the scheme of things.

"I wasn't worried," Flicker said. "Seems like she loves you."

Ethan shrugged. "She also said she'd bust all of you if I ever do anything shady again. It's lucky she's shipping out again soon."

"When she does, you've still got the Zeroes," Flicker said. "We're a kind of family too, right?"

Ethan frowned. Flicker was being awfully sentimental tonight. Because he was doing her a favor? Or was it fear of imminent death?

"The kind of family who pretend to be each other's boy-friends?" Okay. That just got weird. He started over: "Anyway, Jess is the least of our worries now."

Someone went past with a tray of sliders, and Ethan lunged for it. But Flicker stepped in closer, cutting him off.

"Put your arm around me," she whispered. "The cousins are watching!"

"Dude, really?" He wasn't sure what was worse, the judg-ment of the cousins or missing his shot at the sliders. They were disappearing fast. "What if Tee's watching?"

"He's not here. He had to . . ." Flicker sighed. "He's going through some stuff."

"Seriously?" Ethan asked. "I think that applies to most of us right now!"

"Okay, sure." She shook her head. "But he's told you about his family, right?"

Ethan hesitated. When they'd been holed up together in Teebo's hotel room last summer, a lot of stuff had come out. Serious stuff.

"Yeah. But not everything stuck in my head, you know?"

"That's the problem, I guess. But the next time you see him, try to remember something, *anything* more than the usual, okay? Just to make him feel better."

"Whoa. Okay." Ethan nervously filed that under Things Not to Forget.

"Now put your arm around me. We look like a couple of middle schoolers standing here."

"Okay." Ethan nervously put his arm around Flicker's shoulders.

It was too bad the voice couldn't control his whole body. Ethan didn't feel very convincing, and the cutest of the cousins seemed like she was trying not to laugh.

Flicker dragged his hand tighter around her shoulders, lacing her fingers between his. Ethan's whole wrist went rigid.

"Um, are you *sure* Tee's not here?" Ethan muttered.

"I told you, family stuff," Flicker said tightly.

Ethan continued to scan the room. "Can you send him a text and make sure?"

"You're pathetic." Flicker pulled out her phone. "But I should check in with him. Message Nothing."

The phone purred in response and Flicker started texting with one thumb. It was pretty impressive. A lot of people could text without looking, but Flicker took that to a new level.

Ethan's phone fizzed in his pocket, and for a second he thought Flicker's voice-recognition app was taking the fake-boyfriend thing too seriously.

He checked the screen. "Huh. Why would Sonia Sonic wish me a happy festive season? Did you give her my number? I thought she hated me."

"Be nice to her, Ethan," Flicker muttered as she texted. "We still need her on our side."

Another message from Sonia appeared. Seemed like her wrist was on the mend. Which was just more bad news Ethan didn't need.

Coffee sometime? she texted.

Ethan texted back, *I don't do coffee. Makes me hyper.*

Sonia texted back, *MORE hyper, I think you mean. LOL!*

Ethan rolled his eyes and switched his phone to silent. If Sonia was looking for a new story about the Zeroes, he wasn't going to be the one to hand it to her. Not this time.

"Great, the cousins are coming over," Flicker said grimly. "You up to this?"

Ethan steadfastly refused to look in the direction of the group of girls headed their way. He locked what he hoped was an adoring gaze onto Flicker's face.

"My voice is up to anything," he said. "I'm not even here."

"You know, you have a serious dissociative disorder, Scam," Flicker replied.

"I don't even understand what that is," Ethan said, feeling in his pocket for a lozenge.

His throat was already hitting the high burn mark as the cousins descended on them.

CHAPTER 39
ANONYMOUS

THIBAULT'S FAMILY GATHERING WAS IN FULL SWING.
Three generations, from sugar-rushing kids to grandparents,
were piled into the living room to open gifts. Attention lines
flashed everywhere.

None came to rest on Thibault, of course. No different
from his brother's birthday parties. He shouldn't have let
Flicker talk him into coming. Things were bad enough without
reminding himself what he'd already lost.

Thibault's phone chirruped in his pocket. Next to him
Uncle Claude fumbled, pulled out his own. He stared at the
blank screen, then smiled at Thibault, realizing the confusion.
A moment later his eyes slipped away.

Uncle Claude never remembered Thibault, not even for a
second. But at least he'd managed that smile.

The text was from Flicker: *Scam isn't a very good boyfriend. Miss you.*

Thibault felt a glow of pleasure. She *missed* him, after fifteen hours in the car together. After the horror they'd seen this morning.

Another text bubbled up: *Ethan thinks you're here. He's scared you're watching us. :D*

That made Thibault snort. He texted back: *Would LOVE to check out his boyfriend act. But it's time for presents—the little ones are going nuts.*

She replied: *Barbarians! When you open a present on Xmas eve, an elf dies. xo*

It took Thibault real effort to sign off. To pocket the phone and bring himself back to the present, where he was almost invisible.

His littlest brother, Emile, sat by the tree, deciding what to open next.

"You're on number two," Dad said ominously. "No pressure!"

Emile groaned. By family tradition, the little kids were allowed to open three presents on Christmas Eve. The rest had to wait till tomorrow.

After long consideration, Emile reached for a box wrapped in bright red with gold ribbon, and Thibault smiled again. He used the same wrapping paper every birthday.

Emile turned the tag over. "See, Mom, I told you there was a Thibault-present."

A hesitant little shock went through the room, and his parents looked at each other in confusion. But as Emile began tearing the paper, Dad's gaze slid back to his eggnog. Mom looked around the room, as if trying to spot Thibault in the crowd. But her eyes slid off him, her face growing anxious and uncertain.

Maybe he was just torturing them all, being here.

But even so, watching his little brother open the present was worth it.

"Mini geodes!" Emile announced. "Coo-ool!"

"I noticed you didn't have any in your collection," Thibault said, squatting beside his little brother and touching his shoulder. The cousins were focused on their own presents, and the glistening branches of the Christmas tree provided a little shelter. For a moment it was like being alone.

"I don't!" Emile said happily. "These are awesome!"

The bond between them sparkled in the air, thin but clear. He'd had this with both his brothers once; now Thibault only got this connection with Emile.

"I mean, you can't really tell anything from the outside," Emile went on. "It's like a box of chocolates—except you open them with a diamond saw!"

Thibault laughed. The clerk at the lapidary store had made the same joke. Emile must spend a *lot* of time there.

Emile took one of the stones out of the box and weighed it in his hand. "You know how geodes are formed, right?"

"No idea," Thibault lied. "How?"

That was enough to launch five minutes of rock-nerd chatter. Emile's attention came and went—drifting from Thibault to the cousins' presents, to the geodes, and back to his lecture—but the stream of words didn't halt until the lure of another gift to open drew Emile away.

Every now and then Mom, making sure everyone was happy, would watch Emile chattering for a little while. But she never once lifted her gaze from her youngest son to her eldest.

The first Christmas after leaving home had been the worst.

Thibault had stayed away completely that year, still angry at everyone for forgetting him—especially Grand-mère. When she'd moved in after her stroke, her presence had upped the Curve in the household, pushing him out of everyone's minds. Thirteen-year-old Thibault had loved Grand-mère, but that had only made her erasure of him harder to bear.

Sitting here again, he knew he'd been right to stay away. Being ignored at home hurt a lot worse than sitting alone in a hotel room on Christmas Eve, or wandering the empty streets of Cambria.

Had it been the same for that other Anonymous, the one in Portland? Had that poor guy been crowded out of home too?

Had his family even *noticed* that he'd died? If Zero powers still worked after death, a Stalker's body could be found over and over, with no one remembering it long enough to call the cops.

Maybe John Doe made more sense as a code name than Stalker, or Anonymous.

Do you prefer "Forgettable"? He remembered Davey's contemptuous gaze in the rearview. *Homegrown ninja?*

Then suddenly Davey's handcuffed arm was in his mind, the rest of him torn away, the crowd ravening around him, Ren screaming—

No. Running it over in his mind again and again was not the Middle Way.

He breathed deeply of the piney smell, drank in the sight of his blissfully unaware family. It was hard to believe in a Zeroes killer here.

"Oh man, really? For true?" Emile's shouting pulled Thibault the rest of the way back. "A *phone*? Are you *serious*? I love you guys!"

Emile flung himself on Mom and Dad, hugged them, disentangled himself to admire the phone again. "See, Grandmère?"

"How grown-up you are!" she laughed.

Emile's attention whipped around for someone else to share his joy with. It landed on Auguste. "Hardly *anyone* at school has a phone!"

"I hope you guys've porn-blocked that thing," Auguste said with a smirk.

Mom clicked her tongue, and Emile tore his connection off Auguste.

"Thibault, did you see? I got a phone!"

That soft shock went around the room again. Thibault ignored it, more grateful than he could say for this jab of attention.

"Yeah, cool! Welcome to the twenty-first century!"

"Ah, Thibault," murmured Grand-mère. "Of course. There you are."

Again, his mother's attention was the last to drift from him, her face turning anxious again. Emile sat next to Thibault, but as he started the phone's setup procedure, his attention shrank to a short glowing leash between him and the tiny machine.

Prompted by the sight, Auguste started communing with *his* phone, taking pictures of his gifts to send to friends. Grand-mère sat back, smiling gently, her attention a soft net spread so broadly that Thibault claimed some of it. Mom disappeared into the kitchen, muttering about hot chocolate, the troubled expression still on her face.

"Ha!" said Emile as his phone chimed to life.

Thibault bent down to him. "Can I do something?"

"Sure." Emile handed it over.

He watched as Thibault opened the address book, created a new contact—*Thibault (brother)*—and entered his number.

"Like I know any other Thibaults," Emile scoffed.

"You never know, bro. There are a lot of us around."

He chose his moment to join Mom in the kitchen.

She'd mixed all the chopped-up chocolate into the milk,

and there was only the whisking to do. By some miracle Grand-mère wasn't with her, and the aunts were out on the patio, smoking in the cold.

"*Joyeux Noël*, Mom," he said in the doorway.

She looked up, the whisk pausing in the pot.

Her smile, nervous at first, firmed up. She straightened and put her arms out to him. "*Joyeux Noël*, Thibault!"

He held the hug as long as he could. What if it was the last one he ever got from her?

"You've grown so tall!" she exclaimed as they drew apart. Then she touched her mouth, embarrassed. "But why should I be so surprised . . . to see my own son?"

He tried to laugh. "You never remember I'm coming, Mom. That's just how it is with me."

"But none of us got you . . . I don't know if there's anything for you under the tree!"

He shrugged. "Hey, where I'm living, stuff's just a nuisance."

"Where's that again?" she said, hands to her cheeks.

"In the Heights. A really nice place. I'll show you some pictures later, on my phone." But he wouldn't be there much longer.

Keep separate. Be a moving target, Nate had said, his impassive voice as chilling as his words.

The posse of aunts gathered at the back door—soon they'd crowd in here and he'd fall off Mom's radar. "Want me to keep whisking that for you?"

263

"Why, thank you, sweetie." Uncertainly she watched him stirring, glancing at his face with that touch of fear, that touch of shame, that always broke his heart.

Finally she turned to the mugs lined up on the counter, counted them. "Oh, you'll be wanting some chocolate too, won't you?"

"Yes, please!"

And she took down another mug and lined it up with the others, like it was nothing special at all.

CHAPTER 40
MOB

KELSIE HAD NEVER SPENT CHRISTMAS WITHOUT HER dad before.

He was the heart and soul of high spirits. He'd gather all their friends in whatever rental he and Kelsie could afford that year—not for a meal, because food wasn't a big deal for the Laszlos. But there'd be drinks and music and feats of crazy bravery with illegal fireworks. And Kelsie got to stay up all night, riding wave after wave of good cheer.

But all that felt like a long, long time ago. She'd been dreading this first Christmas alone. And since the mall, she could feel the dark chain that connected her to Swarm like an anchor, dragging her down.

Yesterday afternoon, while they were wiping down the stolen car, Chizara had rescued her with a quiet, hesitant invitation.

And now Kelsie was sitting at the Okeke family dining table, trying not to look shell-shocked while Chizara's mom offered her more jollof rice and curry and bread. She'd never seen so much food in one place.

"This is really good, Mrs. Okeke," she said.

"Call me Niyi," Chizara's mom said.

"It's delicious, Niyi," Kelsie said, and meant it. She couldn't believe Chizara got to eat like this all the time.

"Oh, honey, *you* can come to dinner anytime!" Niyi chuckled.

Beside her, Chizara rolled her eyes, but she looked almost as pleased as her mom.

Chizara's mom was sweet and sharp, with a broad smile. And she knew about Chizara's power. Exactly the way Kelsie figured a good mom should just *know* things without her having to explain them like she'd always had to with Dad. Even then, Dad had never really understood.

She liked the rest of Chizara's family too—her father, Sani, and her brothers, Ikem and Obinna. With Kelsie that made six people, enough for the Curve, so she'd taken hold of the feedback loop as soon as she'd stepped into their house. She'd grabbed Niyi's doubt about *one of Chizara's superpowered friends* and smoothed it out. Then she'd tugged on Ikem's Christmas excitement, stretching it like taffy until it wrapped around all of them.

When Kelsie had found a gift under the tree with her name on it, her gratitude had sent the energy in the room spiraling higher. She'd ripped off the bright green paper to find a babydoll sweater inside—embroidered red cherries on a snowy white background. She'd put it on at once.

It was amazing how different Chizara's life was outside the Zeroes. Here there was no hint of Nate's bombastic plans or Ethan's lies. No petty crime or spying through anyone else's eyes. Just nice, happy people sharing a meal.

During dessert Niyi leaned in close. "I was sorry to hear about your father, sweetheart."

It was the first time anyone had brought it up, and Kelsie felt her grief spike hard into the feedback loop. Ikem looked up, confused, and Sani's face rumpled with shared sorrow.

Under the table Chizara's knee bumped Kelsie's.

"Sorry," Kelsie mumbled.

She swallowed her own pain, groping for the happiness of a moment before. The contentment of the Okeke family made it easy to find. Their solidity was a refuge where she could think about bad stuff without bursting into tears. Davey, killed in that fountain. Swarm's power inside her. The way Nate seemed helpless in the face of this new enemy.

She tried to remember something happy. The bike Dad had gotten her one Christmas.

Though, actually, Dad had stolen the bike. Kelsie had ended up riding right past the house he'd lifted it from, and she'd had to face off with a kid twice her size. She was more careful with the skateboard he gave her the next year.

But another year he'd taken her to see the Christmas pageant on ice. For once he'd paid actual money instead of sneaking in, so she'd been able to sit up front. It had been a window onto a strange, other world. One where everyone was beaming with joy, and the audience sang along with the music, their mood as choreographed as the skaters' moves. Where the skilled, graceful, glittering cast was in charge of keeping everyone happy.

Kelsie wished she had even a tiny piece of that kind of control. Skating across the bad emotions. Only ever feeling the good stuff and scattering it out into a delighted world.

After lunch, Ikem and Obinna cleared the table while their parents made phone calls to faraway relatives. That left Chizara and Kelsie in the living room, staring at a tree with lights that shimmered and winked.

"Your family's awesome," Kelsie said.

"Nah. They're pretty normal."

"Exactly." Kelsie felt anything but normal, most of the time. "Is it really okay that I'm here?"

"Are you kidding?" Chizara said. "You're the best thing about this Christmas."

Kelsie nearly burst out laughing. She felt her delight bloom across the family, who were still connected, even spread across the house.

"I mean it," Chizara said shyly. "Mom's always giving me death stares when I mention my friends—a bunch of spoiled white kids with *weird powers*. But then you show up, and she's all smiles."

"I get it," Kelsie said with mock seriousness. "You miss the death stares."

"If you'd *seen* the death stares, you wouldn't joke." Chizara lowered her voice. "It's not fair, though. You use your power to make everyone happy, and you're her long-lost daughter. When I use mine, I'm a moral failure."

Kelsie was stung. "It's not like I'm *making* anybody feel anything. I'm just using what's already here. And imagine if your family wasn't here, Zara. What we'd be feeling now . . ."

Kelsie let the sentence taper off. They'd be feeling Davey die, again and again. And she would be feeling Swarm showing her the dark door in her own soul.

"That's sort of my point," Chizara said. "You amplify happiness. I specialize in property damage! Nate says *crash this fountain* or *fry this cop car*, and I do it. And half of the time, it's to help *Ethan*."

"He'd do the same for you. Any of the Zeroes would."

"We can't keep committing *felonies* for our messed-up friends!" Chizara whispered. "Do you remember what happened last summer? Officer Bright's still in rehab, for a start."

Kelsie was quiet. Maybe Chizara had forgotten, but her dad was one of the prisoners that had escaped that day— prisoners the Zeroes had released. And if he'd stayed in jail, he might still be alive.

She caught hold of her grief before it could flood the family.

"I almost wish Ethan's sister *would* blab to their mom," Chizara went on, lost in her own emotions. "If the cops shut the Dish down, we could all go back to our real lives."

"You can't be serious." Kelsie was horrified. "On top of everything else, you want to lose the Dish?"

"We experiment with people there," Chizara said. "How is that right?"

Kelsie shook her head. She tried to hold on to the cheerfulness of earlier.

"It's not experimenting. It's sharing what we have."

"My mom thinks what we have is evil—bad juju. What if she's right? Think of all those people at the mall. From what I've seen, they *remember* what they did."

Kelsie couldn't breathe. She could remember it all too—every moment of Swarm's dark greed. She hadn't stopped feeling it, ever since the mob had turned on Davey in the mall.

Her anxiety leaked across the house, stilling the laughter from Ikem and Obinna in the kitchen, probably ruining an expensive, precious phone call back to Nigeria. And every minute she didn't rally and bring the happy back, she was only proving Chizara's mother right. Powers were bad. Swarm was bad. And she was another Swarm waiting to happen.

She looked up to find Chizara staring at her.

"The Dish makes people happy," Kelsie said quietly. "And it's my home."

"I know." Chizara took her hand. "In some ways it's mine, too."

That was it, really. The Dish wasn't just a place to entertain crowds, or sleep, or dance. For the first time in Kelsie's life, she had a place that wouldn't suddenly disappear because of a missed rent payment, or one too many noise complaints, or a landlord angry about shady visitors.

Of course, with the Dish on the radar of dirty cops, and Swarm out there looking for other Zeroes to kill, it was just as fragile as anyplace she'd ever lived with Dad.

"It's the first place I've ever been without pain," Chizara said. "But look where we're all going. Nate says the Dish is training, but training for what? You've *seen* what powers can do."

"We're *training* to stand up to whoever messes up our lives!" Kelsie squeezed Chizara's hand, hard. "That's worth it, right?"

Certainty surged through the house, and a whoop came from Obinna in the kitchen. But Chizara didn't look convinced.

Kelsie almost smiled. Chizara's skepticism was familiar, and welcome. Every time Nate made some big speech, you could rely on her to point out whatever was sketchy about the plan.

Chizara shrugged. "Maybe it is."

Kelsie softened. "I've never had anyone I could talk to before, not about my power. I never even *believed* in it till now, and I'm still trying to figure it out. You're so lucky that you can talk to your family."

Chizara laughed. "We don't really *talk* about it. It's more like going to confession. Mom has this truth serum she can deliver through her eyes."

Kelsie got that. There was something sharp and knowing in Niyi's gaze that she didn't want to get on the wrong side of.

"Maybe that's a good thing to have in your life," Kelsie said. "A daily dose of truth serum. No one's ever tried to keep me honest."

"That doesn't sound that hard, Kels. You're a good person."

"Are you applying for the job?" Kelsie asked boldly.

Chizara looked surprised. "Sure. I mean . . . Yeah. I am."

"Good." Kelsie leaned in toward Chizara. In turn Chizara wrapped an arm awkwardly around Kelsie's shoulders.

In that instant the two of them made their own space, separate from the rest of the family. There was no Curve, but Kelsie felt something enfold them, protective and strong.

She relaxed into the embrace. She rested her face against Zara's cheek and breathed her in carefully, afraid to disrupt the moment.

Then somebody's pocket started buzzing.

"Seriously?" Kelsie muttered. "Your phone or mine?"

They listened for the next ring.

"Both." Chizara sighed. "Which means Glorious Leader."

They disentangled from each other reluctantly. Then there

was a moment of self-conscious quiet as they stared at their screens.

Sonia just posted. Huge dump of photos of the Dish.

"What the hell?" Chizara said. "But I bricked her phone!"

The next three texts came fast:

Looks like they were taken by Davey and Ren.

They show all of our faces.

Guess she's got her revenge.

"Whoa," Chizara said. "And I just spent two days feeling sorry for her."

Kelsie couldn't answer. Her fear was spreading out across the house, only a little softened by the happy family.

Chizara felt it, looked up at her. "Are you okay?"

Kelsie tried to swallow. "He'll be coming to Cambria now. Not just to get random Zeroes. He'll know *I'm* here."

She tried to reel it back, the way she felt. Anything to protect this house, this family. They were so good, and she had the power to turn good people into something bad.

They didn't deserve this.

"You can't stay at the Dish," Chizara said. "I'll help you pack."

CHAPTER 41
CRASH

CHIZARA STOOD IN THE DOORWAY OF KELSIE'S room above the Dish, resisting the urge to head back downstairs. The second floor had no Faraday cage, and Kelsie's phone and wireless speakers were needling her bones. A smoke detector in the hallway nagged at her like a whining mosquito.

But this had to feel worse for Kelsie. She was losing her home.

Chizara tried to lighten the mood. "What to wear, when running for your life?"

Kelsie gave a halfhearted snort. She sat on her bed, a black duffel bag unzipped at her feet. She stared dully at her clothes spread out on the floor, along with all sorts of odd treasures from her past—snow globes, plastic figurines, a mini sticker book. How many had her dad given her?

"I can't leave tonight." Kelsie fell backward onto the *Disney on Ice* bedspread. "I'm too jumpy. If I show up like this, Ling will know something's wrong."

"I'm pretty nervous too." Chizara crossed to the window, looked down into the empty alleyway. The city signals massed against her forehead through the cold, rain-spattered glass, a blurry headache. "At least Swarm doesn't know where I *live*. You can come stay with us, you know."

"I can't. We have to stay separate." Kelsie stood up and came to the window, staring down into the lengthening shadows of the alleyway. "How long before he gets here?"

"Hard to say." Chizara tried to sound cool and offhand, like Nate before he'd lost it. "I mean, how famous is Sonia Sonic, really?"

"Famous enough," Kelsie said, and threw herself back down on the bed. "He found Davey and Ren."

"It took us seven hours to drive to that mall," Chizara said. "And he's probably still chasing Glitch."

"He doesn't care about her anymore." A shiver went through Kelsie. "He wants *me*; I felt it. Because Ren was right—I'm like him."

The winter evening darkened another notch. Chizara turned from the window and propped her butt on the sill, taking the haze of electronic pain in her back.

"No, you're not," she said. "You know that."

"All I know is that I love this place." Kelsie looked like a kid lying there, one grubby sneaker crossed over the other. "If I could stay just one more night . . ."

"So stay," Chizara said. "I'll stay with you."

Kelsie lifted her head, her green eyes filling with hope—for a moment. "But what about everyone splitting up?"

Chizara shrugged. "I can't go back tonight. My mom will ask why you had to leave all of a sudden. One death stare and I'd spill the beans."

"Will your mom and dad be okay with that?" Kelsie said. "It *is* Christmas night."

"Mom knows you're upset. I'll tell her I'm staying at your place." Chizara managed a smile. "I may not have mentioned you live above a nightclub."

"Really?" Kelsie hitched up onto her elbows. "That'd be great. I have snacks."

Chizara laughed. "You're still hungry after that lunch? My mom would be scandalized. But what about . . . your house-mate?"

"Anon!" Kelsie said. "Yeah, he left yesterday, right after we got back. He's at Flicker's, I think."

They frowned at each other.

"Let's check," Chizara said.

They went down the hall together, to a door with a hand-written sign.

Anon Exists Here
aka Thibault ("Teebo")
It is polite to knock.

Kelsie banged on the door. "Thibault? You there?"

Silence, except for a last few drops of rain draining from the gutters, and the faint nagging of electronics behind the door. It was kind of creepy, having the whole building empty around them. How could Kelsie stand it, living in such a huge place with only one housemate, who she couldn't remember half the time?

Of course, she wouldn't be living here anymore, would she?

Chizara tried the door. "Locked."

"So?" Kelsie pulled a slender piece of metal from her pocket. She knelt and inserted one end of it into the lock.

"Um, really?" Chizara asked. "Do you *always* carry that?"

"You are *so* straight-edge sometimes," Kelsie murmured, probing delicately in the lock. "And you need a bed."

With a click the door swung open. Even with the lights off, the small dark room looked tidy and ordered. The futon was neatly made, and the books on their crowded shelves were organized by height and color.

"Wow," Kelsie said, switching on the light. "What a neat freak."

"You think?" Anon's room was no neater than Chizara's

own. His airspace was a mess, though. A wifi router and a bunch of other gadgets all pinged at her.

She rubbed her arms. "Think he'd mind if we moved his futon downstairs?"

"Like, you want to sleep in the actual Dish?"

"Yeah, down in the Faraday cage. It's much quieter."

"Sure, awesome." Kelsie tossed Anon's pillow and quilt into the middle of his futon and grabbed hold of one corner. "Would it be weird if we took *my* mattress down there too?"

"Like a slumber party? Hey, it's your last night here. Maybe my last time too." Her throat grew tight as she said the words. "Might as well have fun."

They hauled the futon, thumping down the stairs, then went and got Kelsie's mattress. They arranged it all in the center of the dance floor, surrounded by glorious Faraday cage silence.

"Now go outside and call your mom," Kelsie said, plumping one of her pillows. "She's a nice lady. Don't make her worry! I'll get dinner together."

The streetlights were just coming on as Chizara stepped outside. The street was Christmas-night empty, but Cambria's networks filled the cold air, a storm of insects nipping at her face and arms. She longed to get back inside to the warmth and silence.

Mom was okay with the late notice—of course, she had a fresh houseful of dinner guests to tend to.

"But what about pajamas? Toothbrush?"

"Kelsie's got everything I need," Chizara said. Maybe Anon-a.k.a.-Teebo had an unopened toothbrush in some alphabetized drawer of spare toiletries.

"All right. Call us in the morning if you need a ride home."

"Love you, Mom!" she said as brightly as she could manage.

She powered the phone down and went back inside, shutting the insect storm out of the Dish, locking the door, and pulling the blinds down over glass and mesh.

A few colored spots were wandering around the dance floor.

"Hey!" she called. "Lights are *my* job!"

Kelsie was emptying corn chips into a bowl on the bar. "I was going to put on music, but I want to be able to hear."

"Couldn't you *feel* Swarm coming?"

"Of course. What I meant was, hear you talk." She'd turned off her phone too, leaving the Dish in a state of perfect calm. "It's hardly ever just you and me."

They sat at the bar and crunched into the corn chips, opening jars of salsa and guacamole, washing it all down with beer. Dinner Kelsie-style was just fine with Chizara right now.

"So back at your house," Kelsie said into the silence, "you said something about the mall? About all those people, after Swarm let them go."

Chizara shivered. "I couldn't stop reading about them yesterday—I gave myself such a headache. They remember everything they did. And not only are they traumatized, but they'll remember it every Christmas from now on, you know?"

Kelsie took a drink of her beer. "Yeah. I'm not exactly looking forward to July fourth next year."

"At least none of them will get charged with murder. Everyone's saying it was terrorism, like some kind of gas that makes you violent."

Kelsie's hand was cool on Chizara's sunburned arm. "We're not in that world anymore."

Chizara blinked at her.

"The world where cops and courts decide things," Kelsie said. "With Swarm around, you have to get justice in other ways."

She let go, and crunched another corn chip. The room was big and quiet around them, the spots of light swinging slowly around the walls.

"Thanks for staying," Kelsie said. "I wouldn't have been brave enough to be here on my own."

Chizara attempted a smile, glad to move on from the mall talk. "As if I'd leave you here alone."

"Yeah, but it's nice of you to trust me. After what Ren said . . ."

"About you being a baby Swarm?" Chizara laughed, shaking her head. "She doesn't know anything about you!"

Kelsie scooped up guacamole on a chip, not smiling.

"She just likes making people feel bad," Chizara said. "I mean, her whole superpower is messing with people's heads. She wants you confused about who you are. And a *baby* Swarm? That's not even a thing!"

"But I could feel it." Kelsie looked away. "When they were

killing that guy. I could feel how . . . how *great* it was for him, how satisfying, you know?"

Chizara swayed back on the bar stool.

Kelsie's gaze was far away. "I remember at school, when the mean girls or the jocks would pile on someone. I never felt sorry for the kid in the middle. My power always put me inside the *gang*. I got off on the group vibe. The part of them that wanted blood."

The word hung in the air between them, sprayed and smeared with memories of Davey's death.

"But you like *happy* crowds," Chizara insisted. "That's our specialty here at the Dish."

Reaching toward the dance floor, she sent a pulse of her power through the lighting desk. The rainbow lights spun faster, and the mirror ball began to revolve, covering the walls with sliding white specks of light.

Kelsie glumly watched them.

"That's why people come here," Chizara said. "For *you*. You pick them up, sweep them into the dance."

Kelsie shook her head. "So what happens when my power turns inside out? Yours did. You went from breaking things to fixing them. What if I go the other way?"

Chizara picked up Kelsie's hand from on top of the bar, gazing at her light-stroked face. "When I turned my power around, it was *my will*. I wanted to make up for crashing stuff and hurting people. I wanted to be *good*, Kelsie."

"Sure, but all I wanted yesterday was to go with that crowd, not to care what was right or wrong. I wanted to *take* that life, and—"

"Stop!" Chizara covered Kelsie's mouth with her hand. "No you didn't. Don't psych yourself out. The killer, he made you *think* you wanted that."

Kelsie pulled away, her eyes welling up with tears.

"He swarmed you, is all." Chizara slid off her bar stool and put her arms around Kelsie. "It'll be okay. You're a good person."

"You think?" Kelsie's voice was muffled in her hands. "Because my father wasn't. My mom wasn't. I don't *know* what I am."

"None of us knows who we are." Chizara held Kelsie close, her face in the blond curls. "That's how these powers work— they make your life a mess. But that doesn't mean you're going to turn into a monster."

Chizara gently rocked her, fighting off flashbacks: Davey's last bellow of fear, red spilling from the fountain, the bloodied faces at the center of the crowd.

"But it felt so good. So right," Kelsie said softly into Chizara's shoulder. "Maybe that's what every mob secretly wants to be—something cruel. Something deadly."

"Listen to me!" Chizara lifted Kelsie's head, her hands slipping among the curls. "Maybe crowds don't choose what they are, but *people* do. I trust you, enough to stay here with you even when you're talking scary shit!"

Finally Kelsie was looking at her. "Really?"

"Really. You have my trust."

"I think you're crazy, but thanks." Kelsie's hand rose to

the back of Chizara's hair. Her tear-blurred eyes glanced down at Chizara's mouth before she pressed her own lips, warm and salty, to it.

Every muscle in Chizara's body stiffened—electrified, all of it. But her lips stayed soft, surprised, curious.

Is this allowed? the rest of her body exclaimed, and her throat wanted to cry it out.

But Kelsie seemed so certain, like she'd done this before. Her eyes were confidently closed, her free hand reaching up to stroke the back of Chizara's neck.

Those fingertips sent goose bumps all over Chizara's scalp, then down her spine and washing all over her body. And Kelsie felt so perfect, right here, her slim body pressing close, her strong, thin legs wrapping around Chizara's, her soft tongue calling up Chizara's to join in its swirling game.

It didn't feel wrong. It felt exactly right for this moment, after these awful days they'd been through. The room was full of shadows, from the past and from the future. But somehow they'd found their way to this safe place, this Faraday cage, and within it to this bright and beautiful moment, tinged with tears, heightened by terror.

Kelsie pulled away a moment, touched Chizara's cheek.

"Zara," she whispered. And kissed her again.

Chizara let her eyes sink closed and gave herself over to the spinning light show that was being kissed by Kelsie, and then was kissing Kelsie back.

CHAPTER 42
MOB

KELSIE WOKE UP IN THE DARK.

She was wrapped in Chizara's arms, their legs entwined. Her head was nestled against Chizara's neck, breathing in the scent of her skin.

She'd never felt so protected, so safe. Not without the insulation of a crowd. Every time Kelsie had been in this spot before, waking up in bed with another person, there had been that ache to flee, to get back to the party, the dance, the throng. But this felt like a whole world.

Maybe it was because she and Chizara had worked crowds together, here on this very dance floor. That was what it had felt like last night—lights and music.

Chizara was still asleep, so Kelsie dozed, dreaming of summer. Beach parties and barbecues, sunlight and warmth.

Around them the Dish was restless, the building too old to stay quiet. The roof timbers creaked, and somewhere a crack in a window frame let in a low whistle of breeze. Like the nightclub was breathing.

But then Kelsie felt something else stirring in the distance, outside in the darkness. It felt like the rumble of a crowd that hadn't pulled together yet. All shuffling and unfocused noise, like an orchestra tuning up. Then it gathered into one voice, and her sleep-fogged brain recognized it at once.

Swarm.

She startled awake. For a blissful moment she thought it was just a nightmare. But even after she'd blinked away sleep, the crowd was still there.

Swarm hadn't kept going after Ren, like they'd hoped. He'd read Sonia Sonic's post and rounded on Cambria like it was a five-course meal.

And now he was waiting for her.

She slid carefully from Chizara's embrace, off the mattress and onto the chilly floor. She hesitated, watching Chizara settle with a sigh into the mattress, but there was no way she could take another Zero anywhere near Swarm. He wasn't as ravenous as he'd been in the mall, but hungry curiosity remained. As if every unfamiliar power was a new flavor for him to try.

In the dark Kelsie groped for her clothes. She carried them to the door, alert to the sound of her own soft footfalls, dressed silently, and left without going upstairs for a jacket. Outside in the icy December air, she followed the twanging, discordant trail of Swarm's dark, strange thoughts.

She shivered as she walked. It wasn't just the cold—the Heights felt abandoned. Everyone was fast asleep, hibernating in their beds after a long Christmas Day. Chizara's warmth already felt a thousand miles behind her.

She passed the used-car lot and empty warehouses. Then downhill, along a mix of tiny restaurants and coffee shops, all closed. Somewhere beyond the quiet of the streets, traffic pulsed from the distant highway.

She'd known he'd come for her. Ever since that dark awakening in the mall, where her power had found and fitted into his.

Kelsie came upon him standing in the pool of light from a convenience store's security floods. The store was closed and the metal gate was padlocked. Swarm was alone.

It didn't make sense. The whole way here, she'd felt him as a crowd. Even now there was something *big* about him, something legion. Like there was a brawl inside him, a bunch of people struggling to escape.

From the outside he wasn't anything impressive. Striped blazer, white socks, a carry-on suitcase tilted behind him. Close up she could see that his hair was jagged and unkempt, like he'd cut it himself in a rest-stop bathroom. In one hand he held an oversized phone. The blue of its screen lit his face unevenly. Even as she approached, he kept glancing at it every few seconds.

"You're the first one I've met with a power like mine," he said.

His words were hesitant, like he wasn't used to making conversation.

"I'm not like you at all." Kelsie crossed her arms against the cold. "You're Swarm, right? That's what Davey and Ren called you."

He shrugged. "Just an old screen name. I'm Quinton, actually. And you?"

Kelsie ignored the question. No way would she tell this guy anything about her.

But she felt his power reaching out, like a crowd trying to draw her in. She could sense the strange hum of his emotions. Even with only two of them on an empty street, the Curve seemed to take hold. As if his personality had splintered into a dozen identities, all wrapped up in one worn striped blazer.

She shrank back, reeling in her power until it was safe inside her.

"How could you do that to Davey?" she asked.

He grinned. "It was a team effort. It wasn't just me."

Kelsie felt a tremor go through the air on the word *me*. She could feel the shape of his personal crowd around her. She could hear it in the muffled cries his power sent out as it sought to connect with hers.

"Did you kill Ren, too?" she asked.

"She's not a priority anymore," he said. "What I hated was their lovey-dovey bullshit. Their whiny, clinging love. Always parading it around like it was something special."

"Wait," Kelsie held up a hand. "You hated them because they *loved each other*?"

"Love is vanity," Swarm said. He held his phone high and addressed it, like he was videoing himself. "A selfish parade that people can only join in pairs. Love is showing off the fact you're screwing. And they were doing it to piss me off!"

"It wasn't about you." Kelsie thought about Chizara, asleep in the Dish, and her anger redoubled. "How somebody loves, it has nothing to do with you!"

"Then why be so public about it? You know why they crashed that stupid celebrity wedding, right? A giant *fuck you*, aimed right at me!"

"You're mad because they weren't afraid of you," Kelsie said.

"They *were* afraid," he said, and raised his phone to speak into it again. "But fear is healthy, good and right. It's one of the most powerful engines for moving a crowd. But it's only a means to an end. Love is a blockage in that system."

"What does that even mean?" Kelsie shouted.

"Have you ever tried to work with a crowd that's all about love and peace?" Swarm still addressed his phone. "It's like hammering a nail with wet cardboard. And two people in love? Nothing divides a group faster than couples."

Kelsie didn't answer at first. In a weird way she knew what he meant. She'd watched dance parties splinter as people paired off, group friendships fracture because of a wayward crush. Her friend Fig's thrashcore band had been messily cut in half by an affair between drummer and singer.

"That's part of life," she said uncertainly. "It's not anyone's fault."

"You've swallowed too much of the Kool-Aid," Quinton said with a sneer. "You probably think you're going to find true love. But you know what? It's not for the likes of you and me."

A hard knot rose in Kelsie's throat. Yesterday she might have believed him. Being part of a group had always been more important to her. Having a crowd around her was enough human contact. More than enough. It was everything.

But now . . . it looked like she could be happy with just one person. Couldn't she?

"People like us, we get something bigger than love." Swarm smiled lopsidedly. "We get to be a crowd."

A shudder passed through him and he lowered the phone. His power, the mass of people inside him, rumbled and moaned.

Kelsie swallowed. "Why are you like this? What the hell happened to you?"

"You want my *origin story*?" He sighed, like the question was beneath him, then lifted the phone again. "School didn't brainwash me, for one thing. My parents kept me home till I could see through the bullshit."

Kelsie almost laughed. "Oh, man. You're saying this is because you're homeschooled?"

"*Self*-schooled." He drew himself up. "By the time I was eight, I was teaching my parents algebra. Math wasn't their thing. Self-reliance was. No electricity. No internet. No dependence on strangers or authorities."

"No people," she said softly. No crowds.

Swarm shrugged, and the air rippled, like an avalanche threatening. "There were people. We went to town every Saturday. It was only forty miles."

Kelsie felt an old wound inside her swell. Her dad had taken her to the country once, a half-assed picnic in an old beater he'd won in a poker game. It had been beautiful at first, the national park full of campers and hikers.

But then a wall of rain had moved in, and the two of them had taken shelter while the weekend crowds scattered. For a long hour it had seemed that she and Dad were the only ones on the mountain. Like the rest of the world had emptied out around them.

She'd never been so scared in her life. She hadn't left the city since.

"Do you know what school is like," Quinton asked his phone screen, "when you're twelve and you've never even *seen* one before?"

"I bet that was hard," Kelsie said, though her first day of school had been a relief. Finally she could spend all day wrapped in a crowd, without having to hunt one out. She'd learned to enjoy the quiet attentiveness of a history class, the random spikes of victory from the gym, the wash of relief when the bell rang for the end of the day. It was like being part of something alive.

But she also knew about the other side of school. Where mobs were formed and victims selected. She looked at Swarm's too-tight blazer and his white socks.

She tried to keep her voice soft. "You were bullied."

"I was *taught a lesson*."

The different parts of him, the crowd inside his head, all came together for those last words, and the force of it almost sent her stumbling backward.

"They held me against the lockers to throw basketballs at me. They made speeches before each throw, like a sacred rite. And I kept smiling the whole time, because I'd never felt the crowd's focus before. The time they broke my nose, I laughed with them."

Kelsie nodded, remembering being punch-drunk at age eleven when Sally Jeffers' pigtails had been tied to the back of her chair in homeroom. Everyone had laughed, including Sally. Trying to appease the bullies. Laughing at her own humiliation, because it was better than crying.

The memory made Kelsie sick. "I'm sorry that happened to you."

"I'm not. I was too busy learning about the truth of crowds."

"That isn't how they are," she said. "I mean, that's not how they *have* to be. They do other things. They *dance* . . ."

Suddenly that word, which Kelsie had uttered a dozen times a day since she was fourteen, seemed pitiful. What was dancing compared to all the horrors that groups of people could commit?

"But if you're worried about young Quinton, his story has a happy ending." Swarm finally stopped talking to his phone. He looked straight at her. "I *won*."

"I bet." Kelsie knew the temptation to become part of the darkness.

"Andrew Forster was his name," Swarm said. "New kid at school, tall and strong and good-looking. Showed up in the middle of eighth grade, and right away he told them to stop hurting me."

"A good guy," Kelsie said.

"A morally pretentious *asshole*," Swarm corrected. "I hated the bullies, but at least they knew who I was. Andrew Forster didn't give a shit. For him it was about being a hero."

"He was *helping* you."

"True. Because in that moment when they hesitated and wondered if they should stop, I found my way in." Swarm stared straight at Kelsie, and she could feel the full-bore gaze of the crowd inside him. "And from then on, Andrew Forster was the one against the lockers."

"Oh my God." Another shiver ran through Kelsie.

The more Swarm spoke, the more her teeth rattled. The cold sank through her skin. She wrapped her arms around herself, trying to rub some warmth back into her body.

"Do you know what it's like," Swarm asked, "when you finally find yourself part of something? On the *right* side for a change? After never feeling that before?"

Kelsie nodded slowly. Not the same way Swarm knew. But she remembered finding the Zeroes.

"After that," Swarm said, "I walked into that locker room like a conductor following his orchestra onstage. I made those idiots into something beautiful."

"That's not . . . ," Kelsie said softly. "What you did to Davey—what you forced those people to do—that was brutal and ugly. Not beautiful."

"You're very sweet." Swarm smiled. "But deep down you want to be what I am. You want to level up."

"I don't want that!" Kelsie's throat was dry.

"But it's so beautiful, what we have. The power to make every crowd what it longs to be—a *mob*."

Kelsie wanted to argue, but she could tell just standing here that Swarm's power was bigger than hers, more complete, more *leveled up*. Maybe he really was the end result of her power, what all her training with Nate and the others was leading her to. The other Zeroes had named her Mob, as if they already knew the danger.

Swarm must have seen the fear on her face.

"The temptation is already in you," he said. "You'll join me because I can teach you. And then we can take your friends together."

293

Kelsie almost laughed. "You're crazy! You seriously think you can make me do that? You don't know me at all!"

"I know your destiny," Swarm said casually.

Swarm's power spiked and spun in dizzying patterns. Kelsie tried to close herself against it, but she felt it again—that inner cry that had been under her skin the whole time, unnoticed and unanswered.

"You'll find me when you're ready." He made to walk away, as if the conversation were already over. "Just like Ren and Davey did."

"They *ran* from you!"

"They courted me," Swarm said. "They left a trail of bread crumbs. The wedding was their come-hither glance. The mall, their surrender."

"They tried to sacrifice me and my friends to escape you!"

"Because they wanted *everyone* to join me," Swarm continued. "Ren and Davey wanted to be on the winning team. You will too."

"You're sick," she said.

Swarm grinned his crooked grin, angling his phone toward her. "Maybe *you're* sick. And I'm what you'll become when you choose to get better."

Kelsie stepped forward and pulled the phone from his hand. His palm was slack and damp.

He looked at her in astonishment. "That's my journal. Don't—"

She threw the phone as far as she could. It bounced off a distant wall and clattered down a dark alley.

Swarm crumpled, like she'd ripped out his spine.

"If you're so leveled up," she told him, "go find your stupid phone!"

Then she turned and fled toward the Dish.

CHAPTER 43
FLICKER

"WE MET LAST SUMMER," FLICKER SAID.

Thibault's mother turned to take in her son. Her gaze lingered on him for a long, hopeful moment before drifting back to Flicker. Every time she saw him, her awareness seemed to last a little longer.

"I mean, we got *together* last summer," Flicker clarified, wanting to tell the truth. "We'd met before. We just hadn't realized that we *liked* each other."

"So it snuck up on you." There was a smile in Ms. Durant's voice, a smile Flicker wanted to see. She switched her viewpoint to Thibault's father across the breakfast table, but the man's gaze was still buried in the newspaper. He wasn't actually reading, though. His eyes were fixed on one phrase in a headline—POLICE SEEK ANSWERS.

So maybe he was listening, processing.

"Yeah, Flicker snuck up on me," Thibault said, putting down his tea and laughing. "She was stalking me, in fact."

"*Stalking* you?" Flicker cried. Sure, she'd tracked Anon down to his secret hotel lair, but only in case he needed help with Scam. That wasn't *stalking*, exactly. "You wish."

"He was always so handsome," Ms. Durant said. Her voice was wistful, as if she'd forgotten Thibault was sitting right here.

Flicker took his hand, trying to guide his mother's awareness back to him, but her eyes were fixed on a tiny snag in the white tablecloth. Then the kettle began to hiss, and Ms. Durant was up again, busying herself with cups and saucers.

God, this was hard work.

"See?" Thibault said softly. "There's always something to distract her."

On cue, Auguste came in from the living room, demanding tea. The youngest brother, Emile, was out there too, playing with Christmas toys. With six people, plus his grandmother napping upstairs, Thibault's power had the full Curve to work with.

Maybe this meeting should have waited until the boys were back in school.

But there wasn't time for that. Sonia had posted Ren's revenge dump yesterday afternoon. Swarm could show up any day.

She looked through Auguste's eyes. He stood by the fridge, staring at the food. When he closed the door, his gaze went to

Flicker, like any kid's would to a stranger at the breakfast table. But he left the kitchen without a word, not giving his older brother a glance.

Thibault's father was still reading his paper, but he finally looked up when Ms. Durant settled a tea tray before Flicker. He stared at the four cups.

Flicker's heart lifted a little. But then Ms. Durant only poured tea into three of them.

"Has Auguste drunk all the milk, Mom?" Thibault prompted, and was rewarded with a full cup of his own, and then a splash of milk.

But Ms. Durant never looked at her son, and her husband's eyes were scanning the newspaper now, reading the words. Flicker felt a flash of annoyance and, not for the first time, wished that she could control where other people's eyes looked instead of just peeking through them. If *she* could remember Thibault sitting right here, why couldn't his own parents?

Maybe it was time for some hardball.

"Ms. Durant?" Flicker said. "Emile mentioned you've been feeling unwell."

A little gasp. "Well, I think we're always a little tired the day after Christmas."

"And maybe it's strange, having Thibault here?" Flicker nodded toward him.

"Strange?" his mother asked. The single word hung over

the table, and her eyes met Thibault's for the first time.

He looked so afraid, Flicker wanted to hug him. "Because you can't remember when he went away. When he left home."

"He's so young to be on his own" came the woman's reply. "He's only . . ."

"Sixteen," Flicker provided.

"Oh." Ms. Durant's view blurred a little. Tears of confusion. "I should know that."

Whatever memories his mother had of Thibault, they were from before his power had fully formed, before the grandmother had moved in and pushed the Curve up. Back when he was, what, twelve?

But her gaze stayed on her son, and Flicker suddenly saw the boy in his features. The little kid wondering why his parents had abandoned him in a hospital.

A flash of anger went through her, but she bit down on the words that came with it.

"Maman," Thibault said gently. "It's okay that you don't remember. It's not your fault I left. It's mine."

"You . . . ran away?" Her voice was fragile.

"I had to."

Flicker heard the rustle of newspaper and jumped into the father's eyes. They shifted from his son to his wife uncertainly.

"Then why come back?" challenged a voice—Auguste, from the doorway.

Flicker heard Emile there too, and went into his eyes. They jumped around the table, wary of the unfamiliar sight of his brother and his parents talking.

"Yes," Mr. Durant said. "After you broke your mother's heart, why not stay away?"

Flicker felt Thibault's hand flinch in hers. He'd been knocked speechless.

"He didn't *want* to leave," she said. "He has . . . a condition. It makes you forget about him, sometimes. You have no idea how hard—"

"He left us," his father said, and the newspaper snapped taut.

Shit. Flicker thought she'd been steeled for anything—disbelief, guilt, doubted sanity—but *blame*? Sharp and bitter words rose in her throat, but Emile spoke first.

"When he's here, you just ignore him! And when I ask you where he is, you pretend like you can't hear me!" His voice broke into sobs. "Why are you all so *mean to him*?"

The boy's mother swept in on him, until Flicker could see nothing but the floral print of her dress. She jumped into Mr. Durant's eyes.

He was staring again: POLICE SEEK ANSWERS.

"Listen," Flicker said. "There are . . . techniques for making this work. You can use stories, or mnemonics, like this bracelet of mine with Thibault's name on it. You can get *past* this."

She was babbling now. None of this would make sense if you didn't know about superpowers. But at worst they would all forget what had happened here, and she and Thibault could try again in an hour or so.

But the family disaster seemed to have its own momentum now. Emile was still crying, trying to form words and failing. Auguste was glaring at Thibault, and his mother was looking straight at Flicker.

"What did I do?" her voice reached over her son's sobs. "How did I drive him away?"

"He's right here!"

Thibault's hand wrenched in hers. "Flick, please don't."

"I see pictures of him. And for a second I can't remember! What kind of mother . . ."

"Ms. Durant—"

"I wonder if my mind is *damaged* in some way." She knelt, clutching Emile closer. "Maybe I'm going to forget all three of my sons, one by one."

"Maman." An anguished voice came from Flicker's left.

Flicker realized that she was losing Anon too. Six people here, all their focus on Ms. Durant, all this anxiety. The damn Curve.

But then the woman stared at Thibault. "I'm sorry."

"It's not your fault," he said.

Her eyes moved to Auguste. "I lose track of my boys for a moment—in a store, on the street—and I think I must have forgotten them, too. For a second I worry that I lost them years ago, and I'll never see them again!"

"Stop this!" Mr. Durant cried. "Why do you act like a mad-woman in front of our two boys?"

"*Three* boys!" she cried back at her husband.

The yelling was making it hard to focus. By reflex Flicker's hand went to her bracelet.

T—H—I—

"This is hurting them." Thibault's voice came from beside her. "I have to leave."

He stood and walked away from the table, down the hall.

She followed. "Wait! We can try again in—"

Her phone trembled in her pocket, playing the sound of a car crash—a message from Chizara, who never texted except for emergencies.

"Speak text," Flicker said, and the phone obeyed in its familiar dispassionate tones.

"Swarm. Is. Here. In. Cambria."

CHAPTER 44
ANONYMOUS

THIBAULT STRODE DOWN THE HALLWAY, GRABBING framed photos off the wall. He hardly needed to look, he'd done this so many times in his mind, in moments of rage and frustration when all his Zen deserted him.

"What are you doing?" Flicker stood at the door to the hallway, her different forms of awareness darting after him like bright ghosts.

"I have to fix this," he said.

"Whatever you're doing *sounds* pretty drastic, Thibault. Maybe you should stop and think for a second."

"Think? I've been thinking about this for years. About how one day I might have to erase myself, the way this family erased me four years ago. To disappear, for their sakes."

"We don't have time for this," Flicker said. "If Swarm's

really in town, everyone will be freaking out!"

"Go help them if you want. I have to finish this." Thibault
went farther down the hall, snatching the studio photo of the
three brothers, the blurry snapshot of himself with the seventh-
grade French prize.

His father appeared at Flicker's shoulder, attention spewing
out of him like a firehose. He'd chosen *now* of all times to see
Thibault?

"What do you mean, coming here and making your
mother cry!"

Flicker's mouth fell open with outrage. She would jump in
and start defending Thibault unless—

He chopped at the jet of his father's attention, but it didn't
disappear completely.

"It's okay, Dad," he said coldly. "I'm going."

The jet shrank, and one more hack was enough. The anger
switched off in the man's eyes, and he slowly turned away, took
a step back into the kitchen. "What's upset you, *chérie*?"

It was like being dead, and watching life walk on without him.

"Thibault," Flicker said. "Don't do this now, when you're
hurting."

"I have to, before I lose my nerve. Swarm can wait."

He strode into the home office. There were big shopping
bags folded and slotted down beside the filing cabinet. He
shook one out and thrust it at Flicker, who'd followed him in.
"Hold this?"

With no eyes in the room, she reached out toward his voice. Her hands were shaking. He wanted to hold them, to reassure her. But he couldn't risk losing momentum.

He went through the cabinet like a machine, taking his old school file, his medical insurance papers, anything else that had his name on it, dropping it all in the bag.

Flicker flinched with every *chunk* of weight into her hands.

"I don't understand."

"I'm saving them all pain," Thibault said.

"Looks to me like you're giving up on them."

"That too, I guess." He flicked through the bottom drawer. That folder of memorabilia—drawings he'd done as a kid, pages from composition books when he was learning to write, some hilariously terrible grade-school poems. He dropped it into the bag with the rest.

"But your mom is trying so hard," Flicker protested. "She *wants* to remember you. Can't we work with that?"

"All we're doing is messing with her brain." He took the bag from Flicker's hands. "She doesn't know what's real anymore."

"*You're* real, Thibault. She knows that."

"That's what's driving her crazy," he said. "She lost her son, Flick—as in *misplaced* him. Can you imagine what it's like to realize that a hundred times a day?"

"Kind of," she said faintly. "Same thing happens with my boyfriend every now and then. But I've figured out some strategies. So can she."

"You and I spend time alone," he said. "Too many people live here. I'd always be fighting the Curve."

Flicker's phone erupted in her pocket, a tinny version of "Hail to the Chief." Her ringtone for Nate, but she didn't answer it.

Thibault pushed past her, carrying the bag upstairs. Flicker followed.

Halfway up, there was a buzz in his back pocket. He whipped the phone out as he ran.

Scam, it said. His own family couldn't remember him, but Ethan could?

"Sounds like the Zeroes are panicking," Flicker said.

"Let them."

In his parents' bedroom he dug in the bottom drawer of the dresser, where his father put stuff he didn't want to deal with. Here was that pen set from a long-ago birthday, engraved FOR DAD, FROM THIBAULT. Ancient notes left out hopefully: *Pick up T, soccer, 4pm.* A few letters he'd sent from the Magnifique, when he couldn't stop himself late at night, like drunk-dialing an ex. He grabbed it all, hating how it stank of Dad's confused grief and guilt, and pushed it into the bag.

Flicker stood wary, listening. "Sounds like they have a lot of reminders of you. Maybe they just need you *around* more."

"They need me gone. To be free." Here came that dying feeling again, as he swept into the bag all the pictures and handmade cards Mom had laid out on her bedside table, trying to remember him. She might hunt for these things for a while, but when she didn't find them, her memories would fade.

Peace at last. Closure, of a kind.

"Thibault, listen!" Flicker cried. "I feel like we made some progress down there in the kitchen. We can make this a project." She sat on the bed. "I make you more visible to them. I attach you to something that's easier to remember, the same way Lily's stories about you did for me."

Some small piece of china he'd bought for his mother broke as it fell into the bag. He looked up at Flicker, into the stream of her words, each of them tightening his chest.

"We'll keep trying," she went on. "We'll start with your mom and Emile. And then we'll *make* your dad and Auguste take notice."

"And what if we *die*?" he said.

She jerked back like he'd slapped her.

"You know the stakes here, Flicker. You saw that crowd tear Davey apart. Swarm hunted those two until he caught them. He didn't give up."

"But—"

"But nothing, Flicker. If I die when we walk out of this house in five minutes, or next week, or whenever he gets to us, you think I want to leave my family like *this*?"

Flicker put her hands to her face.

"Dad and Auguste in denial, but finding all this *evidence* around the house for the rest of their lives? Emile confused, calling my number and getting nothing? Mom losing her grip on reality?" He heard the note of despair in his own voice, felt the sting of self-pitying tears.

Get control. Find the Zen. Abjure connections.

He put his hand on Flicker's shoulder—as if to reassure her, but really because she was his lifeline to reality, to still *existing*.

"Maybe I'll come back one day, okay?" He tried to keep his voice steady. "Maybe we'll get a chance to do that project. But with Swarm in Cambria, I can't leave them like this, in limbo."

A sudden tear dashed down Flicker's cheek. He hardly saw it before she wiped it away.

"Okay," she said, her voice collapsing. "But the Zeroes need us now. Let me help you do this faster."

"Downstairs," he said, to steady her. "Where Auguste is watching TV. The photo albums are over the left speaker. Grab the pale blue one and the orange one—shit, can you find them by colors?"

"I'll get Auguste to look at them." Flicker stood up and was gone.

He had everything of Mom's. In Auguste's room there was only that Patty Low poster that Thibault had signed for his birthday. *Love from your bro, T.*

So pathetic. Just one step away from *Remember meeeeeee!*

Emile had made it easy, putting all his Thibault stuff on his desk, like he was trying to remember him these days. The thought of his little brother assembling all these objects hit

Thibault with an anguish that almost stopped his breathing.

He was quick, efficient, as coldly Zen as he could be. Into the bag with it. Gone.

Here came Flicker. Someone was following her up the stairs. God, he didn't want to face Dad again.

But it was Auguste, all busy sight lines. He watched as Thibault opened the pale blue album and started taking out photos.

"What are you guys doing?"

A photo of the family around the campfire dropped into the shopping bag.

"I'm borrowing these for an art project," Thibault said. "Only the ones I'm in."

Auguste's attention flicked from the album to Thibault's face and back. Thibault reached up and snipped that twitching signal. *Dead to you, bro. Don't worry about me even a second longer.*

Auguste's attention slid to Flicker. As Thibault closed the first album, she took it from the pile and held it out.

"Would you mind putting this back on the shelf downstairs, Auguste?" she said calmly.

"Sure." He took it, frowning, and walked away.

A few minutes later Thibault dumped the last album on Emile's desk, stood, and picked up the bag.

It felt as heavy as stones.

"One last thing," he said.

Flicker followed him out and along the hall. Her senses were all on high alert—it was like being wrapped in attentive cotton wool. He pushed through it toward the landing.

But then he passed his old bedroom—Grand-mère's now, the door closed for her morning nap. "Um, two last things."

Quietly he turned the door handle.

The room was dim, curtains drawn. There lay Grand-mère, curled asleep under a throw—small, harmless, breathing slowly. He felt a terrible ache in his chest for her, for all these people he'd perplexed with his power. People he really did love, when it came down to it, and who'd have loved him just fine if they could've held him in their minds.

He bent and kissed Grand-mère's soft cheek, then went back to Flicker, who couldn't see how his eyes swam.

"Almost done," he said in a hoarse whisper, not trusting his voice.

Downstairs he led her, to the kitchen again. Dad had his back to the door. Mom and Emile looked up, but Thibault wiped their attention out of the air, wiped the anxiety from their faces, crossed to the table, and picked up Emile's phone.

"Are you *sure?*" Flicker whispered.

"Shall we make some *chocolat chaud*, Emile?" Mom said too loudly.

"Cool, yeah!" Emile got up and went to the fridge.

Thibault opened Emile's address book, which only held half a dozen names. He found *Thibault (brother)* and hit delete.

310

Delete Contact?

A steadying breath. *Yes,* he tapped.

Then he took his mom's phone and erased himself there, too.

He looked up. He wanted one last hug from his brother and his mom, but he wasn't going to upset them by taking it. Instead he took his father's shoulder. The man looked up, a spark of fear in his eyes.

"No hard feelings," Thibault said, and the look faded to mere bafflement.

Then he went to the door, picked up the heavy bag, and walked past Flicker down the hall.

From now on, to this family he was truly nothing.

CHAPTER 45
BELLWETHER

"GRACIAS, MAMÁ."

Nate watched the coffee pour into his cup, already imagining its taste when he added cream and sugar. Rich and galvanizing, the perfect thing to shake off this looming sense of dread.

The whole family was here at the table. The three sisters were looking at him a little expectantly, waiting for Nate to grace them with his attention. It should have been easy to shelter himself in that glow. Here at home, he was always the golden child.

But he couldn't focus his power. Not since he'd watched a Zero die.

Fixing that seemed like a lot to ask of one cup of coffee, but it was a start. He tipped the sugar bowl, watched the crystals stream.

"My bike has a flat already," Gabby announced.

Nate offered her a sad smile. "And it only took twenty-four hours."

Of course, Papi had bought the Mercedes only a few months ago, and it was gone too. Not just a tire—the whole thing. Now was probably a good time to confess, with the whole family here to cushion the news.

But an unfamiliar feeling settled over Nate—indecision.

Once his father called the cops, they'd start by tracking down the Mercedes. And if Ren wound up in jail, she'd be defenseless against Swarm. Nate didn't want to help kill another Zero, even one who'd painted a big target on him and his friends.

Of course, Ren had been on the run long enough to know about fancy theft-prevention systems, right? By now she'd have ditched the Mercedes.

The family waited, still poised for Nate to break the silence. They always knew when he needed quiet at breakfast, but today his mood had left them uncertain.

Except for Gabby, of course.

"Where did you go shopping with your friends the other night?" she asked. "Like, *all* night—and most of Christmas Eve too!"

The silence tightened a little. Through all the Christmas Day fuss yesterday, he'd managed to hold off awkward questions like this.

"There was a big sale," he said. There was no way around it now. "I had some bad luck with the car."

His mother reached out across the table, took his hand. "Are you okay?"

"I'm fine," he said. "But the Mercedes broke down at Flicker's house."

Papi looked up from his breakfast.

"It wouldn't start," Nate said with a shrug. "We were in a hurry to get to the stores, so Lily drove us. I left it there, and this morning it was gone."

"Gone?" Papi asked.

Both his parents were staring at him now, the concern plain on their faces. But if they checked, the car's nav records would show that he'd driven it to Flicker's first. Whatever happened later would be the thief's doing, of course. Nothing would connect Nate himself to the terrorist attack at the Desert Springs Mall.

That's what the papers were calling it. Straight-up terrorism.

The mood in the room felt wrong, the surprise mixed with something unfamiliar. Disappointment. Those faded little flutterings made it hard to think.

"Someone stole it, I guess."

Nate shut his mouth, but the words had slipped out without any preamble to soften them. A foolish, impatient mistake—the kind he never made. But he wasn't so shaken that he couldn't control a simple family breakfast.

"How crazy is that?" Nate spread his hands, pulling the

threads of their confusion toward himself, leaving them needing an explanation from him, or at least a story.

He sat forward in his chair, drawing his family closer.

"Flicker called just before I came down, wondering why I hadn't said hello when I picked my car up. I was like, 'But I haven't picked it up yet.' And she said, 'But it's gone.'" He looked at Mamá. "It probably just got towed, right?"

"Why would someone tow it?" his mother asked. "Was it parked legally?"

He shrugged. "Right in front of Flicker's. Unless there was some special rule for Christmas Day."

"I'll call the company right away," Papi said. "They'll find it."

"I'll do it." Nate raised his phone. "I'm really sorry I didn't check on it earlier."

This was working. The sisters were bubbling at the possibility that their older brother might be in trouble for once. Papi's face was serious, but also alight with the prospect of the fancy antitheft systems kicking in. He'd paid enough for them, after all.

Their predictable reactions sent relief through Nate. For the two days since Davey had died, reality had seemed broken. He'd had the awful sense that his power was slipping, maybe even turning inside out. But this family breakfast was the perfect place to get his mojo back.

His Zeroes needed him at full strength right now, not wallowing in doubt.

"How did she notice?" Gabby said.

He turned to his little sister. "Sorry?"

"How did Flicker notice your car was missing?" Gabby cocked her head sweetly. "She's blind."

Nate blinked, and revisions of the story flowed easily into his mind: Lily had noticed it missing and asked if Nate had been by. Or Flicker had heard it drive away—blind-people powers, as she liked to say.

Or would too many details clutter the story?

As his mind stumbled, Nate felt his grasp on the room slip a little. He started talking, keeping it vague. "I guess someone else must have noticed. Maybe her sister, or her mom. Anyway, they must have told—"

His phone buzzed in his hand. It was from Crash.

Nate stared at the screen. The letters were tangled, not quite settling on their meaning. But finally his brain worked it out.

Swarm is here in Cambria.

And it came again, that feeling of his power failing. The glistening lances of attention that crisscrossed the table all focused on him, but he sat there powerless and astonished, feeling the full, unbuffered weight of his family's expectations.

He could never live up to them.

Just as he could never keep the Zeroes safe, now that Swarm was here.

"We're all going to die," he whispered, just loud enough that his family heard every word.

CHAPTER 46
CRASH

"THIS RIDE OKAY WITH YOU?"

Kelsie nodded, her eyes screwed up against the winter noon sun, like she wasn't used to being out in daylight.

Chizara reached her mind beneath the silver shell of the Mazda convertible. Zapped open the locks, popped the trunk, quenched the theft-prevention system. "Then let's get out of here, now."

Kelsie pushed the duffel, pillow, and blankets into the trunk. Chizara slid into the driver's seat, squinting through the background Cambria buzz to scan the dash and the systems behind it. Yes, *there* was the roof mechanism, brutish and mechanical.

Kelsie slammed the trunk closed.

"Top down?" Chizara said, poised as Kelsie climbed in and scrabbled for the seat belt.

"No way." Kelsie clicked the belt home and hugged the ever-present snack bag, the wrappers crackling inside. "We're in hiding, remember?"

"Not in hiding—in motion." Chizara gunned the engine. She caught Kelsie's eye, and the girl reached out and pulled her in for a quick kiss.

There was that feeling again—that *this* was everything. That it made perfect sense to leave the rest of her life behind.

"This is the right thing to do, yeah?" Kelsie asked, her face solemn.

"The only way to stay safe is to spread out, to keep moving."

"But we'll be all alone out there."

Chizara shook her head. "Not alone—together. Even if it's just two of us."

Kelsie eyes widened, and they kissed again, and then Chizara pulled the Mazda out into the street.

"To Highway One."

She eyed the road signs, glanced in the rearview, and did a quick lane change. *Yep, Mom, I just stole another car,* she thought wearily. *But not for a joyride, okay? We're running from a killer. It's about survival.*

Also, I need to get away from you while I figure this out—this girl and me.

After the Mercedes, the little ragtop was blessedly straightforward, just the twinge of a chip here and there instead of the full pincushion of computerized everything. Chizara had brain space to focus on holding other stuff together: phone towers and substations they drove past, traffic controller cabinets, fancier cars around them in the traffic.

And she had Kelsie beside her, familiar and yet transformed into something new. Just having someone here who understood the mess they were in was a comfort.

"How far should we go?" Chizara asked.

"Far," Kelsie said. "Somewhere with happy crowds."

"Right." Happy crowds outside a Faraday cage meant assault by phones. But it was worth it to keep Kelsie calm and cheerful. She'd been panicking when she'd returned from meeting Swarm, unable to gather herself until Chizara had said, *Let's just leave Cambria.*

It was that simple. That huge.

"There was that big trance festival last month," Kelsie said, rummaging among the snacks. "Something like that would be perfect."

"I'm not up on the rave scene."

Kelsie snorted, digging deeper. "Get me to a dance party, Zara, or I'm hitchhiking!"

"Good luck with that."

They got on the highway and flew north, back along Swarm's path, to places he'd already hunted and left behind. The traffic was in a post-Christmas lull, the suburbs fizzing with electronic conversations and commands. To their left the Pacific drew closer, azure, shimmering, and vast.

What would it be like to live on a boat? All that glorious signal-free space around her. Of course, Kelsie would go crazy out there.

Like Nate had said about Glitch and Coin—*opposites attract*.

Fifty miles in, Kelsie curled up in what looked like an uncomfortable position, closed her eyes, and fell asleep.

The fizzy suburbs were well behind them, and they were skimming the sea cliffs at speed. This car was a lot more fun than Dad's pickup to drive—low, fast, and sticky on the curves. Chizara's head was clear of electronic interference, of worry for Kelsie, and almost, almost, of her own fear.

Kelsie had wakened her in a panic, all the sweet mischief of last night gone from her face. And she'd only grown more frantic while spilling the story of her meeting with Swarm.

He'd been less than a mile from the Dish last night. Chizara's Faraday cage had gone from a safety zone to a metal-lined death trap. She couldn't believe they were both still alive.

Chizara had sent warning texts to the other Zeroes; then she and Kelsie had fled up to Hill Street to find this car.

Kelsie flailed in her seat, fighting off some enemy in a nightmare. The Mazda swerved a little, and a driver blasted his horn as he passed them.

"Kelsie, wake up!" Chizara shouted, getting control again, her heart pounding. "You're dreaming!"

Kelsie opened her eyes, stared around wildly. "Where are we? Where is everyone?"

Chizara put a hand on her knee. "Highway One, headed north. Just like when you fell asleep."

"God, it's so empty! Zara, you're not taking me camping, are you?"

Even without a crowd around, Chizara felt a glimmer of Kelsie's panic, her fear of being alone.

"We're looking for a happy crowd, remember? One really far away from Cambria."

"Right." Kelsie looked doubtfully at the scrubby green hillside out one window, the gleaming ocean out the other.

"It'll be okay," Chizara said. "If we don't find any beach parties, there's always something happening up in Monterey."

Kelsie closed her window and hugged herself. "Maybe put the radio on? Just for company."

"Sure. Anything left in the snack bag?"

For the rest of the afternoon they snacked and drove and sang along to the radio. Chizara overtook a convoy of trundling RVs, and they traveled along with them, a tenuous community strung along the highway, until the RVs peeled off together at a campground.

Twenty miles after that, Kelsie pushed herself straighter in her seat. "People up ahead."

A half-mile later a beachside parking lot came into sight, a dozen vehicles gleaming there.

Chizara slowed. "A walk on the beach sounds good."

"Yes!" Kelsie was out of the car before it had even rolled

to a stop. Chizara grinned, killed the power, and climbed out. The few signals in the air were very faint. She stretched tall and wide.

"They're building a bonfire!" Kelsie called. Chizara joined her at the fence. Down on the beach, people were dragging chunks of driftwood toward a pit in the sand.

"Lots of coolers and sleeping bags," Chizara said. "Looks like they're planning an all-nighter."

"And they're *happy*." Kelsie took a long breath of the sea air, relief all over her face.

Too happy to turn into a deadly swarm? Chizara wondered.

She swung out her hand and hooked her fingers lightly through Kelsie's. "Okay, I guess we're far enough for one day."

They took their blankets and pillows and snacks down to the sand, leaving their phones, switched off, back in the car. Pacing the beach together, they found the perfect spot—far enough from the party to protect Chizara from the sting of signals, close enough for Kelsie to feel the comfort of the mob.

They explored the rock pools as the light went, and they didn't talk about Swarm, or Davey, or Nate or the other Zeroes, or the future.

Wherever they went, Chizara turned to gaze seaward, the beach party's tech prickling her back, slow-cruising container ships pulsing gently in the distance. But Kelsie always faced the fire and the dancing, loving the company, boosting their good time.

"It feels weird," Kelsie said. "Just leaving the others behind."

"I know. But a big group only makes it easier for him. They're safer with us gone."

"With *me* gone, you mean." Kelsie stared out at sea. "He might even leave them alone once he realizes I'm not there."

Her voice sounded hopeful, but her expression said hunted. Swarm would never stop looking for them.

Chizara would have to text her parents tomorrow morning, after she'd slept on what to say. It wasn't going to be easy, but she didn't have a choice except to save this girl. Chizara's body, her heart, wasn't giving her an option.

Even if it meant leaving everything else behind.

CHAPTER 47
CRASH

AS NIGHT FELL, THEY PULLED TOGETHER THEIR
own little pile of driftwood, and Kelsie ran along the beach to
ask for a burning stick to light it with. She was gone awhile,
bringing the party to a thudding crescendo that echoed across
the sand. Chizara smiled out to sea, listening to the whoops
and cheers.

"I bring the gift of fire!" Kelsie clambered back over the
rocks. She poked the firebrand into the wood. Flames spat and
sparked in the frazzled, dry seaweed at its heart.

The fire didn't last long, and they lay down between the
blankets in the privacy of the darkness and held each other,
kissing a long time, intertwined in the drumbeat of the party
and the empty ocean's soft rushing.

Chizara was more ready than she'd been the night before,

and everything was bigger now. It was as though Kelsie's touch called a giant city into being around them, laced with intricate networks that purred and pressed on Chizara's body in a million different ways, exquisitely almost painful. Together they rippled closer and closer to that city on wavelets that built to waves, lifting them higher and higher.

And at the end Crash jumped from the tip of the highest wave into the middle of the gorgeous, glittering megastructure. She let it all go, crashing through and falling with it, crying out as she did. She was one glowing spark among thousands, sinking, ecstatic, mindless, toward a cool sea waiting below.

Faint bells reached her ears as she drifted on that sea, entwined with drifting Kelsie. She opened her eyes to stars, clouds above. A cold sea breeze touched her face. Oh yes, she was here on this beach with Kelsie.

And she was full of power, like nothing she'd ever felt before. As if she'd crashed a whole city, as if Kelsie's touch had poured a solar flare into her body.

The prickle of phones was gone, as was the nerve-scrape of the party's Bluetooth speaker. Perfect silence.

Except for a distant whooping, and tiny bells clanging, on and on. Chizara lifted her head, looked over Kelsie to the sea.

A cloud slid off the moon and she saw it: a ship, too big, too close, and leaning at a strange angle.

No.

It had run aground on some far-off sandbank under the dark water.

As Chizara sat up, astonished, a container slipped from the stack on the deck, tumbling into the sea with a big, slow-motion, silent, moonlit splash.

"Kelsie!"

The warmth beside her stirred. "Hmmm?"

"Wake up! I think I just—" No. It was too *huge* to be believable.

"What are you yelling about?" Kelsie murmured, struggling to follow Chizara's gaze. But then she stared, mouth open. "Oh my God."

The ship had bristled with tech, but it was all dark now, the pathways cool and empty. The ringing alarms and a few safety lights—on their own circuits, isolated for emergencies—were the only things working.

"It didn't just run aground," Chizara gasped. "I *crashed* it! When I—when we were—I thought I was only crashing things in my head!"

Kelsie clambered up, wrapping the blanket around herself and peering over the rocks at the party. "They're all freaking out. I'll go calm them down."

She staggered away across the sand. Chizara pulled on shirt, socks, pants.

Didn't I tell you to do no harm, Chizara Adaora Okeke?
You did, Mom, you did.

And what's that out there, then?

Kelsie was headed back.

"Their phones are all bricked, Zara," she called. "They can't get help for the ship, and their cars won't start. They think it's some kind of apocalypse! Did you see that oil slick?"

She was right. The ship's fuel was spreading out in the moonlight, flattening the waves.

Do no harm.

"The crew out there, I can feel them," Kelsie said. "They're panicking."

"Everything's down," Chizara said. "Can you calm them?"

Kelsie shook her head. "Too far. Can you fix anything?"

Chizara closed her eyes and splayed a hand at the ship, felt the distant pathways of wiring, the darkened spires of antennae and radar, the dead generators and stilled pumps, the six giant engines cooling.

The fixing power was huge inside her, but she could never rebuild as much as she crashed. And she'd never given a cargo ship a second glance. It was an alien complex of pumps and valves and electronics.

"I wouldn't know where to start," she said.

"But you can fix a phone," Kelsie said in a shivery voice. "We should call someone."

Chizara nodded, gathered up Kelsie's clothes from the blanket, and pushed them at her. "And then we need to go."

Kelsie stared at her. "Where?"

"Home. Back to Cambria."

"But . . . what about Swarm?"

Yes, Swarm was there. But so were Mom and Dad, and Ik and Bin. If Chizara was going to die, she wanted to die near them, with her life still making sense around her, not out on some lonely road, in a stolen car, run down by a killer. Here in this glorious postcrash silence, in the vastness of the power inside her, it was all perfectly clear.

"I can't be out here," she said. "I'm too dangerous."

"But . . . he'll kill you," Kelsie said.

"No. We'll fight him." Chizara picked up one of the blankets and viciously shook the sand out of it. "But it isn't safe for us to be together like this. It feels amazing, but look what it does!" She nodded at the listing container ship. "It's . . . it's irresponsible! Selfish! It *wrecks* things."

Kelsie huddled in the other blanket, dressing inside it, self-conscious now.

"That's what he said," she murmured. "Swarm. That love is bad."

"Losing *control* is what's bad!" Chizara kicked sand over the coals, not wanting to add a brushfire to the night's disasters. "I can't let myself."

It hurt too much to go on, and Chizara turned away to cross the rocks, heading for the car.

A girl from the party was running toward her. "Is your phone working?"

"No, but yours is." Chizara flicked a finger at the dead phone the girl was holding, and it chirruped back to life.

The girl just stared. "What *is* this? Did you see that boat? It's like the end of the world or something!"

Chizara shook her head, stamping away across the sand. "Human error. That's all."

She only had to brush the Mazda with a half thought to bring it back to life. She threw the bedding and bag in the trunk.

Kelsie climbed into view, shrugging on her jacket, trailing the blanket behind her up the path. She looked so forlorn that Chizara's righteous anger died, and she put her arms around her. Kelsie's sandy hair scratched her face.

"Zara, it's not your fault," Kelsie said in a fragile voice.

"It is, because I know better." Chizara stood back and looked at Kelsie, both their eyes welling. "I can't do this. Not with you. Not with anyone. Life's just going to be different for me."

Kelsie reached up and brushed Chizara's tears away with her thumbs. "That's what I always thought. But with you, it's different. Like we make our own crowd."

"I know. But I can't control myself!"

Kelsie blinked back her own tears. "Then we're all dead anyway."

Chizara stepped back. "What?"

"If we can't learn to control our powers, one day I'll be a

Swarm." Kelsie threw her blanket into the trunk and slammed it closed, then spread her hands matter-of-factly. "I'll turn on you, and others, too."

Stunned, Chizara almost let the Mazda's electronics crash.

"So keep practicing, okay?" Kelsie said, her eyes sympathetic but her voice hard. "Now take me back to the Dish. I'll pick up some more stuff and go to Ling's place. Then maybe get a bus out of town. Go and find my mother."

Chizara nodded. Any plan was good if it took them away from the sight of the crashed ship, that reminder of what could happen if she ever lost herself in rapture with Kelsie again.

They got into the car, which now felt too intimate for the two of them, too small for Chizara's power.

She switched her phone on, and the fairy hand of connection, soft and painless in her postcrash state, pulsed into being. As soon as the icons appeared, she called 911.

CHAPTER 48
SCAM

THE DISH LOOKED QUIET FROM THE OUTSIDE. NO lights, definitely no music. Nothing.

Crap, where *was* everyone? It was like being ten again, the day he'd found out the whole class had been invited to Dean Yuen's birthday—everyone except him.

None of the Zeroes had answered their phones all day. Ethan understood the whole together-we're-a-target thing, but seriously, would a single text bring Swarm down on them all?

Surely Nate had a plan by now. Something better than *We'll just show him how awesome the Zeroes are, and he'll totes want to join the club!* It hadn't worked on Ren and Davey. No way was it going to work on a guy who could turn a crowd into a killing machine.

Or maybe the Zeroes were already dead. Maybe Swarm was

picking them off one by one, and Ethan was the only one left alive now.

He shivered and stared at the Dish. He would've heard about that, right? A string of murders would've made the news, or his mom would've told him. She always called him when there was any kind of local crime wave. Supposedly to check that he was okay, though lately it felt like she was also checking to see if he was involved.

Ethan circled around the back of the building, his thumb on his phone, ready to hit 911 at the slightest evidence of Swarm. He quietly let himself in through the back door.

"Hello?" he called into the dark.

Nothing.

He edged along the wall until he found a light switch. In the weak light of the bare bulbs, the Dish's dance floor looked forlorn. No dancers, no light show, nothing but a . . . mattress? And a futon?

Whoever had slept here, they'd left in a hurry. The sheets were tangled and trailing on the floor. It definitely hadn't been Teebo, then. He'd never leave his sweater wadded like . . .

Ethan froze. That was Chizara's sweater. Kelsie's *Disney On Ice* quilt. Here together, on the dance floor, inside Chizara's custom-built Faraday cage. Which meant that this was *Kelsie and Chizara's bed*, and Jess was right.

How could he have wasted all that time thinking Kelsie liked him?

That was hope for you—it made you stupid. Well, from now on Ethan Thomas Cooper was living on the dark side. Wall-to-wall pessimism was way easier than the constant let-downs. Like his dad used to say: *Expect nothing and you won't be disappointed.*

Ethan hated when Dad was right.

He went upstairs to check Tee's room: nobody home. Off canoodling with Flicker, probably. Didn't *any* of these love-birds care that they were all being hunted by a Zero killer?

And where the hell was Nate? He should be fixing all this!

The thought of Swarm made the Dish seem extra empty. What if the guy showed up right now, with a big crowd ready to rip Ethan to pieces?

He headed back down to the dance floor and straight for the back exit. But as he reached for the handle, the door opened on its own.

"Don't kill me!" he cried out.

"Wasn't going to," Kelsie said. She stared at him like he was a stranger.

He'd never felt more awkward than he did right then, standing between the girl he was crushing on and the love nest she'd shared with someone else.

He peered into the darkness behind her. "It's just you?"

"Yeah." She looked past him, winced at the sight of the dance floor. "Mind helping me get my mattress upstairs?"

Ethan minded a lot, but there was no way to refuse without

333

being weird about it. And *technically*, he had no right to be weird at all, because he hadn't even manned up enough to tell Kelsie he liked her in the first place.

"Um, sure."

He followed her onto the dance floor, where she pulled off the tangled sheets and kicked them into a forlorn pile. Together they tipped the mattress on its side and began dragging it toward the stairs. Kelsie looked sad and small at the other end of the load.

Things with Chizara weren't going great, seemed like—not that Ethan's intuitions about Kelsie had much of a track record. In any case, he didn't want to hear about it.

Which was sucky of him. He knew he should be concerned for Kelsie. He should be supportive and understanding and all that friendship crap. He should *not* be a dick about it.

Maybe if they talked about something more romance-neutral.

"Any idea what Nate's anti-Swarm plan is?"

"Running, I guess," she said. "And avoiding each other."

They reached the stairs, and Ethan took the back end, the mattress going *bump, bump, bump* on each step. Just what he wanted to hear, a whole bunch of suggestive mattress thumping.

"That's not a very Glorious strategy," Ethan said loudly over the sound.

"He's still messed up by what happened at the mall." Kelsie dragged the mattress up and over the final step. "He's not used to losing."

334

Ethan exhaled a long sigh. The Desert Springs Mall seemed like a year ago. Weird how a romantic disaster could replace witnessing a mob killing at the top of Ethan's current trauma list.

They made it to Kelsie's room and tipped the mattress onto the bed frame. Then she started dropping stuff into a bag that was already on the floor. Random things: a shirt, a chipped beer mug.

"You packing?" Ethan asked.

"Again," Kelsie replied.

"Where're you going?" Ethan regretted the question as soon as he asked it. She was probably running away with Chizara. Or moving in.

"I don't know."

"Oh." Things *really* weren't going well.

And then, suddenly, Kelsie was crying. She dropped down to sit at the edge of the bed, a rolled-up T-shirt still in her hand.

Ethan lowered himself to the mattress beside her, feeling awkward. He carefully put an arm around her shoulder, ignoring the unkind glimmer of hope that went through him. He was a *good* friend, not some opportunistic butthead.

"What's wrong, Kels?"

"He was right," she said through a sob. "He told me couples ruin everything. Me and Zara, we'll just wind up splitting the group!"

"Nate said that? That's stupid. He's just jealous because he had that crush on Flicker and—"

"Not Nate." Kelsie wiped her face. "Swarm."

Ethan blinked. "Um . . ."

"He said romance divides a group against itself. Couples slice up connections."

Ethan pulled his arm back. "Okay. Is this, like, the same Swarm from the mall? The guy who kills Zeroes?"

She nodded. "He came looking for me."

"And you *spoke* to him? He didn't crowd-smash you into tiny pieces?"

"Ethan—"

"And you guys held a parley to, what, share *romantic insights*?"

"It wasn't like that. He told me how he got like he is, which was sad, actually." Kelsie looked up at him. "But the main thing is, he told me Ren was right. I'm a baby Swarm. One day I'll level up."

Ethan stared. "You mean, you're actually going to turn into . . . *him*?"

His head was swimming with what Kelsie was saying, but that last bit made even less sense than the rest.

"Kelsie Laszlo, killing machine? Forget it."

"But that's why he didn't kill me," Kelsie said. "He has other plans. For when I'm . . . a Swarm."

"Like?" Not that Ethan wanted to know the answer.

Kelsie got up and started going through her closet again. "After I level up, he wants us to be Zero-hunting buddies. He wants me to kill the rest of you."

A short, barked laugh squeezed out of Ethan. "No. Way."

"That's what *I* said." She tossed a pile of underwear into the bag. She was talking like a zombie. "But what if there's no way out of leveling up?"

"That's nuts! You're so . . . sweet. And nice and . . ." Ethan sighed. When did he become so lame? "And the first time we met, you saved me from the Craig! Would a baby Swarm do that?"

Kelsie turned to him. "Back then, I had a dad. And then I had the Zeroes. But what do I have now? Nate's totally ghosting us, Thibault's left the Dish, and Zara's giving up on me and her because she wrecked a ship. Face it, Ethan, the Zeroes are kind of busted!"

Ethan swallowed, afraid to ask about the whole wrecked-a-ship thing. He hoped it was a figure of speech. But whatever it meant, he had to admit the team vibe wasn't happening these days. The empty Dish was proof of that.

"Anyway"—she turned back to her closet—"the truth is, I wasn't really planning on saving you from Craig. I just wanted to find out what you knew about my dad. Just like I was using Chizara to make myself feel safe."

At that moment, a bolt of anger shot through Ethan. Why was Chizara the one to make Kelsie feel safe, and not him? *He* was the one who'd realized that Kelsie had a power, who'd brought her into the group. Who'd waited all this time while she grieved over her dad . . .

Without really meaning to, Ethan opened his mouth, and

the voice spoke. It took all his anger, his frustration about having been silent so long, his desire to be understanding and supportive and *not a dick*, and put it into words.

"We've all been through a lot lately. A broken heart on top of that has got to suck," the voice said smoothly. "And the sad thing is, it's probably always going to be that way for you."

Kelsie looked at him, her eyes wide. "What?"

He had her undivided attention at last. And everything the voice had said felt so true that it even sounded like Ethan talking. That hardly ever happened.

He didn't even pause to think about it. "You're only ever going to be happy in a group, Kels. A crowd. A gang. No one person can ever make you feel loved enough."

"I guess," she said faintly. "That's how it's always been."

"You guys keep telling me *my* power sucks because it only works on one person at a time, but at least I can connect to someone," the voice said. "Maybe *none* of the rest of you will ever have that."

Okay, now the voice was just being cruel. It had sucked up Ethan's stupid jealousy and spat it back into the world, like toxic verbal tar.

Kelsie had grown still. "Ethan, was that you?"

He tried to shake his head. To explain that it was the voice talking crap. But it was *his* anger that had formed the words, and it felt so *right* to say it after they'd all disappeared on him and Kelsie had run off with Chizara.

"You're all made from the same pieces, just rearranged!" the voice blurted out. "You and Swarm. Nate and Thibault. You're just too full of yourselves to see it!"

Ethan clamped his mouth shut. Crap. The voice was in full omniscient mode now, spilling its own brand of truth to get what it wanted.

What *he* had wanted, down at the bottom of his shitty-friend soul.

"You're right." Kelsie grabbed a black hoodie from the closet.

"Wait," he said. "That wasn't me."

She didn't look at him. She slipped the hoodie over her head and turned toward the door, still silent.

"Kelsie? It was just the—"

"I know," she said without turning around. "It was the voice. But that doesn't mean it wasn't true. Just leave me alone, Ethan."

She spun away and slipped from the room, moving like a dancer even when she was hurting. Ethan heard her race down the stairs, and then the back door slammed.

He sat on her bare mattress, breathing hard. His fists were trembling with the effort of fighting the voice.

Kelsie would come back, right? She'd left her bag, so it wasn't like she was leaving the Dish forever.

But *leave me alone*? That was not a Kelsie sentence.

Crap. Was she looking for another conversation with Swarm? There was no telling what that creep would say.

339

And what if Kelsie listened this time?

Ethan ran downstairs and across to the open main entrance. Outside, the winter wind blew newspaper along the front of the used-car lot and rattled empty beer cans beside a row of dumpsters. But there was no sign of anyone.

"I screwed up," Ethan breathed, then shouted, "Kelsie? Kelsie!"

He went left, up the street past a boarded-up building. Nothing. He ran back, skirting the Dish all the way to the wide, vacant streets on the other side. No one. Not even a car at this time of night. He tried dialing her number, but all he got was voice mail.

Crap, he hated himself sometimes. Like when he screwed up so royally that only his superpowered friends could help.

"Someone better pick up the damn phone this time!" he muttered.

He started calling Zeroes.

CHAPTER 49
MOB

KELSIE SHIVERED IN THE COLD. SHE KEPT HER head down and her hood up, trying to disappear in the wide, empty streets of the Heights.

Nothing was moving this late at night. Like someone had hit freeze-frame, and the movie was never going to start again.

Zara had pulled away so suddenly. Because there was nothing important that Kelsie could give her. Nothing that meant as much to Zara as her precious self-control. And then Ethan's stupid voice had truth-bombed her whole damn life.

Nothing divides a group faster than couples.

Love was its own feedback loop, away from everyone else. You stuck with someone and they stuck with you, until your little madness of two overwhelmed everything else and you lost yourself and your crowd. And then the person you loved gave up the first time something went wrong.

Kelsie stuffed down the pain swelling in her chest, keeping it from spreading through the winter-quiet streets. There was no one around to turn into a mob, but she wasn't taking any chances.

She didn't know where to go. The Dish wasn't home anymore. And maybe the Zeroes weren't her family. It had all been a delusion, a way to keep herself from realizing the truth. She had no one. She was a monster and a danger to her friends.

She had to get someplace safe, where Swarm couldn't work his evil. No big crowds. No anger.

If she were on Ivy Street right now, she'd cruise to the front of any line. Everybody knew her there. Everybody expected her to bring a good time. But what if all this pain in her came tumbling out?

Besides, tonight she didn't trust herself to ride any vibe, to be the party girl she used to be. She needed to take ownership of the swirling mess of her own thoughts before she hurt someone.

She reached for her phone and hesitated, wondering who to call. She used to have friends before the Zeroes. Lots of them.

Finally she texted Fig. Of all her friends, he was the guy who knew himself the best. Right now, that was the vibe Kelsie wanted to hook into—certainty and purpose.

Where r u? I need a crowd. Something down to earth.

Fig's reply was immediate. *Got just the thing. Cnr Park &
Washington.*

Kelsie frowned. She'd roamed Cambria's streets since she
was a little kid, in search of a crowd or a good time, or both.
She knew its streets better than she knew her own skin.

Fig was in a church? Whatever.

Be there in ten, she texted back.

She was already moving, racing downhill toward the
highway that cut the Heights from the rest of Cambria.
Her breath was fog flying back over her shoulder as she ran
downtown.

The Baptist church was a plain redbrick building. One of
Cambria's oldest. The lights were on.

Fig met her on Washington Street. He hugged her tight,
practically picking her up off the ground. "I gotcha."

"I know," she said into his shoulder. She was glad it was too
dark for her face to give her away. She jerked her head at the
church. "Is this some kind of Christmas thing?"

"Nope." Fig led her across the parking lot, where empty
cars ticked as their engines cooled in the December air.

There was a blue light on over the narrow basement stairs.

"Oh, right," Kelsie said. "A meeting?"

Fig had been sober since Kelsie's dad had died. It had
surprised her at first, especially since Fig had kept his job at
Fuse. But something about Jerry Laszlo's rapid decline had

started Fig on a new path. One that had led him to Alcoholics Anonymous meetings twice a week.

"Am I allowed in there?" she asked.

"Of course," Fig said. "They'll ask if you want to share. You don't have to."

"But you know I've never—"

"You said you needed a down-to-earth crowd," he said. "This is all I got. You'll like these guys. We're a kind of a fellowship."

Kelsie shrugged. She was okay with religion, as long as it made people happy. Sometimes she'd hang outside a church during service, just for the calm, steady joy it delivered. And she liked the idea of fellowship. Needed it, in fact.

"We can go someplace else if—" Fig began.

"No. This is perfect," Kelsie said.

Fig wrapped an arm around her shoulders and walked her down the stairs.

She was relieved to see that the group inside was small, only a couple dozen people. Three of them were at an old-fashioned coffee urn, filling paper cups with bitter-scented brew. The rest were already seated in folding chairs that faced a small stage.

There was no altar or cross. The floor was concrete and the walls were bare drywall. It looked about as plain as any high school classroom. It was cold, too—was there no heating in this place?

But the crowd itself was warm, and had a certainty that Kelsie clung to.

She accidentally met the gaze of a tall man with long, black hair tied back.

"Welcome," the man called. He headed toward her. "I'm Harold. You must be Fig's friend Kelsie."

She nodded once. "Uh, I don't want to speak. Or share. Thanks."

"No problem—it's an open meeting," Harold said. He had cool blue eyes and a warm palm when he shook her hand. "We'll be ready when you are."

Kelsie felt her gratitude spill out into the room. Harold's smile broadened.

"There's chocolate chip cookies by the coffee," he said.

"Thank you," Kelsie said.

She grabbed a couple of cookies, then took a seat beside Fig in the second row. The knots in her chest began to loosen as the crowd came together. She felt their patience and resilience, and a kind of cautious optimism. Exactly what she craved. She breathed it in, deeply.

Harold got up to speak, and Kelsie felt the room's respect settle around him.

"Good evening," he said. "I'm Harold and I'm an addict."

"Hi, Harold," everyone said in ragged unison.

"Let's start this meeting of the Washington Street Group of Alcoholics Anonymous with the Serenity Prayer. Join me?"

Kelsie knew the words, and halfway through she joined in.

The shared cadence was a little like singing together, and she felt her nerve endings hum.

"Next," Harold said, "I'll remind you that for the protection of the group, we ask that you have no drugs or paraphernalia on your person at this meeting. If you're carrying, kindly dispose of your items outside this safe space and return as quickly as possible."

No one moved. Harold nodded approval.

"Big group tonight. Difficult time of year, Christmas," Harold said, and the crowd murmured in agreement. "We'd like to extend a special welcome to newcomers. Any first-timers here who'd like to share?"

Kelsie looked down at her feet, feeling like a fraud.

She was relieved when someone else got up. The woman had the tough, wizened look of a long-term alcoholic. She gave her name—Tasha—and this time Kelsie joined in with the welcome, feeling a tiny zing of care and encouragement on her tongue as she said the woman's name.

Tasha began haltingly, but the crowd stayed with her. It was like when someone shy gave a wedding speech and everyone wanted them to succeed.

The room's steadiness softened into sorrow. Tasha had been abandoned as a kid, raised in foster homes. Moving around too often was something Kelsie knew well. It must've resonated with some of the others, too, from the low, sad hum of the room.

When Tasha talked about her alcohol abuse, the grief of the crowd peaked, but then it turned inside out into joy when she talked about getting sober. Kelsie had never seen the two emotions connect that way before.

She let her power stretch out, pulling her thinner until she lost track of where she stopped and everyone else began. The room became a shape, all the jagged parts forming a whole.

For a moment Kelsie was that whole, and she wasn't scared of Swarm. She felt sorry that he could never experience anything like this. This certainty of having failed, mixed with determination to do better, be better.

She felt safe here among strangers. Swarm could do what he wanted outside this room, but this place was hers. There was something sacred about the trust they placed in each other.

Then, for one brief, stupid moment, she thought of Zara, and her serenity broke.

Before they'd spent Christmas night together, Zara had been a virgin, she was certain. Kelsie felt a pang of guilt and tenderness at how much that trust had cost her. Chizara had known how dangerous her power could become the moment she lost control. Kelsie had worried about it too, but she hadn't expected the disaster to come so soon, to be so huge and final.

The drive home had been icy, the kiss good-bye distant. Chizara's mind had been blown by crashing that ship, all that power in her body a constant reminder of the responsibilities she carried every day.

But even so, she'd wanted Kelsie to stay with the Okeke family for safety tonight. Kelsie had lied and insisted she would bunk with Ling.

Hardly more than a day since they'd first kissed, and already Kelsie was lying.

Zara was probably lying to her parents, too, or at least not telling them everything. She pretended they were a pain in the neck, but when it came down to it, she wanted to obey her mom and dad and make them happy. Kelsie didn't fit into that picture.

A hot tear rolled down Kelsie's face, and she struggled to keep the pain from spreading into the room. There was enough pain here already.

Fig took her hand, and she regained control.

She kept her head bowed, wiping away tears as the next person got up to share.

"My name's Quinton."

"Hi, Quinton," said the crowd.

CHAPTER 50
MOB

HER SHOCK ECHOED THROUGH THEM, COLD AND hard, with a burning core of hunger.

Harold was staring at Swarm, uncertain what to make of his mocking expression. The rest were trying to welcome him, fighting the sense of danger that they couldn't yet understand.

But then Swarm made it clear—he reached into a plastic shopping bag at his side and pulled out a bottle of cheap whiskey.

"What the hell?" Fig said beside her.

Swarm swung the bottle high into the air and crashed it down before the gathered group. It hit the concrete and shattered, scattering glass and liquid across the floor. The sweet, oaky scent rose up, mixing with Kelsie's fear and panic. People recoiled, knocking over chairs and swearing.

Outrage lit the room like a grass fire. Kelsie felt it spreading through her.

"Aw, hell no!" Fig shouted. He was furious.

"Don't get mad!" Kelsie shouted. "That's what he wants!"

But it was too late.

A tide of horror and vertigo overwhelmed the two dozen people around her, and the shaking began.

Around her, the faces of the swarmed became slack, their arms loose and twitching. Their teeth chattered. She could feel Swarm's power coiling through them all, erasing them, scouring every bit of individuality from them. In a few seconds the crowd's energy became clean and perfect, all those jagged parts tuning to a single frequency, a music of unison.

Ren might've called people dolls, but to Swarm they weren't even that. They were a single, complex instrument.

He spoke with all their mouths at once.

"Who should we kill, Kelsie Laszlo?"

He knew her name. He'd found her here. He knew what she wanted.

Kelsie tried to lock onto something safe. Hope, joy, *love*. But she couldn't remember any of those emotions.

Just this anger. Just this hunger.

The swarm's periphery was abuzz—the people caught at the mad edge of rapture were tipping chairs and bouncing off walls. The coffee urn went over, and scalding water spilled across skin. Nobody even slowed down.

"Stop this!" Kelsie cried out.

But then she felt herself being pulled through the door that had been opened that day in the mall, cast deep into the feedback loop. Her body shook with it, a staccato pulse of need.

She didn't have to search any longer. She didn't have to be heartbroken and hurt and alone. It had only kept her from what was right and pure. Hunger. Want. Anger. Need. This was her real home. She fit right in. There was nothing left in her life but this bitter appetite, no time before this feeling had possessed her, shaken and rattled her. This burning need had been there every moment she'd sought out crowds. Every baseball game, school assembly, poker table, dance party, or club. All of them wanted to become *this*.

She felt the swarm press in on all sides, warming her. Welcoming her. She could feel him harmonizing them. All the dance beats she'd ever used to tune a crowd were clumsy versions of this perfect chord.

There was no Kelsie Laszlo anymore, just Mob. And she was glad for it.

She felt Swarm's hunger rising, and it was her own hunger, the dark union between them finally come.

Her eyes fell on the face next to hers, and chose him. He dropped from the perfect communion, blinking, stilling, becoming prey.

Mob gazed at him. Her victim looked back, utterly confused.

Her mouth watered and her body was locked, ready. This next part would take her over the line, into glory.

The last trace of Kelsie Laszlo inside her let out a cry of panic—she had chosen Fig.

But the swarm buzzed away that scrap of hesitation. She didn't want Fig to run. She didn't want him to be saved.

She wanted to taste his fear.

He cried out at her, but she was beyond language. Words were nothing beside her connection to the whole.

Fig tried to save her. He grabbed her arm and tried to barrel through the people between them and the stairs. He was fit, and he was fast, but he didn't stand a chance, not dragging her along. The crowd brought him down, and his grasp slipped from her hand.

Fig threw them off like a bucking horse. He clawed his way forward as the crowd ripped at his clothes. Someone was kicking him. It slowed him down. But he still didn't stop.

Good. The longer this took, the better.

The swarm had time. Mob didn't need to help—she was all of them, and could feel every foot and fist and fingernail like they were the endings of her own nerves.

She felt a flood of joy wash across the room, the swarm's elation as they beat and slapped and kicked at Fig.

A last surge of desperation went through him, and he sprang up as if out of water, arms swinging, knocking the smaller attackers back.

He spun and reached for Kelsie, still ready to save her.

But when he saw her rapturous expression, the fight faded in him, replaced with a brilliant flavor of horror. She watched in joy as the swarm covered him again.

Then there was a hitch in the kill, a distraction in the room. Someone on the stairs. Mob peered through the buzzing to find a man in uniform, screaming into his radio.

"Request assistance at—"

And then Swarm's voice: "Another hero. Perfect."

Mob felt a twinge in the mob at this change of plan, and through that gap came a shred of relief that Fig was saved.

But then a fresh, searing ecstasy spread through the room. The swarm surged forward at their new target, seeking handholds on his uniform. Something to rip and ruin. Flesh, skin, hair. They tore him open and had at his slippery heart, squeezing it in their fists.

Until he belonged to them, part of the swarm now. He had died at their hands, in their arms. Kelsie felt the bloated satisfaction as they consumed who he had been. She felt the tenderness of his annihilation, and she fed that out into the mob.

Her mob, hers and Swarm's.

CHAPTER 51
FLICKER

"NATE ISN'T HERE, BUT LET'S START," FLICKER finally said, her voice echoing in the empty Dish.

All their bleary gazes went to her sitting up on the bar. They were looking for guidance, for certainty. For any way out from under the pall of Kelsie's sadness and guilt.

"Not fair," Ethan said. "We have to get our butts here at dark-and-rainy o'clock, and Glorious Leader just gets to *sleep*?"

"His phone's probably switched off." Flicker tried to sell it with a shrug, but they all knew that Glorious Leader himself was switched off. At least for now.

But she was here, and she would lead them.

Somebody had to step up and be glorious.

"Last night, Swarm came at Kelsie," she began. "Luckily, she got away."

"I didn't," Kelsie murmured. She was curled up by the wall where the bar ended.

Flicker hesitated. Kelsie still hadn't told the whole story of last night, except to say that a cop had been killed. She'd called Flicker at midnight in shock, and it had taken all night to calm her down and then get the others here to the Dish.

"Well, you're here with us," Flicker said. "That's better than being with Swarm. Or dead."

Kelsie didn't answer, and Flicker quickly scanned the others' viewpoints—Ethan's fluttered with nervous blinks. Maybe that last word had been a bad idea.

God, this must be so easy for Nate, being able to see and feel the effect of everything he said.

"Why *are* we all here together?" Ethan asked. "I thought we were supposed to stay separate! And, you know, *not* in our much-publicized headquarters!"

"It's six thirty a.m., two days after Christmas, Ethan. The streets are completely empty. No crowds anywhere in town." Flicker turned to face the rest of them, trying to keep doubt from her voice. "If he shows up now, we can take him, easy."

Nothing but silence. She'd been hoping for some kind of joke about kicking Swarm's ass, but they were all too scared and exhausted.

And she was about to make things worse, but there was no way around it.

"Swarm killed a cop last night."

"He had help," Kelsie said softly.

"He *used* Kelsie." Flicker plowed ahead. "And he found her even when she was the only Zero around. So keeping apart isn't going to be enough. We can't wait for him to choose his time and place. We have to fight him on our terms."

"Do we even *have* terms?" Ethan asked. "Like, 'Hey, Swarm, meet us alone in a dark alley? Far away from any random people, so we can kick your butt!'"

"Ethan's got a point," Chizara said. "This guy always shows up with a crowd."

Flicker hesitated. If Chizara was agreeing with Ethan, things were bad.

"Like I told you guys last time," Ethan said, "we all should run away. Live someplace no crowd ever goes. I call dibs on Alaska!"

"I tried leaving Cambria," Chizara said. "It did not go well."

Flicker hopped into her eyes, which were on Kelsie. But Kelsie wasn't meeting anyone's gaze.

"You all know what I mean," Chizara went on. "We barely keep it together here in our hometown, a place we understand. Out there, the unknown can sneak up on you, make you lose control."

Then she was looking at the floor.

What *had* happened on Crash's little road trip with Mob? Flicker hadn't checked the news for technical disasters yet. That was another thing Nate would have done already.

"Our powers can do plenty of damage right here," Thibault said.

Flicker went into Scam's eyes, and before they slipped from Thibault, she saw just how pale and harrowed he was. The memory of yesterday morning with his family came flooding back—his poor mom, his confused brothers, his father's anger at it all.

It had been so awful, she kept pushing it away. But she owed it to Thibault to remember every moment. His family never would.

"It doesn't matter where I go," Kelsie said. She was staring at a crack in the floor. "Even if Swarm never finds me, I could do it again on my own."

"That's not true," Flicker said. "You didn't *want* to kill that cop."

"No, I *wanted* to kill my dad's best friend! The cop just interrupted us!"

Kelsie looked up, and Flicker saw her own horrified expression.

"Swarm let me choose who to kill," Kelsie went on. "And I chose Fig, a friend, because I knew how scared he'd be, seeing me *helping*! I knew his was the fear that would taste *best*!"

Kelsie flooded the Zeroes with emotion again—not despair or horror this time, but an exquisite mix of hunger, desire, ecstasy.

A gasp went around the group, and as the elation faded, Flicker felt sick.

What had she done? Bringing them together while Kelsie was still such a mess was a terrible idea, especially without Nate here to guide the group.

Where the hell *was* he?

"Those poor people will always remember what happened, what they did to that cop," Kelsie said. "A lifetime of nightmares, probably a lifetime of prison, too. I'm only free because Swarm let me go."

"It'll be okay," Ethan said. "The people at the mall aren't getting charged with anything."

Kelsie turned to stare straight at him, and Ethan looked scared of her. "Those were nice middle-class people. *This* was alcoholics and addicts, and a cop died. There's not going to be some get-out-of-jail story about magic gas!"

And they'd gone full circle, Kelsie's guilt blanketing the room again with its desolate weight.

"You guys have to stay away from me. I'm a Swarm waiting to happen."

Flicker felt the room shifting, as Kelsie's self-hatred threatened to spill out into the rest of them. She couldn't let that happen. They needed to trust Kelsie for the plan to work.

Flicker channeled her inner Glorious Leader and said, "You're a Zero, Kelsie. That means you don't have to fight this on your own. Together we're going to take this guy down."

A tremor went around the nightclub, as if Kelsie was clamping her fear down to a nervous, lurking shiver.

"How?" came Thibault's voice.

"Not by running away," Flicker said. "We're going to face him, right here, tomorrow night. And we're going to win."

No one answered. She couldn't even see their faces. They were all looking at her, not at each other.

But at least they were listening, waiting to hear her plan.

"He killed Davey with that mall crowd—people who'd waited up all night. They were tired, annoyed, *greedy*. The kind of crowd that tramples people without any help from superpowers. And last night he killed with people whose refuge had been invaded. Who were fragile to begin with."

"A lot of addicts are really strong," Kelsie said. "But not that night. Not after he came in smashing a bottle of whiskey on the floor."

"My point is this," Flicker said. "Swarm doesn't use happy crowds to kill people. He feeds on anger, fear."

"So we hit him with, what, a parade of clowns?" Chizara asked.

"Clowns?" Ethan cried out. "She just said fear is *bad*."

Flicker shook her head. "No, not clowns, or rainbows, or unicorns. We hit him with the crowd we've been training with for the last three months. A crowd we *know* how to make happy."

"Huh," Chizara said. "You mean we hit him with the Dish?"

"Exactly. We face him in our own home, where we control the lights, the music, and the beer. That's how we win."

For a moment Flicker had them all. She could feel it in the room—even Kelsie believed in this plan, or at least she wanted to.

Then Ethan cleared his throat. "But why would he show up here, where we want him, on exactly the right night? He can pick us off anywhere, anytime!"

When Flicker hesitated, it was Kelsie who spoke up.

"That part's easy," she said. "We do what Davey and Ren did. We make him *mad* at us."

CHAPTER 52
SCAM

IN CAMBRIA, WINTER WAS NEVER COLD ENOUGH
for ponds to freeze over. So once a year the county built an ice-
skating rink beside Main Square. The rental skates were crappy,
the music was cheesy, and the hot chocolate was powdered.

But for some reason this was where Sonia wanted to
meet Ethan.

She probably knew the place would annoy him. For a start,
he hadn't skated since he was a kid. And second, nothing said
trying too hard like skating backward to "Jingle Bell Rock."

But Flicker's plan meant he had to go. For the Zeroes to
stand a chance against Swarm, they had to have the biggest,
happiest party ever, and Swarm had to be goaded into coming
to it. And for that they needed something better than handing
out flyers on a street corner.

They needed Sonia Sonic.

When Ethan got to Main Square, however, he started to feel queasy. He hadn't been in a real crowd since that morning at the mall. Right now the skaters reminded him of the frenzied zombies at the outer edge of the swarm. He thought of Davey, ripped apart like a Christmas turkey.

Ethan stood, sweating in the cold winter air. Sonia was late, of course, leaving him waiting with his stomach in knots. He had an awful sensation, like the back of his neck was trying to crawl up to his scalp. His whole body was on the alert for Swarm.

"It's just a bunch of ice-skating idiots," he muttered. "Full of Christmas freaking cheer."

But how could he be sure? The other Zeroes had their magic insight into crowds, but Ethan would never see Swarm coming. They'd all turn into a flash mob of ravening zombies without any warning.

And about the only thing he could imagine worse than running from zombies was running from zombies *with ice skates on*.

He edged toward the rink. A twenty-foot Christmas tree towered beside it, a white star standing out against the dusk. A bank of lights swept red and green beams across the ice. Frank Sinatra crooned through tinny speakers. A food stand steamed near the gate, but it didn't serve beer. Which sucked. Ethan could have done with some liquid courage right about now, if the voice could have managed it.

His phone blipped. Sonia. Crap, she was already out there

somewhere on the crowded ice. So the only way to deliver his message was to strap some knives to his feet and give up any hope of outrunning a swarm.

Well, this was just perfect.

Ethan waited in line, paid his sixteen bucks for a pair of worn-looking rental skates, and struggled into them. He imagined being knocked to the ice by an evil horde and trying to defend himself by slashing at their hands with the old, blunt blades on his feet.

He wobbled out onto the ice, clinging to the rail. He had to shrink aside to avoid skaters moving three times as fast as him.

It was hard to search for Sonia when he was barely managing to stay upright. Why did *he* have to be the one to talk to her anyhow? She hated his guts, and Ethan was sick of people hating him all the time.

With one hand on the rail he managed to turn and examine the crowd. Her hair should be easy to spot, unless she'd dyed it again. Of course, it would probably be fluorescent green or flaming Christmas crimson or whatever, so she might still stand out from the rest of the skaters.

It took five long minutes to locate her. The compression sleeve on her right wrist was covered in glitter stickers. Her hair was tucked into a slouchy beanie, the bleached white of her bangs changing colors with the lights. It was pretty striking, if he was honest. She skated gracefully, while Ethan clung to the rail and pulled himself along one-handed.

"Sonia!"

She saw him, waved her sparkly hand, and one smooth circuit later swept up behind him.

She pulled him into motion. "You made it!"

She looked happy to see him. Ethan didn't like that look. It was usually followed by a rapid shift to disappointment.

"Why'd you choose a skating rink?" he bleated. "I can't skate!"

"I see that." Sonia grinned. She didn't look disappointed yet, even though he was clearly the worst skater on the ice.

"Can we sit down?" he tried. "I need to talk to you."

"You want to talk to me, keep skating," Sonia said.

Crap. Ethan just wanted to deliver his message and go. But talking while staying upright was one thing too many. The voice could handle the talking part, but Sonia was a complicated case. She was wise to the voice, even if she didn't quite understand it yet. She'd work it out eventually, just like Mom and Jess and the Zeroes had. And if he wanted to delay that discovery, he had to watch his step.

"*Slice* with your feet," Sonia said. "Try it with me. First, right."

She linked her good arm through his and Ethan leaned into his wobbling right foot. Or rather, Sonia leaned and Ethan followed because he was holding on to Sonia. But together they slewed rightward.

"Now left," Sonia reminded him, as if there were any other option.

Ethan tilted left.

"Great!" Sonia said. "Now without *leaning* on me so much. You're kind of heavy."

"Sorry." He eased off.

His ankles still wobbled like deboned chicken bits, but he hadn't fallen over yet. And he'd forgotten, mostly, about the ever-present risk of being swarmed.

"How's your girlfriend, the DJ?" Sonia asked.

The question made Ethan's knees shake. Kelsie was a basket case, more convinced than ever that she could go Swarm at any moment. The others were pretty worried too.

But not Ethan. To him Kelsie was still Kelsie. Even if . . .

"She's not my girlfriend."

"Really?"

"Totally. For one thing, she's into girls."

"Oh." Out the corner of his eye he saw a smile creep onto Sonia's face. At his pain, Ethan figured.

He seriously did not want to talk to Sonia Sonic about his defunct love life. On top of everything else, the voice had gone and made him look like a dick, sending Kelsie out into the night alone, and vulnerable enough to wind up at an AA meeting. Add one Swarm, and you had an epic disaster.

At least he was skating half decently. Enough to deliver his message. "Sonia, I need a favor."

"A bigger favor than teaching you to skate?"

"Definitely." Ethan kept his eyes on the skates in front of

him, matching Sonia's rhythm. "We need you to post about a party at the Dish tomorrow night."

"Oh, so *now* I'm useful to you guys?"

Ethan sighed. He'd known he wouldn't get through this meeting without using his power, but he was reaching for it sooner than he'd hoped.

Come on, voice, get to the point, he thought, and the words came leaping out of his lungs. "All those photos you got sent? Of the Dish the night everything went haywire? That was a hit job on us."

"A what?"

"Some people who wanted to mess with us. They set up that whole disaster, and took pictures, then made you their mouthpiece!"

Sonia stared at him suspiciously, and he shrugged.

"It's all true," he said in his own voice.

"That sucks." She thought a moment. "I thought it was weird, just getting all those photos sent to me. And they were behind everyone going crazy?"

"Yep. They're part of what's been going on all over the country."

Way to go, voice! Still kinda true.

"Who would *do* something like that?"

"The bad guys," the voice said. "People who want us good guys out of the picture. And it worked—we're getting major heat from the cops. So we're having a Love Saves the Dish party."

"A *what* party?"

"It's just a fund-raiser, so we can go legit. We need your help to pull a big crowd. But the *right* kind of crowd." He glanced sideways at Sonia. She was still listening. "Otherwise the Dish is dead and we probably all have to become fugitives. Which would leave you nothing to post about."

Sonia's eyebrows shot up. "Is it really that bad? You'd have to leave town?"

"Yep," he said in his own voice. It was just the truth, after all. He let the voice finish up. "You screwed up our thing, so now you gotta help us. Just make it sound like a happy club."

That was the core of Flicker's plan—the crowd's good vibes, along with the music, lights, and Nate's and Kelsie's influence, would win against Swarm's anger. Ethan just hoped she was right.

"Am I invited?" Sonia asked.

"Um . . ." The voice hesitated, and Ethan realized he wasn't sure if he wanted her there.

Sure, Sonia was his enemy, sort of, but this party might turn deadly.

"Well, you had a pretty rough time the other night," the voice said. "We only want people with happy memories of the club."

"Oh, so I'm a bummer now?"

Great. Now she was pissed, and that was a disaster. If Sonia's post brought a bunch of bad vibes to the party, Swarm would turn the Zeroes into pulled pork.

He opened his mouth and let the voice fix it. "Hey, if you

can get the right crowd through the door, I'll personally put you on the VIP list."

He felt a stab of guilt as he said it, but after all, they were risking a lot of other people too. At least this might be the last crowd that Swarm endangered.

And Sonia looked pretty happy. She gestured with her sparkly bandaged wrist. "Just give me a time and date."

The voice was on autopilot now, delivering Flicker's message. "Tomorrow night, starting around eight, and use the word *love* as much as possible in your post. That'll get us a nice crowd, not some random mob of . . ."

Kelsie's code name in his mouth sent a shudder through Ethan, strong enough to make even the voice falter.

"I get it," Sonia answered. "Duh! I'm a woman on the internet. You think I don't know about hate mobs?"

The voice went into sleep mode, and Ethan realized the job was done.

But she was still looking to him for a response.

"Great," he said. "I mean, thanks a lot."

"Did you actually think I *wouldn't* help you?" Sonia rolled her eyes. "Why do you always doubt me, Ethan?"

"I don't know. Because you hate me?"

Her mouth dropped open. "Where'd you get that idea?"

"Because you turned that video of me in to the cops! Because you made it look like I was best friends with bank robbers, when all I was trying to do was save you from getting shot!"

"Hey, you knew their names. What was I *supposed* to think?" She didn't sound angry, but for a moment her balance beside him felt uncertain.

"Yeah, but . . . ," Ethan began, but he didn't have anywhere else to go. It probably *had* been pretty suspicious-looking, chatting with Jerry Laszlo in the middle of a bank robbery. "You really thought I might be a bad guy?"

"Of course! Why else would I turn you in to the cops?"

"Because I didn't like Jay White!"

Sonia stared at him for a long moment; then a sudden peal of laughter spilled out of her. She angled away from him and swooped toward the edge of the rink.

"Whoa, wait up." He followed, shaky without her support. But he made it to the edge without face-planting.

She was leaning over the rail, still laughing.

"Any time you're ready to quit that . . . ," he said.

"It's just," she managed between gasps, "you really thought I was still mad at you for dissing Jay White? I mean, he's *so* last June."

"Okay." Ethan hesitated. "But you looked pretty angry at the time. And then you got me busted!"

She grinned. "You know, whatever it is with you guys, I'm going to figure it out. But until then, it only makes you more interesting, Ethan."

He didn't know what to say to that. He stood with one hand on the rail for balance, as the small army of ice skaters shushed past. No one had ever called him *interesting* before.

Maybe it was some kind of fatalism from the whole Swarm thing, or maybe it was because Sonia was a smart girl with cool hair. But whatever, Ethan wished he could tell her just how interesting he *really* was. How the voice worked, how it always got him into trouble. How he had to fight against it anytime he wanted to really connect with someone.

Which was what he wanted to do now, he realized. He wanted to connect with her—Sonia Sonic. His worst nightmare from last summer.

"Oh, crap," he muttered.

It was totally nuts. Sonia Sonic was a time bomb who could blow up the Zeroes' secrets at any time. She was out to increase her own microfame at their expense.

Plus, there was the fact that he'd just invited her to a party that might become a massacre.

"I should go," he said. "We've got a lot of work to do before tomorrow."

Finally, the look of disappointment he'd been waiting for crossed her face.

She shrugged. "Okay. Hope you had fun skating."

"I didn't fall and slice my fingers off, which I count as a win." He hesitated. "Can you put that post up tonight?"

"Sure. Wouldn't want to ruin your big party." She smiled. "Love Saves the Dish!"

Ethan grinned. Either the voice had done an even better

370

job than usual, or Sonia was in a great mood today.

"Thanks." He felt his smile fade. Part of him still wanted to warn Sonia off the party. But at the same time, he didn't want her to think he didn't like her.

So all he said was, "Stay safe, okay?"

"Okay, freak." She winked.

Ethan skated to the exit, with barely any of the wobble he'd had before meeting up with Sonia.

CHAPTER 53
ANONYMOUS

"HOLD IT STEADY . . ."

Thibault sent the bolt through the steel sheet into the door frame, the drill spitting spirals of metal and wood. When he stepped back, the main entrance to the Petri Dish was smaller, and pretty much indestructible.

"Booyah," the Craig said.

Thibault slapped the man's huge shoulder, keeping physical contact. The six people working in the Dish were too scattered for the Curve to take hold, but he liked to focus the Craig's attention when the guy was swinging big pieces of metal around.

And after what had happened yesterday with his family, Thibault found any connection reassuring.

"Let's get those windows covered."

"You got it, Tee." The Craig led the way onto the dance floor, where the scrap was piled.

Tee, huh? Half a name was pretty good for the Craig. Working together was giving his memory extra grip.

When they had the next sheet in place, Thibault fished in his pocket for another screw, positioned it, and drilled.

It was a relief to be in motion, to have something to do besides think about his family, even if it meant turning the Dish into a fortress. He and the Craig were narrowing the wide, welcoming entrance so a crowd couldn't swarm in all at once. The other Zeroes were setting up escape plans A, B, and C.

Well, not all of them—Glorious Leader was still holed up in his room at home, sending cryptic texts to Flicker. The ones she'd shown Thibault hardly made sense:

Burner phones in supply closet.

Fuel leak off the coast.

Take singles if you need to run.

Working on my old trick.

Thibault wondered what kind of *trick* that was. A new strategy for beating Swarm?

The last thing they needed was Glorious Leader under-cutting Flicker at the last minute. She had stepped up, at least. Fortress Dish was her plan—her gamble.

The whole thing relied on the Dish crowd being too happy, too inherently *good,* to change into a deadly swarm. Even if Swarm brought his own angry minions, they could only trickle in through the narrowed entrance. And as they came, Kelsie would Mob them into the happy dance, with help from Crash's light show.

To be fair, it seemed like a pretty risky plan to stake all their lives on, especially with Kelsie as upset as Thibault had ever seen her. But he'd also seen the right music cue or splash of spinning colors shift a crowd's mood in an instant. The Dish experiments had given them the tools; they just had to make it work.

If all that failed, Ethan and Kelsie were busy narrowing the stairs so a killer swarm couldn't rampage up to the second floor faster than the Zeroes could reach the back-alley fire escape.

Running away was sometimes just as solid as the Middle Way.

"Can I borrow you, Craig?" Chizara called from the second-floor balcony. "We need to rig some more lights up here."

"You got it." The Craig dropped his end of the steel plate, which clanged to the floor.

"Hey!" Thibault said, but the guy was already trotting away like a puppy.

Damn. Disappeared again. And he couldn't lift all this metal by himself.

"Ethan? Kelsie?" he called. "Give me a hand here?"

No answer. Too much Curve.

Story of his life.

Thibault lowered the steel, fighting off despair. He made himself go back to the dance floor. Ethan and Kelsie were working halfway up the stairs, a bright connection crackling between them.

"I shouldn't have said any of that stuff," Ethan was saying.

Kelsie jammed a crate into the barricade. She didn't look at him, but her attention flared.

Thibault cleared his throat. Neither of them noticed.

"Seriously," Ethan said, "I feel really bad about it."

Kelsie straightened up. "Don't apologize. For once your voice was telling the truth."

"There's times to tell the truth, my mom says, and times to shut the fuck up."

Thibault stepped closer. "Um, guys?"

"Your mom says that?" Kelsie said.

"Yeah, except without swearing."

Not a spark of their attention came his way. Too much focus between them.

Thibault balled his fists. He'd spent his whole life eavesdropping, but always with people who would never see him, never know him. Ethan and Kelsie had worked hard to be his friends—he didn't want to spy on them.

But he'd spent all week fighting to be seen. He was done shoving himself into other people's awareness.

He turned back to the pile of scrap. Maybe he could move one of the smaller pieces. . . .

"It was my fault." Ethan's words carried from the stairs. "I can't really control the voice, but it listens to me."

"What do you mean?" Kelsie asked.

"I let jealousy into my head," Ethan said, busily stacking stuff. "Being jealous of you and Chizara, that's what got the voice started."

Thibault looked up at the balcony—maybe he could help Chizara? But she and Craig had disappeared from sight. And to get to them, he'd have to pass Ethan and Kelsie.

He took a few steps toward the stairs, but the brightness of their connection made him pause.

What if they didn't even notice him?

"I don't think there's anything to be jealous of anymore," Kelsie said.

This only deflated Ethan more. "That's rough."

"You're lucky we didn't hook up, Ethan. It's a bad idea getting a crush on me. I'm no good with one-on-one stuff. I only wind up disappointing people. I thought with Chizara it could work, but it turns out I'm still terrible."

"You aren't." Ethan straightened, arms limp by his sides. "But you don't exactly sound surprised I had a thing for you."

"Ethan," Thibault murmured. "She'd have had to be *unconscious* not to know that."

Kelsie didn't even register him. Her awareness had curled up inside her, and her voice sounded tiny. "You were pretty obvious about it."

Ethan kicked at a box embedded in the barricade. "I just wish I'd said something. I was *meaning* to, but the whole frickin' universe kept interrupting me—first Glitch and Coin, then those cops, then Swarm. I mean, whatever you want is cool. *Obviously . . .*"

Kelsie's attention crept out and took hold of him again. "Maybe the universe was trying to tell you something."

"That it hates me?"

"That there's someone *else* out there for you. Someone right in front of you, who's hot for you right back."

Ethan just stared at her.

"Sonia," Kelsie persisted. "With the crazy hair."

"Sonia Sonic?" Ethan squeaked.

Thibault rolled his eyes. *She fixes on you like a spotlight.*

"She did teach me how to skate, kind of," Ethan said.

"Skating's like dancing. It's a courtship ritual." Kelsie picked up another wooden crate and jammed it into the barricade.

Ethan slumped again. "Not that it matters much, seeing as we're all gonna *die* and stuff."

"No, Ethan, don't you get it? This gives you more reason to live!"

It was the first time Thibault had heard a note of hope in her voice since Davey had been killed. It made him feel ashamed at his own despair.

He'd had to walk away from his family, but at least they were all still alive. Kelsie couldn't say the same, and twice this week she'd had Swarm in her head when he'd torn people to pieces.

If she could still muster a smile about Ethan and Sonia, maybe the Zeroes did have a chance tomorrow night. Maybe love really *would* save the Dish. . . .

The Craig appeared at the top of the stairs. "How's it going, guys?"

"Good." Kelsie patted the crate she'd just wedged into place. "No evil horde's getting past this."

The Craig walked down the stairs, inspected the barricade for a moment, then reached out and took hold of the crate. With a single movement he yanked it out, the wooden slats splintering as it came away in his hand.

"Hey!" she cried.

The Craig shrugged. "If I can pull it apart, so can a buncha bad guys."

"Can't argue with that," Chizara called from the second-floor balcony. She and Flicker stood among a nest of new light poles. A tangle of fresh wiring snaked down to the junction box.

"You oughta just block the stairs off completely." The Craig socked his palm with his fist. "Just stay up there and leave me down here to do the dirty work."

"Yeah, except if things go wrong, he'll make you his minion too," Flicker said. "This bad guy *controls* people."

"Maybe other people. Not the Craig."

"Don't worry, you'll get your shot at him," Flicker said. "Hey, you guys, come out where we can see you for a second?"

Ethan, Kelsie, and Craig looked at each other, but stepped out to join Thibault on the dance floor.

Up on the balcony next to Chizara, Flicker held her cane across one shoulder, like a swashbuckler's sword. Thibault felt an actual smile creeping onto his face. She was a glorious leader in her own right.

Now that he'd lost his family, he felt luckier than ever to have her as a girlfriend.

"Craig has a point," she said. "Keeping the crowd happy is only step one. We also have to take out Swarm."

"I'm telling you, no problem." Craig mimed a bear hug, his biceps popping. "Gimme ten seconds and he's out like a light."

"*Ten* seconds?" Flicker laughed. "Five, tops. Trouble is, the moment you start thinking about violence, you'll let Swarm into your head."

"I will?"

"That's the way he works. Your rage is his key to your mind."

"Then how's this gonna happen?" Ethan asked. "What's the point of neutralizing his minions if we can't *do* anything to the guy?"

"We have to switch off his power," Flicker said. "Just for a few seconds."

"I don't see how," Kelsie said. "He has a feedback loop between himself and the crowd, just like I do." She looked around, found Thibault beside her. "Can you cut that kind of connection, Anon?"

He answered slowly, grateful for this moment of the group's attention. "I can't chop away links among hundreds of people, no."

"So we can't get rid of the feedback loop," Flicker said. "But we can *use* it."

She nodded to Chizara, who snapped her fingers. All the new spotlights flashed on, whiting out everything.

"Yeow!" Ethan cried. The Craig grunted, and Thibault shut his eyes, but the pattern of spotlights was already burned into his vision.

Crash laughed her mad-scientist laugh and cut the blazing lights.

"Ow" came Kelsie's voice, tiny and full of pain. Through the spotlight burns, Thibault saw that she'd doubled over and covered her face. "A little warning next time, Zara?"

"Sorry," Chizara said. "We needed to surprise you."

"Mission accomplished."

Flicker was coming slowly down the stairs, her cane tapping now that everyone's vision was fritzed. "We had to test what kind of feedback a surprised crowd would produce. So how was it, Kelsie?"

"Like a grenade went off in my head." Kelsie straightened up, blinking. "I'm still dizzy."

"Me too," Flicker said. "So imagine that times a couple of hundred people."

"And maybe even more light," Chizara said. "I've got power left over from my little . . . accident up the coast. I can pump more watts in and burn out all the lights in a blaze of glory!"

"You think all that would knock you out for ten seconds?" Flicker asked.

Kelsie rubbed her eyes, nodding. "At least."

"I'll be wearing these, then." The Craig pulled sunglasses from his breast pocket and put them on. "Swarm comes in, you guys flash the crowd, I grab him, squish him unconscious. Have I got that right?"

"Sounds like a *plan*," Ethan said.

"But then what?" Thibault stepped into the one remaining circle of spotlight. The others' attention flicked toward him. "What do we do with Swarm once we've got him—besides get him isolated, fast?"

The connections faded as they considered.

"He needs to be away from crowds, like, permanently." Ethan sent a worried strand toward Flicker. "So, lock him up? Somewhere in the country?"

"In the desert. A bunker." Craig's attention fanned out among them. "I might know a place."

"And then, what, spend the rest of our lives taking supplies out there?" Thibault asked, killing the hopeful glow in all their faces. "Hiding the fact that we're kidnappers?"

"Just until we think of something better," Chizara said. "Some way of canceling out his powers."

"What, like putting a big *magnet* next to him?" Ethan snorted.

"Maybe we can cure him," Flicker said. "What if you faced off with him, Kelsie, with the five of us on your side? Could you change his power so he's more like you?"

Kelsie shrank back into herself. "I don't think so. He changes *me*, not the other way around."

"Can we level him *down*?" Ethan said.

Connections spangled at him.

"And how would we do that, Ethan?" Chizara asked.

He threw up his hands. "I don't know. Why even *get* him here if we don't know what to do with him?"

A silence fell, connections probing all around the room.

"Don't worry about Swarm," said a voice from the door. "I know exactly how to deal with him."

Thibault squinted. Nate stood there, framed against the sunlight. He'd snuck in, instead of taking the stage and commanding everyone's attention like usual.

But now he stood resplendent in the sudden fizz of their surprise and hope.

"How?" Flicker asked quietly.

Glorious Leader looked around, deftly connecting with each person—even Thibault. He steadied and brightened each arc of attention, and it felt good. Thibault usually hated Nate's blatant displays of power, but all he could feel was relief at being led with such perfect assurance. At being seen at all.

Damn. He'd really missed the guy.

"Don't worry," Nate said. "I'll handle it."

Uncertainty wormed through the relief in Thibault's gut. He didn't want to think what handling it might mean, and he didn't want to ask.

He waited for someone else to speak up, to insist that Nate say what he was planning. But that round of eye contact seemed to have silenced everyone else's doubts too.

They all wanted to believe that Glorious Leader had it under control.

"Now let's get back to work," Nate said.

CHAPTER 54
SCAM

ETHAN HAD NEVER BEEN SO UNHAPPY TO HIT THE weekend.

But here it was, Saturday, the day of Love Saves the Dish, the world's first party named expressly to piss off an evil super-villain. That was the plan, anyway: lure him in and crush him. If you could call *surround yourself with happy minions, dazzle them with a Dish-tastic dance party, then choke out the bad guy* a plan.

The plan had kept Ethan awake most of the night.

He thought back fondly to the days when corrupt cops were his biggest problem. Or Jess being mad at him. But at least there was one good thing about the likelihood of imminent death—it took his mind off the fact that Kelsie had *known* he had a crush on her, and hadn't bothered to set him straight.

Six months he'd spent pining for her, and the whole time she'd been rolling her eyes about it. On top of which she'd turned out to have an evil power all along.

Gah—no. Kelsie was too nice to make fun of him behind his back. She was *good*. He still hoped that.

Because if she wasn't, they were all going to die today.

Ethan pulled on his best jeans and his favorite hoodie—if he was going to die, he was going to die styling.

"Stop," Mom said as he hurried toward the front door.

Ethan stopped. Mom was usually at the office by now, every day of the week. But today she was still in the bathrobe Jess had given her for Christmas. She was sitting at the dining table with her hands wrapped around a coffee mug.

"Where do you think you're going?"

"Uh," Ethan began.

For a crazy moment he thought about explaining everything, just in case this was his last chance. Maybe it was time she knew about powers and swarms and the Zeroes' busted-ass plan to convert a Heights warehouse into a supervillain trap.

Mom didn't wait for the explanation, though. "Because I *hope* you're going to the funeral."

"The what, now?"

"For Officer Delgado," Mom continued. "Died in the line of duty the night after Christmas."

"Right. The guy who was torn apart by . . . a crowd."

Mom's face fell. "Yeah. Another one, right here in Cambria

this time. He was a good cop and a close friend of mine. He was helping me with an investigation. It would have made his career."

"The Internal Affairs thing?"

She gave him a look and said tightly, "I can't share that information. Only that Marcus Delgado is being buried today with full honors. And you are going with me."

Ethan groaned inwardly. Full-honors funerals took hours. His mom had dragged him to one in Bakersfield two years ago. His swore his butt was still numb. Plus, he did not have that kind of time, not today.

"Can't you take Jess?"

"She's been to enough funerals, don't you think?"

"Oh. Right." Ethan swallowed. "The thing is, I have these important plans with my friends."

"More important than a man who gave his life for this city?"

Ethan was about to say, *Totally, because if we screw this up, we'll all be having funerals.* But any remotely true answer would mean spilling the beans. Besides, Mom looked like she was really hurting, which was kind of weirding him out.

"Ethan, just do this thing for me, okay?" Mom came to stand in front of him, and put her hands on his shoulders. "Please?"

She gave him a look that made him feel small and sad. Just like all those times when she caught him lying about his grades.

But none of this was Ethan's fault. Not directly. Heck, he was trying to *avenge* the guy.

And today of all days, he couldn't abandon his friends for hours of bagpipes and bugles.

So he reached for the voice.

I want Mom off my back. Keep it simple! If the voice got too fancy, Mom would know it was the other Ethan—bad, lying Ethan. And he did not want his last day on earth to include a smackdown from his mom. *Be nice about it. And most of all, voice, be kind.*

The voice leaped up instantly. "Of course I'll go to the funeral with you, Mom."

Ethan clamped his mouth shut. *What part of that was* not *clear?*

Mom smiled gently. She put a warm hand on his cheek. "Thanks, sweetheart. I had your suit cleaned. We'll head to the parade ground in an hour."

She left the room, taking with her any hope Ethan had of being part of the Zeroes' preparations. But the voice had been clear: the only way to get past this ass-numbing funeral was to go.

Watching someone get buried when you and all your friends were probably going to die that night was a seriously depressing experience.

The police parade ground was wedged between the Heights

and a nature preserve. It was infuriatingly close to the Dish, a ten-minute walk at most.

The ground was crammed with uniformed cops standing in formation, hundreds of them. Their faces were rigid with grieving, like this was a grim job that had to be done. Behind them were maybe a hundred civilians in their Sunday best. On the way over, his mom had said there were live feeds all over town in schools and halls and even bars. Seemed like a funeral could really bring people together. Which was too miserable for Ethan to even think about.

Mom found them seats in the grandstand, which was full of suits and cops in dress uniform She stared silently ahead, her hands clenched around a blue rose in her lap.

Mom had lost someone important to her because of a superpowered freak—a Zero, like Ethan. If she ever did find out what he was, would she look at him and think *cop killer*?

Ethan sat, trying not to look at his phone. Nate had been understanding about Ethan missing the party prep, but his calm had sounded more fatalistic than reassuring. Whatever he'd been through after Davey died, Glorious Leader hadn't come back the same.

"Keep *still*," Mom whispered.

The voice leaped to his defense. "Sorry. It's just, I don't know how to act at these things."

Mom's face softened. She put an arm around his shoulders, like she used to when he was little. "You're doing great, kiddo."

She hadn't called him *kiddo* since he was eight. She was going all out with the sentimentality today. She even kissed his cheek, then rubbed at the spot with a thumb.

"Don't want to confuse your girlfriend with lipstick."

"The girls I know are in no way confused," Ethan mumbled, wiping his cheek on the shoulder of his suit.

"You just haven't found the right one yet."

Met her, fell in love with her, was not her type.

His suit cut into his armpits. He'd bought the stupid thing a year ago for Dad's wedding—on sale—and it was too small then. Now the sleeves showed a full inch of his wrists and he hadn't even bothered trying to squeeze into the matching trousers. He was wearing his newest pair of jeans, a blue shirt, and a tie. Exactly the kind of outfit he'd probably be buried in.

He wished he could steal a glance at his phone without looking like a douche. What were the other Zeroes doing right now? How was Nate going to deal with Swarm once they caught him? Ethan hoped Glorious Leader had a real plan and wasn't just hoping for last-minute inspiration.

A procession of motorcycle police rumbled out onto the parade ground, leading the hearse through an honor guard of uniformed cops. The coffin was slid into place at the front of the grandstand while Mom cried silently beside him. Ethan reached for her hand.

They sat through more than an hour of speeches before a lone bugle started playing "Taps." How could an instrument that dumb-looking sound so sad? Even Ethan started choking up, and he'd never met Delgado.

He looked around the grandstand and found Detectives King and Fuentes in their dress blues. They were standing at rigid attention, but even Fuentes looked like he was crying.

"Taps" did it, every time. Turned hardened cops to mush.

Fuentes still managed to look seriously pissed, though. They all did. Too bad the Zeroes couldn't hook into that rage and convince all these angry cops to take it out on Swarm. March around Cambria until they found the guy, and then, *He's your cop killer, the preppy kid with the terrible haircut. He did it with his superpower!*

"Why are those officers staring at you?" Mom asked quietly.

"What?" Ethan followed his mother's gaze to find his old buddies Murillo and Ang, all dressed up in dark blue finery with their hats pulled low. They had blue flowers pinned to their breast pockets, and their gloved hands rested on their sidearms.

Yeah, they were definitely staring at him. They looked angry, too. There were so many local cops who hated Ethan. Maybe he really should think about leaving town.

"Do you know them, Ethan?"

"Um, no?" His real voice was quivering, so he gave himself over to his superpower. *Say anything that makes her stop thinking about Murillo and Ang.*

"Surrender yourself to the rage, Mom."

What the . . .

Ethan turned to his mom. Her pupils were vibrating, the rest of her shuddering so hard that the blue rose fell from her hands. Around them, the senior brass were shivering and jerking. The shaking moved to their teeth and then their whole bodies, until they were practically vibrating.

The voice had done it—she wasn't thinking about Murillo and Ang anymore.

She'd been swarmed.

CHAPTER 55
SCAM

"MOM!" ETHAN CRIED.

She didn't answer.

Come on, voice! Say something to bring her back.

But no sound came. All he could hear was the shuddering breaths and chattering teeth of several hundred swarmed cops.

He took a sweeping look across the parade ground. It was in the midst of a human earthquake. Here by the grandstand the cops had drawn together into one dense, shivering cluster. The civilian audience had been dragged in too, seething and bubbling around the solid blue center. Those outside the chaos were backing off fast, some of them fleeing toward the roads beyond.

Apparently Swarm had decided on an appetizer before the

party tonight. Ethan was doomed to be ripped to pieces. By the looks of it, his own mother was going to deal the first blows.

He twisted in his chair, searching for a way to escape. But he was trapped in the middle of the grandstand, surrounded. These beefy cops would bring him down within seconds. There was only one way left to strike back against Swarm—

He reached for his phone and texted Nate:

Hundreds of cops swarmed!

The message took a long moment to send, and Ethan wrapped his arms around the phone protectively. At least he could sacrifice himself to warn the others.

His phone made a triumphant little *whoop*—the text had sent.

He crumpled with relief, closed his eyes, and readied himself to die. He hoped it was quick. He hoped there was enough of him left to bury. He hoped he didn't have to see his mom covered in blood while she ripped his arms off.

Around him the sounds of the crowd had reached a buzzing crescendo. Swarm was going to slice and dice him. The swarm pressed against him from all sides, so tight he could hardly breathe.

He waited.

Crap. Maybe it took a while to build a crowd to killing pitch, and he had time to get out of here after all.

His phone trembled.

Get back here. Glorious Leader, still giving orders. That figured.

Ethan texted as fast as he could: *Tell Kelsie—*

But he couldn't finish the thought. He was too scared of dying. He sent it anyway. Surely Glorious Leader could come up with some fitting last words on Ethan's behalf.

He tried to meet his mother's eye, but he saw only rage and burning hunger. Then she turned away—

Okay, this was weird. His mother and everyone else in the grandstand were moving in the same direction. Ethan was dragged with them as the shuddering core flowed onto the parade ground.

Then it hit him. They were leaving the funeral. Swarm was steering the whole funeral into the Heights. He was coming to the Screw the Swarm party with his own private army!

The crowd parted, revealing the only other person who wasn't part of the shivering blue horde. Wearing a striped blazer and a curious expression, a guy Ethan's age stood on the stage beside the coffin, staring at him.

This was Swarm? Ethan felt cheated. Wow, so weedy—and yes, that was a seriously bad haircut.

Swarm stared at Ethan like he was a foreign movie without subtitles.

"What *are* you?"

Ethan blinked, about a dozen stupid answers tumbling through his head. *A fellow superpowered freak. A son, a kid brother, a guy doomed to never have a girlfriend.*

He left it to the voice, hoping with all his heart that whatever it said would make Swarm decide not to kill him.

"Mine is the reverse of every power you've ever encountered," the voice said confidently. "I am unique among us all. And if you eat me, I'll turn everyone inside you sour."

It sounded like crazy talk to Ethan. Sure, the others always ribbed him about his power being different, just because it didn't like crowds. But he was still a Zero, right?

Swarm nodded once, as if the voice's words confirmed whatever his Zeroes-hunting nose was telling him. "I'll deal with you later, then. After I tear your friends to bloody pieces."

A stab of anger went through Ethan, and a buzzing darkness appeared along the edges of his thoughts, crowding out all sound and light.

The last thing he could hear was Swarm saying, "Well, that was easy."

Little *twerp*. But the angrier he got, the farther Ethan fell into Swarm's trap.

He fought it, breathing in deep gulps of air, trying to steady his emotions.

Don't be angry. Happy thoughts! Happy thoughts! Dance party in my brain!

But there were no happy thoughts inside Ethan. First this douche had swarmed Ethan's own mom, and now he was headed for the Dish to kill all his friends, way too early for their plan, their *useless* plan, to work.

His anger joined the righteous fury of the cops around him. All that rage carried him jittering along, leaving only one last rational thought. . . .

If only the crowd *had* murdered him. Because alive, Swarm would use him, just like he was using these cops.

He was going to use Ethan to kill the Zeroes.

CHAPTER 56
MOB

IT FELT LIKE GETTING READY FOR A TORNADO.

Kelsie was doing her best to keep her feedback loop with the other Zeroes from descending into dread, but it was wearing her out. She'd been playing uplifting movie themes all day—mostly Bollywood tracks—trying to keep her fear under control. But every time she relaxed, a pulse of anxiety would hit her, then tear through the rest of them.

Maybe the Zeroes trusted her, but Kelsie didn't know if she trusted herself. Not after what'd happened at the AA meeting—what she'd *felt* while the swarm had done its work.

The cops had arrested ten people for the murder, including Tasha, the first-timer. Fig, at least, had been too beaten up to be blamed for Delgado's death.

When she'd visited him in Cambria County General

Hospital last night, Kelsie hadn't even tried to explain what had happened. He thought sooner or later the police lab would identify some kind of poison gas in the whiskey bottle.

But it was so much simpler that that—Swarm was more powerful than her. She had no immunity to his dark control, at least not in a group as vulnerable as an AA meeting. But what if the Dish crowd was no different?

What if Kelsie was helping her friends build their own trap?

Around her, everyone was frantic with activity. She'd barely spoken to Chizara since the beach, but now they were working side by side, wiring the new lights with more power.

Thibault and Craig were building a "shark cage" out of security mesh, a place of last retreat for anyone caught downstairs. Nate and Flicker were arguing about the floor plans spread out across the bar. They all worked with a determination that kept their nervousness under control, barely pulsing against Kelsie's mind. And Nate was at the center of it all, guiding them, his energy back to its full glorious presence in the group.

But then his phone blipped. Nate reached for it, and when he looked up from reading, his face was pale.

"Swarm's headed this way."

The Zeroes all jerked upright.

"He's bringing his own crowd," Chizara said. "I *knew* it."

"Not just any crowd. He took over the police funeral."

"The parade ground isn't far." Flicker swore. "And is that why he killed a policeman? Maybe this was his plan all along!"

Kelsie remembered what Swarm had said when the cop had arrived: *Another hero. Perfect.*

Thibault's voice came from by the windows. "We're not ready. We've got three windows left to reinforce."

"That won't help against hundreds of armed policemen," Chizara said grimly. "And our friendly crowd won't get here for hours."

"Wait a second," Kelsie said. "Isn't Ethan at the funeral?"

"He's the one texting me." Nate looked straight at her. "He got clear. He's fine."

"Kelsie?" Flicker asked. "How close is the swarm? Can you feel them yet?"

Kelsie took a breath and let her perception expand. Ever since Quinton Wallace had arrived in Cambria, he'd been a constant presence at the edge of her consciousness. Like a chronic migraine. But she'd learned to deal with it, blocking him from her awareness.

Now she let her power rush out, seeking him.

A buzzing, angry force was out there. It made the hairs on her arms stand up.

"He's way too close, and getting closer." She turned to Chizara. "I'm sorry. I should've been watching."

"Not your fault." Chizara reached out and took her hand.

Kelsie took a step closer and leaned into Chizara's warmth. All she wanted was to feel safe again, like she had that night on the beach before everything had gone wrong.

"Guys?" Craig spoke up. He stood next to Thibault by the half-covered window, sunlight streaming in around his bulk. "These are cops, yeah? It's not like they'll kill us. I mean, you paid them off with real money this time, right?"

Everyone looked at him. A hammer hung from one of his meaty hands, like he was ready to defend the Dish to the end.

"You should clear out," Kelsie said. "He's not after you."

"Yes, you've helped us enough," Nate said, keeping his tone light. "Head home; we'll see you later."

Craig hesitated, staring back at Nate, as if wondering where Mr. Saldana's usual authority had gone.

Kelsie felt the group wavering between their concern for Craig and a quiet hope that he would stay. He made Kelsie feel safe. He was a link to her past, and he was the one guy outside the Zeroes who everyone trusted. He was also pretty awesome in a fight.

But nobody wanted to put him in danger.

In the end, though, the simple brute force of Craig's loyalty won out.

"If it's all the same to you guys, the Craig will stay. We're a team now, right?"

Nate looked like he wanted to argue. But since Ethan's texts, Nate's usual energy had disappeared from Kelsie's feedback loop.

It was Flicker who argued. "We're talking six hundred cops here, all of them angry about what happened to their comrade. He'll use your anger too, Craig, and he might make you hurt us."

A deep laugh rumbled through the Dish. "You said that yesterday. That's why we have a plan."

"It's fine with me if you stay," Thibault said, and thumped the guy on his massive shoulder. "Seriously, I'm kind of glad."

The Craig grinned. "Then it's settled."

Kelsie felt a weak current of hope flow through the group. She felt them all turn to Nate expectantly, but he didn't move to take hold of this new energy. Since he'd shown up at the Dish yesterday, he'd turned back into Glorious Leader. But he was faltering again, something welling up in him.

Grief. That's what it was. Kelsie recognized the feeling. She didn't dare ask if there was any further word from Ethan. Her throat was clogged with fear.

Flicker took over, as if she felt it too. "Okay. The cops are in uniform, which means sidearms."

"We saw what a swarm did to Davey with their bare hands," Chizara said quietly. "How're we supposed to deal with six hundred people with *guns*?"

"We keep working," Flicker said. "We set the dazzle traps, just like we said. We can still break the feedback loop!"

"It won't work," Chizara said. "It's the middle of the day. The sun's brighter than anything I can throw!"

"There's no time, anyway," Kelsie said. She could feel the dark, buzzing presence of Swarm's murderous army closing in, a sweet, delicious ache in her bones. "They're already surrounding us."

There was silence. Kelsie held Chizara hard.

"Huh," Chizara said softly. "Turns out I hope Ethan made it out of there. I hope he ran."

"Me too," Kelsie said, with a catch in her throat. "At least one of us would survive, right?"

"Guys, we can't give up now," Flicker said. "This is our home. We're ready for this!"

"Get real, Flick," Chizara said. "This plan sucked when it was two hundred happy clubbers. Now it's six hundred pissed-off cops with guns! You can't stop bullets with rainbow lights and wire mesh."

"Stick to the plan," Nate said. A sudden determination filled his voice. "Just pick up the pace. Anon, Craig, finish the cage. Crash, how are the lights?"

Chizara looked like she was about to punch him. She started on a long and pessimistic answer. Kelsie slipped out of her arms and headed quietly for the entrance of the Dish.

It was time.

She could feel Swarm and the broad, dark thrum of the police he'd gathered around him. There was no way out. No last-minute salvation. Everyone she cared most about was at Swarm's mercy, and all the Zeroes' powers meant nothing.

She could feel the siren song of Swarm's power calling to her. Seeking her out, her alone, of all of them.

No point delaying the inevitable. She had to execute her secret backup plan.

She offered up a silent prayer as she unbolted the front door. All day she'd told herself that if the Zeroes' strategy failed, she'd do this—surrender herself to Swarm. Join him and try to push his hunger away from her friends. Anywhere but Cambria.

She hated the idea. Saving her friends meant sacrificing someone else. Some other town, other people's lives. Maybe some other bunch of Zeroes just trying to figure out how to survive.

She turned for one last glimpse of the Dish dance floor.

Nate was right behind her.

"It won't work," he said softly. "He won't let us go, no matter what you do."

"You don't know that for sure," she said.

"I know Swarm," Nate said gently. "There are people just like him in every boardroom and country club my father has ever brought me to. And they're never satisfied until they've taken everything. They think they're the center of the universe. But you're not like that, Kelsie."

She raised her chin defiantly. "My power is just like his, Nate."

"But you're not *him*," Nate insisted. "And you're not your power. You're bigger than that."

Kelsie looked past him to where Chizara and the others were back at work, full of frantic determination. "Then how do we stop him? Because we can't let him destroy all this."

She meant the Dish and everyone in it. But she also meant every gathering, every group, every crowd in Swarm's way, anywhere.

"He'll never stop," she told Nate quietly. "He doesn't know who else to be."

Nate nodded. He looked tired.

"Do you have a better idea than me surrendering?" Kelsie asked. "Come on, Glorious Leader!"

Nate gave her an exhausted look. "I've always hated that name."

"I know." Kelsie smiled. "But right now, that's what we need. A Glorious Leader."

Nate didn't answer. "Ethan said he wanted you to be happy. That's what he was trying for, anyway."

"He did?" she said. "In his real voice?"

Nate shrugged. "They're both real. But he was texting, so it wasn't his power. It was him."

"Please tell me he's okay," she whispered.

"I'm pretty sure he's gone," Nate said. "Don't tell the others."

Kelsie felt her pain bounce around the Dish, hitting all of them. A soft cry even came from the Craig.

She couldn't lose another friend. She stepped to the door and opened it.

Outside, a buzzing, jittering wall of uniformed police stretched from one side of the Dish to the other. The cops wore crisp dress uniform. Their eyes were unfixed, their mouths stretched wide, their holsters unbuttoned and flapping on their hips. They filled the street.

"You can't do this," Nate said.

"I have to."

"Hey, Zeroes!" It was Chizara's voice, calling from the balcony inside. "Come up on the roof—I've got a plan."

Kelsie looked at Nate, and hope bloomed in both their faces.

CHAPTER 57
CRASH

AS SHE STOOD ON THE ROOF WITH THE OTHERS,
Chizara's power built inside her, ready to ignite.

Ever since she crashed the container ship, she'd been carrying a gutload of fixing juice. She'd had to remind herself that it was a *bad* thing to have. To get it, she'd burned out a ship, covered a beach with fuel, and sent millions of dollars in cargo to the bottom of the sea. And learned that the rest of her life would be loveless.

But now that she needed that stored power, it swelled and gleamed, no longer guilty or miserable, a pressing excitement under her ribs. It was huge inside her.

She could feel all things electronic within half a mile. Painlessly. Clearly. Every way she turned, the visible world was just a scrim in front of the nodes, the networks, the teeming chips, the multiplicity of flickering microswitches.

Energy poured underfoot and overhead, in precise, calibrated, controlled, and controllable ways. She could extinguish swaths of systems in a single swipe. She could surge power into them so they blew themselves apart. She could burrow deep and cut a single connection, scorch a single chip. She could reach into a web of dead shadows a mile off and activate it. Any broken system nearby, she could comb its frazzled wires straight, unmelt its burned-out components, knit it together, and bring it back to life.

It was wonderful to feel balanced like this. Her usual pain was transformed into cold, glittering information she could use whenever she chose. Even as she held off on her power, layer after layer of systematic beauty was spread before her, a century and more of trial-and-error design, workings stripped back and re-elaborated, functions given finer and finer form.

She was in command of galaxies.

She was Crash.

"So what's this plan?" Flicker hunkered behind the concrete peak of the facade, her face blank. "Before they start shooting!"

"He still thinks I might join him." Kelsie wiped away tears in that way she had, like she did *not* want you to ask about them. And Chizara wanted to ask, to wipe the tears for her. "While I'm in the way, they won't open fire."

"I hope you're right about that," Crash said. "Because we're driving out."

"*That's* your plan?" Nate cried. "Steal a car and just roll out of here?"

"Not *a* car, no."

Crash waved her hand at the used-car lot across the street. It was so obvious, glistening there, packed with dozens of motley vehicles. Most were new enough to have microchipped starters, but a few had old-fashioned ignition points and coils. It didn't matter—she had power enough for them all.

With a thought, their engines roared to life. She'd surged them slightly too hard—lights flicked on, windshield wipers stuttered into motion, radios blared.

"Holy shit." Flicker jerked her head to one side, listening. "But what about the fence?"

Crash laughed, and one of the big V-8s at the front of the lot accelerated, crashing into a post of the chain link. It bent forward, the web of metal bowing on either side.

"Fifty percent rust," Crash said, and called forward the whole front row. They bashed, retreated, and bashed again, snapping one post, knocking others from their shallow holes in the old concrete.

On the third blow the whole fence collapsed. Revving high, metal scraping, the cars trundled out over the wire.

So much damage, Chizara. So much crumpled metal!

Whatever, Mom. Saving lives here.

She grasped the cars' steering now, which took more effort than mere starter chips, and crept them out into the street. Their thunder shook the Dish roof beneath her feet.

"Don't run anyone down," Flicker said. "Those are still cops down there."

"I'm not a monster." The first cars reached the shuddering lines of blue, and gently pushed into the policemen. It was like nudging spinning tops—the cops wobbled and corrected. Nudge, wobble, correct. Nudge, wobble—

"Perfect," Nate said, peeking over the parapet. "Swarm can take over people, but not cars!"

"Exactly," Crash said. "And he's not used to anyone pushing his toys around, so he can't hold a line firm. The only settings he's got are shuddering standby and murderous rage."

But she couldn't give him time to figure out a counterstrategy. She pressed the cars through the lines of blue. Soon the space in front of the Dish looked like an angry rush-hour traffic snarl.

The sound of battering came from below. A phalanx of police were bashing at the Dish door.

"They won't get through the steel," the Craig said. "Not unless they brought C4."

Flicker swore. "But that's one less exit we can use."

"We can't get out of here in cars anyway," Nate said. "If

he turns those cops murderous, they'll just haul us out the windows!"

"Everyone relax," Crash said. "We just need something *big enough*."

She flung her mind outward, searching the surrounding blocks.

More tech was arriving beyond the dithering edge of Swarm's crowd. Cars bringing on-duty cops in. News vans with satellite dishes flowering on top, ambulances and—was that a fire engine?

They were all too far away, and full of passengers already.

A news helicopter hovered overhead, lousy with tech, filming the strange behavior of Cambria's finest—and those kids on the roof, probably. Crash eyed it longingly.

But helicopters were sensitive beasts—one wrong twitch of the tail rotor and the torque would smack them into the crowd.

She needed something simple, solid, and muscular. An automotive version of the Craig.

And there it was, at the construction site three blocks away—a dump truck.

She started it, backed it out, crashing through the wooden safety fence. It was an old-style lump of a thing, its tires as tall as a person. As she trundled it toward the Dish, she worked her battalion of cars through the blue throng, clearing a lane for the truck.

It was like playing some old video game in her head, big bright hieroglyphs making gentle headway against many smaller, finer ones.

Carefully she slowed and steered the dump truck around the corner. Beside her the Craig nodded. "Good choice."

"He's not going to just let us do this," Nate said. "He must be planning something else."

"Let's not stick around to find out," someone said— Thibault, almost faded into the throng surrounding them.

"Not planning to stick around," Chizara said, hauling the truck forward, her cars clearing the street of cops.

A sudden volley of gunshots rang out, and they all ducked. Then a second roar of gunfire crackled up from the street.

"Damn it," Flicker said. "Shaky eyeballs down there. But it looks like he's shooting up your cars, Crash."

Crash could already feel the damage, could hear the windows shattering, the tires hissing flat, the fuel tanks leaking, even as she healed silicon and metal to keep as many vehicles going as she could. She wouldn't be able to keep this up for long. But how much ammo did cops bring to a *funeral*?

Chizara, a whole car lot, completely destroyed!

Not my fault, Mom. Talk to the bad guy.

She lumbered the dump truck closer, its reassuring weight, its bulletproof hide. She guided it in among the stalled cars, which offered no more resistance than traffic cones.

Flicker spoke up. "How about this? We can drop into that truck bed from the second-story window, and they won't get a clear shot. They're not really aiming with their eyeballs jittering like that."

"Perfect," Crash said. "Everyone down to the second floor."

CHAPTER 58
CRASH

THE SECOND-FLOOR OFFICE FELT DARK AND boxed-in after the rooftop. Crash quelled her claustrophobia and ran straight for the window.

Someone pulled her to a stop. "Let me."

Thibault stepped forward and peered through the window shades. "Whoa. That thing is a *tank*."

"The dumping bed is thick enough to block signals," Crash said. "It'll stop bullets."

Crash reached outside and backed up the dump truck like the overgrown toy it was. Its engine ground closer until its rear thudded into the wall, shaking the building around them.

"Okay," she said. "I guess we jump now."

"Yikes," Thibault said. "That's a ten-foot drop."

"No problem," said the Craig. "I'll catch you."

He ripped the shade down, and winter sunlight streamed in. Then he threw open the window, and leaped onto the sill with surprising lightness.

"One by one," he said, and dropped out of sight, landing in the truck bed with a resounding metal boom.

Thibault rushed back to the window. Looked down.

"You okay, dude?"

"Jump!" came the answering cry.

Thibault took Flicker by the arm, guided her up. For a moment they kissed, silhouetted by sunlight, her hair tossed by the cold wind.

Then Flicker leaped from the sill with a cry.

"He got her!" Thibault said. "You next, Kelsie."

"I have to go last," Kelsie said, pushing Crash forward.

"Busy!" Crash said. Her cars were dying out there, blinking out of the video game. And now she could see the distant edges of her fixing power, where before it had seemed limitless.

Yet with all this going on, she still managed to feel a spark of pleasure at Kelsie's body pressing against hers.

Stay focused, Crash!

"He's only holding his fire while I'm up here," Kelsie said. "As soon as I'm safe in the truck, they'll start shooting again. *Go*, Zara!"

Crash obeyed, stepping onto the sill. For a moment the whole insane tableau spread out below her, real objects matching the filigree maps of circuitry and pulsing electrons in her mind.

So *many* cops. Could she push this monstrous truck through without crushing a single one?

Still watching the game in her head, she dropped into the Craig's waiting arms.

"Oof! Thanks, Craig."

Craig set her gently onto the sun-warmed metal of the truck bed. She slid down to join Flicker in the corner near the cab, casting her mind along the escape route, now littered with dead cars, delicate little phones in police officers' pockets filtering in among them.

There is going to be loss of life, Mom.

You cannot, Chizara. I'm serious now. Look into my eyes.

"What's taking so long?" Craig said.

"They're just up there talking," Flicker said. "Nate! Kelsie! Thibault! Come *on*!"

Endless moments passed. Then Kelsie was swinging her legs over the sill. Chizara imagined bullets flying.

"Just jump!" she cried.

Kelsie pushed off and Craig stepped forward and caught her.

"Nate wouldn't come!"

"What?" Flicker said. "Bellwether, get *down* here! We all go together!

Chizara put out her arm and scooped Kelsie into the corner with them.

"He said he has to fix this," Kelsie wept. "Said it's not enough for us to get away. Thibault's arguing with him!"

"Nate! You butthead!" Flicker yelled up at the window. "Cut this macho shit *now*!"

A roar of gunfire answered her, the windblown curtain flailing and tearing. The truck rattled around them. Sounds of shattering glass came from the cab, and the two-way radio fizzled and died.

"Thibault!" Flicker cried.

The engine felt indestructible, but Chizara could feel the fuel tank beneath her. One bullet hole and the truck's lifeblood would start to leak.

Did fuel tanks really explode if you shot them?

"I hate you, Nate." She started to pull the massive machine away from the wall. "Hang on, everyone."

The gunfire choked off.

"Wait! Wait!" Flicker cried out. "Something weird's happening!"

Chizara braked the truck, clenching her teeth with the effort.

"All I can see is sky," Flicker said. "Everyone's looking up!"

"What, is he *flying* in reinforcements?" Kelsie cried.

"Shit." Flicker held her head, concentrating. "They're all lying down. Hundreds of them."

"What?" Chizara asked. "He can make them *lie down*?" But she could see, by the stilled phones in their pockets, that the cops around the truck had stopped moving. Two clusters of them were positioned right under the front wheels.

A massacre waiting to happen.

Kelsie stared at her, tearless, terrified. How could Chizara tell her that they weren't going to escape, that Swarm had countered all her glorious power with a bunch of soft-bodied humans *lying on their backs*?

"I'm sorry," Chizara said. "I tried."

Wordlessly, Kelsie put her arms around her.

"Let me take a look," the Craig said.

"No!" all three of them screamed. They threw themselves at his back as he pulled himself up to the rim of the truck bed.

But a volley of shots rang out, and the big guy went limp.

He fell back into their arms, a bullet through his neck.

CHAPTER 59
GLORIOUS LEADER

ANOTHER BURST OF GUNFIRE SOUNDED AS NATE approached the front door of the Dish, but he hardly flinched.

It didn't matter if bullets found him.

Ethan was dead, torn to pieces like Davey. The blood of another Zero was on his hands.

He let the guilt and misery of it overwhelm him. He forced the shame of it through his mind again and again, until his heart broke. Until he was certain that as a leader he was nothing.

The he listened at the door. The banging had stopped.

He opened it.

Two dozen cars filled the street before the Dish, bullet-riddled and window-shattered, leaking fuel that smelled bright and dangerous in the hot sun.

The dump truck was idling, not moving, and a moment later Nate saw why.

A carpet of blue covered the street. Hundred of cops lay on their backs, shuddering and twitching, staring at the sky.

Another jolt of despair went through him. Crash's escape plan had failed. Only he could fix this.

And he was nothing.

He stepped gingerly among the prone policemen. They stared up at him, their eyes bulging with rage, their anger over their fallen brother focused straight at Nate. They were dying to tear him to pieces.

Nate let their hatred come. He deserved it. Glorious Leader that he was, he had lost *two* Zeroes.

It only took a few moments in that concerted glare, and he was ready.

The earth dropped out beneath him, and he was falling, tumbling, lost. That part of him that was hungry for all that attention, even if those hundreds of eyes were glaring pure loathing, stuttered for a moment.

Nate flipped his power inside out.

Making a fist of his shame, he crumbled his ego, already battered and broken by his failure to save Davey and Ethan. All his expectations of obedience, attention, and worship flew apart like thrown sand.

Look on my works, ye Mighty, and despair!

Nate had always hated that poem. But holding it in his

mind helped. *The lone and level sands stretch far away. . . .*

The pure beams of hostility burning from the police faltered and frayed, then began to slide off him, to point back at the sky.

He was beneath their notice.

Nate walked through the vibrating field of blue, right up to the closest officer in his starched dress uniform. He knelt down to the man's face, staring into his jittering, wrathful eyes.

"I'm not here," Nate said. "I'm nothing."

The man kept staring, as if Nate *were* actually nothing, invisible before him.

It was working, but even a whiff of satisfaction would be the end. Nate kept his mind on one simple thought: *I lost two Zeroes. I'm worthless.*

He stepped gently over the man. Shuffled his way through the rustling mass of blue, never letting himself feel a moment of certainty, or confidence, or rightness in his actions.

No one stopped him. No one saw him.

A slow minute later and he was in the rearmost ranks of the swarm. Back here the cops were standing, shaking and staring and angry.

Among them stood Quinton Wallace and the senior brass, with the fanciest uniforms, the most medals.

Swarm himself looked bored, staring at the giant dump truck, chewing his lip, planning something.

I'm worthless, Nate reminded himself. *I'm nothing.*

He shambled forward, gathering no attention. Not a glance.

But when he was only a few yards from Quinton Wallace, something wonderful and disastrous happened—a spark of hope shot through Nate.

He saw Ethan.

He was among the police brass, in jeans and a tight suit jacket and tie. His mouth was slack, his eyes vibrating in his skull, his body shuddering and his limbs twitching. He was Swarm's zombie, but he was alive.

Nate tried to stifle the moment of elation. But it was too late.

"Did you think I wouldn't see you?" Quinton Wallace said, his gaze shifting from the Dish.

He laughed, and Nate let the harsh sound burn him even further down. *I'm useless. A danger to the Zeroes. Nothing.*

"Be serious," Swarm said. "I've killed a Stalker before."

Stalker. Nate's brain reeled at the word.

It was so obvious now. His and Thibault's powers were the same, turned inside out. This abject Nate was nothing more than another version of Anonymous.

Not Anonymous—Thibault Emmanuel Durant, who never used his hated middle name. Memories flooded in now: every detail of Thibault's face, the conversations they'd shared camping in the Redwoods, all the times here in Cambria when Nate had cut him off, forgetting he was there. The awful thing Ethan's voice had said two summers ago, about Thibault having been abandoned at the hospital by his parents, like they'd never had an oldest son.

For the first time, Nate really remembered his friend. And finally, having become like him, it was possible to understand that Zen, that rage, that pain.

Nate was learning so much, just as he was about to be torn to pieces. When all he wanted was to know *more*.

"How can you see me," he asked, "in a crowd this big?"

Quinton Wallace shrugged, waved dismissively at the cops around him. "What crowd? This is all me. Smooth pieces of the whole. As long as I focus, I won't forget you're there."

Of course. Like being alone with Thibault—tricky, but not impossible. So his plan . . .

Nate's eyes went to the holster of the nearest cop. It was unbuttoned, the gun right there.

The officer took a neat step backward.

"Too late for that," Swarm said.

Defeat churning in his stomach, Nate let his gaze fall to the ground, to the cops' freshly shined shoes, all exactly the same. He didn't deserve to win, to avenge Davey. He didn't even deserve to live.

"I'm sorry," he croaked.

"It's okay," Swarm said coolly. "Trying to shoot me was

something, at least. It was so disappointing, finding Davey hand-cuffed and waiting. No challenge at all."

Nate swayed, tears of shame welling up. "That was my fault too. I told Anon to—"

"Not interested. I think I'll kill you now." Swarm smiled. "I've never shot anyone before."

He pointed at Nate's heart, and two dozen police drew their weapons, all aimed at the same spot, fury making their hands shake.

"They'll hit each other," Nate said, hardly more than a whisper.

"Like I care," said Quinton Wallace, but then he was frowning, staring at the trembling, extended hand of the officer beside him.

It was empty.

It took a moment, but then Nate understood. He pulled in a ragged breath. "I guess you've never faced two Stalkers before, have you?"

"What do you—"

A shot sang out, its vast and sudden crack erasing all sound from the world, till it came echoing back from the high brick walls of the Heights.

With a look of astonishment Quinton Wallace fell to one knee. He coughed, and blood flew from his mouth, spattering down his blazer and onto the asphalt.

Behind him stood Thibault Emmanuel Durant. Smoke drifted from the barrel of the gun in his hand, and his eyes were wide, fixed, staring down at the kneeling boy.

Wallace raised his hand. His eyes met Nate's, and his bloodied lips moved, trying to say something but only spilling more blood—

The gun roared again, flattening him to the ground.

CHAPTER 60
ANONYMOUS

AS QUINTON WALLACE DIED, THE COPS WOKE UP.

Thibault saw them jerk to consciousness, heard them gasp. They all stared at the weapons in their hands, uncertain why they'd drawn them, why they'd marched a mile in dress uniform, full of anger. The air flicked and zotted with attention strands as they tried to read the situation.

They saw the dead body, and the gun in Thibault's hand, smoke wisping up from it. They didn't need to see Thibault himself—the gun was enough. Their weapons swung around, the muzzles in a jagged row, aimed at his chest.

Their attention blazed so bright, so thick, he didn't even think to start chopping it away. The instant he moved, bullets would fly.

He stood blinded, stiff, waiting to be blasted into oblivion—

true nothingness, the kind his mind would never reach. His hand still ached from the kick of the gun, but it felt impossible to drop it and save himself. It was like he'd shot his own will away, along with Wallace's life.

He was going to die right here, right now.

The police would finish what he'd started two days ago—erasing Thibault Durant from the world.

"Don't shoot!" came Nate's voice, ringing into the silence with its old commanding tone. After those moments of anonymity, he was flipping back to his natural state as the radiant, glorious center of attention.

Like the first spits of a sparkler, his power flew out into the darkness that Swarm's influence had created. It arced across the phalanx of police. Thibault felt himself fade as all that fierce, confused attention left him, shifting to Nate until the guy was lost in its dazzle, his raised hands marshaling every shimmer.

"I'm surrendering! Don't shoot."

The muzzles swung away from Thibault, and air rushed into his lungs, as if the guns had been squashing them flat. Maybe he wasn't going to die today.

"I had to do it." Nate's calm voice sounded small after the gunshots. "He was controlling you. But I give up."

He was taking the rap.

"No, wait!" Thibault shouted. "You can't—"

"On the ground!" a dozen voices cried, at the roaring edge of panic.

Nate sank to his knees, his expression splendidly confident that none of them would dare pull a trigger.

But the cops were scared and confused, their focus fitful, like the swarmed people at the mall—and they were afraid. In a clattering storm of safety catches, more pushed forward to get guns on Nate. Bumped from behind, Thibault stumbled and fell across Wallace's body. He tried to scramble off the bloodied blazer, away from the ghastly head wound, but the cops were in a fever now, too dense a crowd to see Thibault at all.

Their frenzy overwhelmed Nate's power, and they piled in on him. Through the milling legs Thibault glimpsed his friend on the ground, his cheek scraping on asphalt as they held him down. A kick went into his side.

There were still a dozen guns on him.

"Flip yourself back, Nate! Disappear!" Everything sounded soft and foggy through Thibault's gunshot-deafened ears, and there was Quinton Wallace's ruined face staring up at him.

But much worse, it was gone—that moment when Nate, his power inverted, had joined Thibault in anonymity. Had actually *seen* him. Had *remembered* him, right here in the middle of a crowd. Thibault had met the gaze of another Anonymous . . .

Who was about to be killed, if Thibault didn't do something.

He still had the gun. If he shot it in the air, would that break their fever, or at least give them a new target? Thibault

427

dragged himself up and charged at the unseeing cops. "Leave him alone!"

"Shut the hell up, Tee." Ethan was holding him back by his belt, the effort popping a button on the too-tight jacket he was wearing.

"Scam," Thibault said. "You can see me?"

"Dude, you just fired a gun—*everyone* saw you." Ethan peeled Thibault's fingers from the cooling weapon and dropped it on Wallace's body with a thud. "And we're buddies. Come on."

"But Nate! They're going to—"

"We can't help him now. Can't even see the guy under all those cops!"

Ethan pulled Thibault, stumbling, through a solid nightmare of blue-dressed officers, jabbed by their fists and shoulders as they strained to glimpse what was going on in the middle of the pile:

Nate, kicked and crushed, taking the blame for what Thibault had done.

"Keep moving!" Ethan called over his shoulder. "We need to get to the Dish. Get the others and rescue Nate together—"

"Ethan!" A woman grabbed Ethan by the shoulders. "You're okay!"

She wore a narrow black skirt suit and a dark cloche hat. Deputy District Attorney Cooper, a.k.a. Ethan's mom, breathless and worried.

"I'm getting you out of here! This was some kind of attack. Hallucinogens, or maybe—" She stared through the crowd beyond them at the blood pooling out from Wallace's body.

"Mom, it's under control." Ethan's real voice was all doubt and nerves. "I gotta help my friend here."

"Your friend?" DDA Cooper stared at Thibault, her attention bright and sharp for a moment. He knew he looked bad, shocked and guilty. "Is that blood on you, son?"

Thibault looked down. A smear of red on his shirt, from when he'd fallen on Wallace, made his head swim, but he managed to reach up and snip away DDA Cooper's attention.

She turned back to Ethan. "Come on. It's not safe here."

She started to drag him away, pushing past Thibault like he was just another bystander.

And not a cold-blooded murderer.

Horror yawned in him. With a tiny movement of a finger he'd snuffed out everything Quinton Wallace had ever been. It shouldn't be that easy, just to point at a person and blast them out of the world.

And his power was going to let him get away with it. He could walk out of town right now if he wanted, away from this or any other crime. His knees almost buckled under the weight of that license.

Thibault could erase *anyone* without consequence, just as he'd erased himself from his family's memory.

But a spindly lifeline of attention was wavering his way.

"Mom, please. *My friend needs me.*"

My friend. Thibault fell on the words gratefully—he had friends to keep him from walking away from what he'd done.

Ethan's mother came to a halt, but only because a pair of cops in dress blues had blocked their way.

"What is it, Detective King?" she asked.

King nodded at the scrum of cops arresting Nate. "Have you seen the suspect, ma'am?"

"No, who is it?"

"Nataniel Saldana," the male detective said. "Same guy your son called after the bank job last June."

DDA Cooper looked at Ethan, then back at the detectives. "Are you sure?"

"It's Saldana, all right," King said.

All three of them stared at Ethan, who opened his mouth. Thibault knew that expression, the expectant look in the eyes—waiting for the voice to step in and save him.

But Ethan's mom was faster.

"Don't you *dare*," she said. "What do you know about this?"

"Um, nothing!" Ethan blurted in his real voice.

His mother's eyes narrowed. "This morning, you said your friends had big plans today."

"Yeah, like, *party* plans."

"Ethan, your friend just shot someone! The time to stop lying is *now*."

"Nobody meant this to happen!" Ethan cried. "It just—"

"Ethan, I swear to God I'll have these detectives arrest you!"

Not again. No one else is taking the blame.

This is on me.

Thibault touched his fingers to Swarm's blood on his shirt, rubbed a streak across his forehead, and stood right in front of DDA Cooper.

"Forget about your son," he said. "It was *me.*"

CHAPTER 61
ANONYMOUS

DDA COOPER STARED AT HIM, HER EYES TRACING the stripe of blood, horror building in her face.

The shame inside Thibault gaped wider, and he remembered the roar of the gun in his hand, the sick satisfaction of obliterating an enemy, of answering savagery with even greater violence. Her eyes began to dull—it was working.

As he reached out to grab Ethan's arm, Thibault felt his power lurch, the force of his self-disgust slicing at the web of connections around them. The lines of the three adults' attention trembled and frayed, until they were staring at each other, confused.

"Detectives," Ethan's mother said. "I need to find my son."

"He was at the funeral?" King asked.

DDA Cooper looked uncertain for a moment and said, "I think so. Please help me."

And all three turned away and plowed toward the center of the turmoil.

Ethan stared at Thibault.

"Whoa." His focus stayed rock steady. "Did you do that?"

"I did." Sight lines were sliding off Ethan, falling away on all sides. "They can't see you at all."

"Dude. You rule!"

Thibault shook his head. This didn't feel like a victory. More like he was sinking into oblivion and dragging Ethan with him.

"Come on. We have to get back to the others." He had to stay connected with *something*. His friends were all he had left.

"But, Thibault, you *leveled up!*"

Thibault gave him a brief smile—Ethan had said his name with the right accent, in his own voice, for the first time ever.

"I *remember* everything now!" Ethan crowed. "That day I was stuck in your hotel room. All those *Red Scepter* games!"

Thibault looked down at his hand gripping Ethan's arm. "I got blood on you. Sorry."

"But you beat *Swarm*," Ethan said, as if it had been just some boss fight in *Red Scepter*. He waved his hand in front of a passing cop's eyes. The man knocked it away in annoyance but kept striding without giving Ethan a second glance. "This is so *weird*."

"I'm telling you," Thibault said, "you don't want to live here. Let's get back to the Dish."

Ethan started to walk but then pulled up, pointing. "Oh crud—Ang and Murillo."

Deeper in the scrum of police, two cops were staring straight at the Dish's battered facade. It took Thibault a moment to recognize them—from almost a week ago when Ethan had handed them a bag of money.

"They know Nate, too," Ethan said. "He talked to them at that stupid hockey game!"

Thibault felt himself sinking again. "They're going to connect the Dish to all this."

"But we bribed them to stay quiet!" Ethan said.

"That money covered an illegal nightclub," Thibault said. "Not a terrorist attack at a police funeral."

One of the two officers pointed up at the club, and they fell into what looked like a heated argument.

"We're screwed," Ethan said.

Shame hit the hollow of Thibault's stomach. It wasn't just Nate taking the blame anymore. Ang and Murillo could implicate Ethan, and everyone else at the Dish. Sonia's post had pictures of Chizara and Kelsie running tech, of Flicker tending bar.

Thibault could walk away from this murder, but he'd brought the whole world down on his friends.

"Move it, Tee." Ethan was pulling him along. "We have to warn them!"

Thibault floundered after him, unable to speak. He felt as if he'd never speak again, his voice drawn away deep inside him, and all other sound with it.

There stood the Dish, in the middle of a great silence.

Thibault might as well have burned it down.

The dump truck loomed as they drew near, the passenger window frosted around a bullet hole, the windshield shot away. The dumping bed was tilted, making it possible for someone to clamber out across the tailgate—

Flicker, her hands streaking the metal crimson, the front of her bright orange dress soaked with blood.

She'd been *shot*? The silence thickened around Thibault, his attachments to reality fraying.

Then Ethan wrenched himself from Thibault's grip, tearing away another thread of connection. Flicker was calling to Ethan for help, but still there was no sound. She dropped to the ground, steady on her feet.

Maybe it wasn't *her* blood. . . . Thibault felt a scrap of hope.

But then Flicker looked up, and behind her came Chizara and Kelsie. And heaped against the tailgate by the truck bed's angle and gravity, something hulking and still.

A body.

The solid, reassuring presence that had been Craig, now cut off forever from the web of humanity. No glimmer of attention came from his eyes. No connection to the lacework of grief and shock among the others.

Thibault felt himself disconnecting too, moving past horror

and shame until everything paled, bleached, faded around him. This wasn't leveling up. It was something more vast and awful—and at the same time insignificant, one inglorious human winking out.

His real name floated out of his reach—it had never mattered, and he let it go. He was stretching taut and thin. Now holes were opening up in him, spreading, until he shimmered like a cobweb across the face of the universe.

Something to be casually brushed aside.

Anonymous rose, too insubstantial even to be grateful, into the Nothing that had always waited for him.

CHAPTER 62
FLICKER

FLICKER FELT A PIECE OF HERSELF TEARING AWAY.

The feeling came from nowhere and everywhere—the dread of this awful day taking form, reaching out, pulling her heart from her chest.

More noises then—Kelsie crumpling against the truck, Chizara grunting, barely catching her.

For a moment Flicker thought Kelsie had been hit by a stray bullet, but she'd heard no shots, just police sirens, shouts, helicopters overhead.

"Did you feel that?" she asked Ethan.

"Like someone punched my brain?"

From Kelsie, a murmur: "Someone just *left*."

An aftershock, maybe? When that pair of shots had rung out a few minutes ago, a cry had come from Kelsie, and she'd fallen to the bed of the dump truck, repeating, *Swarm's dead!*

Flicker had thrown her vision out into the throng and found Quinton Wallace moments later—shot in the head and in the back. By then the police were waking up, rising from the ground with their eyes casting about in confusion, no longer vibrating with the wild energies of the swarm.

Now, a block away from the Dish, cops milled thickly around someone pinned to the ground. Metal flashed—handcuffs coming out. A few yards away lay Swarm's dead body.

Flicker tried to get her vision into the center of the pack, but it was all a flurry of motion and violence.

"Craig!" Ethan shouted up at the tailgate. "Guys. He's not moving!"

Flicker's vision came reeling back. Shit—Ethan didn't know. He hadn't hunkered long minutes in the truck bed, blood pooling underfoot. Listening to Kelsie fight with all her soul against becoming one with the swarm. Waiting for those zombie cops to rise up and come scrabbling across the tailgate.

"Ethan. He's dead."

Ethan went silent, and Flicker didn't have time to find eyes on him.

Kelsie was still mumbling nonsense. "When Swarm died, they disappeared. *Hundreds* . . . and one more, just now."

None of it made sense. But Flicker still felt that last aftershock, an icicle through her heart.

"They were *inside* him, the people he killed," Kelsie said, muffled by Chizara's embrace. "Regular people, Davey, other Zeroes. And now they're all gone."

"Hang on, Kelsie, please," Chizara said. "I'm trying to keep from crashing this whole block!"

"He's *dead*?" Ethan cried.

Flicker took hold of him. "What happened out there? Who shot Swarm?"

"I think it was Nate."

Another piece of Flicker's heart broke. "*Nate* shot him?"

"It must have been. The cops took him down, hard." Ethan gripped her arm, started pulling. "We have to get out of sight. They could be here any minute!"

"Why would they come here?" Flicker demanded.

"Ang and Murillo know Nate! The Dish is in the middle of all this, they know it's his club, and he just shot someone!"

It churned through her brain again. *Nate killed a Zero.*

She let herself be pulled along, remembering his stone-cold confidence at the Dish yesterday. *I'll handle it.*

When he hadn't jumped down into the truck to escape, she'd thought Nate had simply given up. But he'd had a plan. The most basic, awful plan: kill a Zero, along with the hundred stolen souls he was freighted with.

"You get why he did it, right? Someone had to," Ethan argued with Flicker's silence. He was pulling her toward the alley behind the Dish, and she heard Chizara and Kelsie behind them. "I mean, he must've planned this all along—charm his way in close, grab a gun, blow the guy away!"

Blow the guy away—like Swarm had been dead leaves. He was a killer, but also a Zero like the rest of them, born with more power than he knew how to control.

The smell of garbage bags and old cigarettes hit, and the sirens and shouts grew muffled by high brick walls.

"Okay, nobody can see us," Ethan said. "How do we rescue Nate?"

"Rescue him?" Flicker sent her vision questing out into the chaos.

Among the flashing emergency vehicles, two officers were yanking Nate to his feet. He strained to look back at the Dish— his hair mussed, his face blank, pale where it wasn't bleeding.

They were dragging him toward a police van.

"Too late," she said. "They're taking him away."

"We can't let them!" Ethan cried. "You should've heard the theories my mom was coming up with—terrorism, or a gas attack! They'll put him in a supermax!"

"I can crash every engine out there." Chizara had an edge in her voice, like she was dying to. "Just say the word."

Shit, thought Flicker. They were talking like she was the leader now. They'd seen how pathetic her plans were. Defeat the Swarm with lights, music, a happy crowd—

When brute force, deadly force, had been the answer.

Focus on the present. Fix this.

She let her vision swell, taking in every set of eyes within her range, block after block of policemen, gawkers, drivers caught in traffic, even people peering down from news helicopters.

It almost burst her head, but it made the answer clear.

"There's nothing we can do," Flicker said.

"What do you mean, *nothing*?" Ethan yelled. "We have to go and—"

"There are a dozen cameras pointed at him. They know his face, and your mom knows his name. If we bust him out, he'll be a fugitive, a wanted man, forever."

Ethan's grip tightened. "That's better than doing twenty years for murder!"

"We already tried to take on six hundred cops today," Flicker said. "And we failed."

"But we can't just . . ." Ethan's voice faltered. "Nate would never let one of us get taken away!"

Flicker leaned a shoulder against rough brick, too exhausted to stand. But she spoke with all the certainty she could muster.

"Nate would do the smart thing. Even if it sucked."

"Damn it," Chizara said. "He probably would."

Flicker watched them put Nate in the van, and she felt it again, that tearing away. More like she'd lost her true love than a friend. Too much to bear.

Around Nate the crowd was loosening. A few cops in dress uniform moved slowly off in the direction of the funeral they'd abandoned. Others bunched in the middle, making radio calls and running yellow tape around Swarm's body. Normalcy was returning, which meant they had to move fast.

But she had to watch as Nate was pushed inside the van, and the door slammed closed. It crept through the milling crowd and out of sight.

"Okay," Flicker said, pushing herself from the wall. "We have to run. But we need a few things in the Dish."

CHAPTER 63
FLICKER

"MONEY?" CHIZARA ASKED. "*THAT'S* WHAT WE came for?"

Flicker knelt by the boxes of cleaning supplies, digging for the roll of singles Nate kept so the Dish never ran out of change. His texts had seemed so random yesterday, but they were coming into focus now.

"Yeah, we gotta *run*!" Ethan cried from the alley door.

Flicker didn't answer. If they thought cash wasn't important, they didn't understand how bad this was.

Kelsie spared her the trouble of explaining.

"We need money, guys," came her small voice from beside Chizara, across the bar from Flicker. "We're not just running away from the Dish. We're leaving Cambria—forever."

"Wait," Ethan said. "Which kind of forever?"

"The only kind." Kelsie's voice was soft, but it echoed across the empty Dish dance floor. "None of us can go home."

"Why not?" Chizara said. "Those dirty cops know Ethan and Nate, but they never met the rest of us."

"His sister did," Kelsie said.

"Crap. She's right." Ethan's real voice cracked a little. "The second Jess sees Nate's face on TV, she'll spill."

Flicker's fingers found it—a fat roll of rubber-banded bills. Enough for a couple of tanks of gas, at least. They'd have to risk Ethan's voice for everything else.

This was going to be one hell of an uncontrolled experiment.

"Jess said if anything weird happened, she'd tell Mom everything! Even about our superpowers!" Ethan was hyperventilating. He needed a task to focus on.

"Scam," Flicker said. "There are some burner phones in the supply closet. Under the paper towels. Get them."

As he stormed away, Flicker realized why Nate had planned for this escape—because he planned for *everything*.

How was she supposed to replace someone who was born to lead?

"I'll grab you a tee and one of my skirts," Kelsie said. "You can't go outside covered in blood."

Flicker nodded. "Two minutes."

Her hands were sticky too. She moved toward the sink behind the bar.

Chizara was pacing now. "I can't just leave again! After everything that happened today, why would the police care about some kids throwing illegal parties?"

"They'll take a hard look at this club because of Nate." Flicker ran water and started to scrub. "They'll see thousands spent under the table on electronics. They'll see a Faraday cage to block surveillance, because *every* nightclub has one of those. And reinforced metal doors and windows, enough to withstand a siege from a SWAT team. Does that sound like a *party* to you?"

There was a charged silence as Chizara tried to resist the awful logic of the situation. Flicker had spooked herself, and she cast her eyes outside to see if the police were coming already.

Not yet. Confusion still reigned out there. The media was arriving in hordes, trying to untangle the story. Onlookers gathered, pressed against the line of police tape to gawk at the tape outline of Quinton Wallace's body on dark asphalt.

A command area was already set up—

"Shit." Flicker turned off the tap. "You should see the texts the police brass are sending each other. CCPD can't investigate what happened, because every cop in Cambria was involved."

"Of course." Ethan was back from the supply closet. "They'll call in the Feds!"

"They know it's the same thing that killed Delgado, and that hit the Desert Springs Mall. And . . ." Flicker tried to keep her voice steady. "They're talking about the police station meltdown last summer."

"No way," Chizara said. "Why?"

"Because that's how my mom knows Nate!" Ethan cried. "She tracked him down after I called him from the police station."

"God," Chizara said. "Everything we've ever done has made this *worse*."

"Pretty much." Flicker shut her vision down, trying to process it all. "Ethan called Nate from the cop shop, and Nate called the rest of us minutes later. Even Kelsie's in his phone records now."

"We're all connected." Kelsie's feet were thumping down the stairs.

"Which means we're all leaving." Flicker fished her phone out of her pocket and put it on the bar. "We can't take these. They're just tracking devices now."

"I'll nuke them," Chizara said, her voice hollow. "Get rid of our texts and photos, at least for now."

As Kelsie's footsteps approached, Flicker turned away from Ethan's voice and pulled off her dress, trying not to get blood in her hair.

A whiff of burned microchips filled her nostrils.

Flicker sighed as she took the shirt from Kelsie and put it on. All that time spent training her voice-recognition software, gone in a puff of Crash juice.

"You're really coming, Zara?" asked Kelsie softly. "Leaving those two perfect little brothers behind?"

"Daughter takes unexplained road trip, or Homeland Security

arrest, her in front of said brothers." Chizara's voice was flat. "I know which my mom would prefer."

"Me too," Kelsie said.

All dressed now, Flicker cleared her throat. "Crash, can you find us a working car?"

"On it."

Flicker checked her bag. Yes, her folding cane was in there, along with an extra pair of dark glasses. Lots of credit cards that were useless now. Unless she handed them to someone headed in another direction, just to give the Feds some false leads.

"We're going to rescue Nate *soon*, right?" Ethan said from the front window.

"We'll get him out some way." Flicker put all the certainty she had left into the words. "Without him we wouldn't have survived today."

"Same goes for the Craig," Kelsie added softly.

"Oh, crap." Ethan started to hyperventilate again, as if he'd managed to forget already.

Flicker hadn't—she still smelled his blood, and felt it under her fingernails.

The empty feeling hit again, the one that kept cutting through her. Because this was all her fault. She was the one who'd decided to confront Swarm, when they all should have run the moment he showed up.

"Found a ride," Chizara said. "Just this side of Hill Street. Is the way clear?"

Flicker sent her vision searching behind the club and found no police barriers. Just onlookers and gawkers, and the slow return of normal traffic.

"Clear enough," she said.

Kelsie was right next to her, a featherlight touch.

"You're doing good," she said softly. "Just as glorious as Nate."

Through all her exhaustion Flicker felt a shred of solace from the words. And yet, as she made her way to the alley door, she couldn't shake the nagging feeling that she'd forgotten something.

Something really important.

There was an absence in her, a gap where a vital spark had lived and was missing now. A nothingness that couldn't be explained, not even by Nate's arrest or the awful fact that Craig was dead.

Unbidden, her right hand went to her left wrist and found a bracelet there. She felt braille dots, punched into the leather.

T—H—I—B . . .

Nonsense letters. Where the hell had this bracelet come from? Flicker pulled it from her wrist and dropped it on the floor.

She tried to send her vision out into the alley but found no eyes.

"All clear," she said.

The door yawned open, and the four remaining Zeroes left the Dish forever.